The
Story
of
B

PROPERTY OF
BOGOTA PUBLIC LIBRARY
(201) 488-7185

BANTAM
BOOKS

New York

Toronto

London

Sydney

Auckland

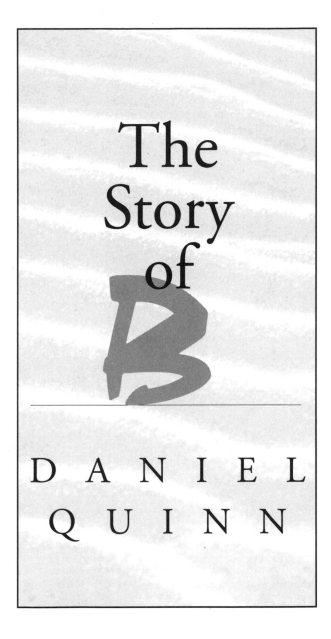

The
Story
of
B

DANIEL
QUINN

This is a work of fiction. The characters, events, and incidents in this novel are wholly the product of the author's imagination, as are the educational institutions and religious orders with which they are affiliated. Any resemblance to actual persons or real organizations, whether a similarity of name or description, is entirely coincidental.

THE STORY OF B
A Bantam Book / December 1996

"Population: A Systems Approach" was published in a slightly different form by the Center for Biotechnology Policy and Ethics, Texas A&M University.

All rights reserved.
Copyright © by Daniel Quinn.
Cover art copyright © 1996 by Alan Ayers.
No part of this book may be reproduced or transmitted in any form or by any means, electronic or mechanical, including photocopying, recording, or by any information storage and retrieval system, without permission in writing from the publisher.
For information address: Bantam Books.

Library of Congress Cataloging-in-Publication Data
Quinn, Daniel.
The story of B : a novel / Daniel Quinn.
p.   cm.
ISBN 0-553-10053-X
I. Title.
PS3567.U338S76   1996
813'.54—dc20   96-21664
CIP

Published simultaneously in the United States and Canada

Bantam Books are published by Bantam Books, a division of Bantam Doubleday Dell Publishing Group, Inc. Its trademark, consisting of the words "Bantam Books" and the portrayal of a rooster, is Registered in U.S. Patent and Trademark Office and in other countries. Marca Registrada. Bantam Books, 1540 Broadway, New York, New York 10036.

PRINTED IN THE UNITED STATES OF AMERICA

BVG   10 9 8 7 6 5 4 3 2 1

For Goody Cable
and of course Rennie, always

When one does not see what one does not see,
one does not even see that one is blind.

—Paul Veyne

part
one

Friday, May 10

A Diary

Today I ducked into a drugstore and bought a notebook—this notebook right here that I'm writing in. Clearly a momentous event.

I've never kept (or been tempted to keep) a diary of any kind, and I'm not even sure I'm going to keep this one, but I thought I'd better try. I find it's a peculiar business, because, though I'm supposedly only writing for myself, I feel impelled to explain who I am and what I'm doing here. It makes me suspect that all diarists are in fact writing not for themselves but for posterity.

I wonder if there's a child anywhere who hasn't, at some stage of awakening consciousness, incorporated into his/her address "The World" and "The Universe." Having already done that (almost three decades ago), I begin this diary by writing:

I am Jared Osborne, a priest, assistant pastor, parish of St. Edward's, professed of the Order of St. Lawrence, Roman Catholic Church. And having written that, I feel obliged to add: not a very good priest. (Wow, this diary business is hot stuff! These are words I've never dared to whisper, even to myself!) Without examining the logic of this too closely, I can say it's precisely *because* I'm "not a very good priest" that I feel the need to start this diary at this point in my life.

This is excellent. This is exactly where I have to begin. Before I go on to anything else, I have to put it down right here in black-and-white who I am and how I got here, though thank God I don't have to go back as far as my childhood or anything like that. I just have to go back far enough to figure out how I came to be involved in one of the strangest quests of modern times.

Recruiting Poster: Why I'm a Laurentian

By long tradition, we Laurentians have been defined in terms of our difference from the Jesuits. Some historians say we're not as bad, some say we're worse, and some say the only difference between us is that they have a better instinct for public relations. Both were founded at roughly the same time to combat the Reformation, and when that battle was lost (or at least over), both redefined themselves as elitist educators. And where do little Jesuits and Laurentians come from? Jesuit recruits come from Jesuit schools, and Laurentian recruits come from Laurentian schools.

I came to the Laurentians from St. Jerome's University, the intellectual hearth of the order in the United States. This may explain why I became a Laurentian, but of course it doesn't explain why I became a priest. All I can say on that point right now is that the reasons I gave when I was in my early twenties no longer seem very persuasive to me.

The important thing to note here is that I was considered a real comer when I was an undergraduate. I was expected to be another jewel in the crown—but by the time postdoctoral studies rolled around, I'd been spotted as a rhinestone—plenty of flash but pure paste. I was a big disappointment to everybody, most of all to me, of course. My superiors were as nice about it as they could be. I was never going to be invited to join the faculty at St. Jerome's or any other of the order's universities, but they did offer to find a place for me at one of their prep schools. Or if I didn't care to be humiliated quite that much, I could be loaned out to the diocese for work in the parochial trenches. I chose the latter, which is how I ended up at St. Ed's.

I say I'm not a very good priest. I suppose this is a bit like a cart horse saying it's not a very good horse, because it expected to be raced but couldn't make the grade. The blunt truth is that you don't *have* to be a very good priest to make the grade at the parish level. This observation is not as cynical as it sounds—the priest is only a mediator of grace, not a source of grace, after all. Sure, you've got to be even-tempered and patient and tolerant of human shortcomings (which says a lot), but nobody expects to you be a St. Paul or a St. Francis, and a sacrament that comes to you from the hands of an utter swine is every bit as efficacious as one that comes to you from the hands of a paragon. The way things are going nowadays, you'll be considered a bloody treasure if you don't turn out to be a child molester or a public drunk.

Enter Fr. Lulfre

Six days ago I got a nice little note from the dean's secretary asking if I would be so kind as to present myself next Wednesday (day before yesterday) at the office of Fr. Bernard Lulfre at three o'clock in the afternoon. Well, now, *that* was interesting.

Dear Diary, I can tell right off the bat that you don't know who this Bernard Lulfre is, so I'll have to enlighten you. In a word, Pierre Teilhard de Chardin was the Jesuits' superstar, and Bernard Lulfre is ours. Teilhard de Chardin was a geologist and a paleontologist, and Bernard Lulfre is an archaeologist and a psychiatrist. The difference, typically, is that Teilhard de Chardin is world famous, while Bernard Lulfre is known to about ten people (with names like Karl Popper, Marshall McLuhan, Roland Barthes, Noam Chomsky, and Jacques Derrida). Never mind. To those who breathe the rarefied air of the scholarly Alps, Bernard Lulfre is a heavyweight.

While an undergraduate at St. Jerome's, I wrote a paper proposing that, although belief in an afterlife may have given rise to the practice of burying the dead with their possessions, it's just as plausible to suppose that the practice of burying the dead with their possessions gave rise to a belief in an afterlife. The course instructor passed it on to Bernard Lulfre, thinking it might be publishable in one of the journals he was associated with. Of course it wasn't, but it brought me to the great man's attention, and for a season I was shown round as a promising youngster at faculty teas. When I entered the novitiate a year later, it was imagined by some that I was a sort of protégé, a misconception I foolishly did not discourage. Fr. Lulfre may have followed my progress in the years that followed, but if so, he did it at a very great distance, and when my academic career began to falter, his remoteness began to be interpreted (with equal imaginativeness) as a withdrawal.

In the five years since my ordination, until that nice invitation arrived from the dean's office, I hadn't heard from him once (and hadn't expected to). Naturally I was curious, but I wasn't exactly holding my breath. He wasn't going to offer to send me to the ball in a coach-and-four. Probably he was going to ask for a small favor of some kind. Maybe some folks at St. Jerome's wanted to know something about somebody at St. Ed's, and they said, "Why don't we have Fr. Lulfre contact that young Fr. Osborne who works there?" No one would hesitate to ask me to do a bit of spying for the order if spying was needed. We've had our own private espionage network for centuries and think of it as being not one whit less honorable than that of MI16 or the CIA. (We're quite proud of our intrigues—in a quiet way, of course. During the last decades of Elizabeth's reign, for example, our "English College" at Rheims infiltrated scores of priest spies into Britain to keep the spirit of insurrection alive among English Catholics. Our greatest coup was achieved in 1773, when Pope Clement XIV was feeling some scruples about destroying his old friends the Jesuits; it was one of our own who showed him how to reason with his tender conscience and get the job done.) The order is our homeland, after all, and it would be taken for granted that, even in exile, I would never allow some paltry diocesan or parochial concern to supersede my loyalty to it. On the other hand, if it was something as simple as this, then a phone call would have been sufficient. The more I pondered the problem, the more intrigued I became.

At Fr. Lulfre's office

Nothing had changed at Fr. Lulfre's office since I'd last visited it some ten years before: It was in the same corner of the same floor of the same building. Fr. Lulfre hadn't changed either: Still six and a half feet tall, as broad as a door, with a massive, rough-hewn head that might belong to a stevedore or a trucker. Men like him somehow don't change much till they reach an age like seventy or eighty, when they fall apart overnight and are whisked away.

I've been around enough brilliant men to know that they're seldom brilliant in real time, and Fr. Lulfre is no exception. He greeted me with unconvincing heartiness, made some awkward small talk, and seemed ready to beat around the bush for hours. Unfortunately, I wasn't in the mood to collaborate with him on that, and after five minutes a dreadful silence overtook us.

With the distinct air of someone biting the bullet, he said: "I want you to know, Jared, that there are many men in the order who know you're capable of doing more than you've been asked to do."

Well, shucks, I wanted to say, but didn't. I murmured something or other to the effect that I was gratified to hear this, but I doubt if I managed to keep every trace of irony out of my voice.

Fr. Lulfre sighed, evidently realizing that he still had some biting to do on this bullet. Deciding to give him a break, I told him, "If you've got a different assignment for me, Father, you certainly don't have to be shy about proposing it. You have a ready listener here."

"Thank you, Jared, I appreciate that," he said—but still seemed reluctant to go on. At last he said, rather stiffly, as if he didn't expect to be believed, "You will remember the special mandate of our order."

For a moment I just stared at him blankly. Then of course I *did* remember it.

The mandate about the Antichrist.

The "Special Mandate"

In studying the history of the Laurentians, every novice learns that the original charter of our order includes a special mandate regarding the Antichrist, enjoining us to be in the vanguard in our vigilance. We're to know before all others that the Antichrist is among us—and we're to suppress or destroy him, if that should prove to be possible.

At the time the mandate was written, of course, it was taken for granted that the identity of the Antichrist was a settled matter: It was Luther and his hellish company. As this confident understanding gradually became unfocused, the Laurentians began to argue among themselves about the means by which the mandate was to be fulfilled. If we were to be vigilant, what were we supposed to be vigilant *for*? By the middle of the seventeenth century, everyone in Europe had heard so many people accused of being the Antichrist that they were heartily sick of the whole subject, and speculation along those lines became more or less what it is today, the domain of religious cranks—except among the Laurentians, who quietly developed their own distinctive (and unsanctioned) Antichrist theology.

The Antichrist comes to us from a prophecy of John, who wrote in his first letter, "Children, it is the final hour. You've been told that the Antichrist is coming, and now not one but a multitude of Antichrists have appeared, so there can be no doubt whatever that the final hour is upon us." When this "final hour" failed to arrive during the lifetime of John's contemporaries, Christians of each succeeding generation looked for signs of the Antichrist in their own era. At first they looked for persecutors of the Church, preeminently Nero, who was expected to return from the dead to continue his war against Christ. When Roman persecution became a thing of the past, the Antichrist degenerated into a sort of folktale monster, a huge, bloody-eyed, donkey-eared, iron-toothed bogeyman. As the Middle Ages wore on and more and more people became disgusted with ecclesiastical corruption, the papacy itself began to be identified as the Antichrist. Finally popes and reformers spent a century belaboring each other with the bad name. When the Laurentians, with their special mandate, began to rethink the matter in the centuries that followed, they went all the way back to fundamentals and took note of the fact that prophecies are seldom literal predictions of future events. Often they're not even recognized as prophecies until they're fulfilled. Numerous examples of this occur in the New Testament, where events in the life of Jesus are described as fulfilling ancient prophecies that were not necessarily understood as prophecies by those who enunciated them. Laurentian theologians reasoned this way: If prophecies about Christ must wait upon their fulfillment to be understood, why shouldn't the same be true of prophecies about Antichrist? In other words, we can't really know what John was talking about until it actually happens, so the Antichrist is almost certain to be different from whatever we imagine him to be.

If someone tells you that Saddam Hussein is the Antichrist (and he has in fact been nominated for that honor), you're absolutely right to laugh. The Antichrist isn't going to be a worse sort of Hitler or Stalin, because worse than them will just be more of the same in a higher degree—sixty million murdered instead of six million. If you're going to be on guard against the Antichrist and not just some ordinary villain, you have to be on guard against someone of an entirely new order of dangerousness.

And that's where things stand at the end of the second millennium. But not exactly. This is just the "official" word, and the impression you get on receiving it in the Laurentian novitiate is that the Antichrist thing is a dead issue and has been so for nearly two centuries.

What I now learned from Fr. Lulfre was that this impression is a false one, engendered as a deliberate policy in the novices, primarily to forestall babbling that could end up as an embarrassing story in the sensationalist press. The policy works. Among the peasantry of the order, the subject of the Antichrist never comes up. At the topmost levels, however, a discreet watch is still kept. Very occasionally—maybe once in fifty years—a worrisome individual pops up, and someone from the order is sent out to have a look.

Someone like me. Someone *exactly* like me.

The candidate

The candidate was one Charles Atterley, a forty-year-old American, a sort of itinerant preacher who had been circling the middle states of Europe for a decade, picking up a fairly large but unorganized following that seemed to defy all demographic sense and wisdom. It included young and old and everything in between, both sexes in roughly equal numbers, mainstream Christians and Jews, clergy of a dozen different denominations (including the Roman Catholic), atheists, humanists, rabbis, Buddhists, environmentalist radicals, capitalists and socialists, lawyers and anarchists, liberals and conservatives. The only groups notably unrepresented in the mix were skinheads, Bible-thumpers, and unrepentant Marxists.

Atterley's message seemed difficult to summarize and was typically characterized as "mind-boggling" by those who were favorably impressed and as "incomprehensible" by those who weren't. I told Fr. Lulfre I didn't understand what made him seem dangerous.

"What makes him dangerous," he said, "is the fact that no one can place him or his product. He's not selling meditation or Satanism or goddess worship or faith healing or spiritualism or Umbanda or speaking in tongues or any kind of New Age drivel. He's apparently not making money at all—and that's disquieting. You always know what someone's about when he's raking in millions. Atterley's not another example of some familiar model, like David Koresh or the Reverend Moon or Madame Blavatsky or Uri Geller. In fact, his presentation and lifestyle are more reminiscent of Jesus of Nazareth than anyone else, and that too is disquieting."

"Disquieting I understand," I said. "Dangerous I don't."

"People are *listening*, Jared—possibly to something quite new. *That* makes it dangerous."

This I could understand.

Anyone who thinks the Church is open to new ideas is living in a dreamworld.

The assignment

Atterley was presently in Salzburg, Fr. Lulfre said. I was to go there, listen, watch, hang out, and report back. When I asked who my European contact would be, I was told there would be none. I was to contact no one in the order under any circumstances. I would travel under my own name, making no secret of my priesthood but not broadcasting it either. I would travel in civilian clothes, as if vacationing.

"Why doesn't someone in Europe handle this?" I asked.

"Because Atterley's an American."

"But he's talking to Europeans."

"Don't be simple, Jared. Europe is just a rehearsal. Whatever else the United States has lost in the last three or four decades, it's still the world's style setter, and nothing will catch on everywhere unless it catches on here first. Atterley knows this, if he's half as bright as people think he is, and when he's ready for us, he'll be here, count on it. And that's why you're going to Europe: We want to be ready for him before he's ready for us."

"You seem to be taking him very seriously."

Fr. Lulfre shrugged. "If we don't take him seriously, then we might as well not take him at all."

After discussing a few mundane matters, like travel agencies and credit cards, I got up to leave, a heavy question in my mind causing me to drag my feet. At the door I finally got it out.

"And what happens afterward? To me, I mean."

He chewed on this for a minute, then asked me what I *wanted* to happen.

"I don't know," I said. "If you think I'm being wasted at St. Ed's, then what's the plan? Were you thinking I'd go back and waste myself some more?"

"You're right to ask," he said, as if I didn't already know it. "There is no plan as such, but I feel it's an unspoken assumption that this would mark the beginning of something new for you."

"I'd rather hear it as a spoken assumption, Fr. Lulfre."

"You've heard it spoken by me, Jared. Won't that do?"

I wouldn't have minded hearing it spoken by a few other people, but he didn't offer to arrange such a thing, and I didn't want to be churlish about it, so I told him sure.

The end of the beginning

That was the day before yesterday. Yesterday and today I've spent canceling appointments, parceling out my duties at St. Ed's, making travel arrangements, and bringing this diary up to date. There's something else on my mind that should go in here (maybe a lot), but I don't quite know what it is and won't have any leisure to look for it till I get on the plane to cross the Atlantic.

Tuesday, May 14

Salzburg

If a spymaster in Len Deighton or John Le Carré sends you to have a look at a man in Salzburg, chances are the man will be found in Salzburg. Real-life spymasters are not as reliable as this. Charles Atterley is not in Salzburg. As far as I've been able to learn in two days, he's *never* been here and isn't *expected* here. In fact, no one has ever heard of him.

Salzburg, however, is very cute and full of Olde Worlde Charm, and the locals tell me again and again, "Your friend is probably waiting for you in München." They make it sound as if Munich is packed solid with American friends that have been mislaid in Salzburg, and one of them is bound to be mine.

I may as well have a look.

Thursday, May 16

Munich

I haven't been able to turn a trace of Atterley here, and I'm beginning to feel rather stupid. I didn't come to Europe prepared to play detective, and I haven't got a single "in" anywhere.

I did manage to find a friendly librarian with a computer, and she gave the problem half an hour, but you can't be very inventive when all you're drawing is a blank. What do you do after you've checked all the newspaper files back to the Beer-Hall Putsch? Ask the concierge, I suppose. The concierge knows everything. But what do you do after the concierge gives you a vacant stare?

I suppose I should call and confer with Fr. Lulfre, but this isn't an idea that appeals to me.

To this point, I've been behaving rather compulsively (though that may not be quite the word I'm after). I've been acting as though I could find Charles Atterley by dint of sheer, unremitting determination. This strategy certainly hasn't worked, and pursuing it has left me feeling ridiculous and inept.

The following are facts: I wasn't given a deadline, no special urgency attaches to my mission, and I have no idea what to do next. Therefore (therefore!) I might as well relax and go with the flow for a while.

Adieu.

An invitation

I went for a walk.

I'm not, in truth, an adventurous traveler. As I say, I went for a walk in the vicinity of my hotel and looked in shop windows. I paused here and there to study a menu in a restaurant window, as if I knew what any of it meant. There went an hour, frittered away like a carefree vagabond. I slunk back into my hotel and hung around the desk in the absurd hope that someone would tell me a message had come during my absence. Finally, hopelessly, I slunk into the bar, sat down at a table, and ordered a beer. After a few minutes the barman brought over a bowlful of salted peanuts and said the gentleman at the bar wondered if I was American, and if so, would I object to his joining me?

The gentleman at the bar was a spare, bright-eyed person in his sixties, European, from the cut of his elderly but very respectable suit. I wondered why he would want to join me if I was an American but presumably not if I wasn't, but gave him a nod and a welcoming smile, and he brought his drink over, introduced himself with Teutonic formality, and sat down.

I was ready for some sympathy and suggestions, and Herr Reichmann didn't have to pull out my fingernails to get me to talk about my quest for a man named Charles Atterley (though of course not a syllable of the word *Antichrist* passed my lips). I had long since invented a flimsy but apparently adequate cover story to explain my interest: I am a freelance writer investigating a man said to be leading a new religious movement.

"A new religious movement?" Herr Reichmann inquired with amused incredulity. "You know, we Europeans are not so gullible as you Americans, with your angels and your magic crystals."

"Exactly so," I replied smoothly. "That's just why Atterley seems so significant."

We made polite small talk for a few minutes, then Reichmann paused and gazed thoughtfully into a distant corner of the room. "I can put you in the way of someone far more significant than this Atterley," he said. "And possibly a member of his circle will be able to advise you."

"I'd be most grateful for that," I told him earnestly.

He wrote down a name on a beer coaster and handed it to me, saying, "Der Bau, nine this evening. The concierge will be able to give you directions."

He stood up and began to walk away, then suddenly turned about-face and bowed.

"Make him give you a map," he said.

A few minutes later I obediently carried the coaster to the concierge and demanded directions and a map. He thought the map unnecessary but grudgingly produced one when I insisted. I asked him what a Bau is.

"A Bau is a tunnel," he said, then, after a moment's thought: "No, I am mistaken. A Bau is like . . . is like an underground hiding place."

"A catacomb?"

"No, an animal's hiding place."

"A burrow?"

"That's it. A burrow."

In the burrow

I can't imagine that such a place as Der Bau exists anywhere in the New World, though there might be places created to look like it. When it was built, not far from the Karlstor, c. 1330, it was the cellar of a noble's palace. The level of the streets around the palace rose with the accretions of centuries, gradually turning the ground floor into a cellar and the original cellar into a subcellar. During World War II the subcellar housed treasures from nearby churches and museums. Afterward the palace stood in ruins until 1958, when it was razed and replaced by a commercial structure. The subcellar was preserved as Der Bau, a cabaret along classic lines, a boozy laboratory of artistic and intellectual experiment rather than a venue for popular entertainment. It was accessible from the lobby of the new building by means of a winding staircase that seemed to descend into the bowels of the earth.

At the entrance, a pleasant young woman tried to persuade me I'd come to the wrong place and would have a much better time anywhere else in Munich. I insisted I knew where I was and had been specifically invited to the evening's presentation. The name Reichmann bounced off her without effect, but she cheerfully passed me through when she saw I wasn't going to be deterred.

The room itself was of course abysmally dark but, thankfully, without the usual bohemian touch of candlelit tables. The ceiling, a surprising five or six meters high, teemed with tiny track lights, at the moment dimmed to near extinction but capable of producing the blaze of noon. The room was difficult to size, since its boundaries disappeared in the gloom, but was probably not more than thirty meters square.

A low, circular stage revolved slowly in the center of the room under a stationary, four-sided marquee of video screens. In the center of the stage stood a sort of combined lectern and computer keyboard. I groped my way forward till I found a seat at a table not much bigger than my notebook. One of my keys to early success as a scholar was the ability to listen to a lecture while taking it down verbatim in shorthand. I perfected this trick to such an extent that I could perform it in the dark (as I'd have to tonight) and without even thinking about it. Having made my preparations, however, it suddenly occurred to me to wonder if I wasn't wasting my time. Herr Reichmann hadn't given any indication that tonight's lecture would be in English. Indeed, why would it be? I looked around for someone to ask but quickly found I didn't care to reveal the fact that I was such a fool as to attend a lecture in an unknown language. I didn't even know the speaker's name, for God's sake.

These fretful thoughts were cut short when the lights under the marquee brightened, marking the arrival of the man himself—the arrival of a man and a woman, as it turned out. They stepped onto the stage, and the man took his place at the lectern and turned on the keyboard. As he worked at the board with silent concentration, oblivious of the audience, he reminded me of a large bird of prey, with his black suit, piercing eyes, and beaky nose. He also reminded me of a gargoyle, with his broad cheekbones and wide mouth, and of a lanky Parisian gangster I'd once met at a cocktail party who quoted Augustine and Schopenhauer and bore in his face the shadows of a terrible past. I thought he looked to be in his early or middle forties.

The woman—tall, athletically built, in her early thirties—took a position at the opposite side of the stage, facing the audience. Wearing jeans tucked into boots, a black silk shirt, and a tawny rawhide jacket that matched the color of her hair, pulled back into a ponytail, she looked out solemnly over the crowd. As the revolving stage slowly brought her round to my side of the room, I saw she had an extraordinary tattoo across her face—a red butterfly. From her rich complexion and exotic features, I felt sure some parent or grandparent had given her an infusion of Africa, Asia, or pre-Columbian America.

Suddenly the video screens popped into life bearing a title:

THE GREAT FORGETTING

The man gave the audience a moment to look at it, then began to speak.* I felt the woman's eyes on mine as she, too, began to speak . . . in sign.

Almost from the first words out of his mouth, I knew I'd been deceived—mysteriously and gratuitously. This could be no one but Charles Atterley. I knew this not by any strictly logical process, though logic certainly played its part. That he was an American was beyond doubt. That was enough. It wasn't possible that two different speakers from America could be spreading inflammatory ideas around Central Europe at the same time.

It seems strange to me now, after the event, that this revelation should have upset me so. I simply couldn't fathom why Herr Reichmann had taken the trouble to mislead me. It seemed completely pointless, and it was this pointlessness that stunned me. Luckily, my training didn't fail me. Even if my brain was stalled, my hand continued to work. Atterley's words marched across the page as if awakened by magic, as if they'd been written in invisible ink and were being drawn up out of the paper by the action of my pen. I realized I was watching my hand when it suddenly stopped—because Atterley had stopped. I looked up to see a new set of words forming on the screen:

VERILY I SAY UNTO YOU . . .
AGAIN AND AGAIN AND AGAIN

For some reason, this succeeded in jolting me out of my trance. I'd missed the first four or five minutes of Atterley's talk, but of course I hadn't missed them entirely. The minutes were there as a sort of echo that I was able to play back for the gist of his message.

* The text of this speech will be found on pages 237–255.

Atterley was talking about matters close to my life and even closer to my work—and I didn't like what I heard. This wasn't because it wasn't true but for exactly the opposite reason: because it was true and I'd missed it. He was making acute observations about phenomena I'd witnessed a thousand times and never thought to notice. I'd been living like a horse in the winner's circle at Ascot; the horse isn't at all impressed if he receives a royal visit, but this isn't because he's a republican, it's because he's a dimwit.

Everything Atterley was saying was obvious, and all of it was new. This made it maddening, because what is obvious should be *old*—and therefore well known, boring, and unnecessary to say. I glanced at the listeners around me, and seeing them riveted by Atterley's words, I wanted to kick them in the shins, grab them by the hair, and shake them, screaming, "Why are you paying attention to this? You *know* this! You could have worked it out yourself!"

But they hadn't worked it out—and I hadn't worked it out either.

The stage revolved, bringing me first Atterley then the woman, speaking with her hands. It got so that I hated seeing them coming and going—the two of them somehow being worse than twice as bad as one of them alone.

I hated seeing them coming and going—but I also just hated them, for what they were doing. They were showing me I was exactly like that goddamned horse in the winner's circle at Ascot. I may toss my head and prance like a champion, but when it comes right down to it, I can't make out any difference between the Queen of England and a stable boy.

They had found a sore spot in me that I didn't even know I had—and I detested them for it. They went on for another forty minutes or so. I heard it all, and I closed my ears to every bit of it—though my hand went on taking it down. Then suddenly the screens went dark, the lights on the stage dimmed, and Atterley and his pal stepped off into the darkness.

I got out of there like a drunk who has just remembered where he stashed a bottle. In fact, I needed a drink, but I didn't want one there or at my hotel, where I might conceivably run into Herr Reichmann again.

No problem. Munich is a big, big city, with plenty of drinks in it.

Friday, May 17

Aftershocks

Quite probably I've screwed up, though I don't suppose I've screwed up irrevocably. I came, I saw, I ran away. I'm obviously not going to make a point of reporting this to Fr. Lulfre.

It's also obvious that I have to get back on Atterley's trail.

Later

Herr Reichmann isn't registered at the hotel, and the barman who introduced us says he'd never seen him before. I didn't really expect it to be that easy. The concierge looked up Der Bau and learned that it opens at three in the afternoon, information that proved to be false or outdated. It opened—rather reluctantly, it seemed to me—at around five-thirty. The staff on hand for this event didn't have enough English to be of any help, but they managed to make it clear that they would send me someone named Harry if I'd sit down and wait for an hour or so.

I sat down and waited for an hour or so, and, surprisingly enough, they sent me someone named Harry, who turned out to be an Englishman or maybe a German who had schooled in England. I told him I was trying to find Charles Atterley.

"The name isn't familiar to me, I'm afraid," said Harry.

"The man who spoke here last night," I said.

"Ah. Is that his name?"

I looked at him incredulously. "You don't know his name?"

"I don't know *that* one."

"What do you mean?"

Harry shrugged. "The name I know may not be a name at all. He's known as B."

"B? B as in *boy*?"

"That's right."

"Why does he call himself that?"

Harry gave me the sort of smile you give a toddler who inquires about Santa's elves. I asked where I might find him.

"No idea at all," Harry said.

"Do you know where he might be speaking next?"

"No."

I thought for a moment. "How did you happen to book him into Der Bau?"

He frowned over this question as if I might be approaching the boundary between curiosity and presumptuousness. "This isn't Caesars Palace here, my friend. Arrangements are made in all sorts of ways and are usually very offhand. We don't go through any process you would recognize as 'booking acts.' "

"But you must have had some way of reaching him. . . ."

"We might have had, and if you put a gun to my head, I might be able to dig it up, but short of that, I'm not likely to." He shrugged again. "That's just the way it is. This isn't a missing-persons bureau, and I've got other things to do."

I told him I understood, thanked him anyway, and got up to leave.

"Come back later," Harry said. "You can always find people to talk to if you're buying drinks, and someone in the crowd may know more than I do about this guy."

I thanked him again and went back to the hotel.

Sitting here in my room—sitting, pacing, staring out the window—it suddenly popped into my memory that, when the heroes of fairy tales don't know what to do, they just sit down and weep. In the same circumstances, a modern hero can slug somebody or go out and get drunk, but he can never just sit down and weep.

I've read enough detective stories to know I should go pry some information out of somebody, but whom?

Sitting here staring at this notebook, it has finally occurred to me there's something I've *avoided* doing, and that's reading the talk I took down in my other notebook last night at Der Bau. I confess to having a strong reluctance to do that.

Interesting: I remember the title of the talk ("The Great Forgetting"), but I've forgotten what The Great Forgetting is. I haven't really forgotten it, of course, but I've shut the door of my memory on it, which means that—

Saved by the telephone bell. As I should have been. When the hero sits down and weeps because he doesn't know what to do, the fairy-tale universe sends magical helpers. Mine wasn't very magical but he was certainly mysterious. I think I can put it all down verbatim.

ME: Hello.
HIM: Fr. Osborne?
ME: Yes. Who is this?
HIM: What the devil do you think you're doing?
ME: What?
HIM: Do you understand what you're supposed to be doing here?
ME: Who is this?
HIM: I was led to expect someone marginally competent.

It was impossible to miss the drift of the conversation, and I was certainly getting the rough end of it. I tried to rally a bit of self-defense.

ME: I don't know who you are or who appointed you my housemother, but I know who I am. I'm a parish priest. If you were expecting James Bond, either you were misled or you misled yourself.
HIM: Does being a parish priest mean you live in a coma?
ME: I'm sorry to have been a source of disappointment for you.

With that crusher, I hung up, something I don't think I've done to a caller since junior high. There's nothing to beat it when your back is against the wall. As expected, he called back immediately.

"The girl is sick," he told me, sounding as if nothing had happened. "The girl is dying."

"What?" For a second I thought he was giving me a password of some kind. Maybe I was supposed to reply with, "But the swallows will return to Capistrano anyway." Luckily I caught myself and said, "You mean the one who was signing?"

"Of course. Didn't you see her face?"

"I saw her face. I just didn't realize it was— What is it, lupus? Lupus isn't fatal, is it?"

"It's scleroderma, or possibly mixed connective-tissue disease. They're all in the same family, including lupus. It's an autoimmune collagen disease, degenerative, incurable."

"Okay. And what am I supposed to do with this information?"

"Radenau has a research facility devoted to the study and treatment of collagen diseases. That's what the two of them are doing in Central Europe. Radenau is the center of the circle, ninety kilometers south of Hamburg."

"So what are you saying? When in doubt, head for Radenau?"

"When in doubt, remember that Radenau is the center of the circle."

"Somebody could have told me this at the outset."

My caller sighed. It made him sound almost human. "Somebody could have told it to me too, but nobody did. I dug it out for myself."

This news did not make me happy, but I managed to keep it to myself. I said, "That brings me back to my original question. Who the hell are you? And if you're taking care of this, what am I supposed to be doing?"

"You're supposed to be leading and I'm supposed to be following. You're not even supposed to know I'm here."

"Why am I not supposed to know you're here?"

"I don't know. Maybe the idea is not to tax your powers of dissimulation. Or maybe the idea is to make you take some initiative."

"Fuck you, Charlie," I said. Some people are shocked when they hear a cleric talk as dirty as a third-grader, but this one just waited. "Listen," I told him, "I'm not a detective. I admit it. I could use some help."

"Not from me. Get out there and do some work."

The line went dead.

Detective work

I got out my map, and that helped a lot. In a circle around Radenau there were fifty major cities where B might be speaking—Nuremberg, Dresden, Berlin, Kiel, Hamburg, Bremen, Essen, Köln, Frankfurt, Heidelberg, and Stuttgart, to mention just a few. There would have been nothing to it if Billy Graham had been out there touring, but how the devil was I supposed to track the speaking engagements of a virtual unknown named B?

Finding no inspiration in geography, I spent some time wondering who Charlie is. A civilian, surely. As people will, I conjured up a figure to fit the voice. I put him at age thirty-five, wiry, of middling height and weight, some sort of military or paramilitary type with a ratlike face and cheap clothes dating from the 1950s. As is evident from all this, Charlie had failed to win my affection. I toyed briefly with the idea of calling Fr. Lulfre and asking what the deal was but couldn't find a shadow of an argument to support it.

If Charlie knows where B is, what does he gain by withholding this information from me? If he wants to make me look bad, why call and give me hints? On the phone he tried to sell me an explanation for these mysteries: He was dealing with a lazy schoolboy; I'd done my homework poorly, and he wasn't there to give me the right answers, he was there to give me a taste of the stick. That makes sense if he really is a military type. He's treating this like boot camp. Okay.

As far as I can see, there's only one fact in everything he told me that is both hard and relevant: Wherever else B and "the girl" go, they eventually end up back in Radenau. I have to assume this is the best information Charlie has. If he knew for a fact that B is going to spend the summer in Spitzbergen, for example, he certainly wouldn't give me all this dizdazz about Radenau. If I'm right about this, then Charlie himself is heading for Radenau.

And that, I have to suppose, is what he called to tell me.

Isn't it grand to be educated?

Saturday, May 18

Radenau

Departing after a late, leisurely breakfast, I was in Hamburg by midafternoon. Germany is smaller than Montana, and traveling from one end of it to another on the high-speed intercity express makes it seem even smaller. Having a couple hours to kill before making a connection to Radenau, I visited the tourist office at the Hauptbahnhof and was earnestly advised not to miss the Jungfernstieg, an easy walk away, which would give me the city's magnificent artificial lake on the one hand and its most elegant shops on the other. I took the advice, and there it was, by golly, exactly as advertised.

Not much of Radenau predates the 1940s. Albert Speer, Hitler's architect and technocrat-in-chief had something or other in mind for it during the late stages of the war but certainly not a fine-arts center. I think it was going to be a place where factories would really feel at home during the Thousand-Year Reich. Now it's a sprawling industrial park dotted with apartment complexes indistinguishable from barracks. The only good things my guidebook could find to say about the hotel where I'd booked was that it was modern and scrupulously clean, and it was both of those. It was also "downtown," which is to say in the older part of the city. Old Radenau doesn't even pretend to be quaint.

I'd spent my time on the train making a readable longhand copy of "The Great Forgetting" to send Fr. Lulfre. When I checked in at the hotel, I asked the desk clerk if they had a fax machine, and he drew himself up as indignantly as if I'd asked about indoor plumbing. I'm glad I had a fax to placate him with.

I'm going to have a bath, a long, meditative dinner (meditating about as few things as possible), and perhaps a stroll before bed. No more than that. No work till tomorrow.

A long night begins

As I said I might, I took myself out for a walk after dinner. The night was pleasant, the streets were quiet. I'm not a big explorer. About three blocks out (in other words, near the limit of my adventurousness), I heard a mild sort of hubbub somewhere ahead. If this had been Beirut, naturally I would've just turned around and gone back to the hotel, but since it was Radenau, I was curious. I let the noise guide me to a nearby side street where a small theater was being picketed by forty or fifty citizens who seemed rather stunned to find themselves employed in such a vulgar display of rowdiness. They were milling about in an undisciplined way, parading crudely scrawled signs to nonexistent witnesses and halfheartedly chanting slogans whose exact wording was still being worked on.

It took me about three seconds to realize that I'd found B, or at least the site of his next gig. A favorite activity among the sign makers was to publish the supposed meaning of B's name. Thus he was named as the blasphemer, the bastard, the bunghole, the bigmouth, the blowhard, the bonehead, *le badaud, la bête, le bobard, le boucher, le bruit, die Beerdigung, der Bettler,* and *die Blattern,* among others I no longer recall. Still others identified him as Beelzebub, the Beast, Belial, and Barabbas, and two or three, ignoring the initial problem altogether, confidently dubbed him the Antichrist, which I must say surprised me on the basis of what I knew so far. Really, the whole thing surprised me.

The theater entrance was being defended by a uniformed guard who looked both more fierce and more worried than I thought necessary under the circumstances. The only rule he seemed to be enforcing for admittance was that protest signs had to be left outside. Watching the traffic at the door, I soon saw that the procedure was to picket for a while, then to go in and heckle the speaker for a while, then to come back out and picket some more. I pushed my way in.

First I took in the fact that the lecture hall wasn't very large, seating some three or four hundred, then I took in the much more important fact that the hecklers were definitely not putting their hearts into their work. Perhaps it's true that Germans are uncomfortable defying authority. The first twenty rows pretty clearly held B's supporters, looking sullen and tense, while behind them—and everywhere else—were arrayed his glowering (but largely silent) antagonists. There was an empty seat near the front, and I headed for it after grabbing a stack of handbills to use as writing paper. I was disappointed to see that, except for B, the stage was empty.

B lifted his eyes to mine as I sat down, and an electric charge of recognition flashed between us, or so I imagined.

He was sideways to the audience, slouching against the podium and leaning forward to bring his lips to within a millimeter of the microphone. I bother with these details in an effort to recreate the impression he gave of being entirely indifferent to conditions that might have silenced or intimidated other speakers, for while the hecklers were not very noisy, their hostility was palpable. His hands were still and relaxed, and he seemed wholly focused on his thoughts, which he was sharing with the audience as intimately and spontaneously as if in private conversation.

I had no idea how long he'd been talking, but as I listened I began to recognize familiar ground within "The Great Forgetting." But though the ground was familiar, it was less extensive. In other words, this was just a review. Eventually he paused and sent his eyes deliberately around the auditorium.

"Tonight," he said, "I'd like to talk to you about the boiling of a frog."

I uncapped my pen and started taking it down.*

An invitation is issued

Till now I've never had reason to examine it (or even to notice it), but I go into a sort of trancelike state when I start transcribing a lecture. There is a very pleasant sensation (now that I look at it) that the words coming off the end of the pen are my own. I have the illusion that my hand is anticipating what my ears hear—that I know the words before they're spoken and could transcribe the lecture even if the lecturer stopped speaking. I experience a strange sense of intimacy with the speaker. I may have no very exact understanding of what he's

---

* The text of this speech will be found on pages 256–273.

saying, but I imagine I have a profound perception of his meaning. When he stops speaking, I may be unable to answer the simplest question about his topic, but this doesn't worry me, because I know it's all securely locked away in my transcription.

Since on this occasion B was using no visual aids, I closed my eyes, which usually helps concentration. About half an hour later, however, they popped open quite involuntarily. I looked up at B, he looked down at me, and our eyes met briefly, without special acknowledgment or recognition. Without a pause between words, he swept his eyes over the crowd, registering no difference, as far as I could see, between friends and foes. Then, in a gesture that had no evident correlation to anything he was saying, he lifted the index finger of his left hand straight into the air, held it there for a moment, then decisively angled it to his right. It was unmistakably a signal of some kind, but I couldn't spot anyone who had caught it or seemed be reacting to it in any way. I considered the idea that the signal had been picked up only by me because it was *meant* only for me.

He went on speaking. I closed my eyes to shut out the relentless noise of the crowd and went on transcribing. Minutes passed. Suddenly I noticed that my hand had stopped moving, and I actually wondered why. Opening my eyes, I saw that B was finished. Even so, it wasn't till he'd gathered up his papers and stepped away from the podium that the audience seemed to waken to the fact that B's talk was over. His hecklers sent up a cheer of self-congratulation for a job well done, while his supporters hurried to organize some applause. Already moving, B gave them an indifferent nod and disappeared into the wings.

Pilgrimage

By the time I got outside, the protest had turned into a party, with hugs and kisses and wine-filled paper cups for everyone who had taken part in the mighty deed. B's supporters straggled into the night unmolested except for teasing catcalls and jeers. As I watched from across the street, I soon realized that the protesters were doing the same thing I was: keeping an eye on the stage-door alley beside the theater, waiting for B to emerge. After a few minutes a car pulled up—not a limo by any means, just a middle-aged Mercedes sedan. A second later a flying wedge cut through the crowd, muscled its passenger into the backseat, and stood guard as the sedan sped off to the right.

Having missed its chance for a last little *coup d'éclat,* the crowd quickly lost its buoyant mood and began to break up. Bottles were corked, cups were collected, and naturally everyone had to shake hands with everyone else before departing. While this was going on, the uniformed guard reappeared at the theater entrance to usher out one last patron and lock up behind him. The patron thanked the guard with a nod, flipped up the collar of his topcoat against the night air, then turned to his left and made his way through the crowd into the darkness beyond. He would have been easily recognized had anyone bothered to look. I waited until he had a head start of fifty meters or so, then followed.

Obviously I had no idea where he was leading—if he was leading at all. Less obviously I had no idea why I was following, except that I imagined I'd been invited. At first I thought it likely that the Mercedes would circle the block to pick him up, but I was mistaken. Then I thought it likely that he was headed for some nearby tavern or coffeehouse, but again I was mistaken. He walked on—and on and on—gradually leaving the downtown area of the city behind.

I began to have second and third thoughts about this adventure. If suddenly abandoned, I wouldn't have an easy time finding my way back to the hotel. The buses were no longer running—or at least not here—and I hadn't seen a cruising taxicab in half an hour. Even worse, from my point of view, we'd entered an area of the city that I supposed would be called light industrial. There were no apartment buildings, no shops, no cafés, no all-night drugstores with convenient telephones and possibly helpful clerks. This was the home of factories, machine shops, brickyards, and warehouses, inhabited at this hour only by night watchmen and guard dogs.

A reasonable question would be, Why didn't I catch him up and ask where he was going? I wondered about that. Would that be the ordinary thing to do—or the extraordinary thing? The normal thing or the odd thing?

Thinking about it didn't help, of course. The natural thing is always the unstudied thing, the unselfconscious thing. This particular thing was something that, if done at all, should have been done right away. What sense would it make to follow blindly for an hour, then rush up and demand to know where he was leading me? It was an absurd situation, which I—being grown-up, male, competent, etc., etc.—should somehow have handled in a different and better way (though even now I can't say what way that might have been).

Looking up from my gloomy thoughts, I saw that B was entering a small, nondescript building just ahead. It looked like a leftover shed of some kind, sandwiched between a warehouse and a railroad yard. I hurried on, hoping this was B's destination. I was startled and amused when I reached the door and found an artfully rough sign next to it reading LITTLE BOHEMIA.

Little Bohemia!

When I opened the door and stepped inside, a laugh burst out of me like a bird startled from a tree. Little Bohemia was a tavern, but a tavern unlike any I'd ever seen, except perhaps in dreams or imagination. It might have been a set designer's creation for a film biography of Amedeo Modigliani. It was low-ceilinged, full of cobwebs and smoke, and would have been pitch-dark except for a few candles stuck in the necks of wine bottles. The walls were thick with sketches, caricatures, and paintings, most so blackened by smoke that they were little more than post-impressionist smudges. Incongruously—yet somehow perfectly—a rainbow-lit jukebox near the door was hissing its way though an ancient, scratchy Piaf record, which had to be, could only be, and indeed was . . . "La Vie en Rose." Spending a million, Disney couldn't have made it better or more archetypal, though the dust and cobwebs would have been created from antiseptic plastic and the song would have been sung by a clone of Piaf herself, wearing a perfect reproduction of the Sparrow's famous old sweater.

The clientele, however, weren't *en rôle,* or at least not self-consciously so. There were no berets, no Basque fisherman's jerseys, no artistic goatees. These folks, murmuring at their tables or hunched over their chessboards, might have been anything—poets, novelists, playwrights, actors, artists, models—but who knows? Nowadays, public-relations flacks look like artists, artists look like truckers, and truckers look like off-duty soccer champions.

B was seated at a table at the back, and I gathered that he must be an old customer and one of settled habits, for a waitress was already in the act of serving him, not sixty seconds after his arrival. Catching sight of me, he summoned me with a nod to the chair at his right. As I approached, I heard him say to the waitress, "Theda, bring my friend one of these as well, won't you? He's had a long walk." And then to me: "It's a single-malt Scotch, Lagavulin sixteen-year-old, and will restore the dead to life, if administered within a reasonable amount of time."

I sat down and looked, probably rather blankly, into his strange, gargoylelike face.

"Well, what did you think of my lecture?" he asked.

"I don't know," I said, then added: "I'm not being coy. I'm still working on it."

"You were at Der Bau."

"That's right."

"But not at Stuttgart or before?"

"No."

"That's good. By chance or design, you've begun at the beginning of the cycle."

"It was by chance," I told him, and he smiled politely, as if it made no great difference.

"What's your name, by the way?"

I told him, and Theda chose that moment to arrive with my drink, a dark amber liquid in an oversize shot glass. I took a sip and blinked in astonishment at its weighty, charged smokiness.

"Wonderful, isn't it?"

I nodded, suddenly feeling oddly detached, like a page torn from one book and inserted in another. "And 'B'?" I asked. "Why are you called B?"

He gave me a twisted smile. "Do you know—I'm not entirely sure! This was a name the crowds chose for me, in answer to some deep, unconscious perception. When the name stuck, I did some research, as much as is possible about something like that. If, in ancient times, you met a man or a woman branded with the letter *A*, you knew that their sin was . . . ?"

"Adultery."

"Of course. That wasn't just Hawthorne's invention for *The Scarlet Letter*, you know. If you met someone branded with the letter *B*, you knew that his sin was blasphemy."

"And is that in fact your sin?"

"Oh yes. But I can't believe the crowds chose the letter for that reason—or at least not deliberately."

"Then why?"

He shrugged. "I simply don't know."

"May I ask your real name?"

"I'd rather you didn't. I no longer use it, except on hotel registers."

"All right. Why did you signal me to follow you?"

He smiled in a new way, as if out of real pleasure. "Do you know the ancient Chinese novel *Monkey*? It's the story of a scamp of a stone ape hatched as a sort of divine accident from a stone egg on a mountaintop. After living a carefree life for many years he suddenly became aware that there's a great deal to learn that he knew nothing of, and he set off across the world to find a teacher. At last he came to a monastery ruled by a famous sage, who let him attend classes with the other novices while serving as a sort of chore boy. One day after several years the master asked Monkey what sort of wisdom he was searching for. Monkey asked in turn what sorts were available, then proceeded to reject each one as it was described. The master became enraged, cracked Monkey three times over the head with his knuckle-rapper, and stomped off. The other pupils were furious, but Monkey wasn't dismayed, for he understood the language of secret signs and knew that the master had ordered him to come to his quarters at the third watch. When he arrived, the sage commended Monkey for insisting on a wisdom beyond what others would accept and made a magical revelation so powerful that Monkey received Illumination on the spot."

Teachings: public and secret

I gave B a minute to go on, and when he didn't, I asked him if I was a monkey he'd selected for special instruction.

"Possibly," he said, "but that isn't why I told the story."

"Go on."

"Why did the sage have two sets of teachings, public and secret?"

"I don't know."

B lowered his chin to his chest and gave me an ironical "up-from-under" look. "Give it some thought," he told me. "Play along with me."

"Why did the sage have two sets of teachings? I'd say it was because he wouldn't be much of a sage if he didn't. The public teachings are the ones that everyone hears, because those are the ones that can be articulated. The secret teachings are the ones that cannot be articulated at all—because they don't exist."

B nodded thoughtfully. "A very good, modern answer. The answer of a cynic."

"I don't think of myself as a cynic."

"But you're quite certain there are no secret teachings."

"Absolutely certain."

"Jesus didn't have any special nuggets for his disciples."

"No."

"Nor did Gautama Buddha or Muhammad for theirs."

"No."

"You may be right, of course, but this misses the point of my story."

"Okay. Why *did* the sage have two different sets of teachings?"

"One was a set of teachings that are easy to disclose, the other a set of teachings that are very difficult to disclose. The first was the public set, of course—the set to which all the novices were exposed. The second was the secret set, the set that only exceptional students can aspire to—or accept."

"In other words . . . ?"

"In other words: Secret teachings aren't ones that teachers keep to themselves. Secret teachings are ones that teachers have a hard time giving away."

I shook my head. I damn well *had* to shake my head, of course. I've never seen it spelled out, but it's implicit in every text that—aside from forbidden (and probably illusory) lore like witchcraft and necromancy—there are no *relevant* secrets. There are plenty of things we don't know and will never know, but everything we *need* to know has been revealed. If this isn't the case, if Moses or Buddha or Jesus or Muhammad held something back for an inner circle, then revelation is incomplete—and by definition useless.

I said, "I'm not sure how this answers my original question. Why did you invite me here?"

"I invited you for the same reason the sage invited Monkey. I hope to make you take away some of the teachings I can never get to at the podium."

"I don't understand. Why can you 'never get to them' at the podium?"

My question seemed to defeat him. He sighed, collapsed in on himself, and looked around bleakly in a sort of pantomime of pedagogical despair. "I thought you understood what was going on here."

"I'm sorry. I thought I did too."

"Every time Jesus stood up to speak to a group, he was speaking to a thousand years of shared history, shared vision, and shared understanding. The people in his audiences were Jews, after all. They didn't just speak the same language. Their thoughts had been shaped by the same scriptures, the same legends, the same worldview. He didn't have to teach them who God was, who Abraham was, who Moses was. He didn't have to explain concepts like *prophet, devil, repentance, baptism, scripture, Sabbath, commandment, heaven, hell,* and *messiah.* These were all commonplace notions in their culture. Whenever he spoke to them, he knew with absolute certainty that his listeners came to him prepared to understand what he had to say."

"Yes, I see that."

"Jesus didn't have to lay a foundation every time he spoke. Others had done that for him through a hundred generations, literally from the time of Abraham. But I *do* have to do that—with every single audience I face. You've heard me in Munich and here in Radenau, but you haven't heard what I have to teach. All you've heard so far is the foundation—and it's far from finished."

"But eventually . . ."

"Yes, I get there eventually, and that's why crowds call me Blasphemer and Beast and Antichrist. But I never get to the *end* of what I have to teach—not in public."

"Why not?"

"Because there's no continuity among my listeners from one audience to the next. This means that, in each succeeding audience, fewer and fewer people have been with me from the beginning and more and more of them are getting lost. After five or six lectures it's point-less to go on. The end is still out there, but I've no hope of reaching it with this audience—and even less hope of reaching it with the next audience. I have to go back and begin all over again, which is what I did in Munich."

Then B nodded in my direction and said: "And I have to wait for the arrival of someone like you."

I felt a pang of fear at these words, the very same pang I feel when I picture myself falling from a tall building.

The unmasking

We sipped our life-restoring drinks. We listened to Piaf and other singers of her era, all French or German. We inhaled vast quantities of secondhand smoke. After a few minutes I said, "That still doesn't explain why you chose me in particular."

B frowned and scratched vaguely at the corner of his right eye—a gesture I would soon get used to seeing. "This clearly troubles you," he said at last, "and I'm trying to imagine why." I opened my mouth to deny it, but he stopped me with a shake of his head. "You're *not* a good liar, you know."

I gawked at him.

"Not enough practice, I'd say."

"What makes you think I'm lying?"

He shook his head again. "Don't do that, Jared, you're really terrible at it. Either lie with conviction or speak the truth."

"You're right," I confessed. "I'm not a good liar and I don't get enough practice. But, even so, what made you decide I was lying?"

"The very persistent trend of your questions—your insistence that my invitation needs to be explained. You're obviously wondering how you managed to fool me."

I wasn't sure he was right about this, but I was too thick-witted—too clogged with smoke and booze—to think about it clearly.

Suddenly there was a third person sitting at our table. I took it in that way: first, that it was a person; second, that it was a woman; third, that it was a woman I'd seen before. It was the woman from Der Bau—the woman who had translated B's talk into sign language, the woman in the rawhide jacket with the strange butterfly opened across the center of her face. The woman (I suddenly realized) who had exerted a powerful attraction on me from the moment I saw her, with her broad, athletic shoulders, her ranch-hand clothes, and her wild tawny hair.

She was talking to B—with her hands. He was "listening" intently. Suddenly a big smile swept across his face, and he looked at me . . . and laughed: "A priest!"

I said, "What?"

"You're a priest?"

I looked at the woman and she met my gaze without expression, as if I were a lizard or a fish.

B said, "She found your breviary."

I stared at him without comprehension until he added: "In your room at the hotel." Even then it took me most of a minute to figure it out. He had invited me for a hike across Radenau so his assistant would have time to find my hotel, work out which room was mine, and go in. I was grateful she hadn't found my diary; that travels with me.

I didn't know what to say. I felt profoundly stupid and incompetent, like a kid who might pick Tiffany's as a terrific place to make his debut as a shoplifter.

"Are you an assassin," B asked, "or just a spy?"

The woman laughed—not sarcastically, it seemed to me, but with genuine amusement. I was surprised when she spoke—that she *could* speak.

"Not an assassin," she said, looking at me now as if I were a cocker spaniel that someone had just mistaken for a pit bull.

"No, I'm sure you're right," B said. "Not an assassin. What then?"

It was almost funny. At that very moment Piaf started singing "Non, Je Ne Regrette Rien"—no, I don't regret anything! I couldn't think of a single thing to say.

The next few minutes passed (as they say) as in a dream. Theda got paid. B and the woman stood up to leave and seemed surprised when I didn't follow their example.

"Are you going to spend the night?" B asked.

"No."

"Then come on, we'll give you a ride back to your hotel."

Feeling even more idiotic than before, I rode in the backseat of the Mercedes I'd seen earlier outside the theater. The woman drove.

"This is Shirin, by the way," B told me.

I nodded mutely.

Fifteen minutes later we pulled up outside the hotel. I struggled out of the backseat and thanked them for the ride.

Shirin gave me a shake of her head and a pitying smile, then drove off.

I trudged gloomily into the hotel.

Saturday, May 18 (cont.)

The night should have been over then . . .

But it wasn't.

As I passed the desk, the clerk stopped me to deliver a message, neatly sealed in an envelope. Someone more experienced might have shoved it in a pocket and forgotten it, but I'm not used to receiving messages at hotels. I ripped it open and read:

> Jared:
> Call me immediately on receiving this message, day or night. Immediately.
>
> Bernard Lulfre

I crumpled it into a ball and shoved it in my pocket. As I turned to resume my journey toward the elevators, the clerk said, "He was very insistent, sir."

I turned back and was surprised to see that it was the same clerk who had been wounded by my wondering if the hotel had a fax machine. Possibly he was a cyborg, tireless and efficient.

"Very insistent, was he?" I asked.

"Very insistent, sir."

"I'd like a bottle of whiskey in my room."

A tiny frown line appeared in the middle of his forehead. "I'm afraid the bar is closed, sir."

"I don't want a bar, I want some whiskey in my room. Half a liter, or however you bottle it over here." I shoved a hundred marks at him and walked away.

. . .

Was I going to call Bernard Lulfre in this state of mind? It really made no sense, but I wanted to have a drink, go to sleep, and wake up without this hanging over me, so I placed the call. Fr. Lulfre himself answered the phone.

"Jared!" he said. "It must be the middle of the night over there."

"It is, yes."

"What's going on? Bring me up to date."

"I've attended two of B's lectures, and I've—"

"Two of whose lectures?"

"B's. He's not known as Atterley over here. To the public he's known as B."

"B as in *boy*?"

"B as in *blasphemer*."

"I see. You've attended two of his lectures, and . . ."

"And I've spent an hour talking to him."

"Really! As what, a fan? A follower?"

"Yes, possibly," I replied vaguely.

"And what's your impression?"

"That he's very bright. Completely sincere."

"Not your impression of him, your impression of what he's saying."

I was too tired to think about this. "I don't know. It seems harmless enough."

"Harmless? That can't be right."

I shrugged at him over four thousand miles of cable.

"Have you been taping him?"

"That's not practical. Unless he was wearing a mike, I'd just get crowd noise."

"Have you been taking notes at least?"

"Better than that," I snapped. "I have it down verbatim, in shorthand. Didn't you get my fax?"

"I haven't been down to my office today. Is it all there?"

"Just the first lecture. I'll have to make a longhand copy of the second one. That'll take a few hours."

"It's not some exotic personal shorthand, is it?"

"No, just ordinary speed writing."

"Then my secretary can figure it out. Go ahead and fax it."

I started to object on the grounds that the notebook would have to be photocopied first, since it couldn't be faxed directly, but quickly realized I was just being childish. Resigning myself to the inevitable, I went downstairs and got it done.

A bottle of Cutty Sark was waiting for me in my room when I got back.

I started drinking and I started writing. I don't know what the hell is going on, but I do know this diary's going to be useless if I don't keep it current as I go along.

Brought it up to the present just in time to close the drapes against the rising sun. Hope I remember to put out the "Disturben Verboten" sign before crashing.

Dangerous questions

The fax machine in this joint runs round the clock, but lunch is only served till two, and I barely managed to get seated. It's now 2:47. I suppose I note the time as a means of procrastination. I don't want to think, I don't want to write, so I make careful records of the time.

It's 2:50, and I wonder what's wrong with me.

It's 2:52, and I think my life is falling apart.

Falling apart under what stress? I can't quite figure it out. Or I don't quite *want* to figure it out. Certainly the largest part is B, but I can't figure out why. I'm extremely reluctant to reread his lectures. His message is like a shadowy figure standing at my shoulder. I can catch it out of the corner of my eye, and it troubles me, because I can't see it clearly. I know I could turn around and face it directly, but, as I say, I'm reluctant to do that.

I told Fr. Lulfre that B's teachings are harmless. What did I mean by that? I think it was something like this: B is harmless, because he's just calling into question the entire foundation of Christianity—not to mention Judaism, Islam, and Buddhism.

No harm in that, is there?

No harm at all, Fr. Lulfre, because you taught me yourself that no question is dangerous—for *us.* We've got all the answers, so ask away. We can answer anything. Absolutely anything. For *us,* questions aren't hazards, questions are opportunities.

Isn't that right, Fr. Lulfre?

So what's your problem, Fr. Lulfre?

On the phone I said to you, "B's teachings are harmless," and you said in reply, "That can't be right."

What?

What does this mean, Fr. Lulfre? Does it mean that some questions are dangerous after all?

The good soldier Jared

The fact that I find anything here to be disturbed about . . . disturbs me. I shouldn't be disturbed at all. I mean, I'm a good soldier, aren't I?—smart as hell but basically a simple, uncomplicated kind of guy. What's the name of the tormented preacher in *The Scarlet Letter*? Dimmesdale? I'm no Arthur Dimmesdale, not by a million miles. I'm no tormented anything. You want me to spy on some guy who's being talked about as the Antichrist? Sure, why the hell not? Where's my plane ticket? What's the limit on my credit card?

Hey, that's why the great minds of the Laurentians chose me, isn't it? They wanted someone bright, controllable, and loyal—not necessarily strong in faith but maybe just a bit weak in imagination.

The joke is, however (and it really is a terrific joke), that, because I'm just a good soldier, simple and uncomplicated, I *listen* to the guy I'm supposed to be spying on. And, having listened, I say, "Yeah, I see what he's saying. This is something new. This is something *really* new. This guy is making sense. He's making as much sense as I've ever heard *anybody* make. What's the problem?"

Then the guy takes me aside and says:

Then the guy leads me halfway across the city on foot and says:

Then the guy buys me sixteen-year-old Scotch and says:

"There are some teachings that only exceptional students can handle. I hope to lay some of those teachings on you."

I think maybe the great minds of the Laurentians should have found themselves a soldier who was not quite so good—or perhaps much better.

Of course, I'm not quite sure where I stand with B at this point. Looking back on it now, I see that I was a lot more upset by Shirin's revelation than he was. The truth is, I was just projecting. Having been found out, I took it for granted that he'd be disgusted or disappointed. In fact, he was neither. He was *amused.*

Okay, I'm still not sure where I stand with him, but I don't think I'm exactly in the trash heap. I didn't come off looking brilliant, but I'm pretty sure I didn't come off looking like scum.

Sunday, May 19

Radenau: Night Two

When I arrived at the Schauspielhaus Wahnfried at nine o'clock, I almost thought I'd come on the wrong night or to the wrong place, because the protesters were gone. Perhaps this second night of speaking wasn't on their schedule or they thought one night at the barricades was sufficient; perhaps there was a heckler shortage at some other site. Nonetheless, the door was being guarded by a vestige of the group, an angry-looking woman passing out angry-looking flyers. I accepted one, but it was in German.

On the previous night the houselights had been turned up as if for a quick evacuation. Tonight they were turned down as if for a quiet reading. The stage was dimly lit and empty except for its speaker's podium. There were perhaps a hundred people in the audience. Not wanting to be recognized from the stage, I took a seat well back. It was a quiet crowd, patient, subdued—a crowd of strangers and, for the most part, I thought, loners.

After a few minutes B walked onto the stage, stepped up to the podium, and began arranging papers. For a public speaker, this is just technique. After a few moments the audience registered his presence and subsided into silence. B began, as I assumed he would, at the beginning, summarizing not only the previous night's talk but the one he'd given in Munich, extending the process of diminishing returns that he'd described at Little Bohemia. With each successive talk, this summary would grow in comprehensiveness—and proportionately diminish in effectiveness.

When he was finally ready to step off into unexplored country, he paused and looked around, gathering up everyone's attention, and I took out my pen.*

---

* The text of this speech will be found on pages 274–284.

.   .   .

I think that my true situation came to me then in the next forty minutes, as I was scribbling away, fiercely concentrated on hearing and on making out the words (for you can't really hear if you don't get the words—it all just turns into gibberish). Pious souls often imagine that being a priest automatically puts you miles ahead of everyone on the wisdom track. Listening to B, I realized that I'm not an inch ahead of anyone on that track. I'm in the dark. I'm at the beginning. For all intents and purposes, I'm still nineteen. At one point, my hand wavered, and I said to myself, "I don't need to take this down. All I have to do is listen." But I was sufficiently doubtful that I kept going. I'm glad I did, now, of course. At the time I felt like a man at the wheel of a sinking ship—purposeless, since any ship can find its way to the bottom.

After half an hour I also felt like a losing boxer in the eighth or ninth round of a ten-rounder. I'd been hit everywhere it's legal to be hit—every square inch. The sentences came at me like punches, and I read them and took them in like punches. "Oh yes, there's another one to the kidney. I remember one like that in round three." "Oh yes, and there's one to the biceps—that's not supposed to hurt, but god-dammit it does!" "And here comes one I was sure was going over my shoulder, but instead it caught me right on the ear."

When it was over, I staggered outside with everyone else and planted myself across the street, assuming B would make his appearance in a few minutes. This gave me some time to think, and here's what I thought:

I've been living in a sort of time capsule, or perhaps in a special ward of the hospital that hadn't changed since, oh, the 1950s. It was a ward in which my parents and their friends would have been happy. I'm not sure what I mean by this, I'm just groping. In this ward, Glenn Miller is still cool, not as a figure of nostalgia, but as he was to my parents when they were in college. In this ward, kids have big weddings and spend their honeymoons trying to figure out what it's all about. In this ward, they use the rhythm method and have kids when it fails. In this ward, there are no crack babies, no lunatic cults, no terrorists. In this ward, if someone happened to tune in a radio station carrying B's talk, he would have dialed up something else—something relevant to life in the ward.

I don't suppose I actually had these specific thoughts while I was standing outside the theater. I'm not sure a single coherent idea passed through my head, I was just standing there feeling doomed. At some point unnoticed by me, someone turned out the marquee lights and the lights in the lobby. Perhaps ten minutes passed. Finally I came to and realized that the preceding night's pattern was not going to be repeated. B was still inside, and if I wanted to talk to him, I'd have to find him there. I slunk my way over to the dimly lit stage door and found it prepared as a smoker's bolt-hole, a book of matches holding it open a crack. I went in, discarded the matches, and let the door close and lock behind me.

Far, far away there were voices. There was nothing unusual about them. They didn't sound particularly happy or sad, excited or calm. They might have belonged to people discussing a housing ordinance or the end of the world. There was no way to tell, though I stood there listening through a full minute while my eyes tried to find a glimmer of light to see by.

The stage was obviously going to be more or less directly in front of me, on the other side of some unknown collection of corridors, dressing rooms, waiting areas, and finally the wings overlooking the stage area itself. Since no helpful angel was there to guide me, I began groping my way forward, and after a couple of minutes was rewarded with a glimpse of gray light to my left. It was a bare bulb hanging over a bare stage and dimly illuminating the empty auditorium.

Into the underworld

The mutter of voices was as distant as ever. I followed it backstage to the well of a circular iron staircase and descended into the darkness. I didn't need my eyes; the steps were regular, the railing solid. I'd seen once, somewhere, a cross-section diagram of a theater, showing a first below-stage, a second, a third, and a fourth, and I remembered wondering what could be usefully stored at such a depth. Soon the klink-klunk of my footsteps was heard below, and the muttering stopped. The fourth below-stage, where the stairs came to an end, was vast and high-ceilinged. At a far end of the space, set atop boxes and tables and shelves, a hundred candles illuminated an area that looked like a living room carved out of the middle of an antiques shop.

B was seated in an armchair facing me. He waved and called out, "Don't worry! There are no rats!" as if encouraging me to come forward. Suddenly a dozen faces bobbed up out of the flotsam to stare at me dimly from behind ancient, battered furniture, rolled-up rugs, moldy dressmaker's dummies, rotting displays of taxidermy, towering wardrobes, stacks of books and magazines, and racks of faded costumes. B seemed to sense my self-consciousness and made my approach less awkward by explaining the absence of rats.

"The management is careful to mount a performance of *King Lear* at least once every second year," he said. When he had everyone's eyes, he went on: " 'Mice and rats and such small deer have been Tom's food for seven long year.' *Lear,* Act III, Scene 4"—as if this would make it all plain.

He gestured to a chair at his right, a wonderful old Biedermeier fauteuil with cushions of faded pale green velvet. He himself occupied an even more wonderful Regency *bergère* in gilt and ebony with clawed feet and handrests modeled as lions' heads. I sat down and looked around.

There was an extravagant Directoire ottoman at my right, and Shirin was curled up at one end of it, dressed as always in tan jeans, boots, and a silk shirt (this time dark green instead of black). She was looking at me with polite interest, and I wasn't entirely sure she recognized me. The other end of the ottoman was occupied by an intense-looking teenage girl in blue jeans and gray sweatshirt.

"This is Jared Osborne," B said to the others, who nodded—without any sign of enthusiasm, I thought. "I'll let everyone introduce himself or herself later." He turned to me and said, "We were still discussing the question that was raised at the end of tonight's talk, about the need for a program. How would you have answered that question?"

"I'm afraid I don't remember it."

"In essence, the questioner asked what we should *do,* now that we see the people of our culture careening toward self-destruction."

"And you're asking me how I would answer it?"

"I should explain," B said to his audience, "that Jared Osborne is a Roman Catholic priest."

"I'm not here in that capacity," I told him.

B shrugged. "I would assume that a point of view remains even if the capacity is left behind."

"Yes, it does, but I came here to listen, not to talk, if that's all right."

"Of course . . . Just before you arrived, I had made some remark about saving the world, and Michael there"—he nodded at a tall man in the audience—"had objected to this language on the grounds that the world doesn't need us to save it, it only needs us to leave it alone. I was explaining that I hadn't been using the word *world* in a biological sense but rather in a traditional biblical and literary sense, which doesn't refer to the planetary biosphere we call the world but rather to something that would be better described as 'the sphere of human material activity.' This is the world Wordsworth meant when he wrote, 'The world is too much with us.' This is the world Byron meant when he wrote, 'I have not loved the world, nor the world me.' This is the world John meant when he wrote, 'Anyone who loves the world is a stranger to the Father's love.' Wouldn't you agree, Fr. Osborne?"

"Yes. John certainly wasn't referring to the biosphere."

"What I said was this: If the world is saved, it will be saved by people with changed minds, people with a new vision. It will not be saved by people with old minds and new programs. It will not be saved by people with the old vision but a new program."

Everyone in the room seemed to be looking at me, awaiting my reply. I couldn't imagine why this was so, but there was no mistaking it. I said, "I'm not sure I know the difference between a vision and a program."

"Recycling is a program," B said. "Supporting earth-friendly legislation is a program. You don't need a new vision to engage in either of these programs."

"Are you saying that such programs are a waste of time?"

"Not at all, though they do tend to give people a false sense of progress and hope. Programs are initiated in order to counter or defeat vision."

"Give me an example of what you mean by vision."

"Vision in our culture supports isolation, for example. It supports a separate home for every family. It supports locks on the doors. It powerfully supports staying isolated behind your locked doors and viewing the world electronically. Since this is the case, no programs are needed to encourage people to stay home and watch television. On the other hand, if you want to get people to turn off their television sets and leave their homes, that's when you need a program."

"I see—I think."

"Isolation is supported by vision, so it takes care of itself, but community building isn't, so it has to be supported by programs. Programs invariably run counter to vision, and so have to be thrust on people—have to be 'sold' to people. For example, if you want people to live simply, reduce consumption, reuse, and recycle, you must create programs that encourage such behaviors. But if you want them to consume a lot and waste a lot, you don't need to create programs of encouragement, because these behaviors are supported by our cultural vision."

"Yes, I see."

"Vision is the flowing river. Programs are sticks set in the riverbed to impede the flow. What I'm saying is that the world will not be saved by people with programs. If the world is saved, it will be saved because the people living in it have a new vision."

"In other words, people with a new vision will have new programs."

"No, that's not what I'm saying. I repeat: Vision doesn't need programs. Vision is the flowing river. The Industrial Revolution was a flowing river. It needed no programs to get it going or to keep it going."

"But it wasn't always flowing."

"Exactly. It wasn't a river in the second century or the eighth or the thirteenth. There was no sign of the river in those centuries. But, one after another, tiny springs bubbled up and began to flow together, decade after decade, century after century. In the fifteenth century, it was a trickle. In the sixteenth, it became a brook. In the seventeenth, it became a stream. In the eighteenth, it became a river. In the nineteenth, it became a torrent. In the twentieth, it became a world-engulfing flood. And through all this time, not a single program was needed to further its progress. It was awakened and sustained and enhanced entirely by vision."

"I understand."

"It's a sign of our cultural collapse that supporting our vision has come to be seen as wicked, while undermining that vision has come to be seen as noble. For example, children in school are never encouraged to want the material rewards of success. Success is something to be sought for its own sake, certainly not for any wealth it might bring. Business leaders might be offered as role models because of their 'creativity' and their 'contributions to society,' but they would never be offered as role models because they have luxurious homes, exotic cars, and servants to attend to every need. In the world of our children's textbooks, an admirable person would never do anything just for money."

"Yes, I suppose that's true."

"The people of our culture are tremendous bullet-biters. For those of you who are unfamiliar with this idiom, 'biting the bullet' supposedly helps one tolerate pain. One first tries to avoid the pain, but if the pain absolutely must be borne, then one must 'bite the bullet.' For most who write and think about our future, it's a foregone conclusion that we're all going to have to bite the bullet very hard in order to survive. It doesn't occur to these thinkers and writers that it would be far less painful to start fresh. As they view it, our task is to grit our teeth and cling faithfully to the vision that is destroying us. As they see it, our doom is to go on indefinitely hammering ourselves in the head with one hand while using the other to dispense aspirin tablets for the pain."

I asked, "Is it so easy to change a cultural vision?"

"The relevant measures are not ease and difficulty. The relevant measures are readiness and unreadiness. If the time isn't right for a new idea, no power on earth can make it catch on, but if the time is right, it will sweep the world like wildfire. The people of Rome were ready to hear what St. Paul had to say to them. If they hadn't been, he would have disappeared without a trace and his name would be unknown to us."

"Christianity didn't exactly catch on like wildfire."

"Considering the rate at which it was possible to spread new ideas in those days, without printing presses, radio, or television, it caught on like wildfire."

"Yes, I suppose it did."

"The point I want to make here is that I have no idea what people with changed minds will do. Paul was in the same condition as he traveled the empire changing minds in the middle of the first century. He couldn't possibly have predicted the institutional development of the papacy or the shape of Christian society in feudal Europe. By contrast, the early science-fiction writer Jules Verne could make a century's worth of excellent predictions, because nothing changed between his time and ours in terms of vision. If people in the coming century have a new vision, then they'll do what is completely unpredictable by us. Indeed, if this were not the case—if their actions *were* predictable by us—then this would prove that they didn't have a new vision after all, that their vision and ours were essentially the same."

I said, "It seems to me that you do, however, have a program. You mean to change minds."

"Would you say that Paul had a program?"

"No, not really. I'd say he had an objective or an intention."

"I'd say the same for me. *Program* isn't the right word for what I'm doing, though I know it's the word I used in answering that woman's question tonight. In our culture at the present moment, the flow of the river is toward catastrophe, and programs are sticks set in the riverbed to impede its flow. My objective is to change the direction of the flow, away from catastrophe. With the river moving in a new direction, people wouldn't have to devise programs to impede its flow, and all the programs presently in place would be left standing in the mud, unneeded and useless."

"Very ambitious," I remarked dryly.

"You could call my delusions messianic," B said with a smile. "Others have—those who denounce me as the Antichrist."

Those words came to me with a little shock, and I spent a moment mulling them over before replying that I didn't see what the Antichrist had to do with it.

"That's because you haven't heard enough—or haven't followed what you've heard to its logical conclusions."

He had me there. There was no doubt of that. Or at least, so I thought.

Sunday, May 19 (cont.)

The Inquisition

"I'd like to know why Fr. Osborne is here." That came from Shirin. I looked at her, but her eyes were on B.

"Shall we see if he'll tell us?" B asked.

Shirin exchanged a glance with the girl at the other end of her elegant Directoire ottoman. Everybody in the audience seemed to exchange a glance with his or her neighbor. Apparently their answer looked like a yes to B, who turned and nodded the question to me.

I figured I must have good espionagic instincts, because I saw in an instant that there was a lot of safe truth I could tell them without coming within miles of a lie that might trip me up later. My dialogue with B had kept my attention focused on him up to this point. Now that it was my turn, I had a look around. Shirin I've already described. She was to me sphinxlike and inscrutable, with her strangely marked face and intense eyes. Bonnie, the girl at the other end of the ottoman (who I later learned was the daughter of an American businessman), was even more overtly suspicious and hostile. The audience behind them (outside what I took to be an inner circle) seemed more neutral. The man B had called Michael was someone I felt an instinctive liking for, I'm not sure why. He gave the impression of being tall, clumsy, and slightly funny looking, with big, fleshy ears, a long face, sleepy eyes, and rubbery, humorous lips, but at the same time both highly intelligent and naturally modest. His clothes were so nondescript that I have no recollection of them at all. There was a short, crafty-looking woman in her fifties that for some reason I pegged as a school principal. There was a distinguished-looking man in his seventies, a physician perhaps, or a retired librarian; later I found out he was a baker. There was a young working-class couple who seemed nervous and slightly alarmed; they were the Teitels, Monika and Heinz. There was a smirking twenty-year-old who looked like he was just itching for a chance to crush me like an insect with his giant intellect; that was Albrecht.

"Let me start by saying why I'm *not* here," I told them. "I'm not here as a Vatican emissary. If I were, I'd look like one—I'd be wearing a black suit and a Roman collar. It's true, on the other hand, that I was sent here by my order, but not as a missionary or a polemicist. I'm not here to make converts or defend the Faith. I'm here to listen and understand."

"What order?" Shirin asked.

"The Laurentians." The name clearly rang no bells. I told her it was a teaching order similar to the Jesuits.

"Why do the Laurentians want to 'understand' B? Why them rather than the Dominicans or the Franciscans?"

"I'm afraid I can't speak for the Dominicans and the Franciscans."

"The question is, why are the Laurentians curious? I assume you can speak for them."

Well, she had me there, of course. I was not far from admitting that the Laurentians wanted reassurance that the Antichrist charge being made against B was unfounded, but he had just finished telling me I was still not up to speed on this issue where he was concerned.

"I feel like I'm being pulled in two directions," I told her. "Is your question why anyone in the Church is curious or why the Laurentians in particular are curious?"

"Are the answers different?"

"Yes, they certainly are."

"Well, start by telling us why anyone in the Church is curious."

"You're attracting attention, evidently on religious grounds, that's why. Anyone who walked by the theater last night could see this and would be curious to know what it was all about."

"Okay. And why are the Laurentians curious?"

"I'll answer that very bluntly. We like to be ahead of the rest. We like to be a little nimbler, a little more alert, a little more curious, and a little more avid to have our curiosity satisfied."

"Cutting-edge types."

"That's how we like to see ourselves. Is that reprehensible?"

Shirin smiled and shook her head. "Neatly done," she said.

I looked over at B, who was nodding with approval. "Very neatly done indeed," he said. "Really smart wolves know that the most suspicious-looking wolf in the pack is the one disguised as a sheep."

"So you're saying what? That really smart wolves don't fool with disguises?"

B looked around the room and finally nodded at Michael, who grinned at me goofily and said, "Really smart wolves disguise themselves as *friendly* wolves."

Three snappy comebacks flashed through my mind, but I knew that nothing I could say was going to shake the truth of the implied charge.

The woman I'd thought of as a school principal piped up at this point in heavily accented English. "Always has been my guiding principle for forty years to say 'Never trust a Christian.' Not once has ever Christian given me reason to change."

"May I ask why?" I said (glad for the diversion).

She stared at me with frank loathing. "Always your allegiance is in doubt, is . . . tainted."

Unable to find the words she wanted, she spoke in German to Michael, who translated: "Your loyalty is always subject to change, Frau Hartmann says. Always subject to revision according to some undisclosed standard. Today you're my friend, but there's a hidden line inside of you that marks the beginning of your allegiance to God. If I unknowingly cross that line, then, although you continue to smile at me like a friend, you may see that it has become your holy duty to destroy me. This week you're my friend, but next week they say I'm a witch and God wants witches to be burned, so you burn me. This week you're my friend, but next week they say I'm an Anabaptist and God wants Anabaptists to be drowned, so you drown me. This week you're my friend, but next week they say I'm a Waldensian and God wants Waldensians to be hanged, so you hang me."

Michael gave me an apologetic smile and explained that Frau Doktor Hartmann was a historian.

Since I couldn't think of any defense to make to her charge either,

I turned back to B and said, "So I'm a wolf trying to pass himself off as a friend, and, being a Christian, I have an allegiance that is unreadable to outsiders. Where does that leave us?"

"I don't know. Shirin?"

"What do you do with the notes you take when B talks?"

"They aren't notes," I told her, "they're shorthand transcriptions."

"All right. What do you do with them?"

Shirin had already visited my hotel once, to search my room. If she could manage that, it would be no great feat to find out what I did with my transcriptions. (In other words, I had to assume she already knew.)

"I fax them to my superior in the United States."

"Why does he want them? And please don't tell me how much he yearns to be on the cutting edge of religious thought."

I turned back to B and said, "What comes next? Splinters under the fingernails? The rubber hose?"

B's gargoylish face twisted into a scowl that seemed half-serious, half-humorous. "Why do you keep referring your problems to me? It's Shirin you have to satisfy. Talk to her, not to me."

I was stunned by this gender betrayal, and equally stunned by my own self-betrayal. I had tried, unconsciously, to nudge B into lining up on my side—us guys against the common enemy. I was profoundly disappointed in myself; I'd imagined I was at least a decade beyond such schoolboy games.

I looked at Shirin, and my priesthood slipped off my shoulders like a cloak with a broken clasp. In an instant she became a person in my eyes and ceased to be a troublesome, irrelevant parishioner that I had somehow to placate and get round. What was in her eyes, I now saw, was not hostility and suspicion but, amazingly, fear. For some reason inconceivable to me, I was a source of terror to this sinewy, competent woman. My heart melted with pity for her and remorse for the calculated deception that had brought me face-to-face with her.

I really intended to answer her question now, and I may even have thought I was doing so as I began to speak.

Some truth comes out

"B is telling me the world I belong to is extinct," I said to her. "It's been extinct for decades, and we didn't even suspect it."

Shirin was frowning hard, struggling to make sense of my words but not wanting to distract me, now that I was evidently coming clean with some sort of truth.

"That's not quite right," I went on. "We *suspect* that we're obsolete, but we're confident that our suspicions are groundless. Do you see what I mean?"

Shirin shook her head helplessly.

"I'm talking about us guardians of the faith, you understand. The professionals. We know how to deal with our suspicions—we have to, because it's our job to deal with the suspicions of *other* people. We are, in large part, professional soothers, professional reassurers, professional dispellers of doubt."

Shirin nodded faintly, a millimeter or so, to let me know that she was beginning to follow me now, shakily.

"Our message to those we must reassure is: 'Don't worry, nothing's happened. The world is just what it was. Don't be anxious, don't be alarmed. The foundation is solid. The pillars are still standing. Nothing has changed since . . . the year 1000, the year 200, the year 33, when the gates of heaven were opened for us by Someone who laid down His life for our sins and on the third day rose from the dead. Not a thing has changed since then. Though we go to war with smart bombs and nerve gas instead of swords and rocks, and write our thoughts on plastic disks instead of parchment scrolls, these days are still those days.'"

Suddenly it was Shirin's turn to look to B for help. When he offered nothing, she turned to her friend at the other end of the ottoman, to Mrs. Hartmann, to Michael. No one seemed to have anything like a suggestion to make. With no more prospects in sight, she was forced to come back to me.

She said, "I'm afraid I don't understand why you're telling me this."

"I had the impression you wanted the truth."

PROPERTY OF
BOGOTA PUBLIC LIBRARY
(201) 488-7185

"I do."

"You can't just say, 'All I mean by truth is this one piece of the puzzle. If it isn't this one piece, I don't want to hear about it.'"

Shirin blinked and nodded. "I'm sorry," she said. "I didn't understand what you were doing."

"These days are still those days. Do you understand what these words mean?"

"To be honest, I'm not sure."

"You've asked why my superior is interested in what's happening here in Radenau. I'm explaining: He's interested because these days are still those days. Nothing has changed. The foundation is solid. The pillars are still standing."

Shirin struggled with it for a moment, then appealed to B for help.

"I think Fr. Osborne is on the verge of clearing it up now," B said.

"I'd appreciate it if you'd drop the title," I told him, looking around to include everyone in the room. "By calling me Fr. Osborne, you continually insist on my status as an outsider, a probationer."

"What would you prefer?" B asked blandly.

"If you generally go by first names, as you seem to, then I'd prefer to be called Jared."

"Jared's all right with me," B said, "but the others will follow their own inclinations."

"Fine," I replied, and turned back to Shirin. "Four hundred years ago, when our order was founded to defend the Church against the forces of Reformation, it took on an additional, exceptional mission, little talked about in recent centuries. That mission was to maintain a special vigilance, a special watch. We were to be the first to recognize the Antichrist."

A dead stillness fell over the room. It was finally broken by Frau Hartmann, who croaked, "Surely you are joking."

"If you think that," I told her, "then you haven't been listening. These days are still those days."

"You mean the watch is still being maintained by the Laurentians?" This was from Shirin.

"It is, though I didn't know it until recently, to be honest with you. I thought it had been forgotten centuries ago. Even I had begun to forget that these days are still those days."

"But this is nonsense," Frau Hartmann said. "This is what the rabble say in the streets."

"For them too, these days are still those days."

"You must deny it," she told B firmly. "When next you speak, you must deny it."

"Deny it how? Do you think I should pass round my birth certificate, which indicates that I'm a perfectly ordinary person?"

"You must attack the idea itself."

"On what grounds? If it's thinkable to posit the existence of a Christ (as it obviously is), then why shouldn't it be thinkable to posit his antithesis?"

"But you are not his antithesis."

"So you say. Others say that I am, as you know."

"They have no grounds. No grounds that are . . . *fernünftig.*"

"Rational," Michael supplied.

"Perhaps Jared will tell us how the Laurentians view the grounds."

I said, "I'm like Frau Doktor Hartmann—I see no rational grounds for associating you with the Antichrist. I told you this twenty minutes ago, and you said I hadn't heard enough to decide."

"That's not exactly responsive," B said. "Shirin's original question seems more relevant than ever: What does your superior want with your transcripts?"

"I thought that was clear by now. He wants to know what you're saying, because people are calling you the Antichrist."

"But what does he make of what he reads? And, by the way, does this person have a name you can share with us?"

"His name is Bernard Lulfre."

B looked momentarily stunned. "Do you mean the archaeologist?"

"Yes. Do you know him?"

"I know his work. I didn't know he was a Laurentian."

"What work of his do you know?"

B produced a smile that made him look as if he was remembering something pleasant. "He allied himself a bit too inflexibly with the theory that the Dead Sea Scrolls were produced by an Essene community that was resident at Qumran."

"I didn't realize the theory was in doubt."

"It's very much in doubt, despite Fr. Lulfre and other old hard-line supporters."

"Obviously I don't read the right journals anymore."

B shrugged. "How has he reacted to your transcripts?"

"He hasn't, as yet."

"How *will* he react?"

"I honestly don't know. Certainly not in any crude or obvious way."

"Oh no," B said, with a small, private smile. "I'm sure Fr. Lulfre wouldn't react in any crude or obvious way. Fr. Lulfre is nothing if not subtle."

Sunday, May 19 (cont.)

The Antichrist over coffee

Heinz and Monika Teitel had disappeared without my noticing it. They now reappeared wheeling a coffee cart down a dim corridor that opened up behind B's chair. Incongruously, I thought, it was time for a little kaffeeklatsch. I accepted a cup, along with a small, flavorless pastry dusted with powdered sugar, and retreated to my seat while the others engaged in low, apparently inconsequential conversation around the cart. Shirin alone ignored the whole thing, staying where she was in order to think her own thoughts.

I closed my eyes and found the interior rooms of my head quite thoroughly deserted.

When, after ten or fifteen minutes, everything was cleared away and everyone was seated again, B began to speak in his normal, unhurried way.

"In light of what we've heard here tonight," he said, "I've decided to alter my plans for the next few weeks." Except for Shirin, who reacted to his words as blandly as if she'd spoken them herself, his listeners were clearly astonished.

"Everyone here, except, I believe, Albrecht, has been with me through at least one full series of lectures. This means you know what Jared doesn't know. You know why there are pickets out there denouncing me as the Devil's Spawn, Beelzebub, the Beast, and indeed the Antichrist himself."

"They picket because they do not understand," Frau Hartmann grumbled.

"What do you think, Shirin?"

"They picket because they *do* understand," Shirin replied grimly.

B said, "I'm afraid Shirin is right, Frau Hartmann. But whether she's right or you're right is beside the point. Fr. Lulfre and probably others of his rank have made themselves our judges, and these men won't be polling the masses for their views. Don't you agree?"

This question was for me, and I told him he was absolutely right.

Heinz Teitel raised his hand. This awkward young man, along with his wife, Monika, seemed the least at home of anyone in this oddly assorted group. With apologies for wasting the others' time with a question they probably didn't need answered, he asked if I would explain briefly the meaning of the term under discussion. "Neither of us was brought up in a religious household," he said. "I think we have always assumed that the Antichrist is more a symbolic person than a real one, like Mammon or Pandora."

• "That's not at all an easy or obvious question," I told him, "and I'm not an expert by any means, but I'll do my best. The Antichrist is a central figure in the mythological history of the cosmos as it was widely understood in ancient times—in our culture, as B would say. The culture of the Great Forgetting perceived the universe and humankind to be the products of a single creative effort that had occurred just a few thousand years ago. It perceived the events of human history to be the central events of the universe itself, unfolding over a fairly brief period of time. Only a couple hundred generations of humans had lived from the beginning of time, and it was imagined that only a couple hundred more would live before the end of time— perhaps even less than that. It's important to realize that the people of this time had no conception of a universe billions of years old and with more billions of years ahead of it. As they imagined it, the cosmic drama was only a few thousand years old—and was not far from being over. The central issue of this cosmic drama was a struggle between good and evil being waged on this planet. Among the Jews, who were probably the most potent religious mythologists of the age, the issue would be settled by two champions. God's champion, the messiah, was expected momentarily, and his appearance would mark the beginning of the final days. An adversary would also appear— Satan's champion, a Man of Sin. The two champions would battle, the forces of evil would be vanquished, and history and the universe would come to an end.

"Early Christian authors had the same vision of history, but for them, of course, the messiah had already come, and all that remained was for the Man of Sin to come. Now that the messiah had been named as the Christ, his adversary could be named as the Antichrist. Now that the messiah's mission was plain, his adversary's mission was plain. Since Christ came to lead all humanity to God, Antichrist will come to lead all humanity to Satan. And Antichrist will not fail, any more than Christ failed. Antichrist will be loved and followed as fervently as Christ—but only for a time, of course. Ultimately, after a cataclysmic battle, the forces of God will triumph, bringing history to its conclusion.

"This clear vision of the Antichrist became muddled and trivialized in succeeding centuries as one generation after another found someone to lambaste with the name. Anyone widely feared or hated could expect to be called the Antichrist, and eventually both sides of the Reformation had to bear the label. After this period, from the seventeenth century on, people were sick of the whole idea. Every generation continues to nominate a candidate of its own—Napoleon or Hitler or Saddam Hussein—but no one takes it very seriously."

A restless silence greeted this summary. Everyone seemed to wander off mentally for about a minute and a half, then Heinz was ready to go on.

"I can understand why no one takes it seriously," he said. "What I cannot understand is why *you* take it seriously. You and your order and your Fr. Lulfre."

I admitted it was a good question. In fact, I admitted it in several different ways as I tried to figure out how to explain why it was possible to continue to take the Antichrist seriously. Finally, I said, "This situation was foreseen by the early Christian theologian Origen. I don't mean this exact situation. I mean that what he foresaw is applicable to this situation. He said, in effect, that every generation will produce forerunners and prefigurements of the Antichrist, and these will deserve the name insofar as they embody the spirit of the Antichrist. It's from among this number that at last *one* will come who deserves the name in its proper sense. It is for this *one* that we maintain our vigilance."

"What does that mean—one who deserves the name in its proper sense?"

"This is precisely what can't be known in advance. It can only be known in the event itself. That is, when we see the *real* Antichrist, then we'll know what the name means. Then we'll say to ourselves, 'How could we have imagined that Nero was the Antichrist—or the pope or Luther or Hitler?' The real Antichrist will reveal to us the meaning of the prophesy itself. Indeed, that's how we'll know him. He'll be the one who shows us what it *means* to be the Antichrist."

The condemned is sentenced

The silence that followed this speech was a deadly one. At last young Albrecht broke his silence to ask B why he would change his plans for my sake. I was surprised when he spoke not with a German accent but with an English one.

"To get rid of him the sooner," B said simply.

"If you want to get rid of him, let us do it—Heinz and Michael and me. We could take him out and dump him in a lake or something."

"I doubt if that would do much good. What do you think, Jared?"

"I agree, it wouldn't do much good. I'm infinitely replaceable, and if I went missing, suspicion would fall on you almost immediately."

"I'm afraid Jared is right," B told the boy.

"I still don't see what's to be gained by helping him."

"Show me how hindering him will gain more, and I'll hinder him."

Albrecht gave it some serious thought but evidently couldn't come up with anything.

B stood up and said, "I think we'll stop here. Shirin or I will be in touch with you." Then, turning to me: "Shirin will walk you to your hotel. Come back tomorrow at six or seven."

I opened my mouth to say that it was hardly necessary to provide me with an escort for a four-block walk, then realized that B knew this as well as I did.

The prisoner is released

I was surprised to find that it was still dark night when we emerged from the theater. Although I could see the time on my wrist, I had the feeling dawn should be well advanced after that prolonged Sturm und Drang.

We walked in silence for a few moments, then I remarked that they seemed very much at home at the Schauspielhaus Wahnfried.

"The director of the board is a supporter," Shirin said without elaboration.

"You actually live there, then?"

"It's our home base, yes."

"But why in Radenau?"

As soon as I said it, I remembered that I knew why. The "mysterious caller" had explained it to me over the phone in Munich. For a second I was in an icy panic, then I realized it was a perfectly natural question. To avoid asking it might well have seemed more suspicious than asking it.

She said, "There's a medical center here devoted to the study and treatment of mixed connective-tissue diseases."

I said, "B has a mixed connective-tissue disease?"

"*I* have a mixed connective-tissue disease. Scleroderma, in fact."

"I'm sorry," I said. "My medical education is pretty spotty. Is that connected to *this*?" I waved a finger over my nose and cheeks.

"The lupus butterfly," Shirin said.

"Lupus. I'm sorry: What's lupus?"

"Another mixed connective-tissue disease. I have symptoms of both."

"I hope it's not serious."

"Do you?"

"Yes, I do. Believe it or not, priests are occasionally capable of normal human feelings." Aiming for a light touch in my welter of lies.

"It all depends," she said, "on how involved other organs are— heart, lungs, kidneys. Unfortunately, in my case, it's very serious indeed. No one expects me to see the new century. On the bright side, in my case, the end will probably come suddenly, and I should be quite active until then. It's not a pretty disease to linger with."

Clergy are trained to have plenty of good, solid things to say at moments like this, but I didn't reach for any of them. I didn't even want to say—for the third or fourth time—that I was sorry. We walked on for a bit in silence.

Finally she asked me if I knew why B had told her to walk me home. I said I didn't.

"I didn't either, at the time," she said. "Now I do. He knew I'd be able to think about the unthinkable and to ask the unaskable. People in my position have practice at that."

"You have an unthinkable question for me?"

"That's right."

"Go ahead."

"What will your Fr. Lulfre do if he decides that B is the Antichrist?"

I laughed, sort of. "I see what you mean. That's completely unthinkable."

"It would be unthinkable for him to decide that B is the Antichrist?"

"Yes."

"Then what's the point of sending you here?"

It took me a minute or two to work that out. Incredible as it may seem, I hadn't seen any reason to work it out before then. I said, "If a stain that looks like a weeping Madonna one day appears on Mr. Smith's living-room wall, and everyone swears they see tears flowing down her face every Friday at three o'clock, and thousands of pilgrims are streaming past day and night, week after week, and people are claiming that the sick are being miraculously healed at this shrine, then eventually somebody from the Church is going to be sent to look into it. This will be some unlucky priest like me, sent from afar, because it would be too painful for the local priest to point out to his neighbors that this stain appeared right after that big rainstorm last spring, and the Smiths had in a local handyman to fix their leaky roof the same week, and no one is allowed to get near the Madonna on Friday afternoons but Mr. Smith, and the vial he uses to collect the teardrops could just as easily be used to put the teardrops in place, and even though Mr. Smith doesn't actually charge anyone to go through his house, there's a bushel basket by the door and it's always full of money, and though one or two have claimed to be healed of something, they never stick around long enough to be checked by any doctor."

"So this priest *isn't* sent to see if there's been a miracle."

"Of course not. He's sent there to make sure there *hasn't* been a miracle."

"I've afraid that's too devious for me. If everyone assumes there was no miracle, why send a priest?"

"Because *someone* has to be sent. No matter how unlikely, no matter how improbable, someone has to be sent."

"And someone has to read his report."

"Absolutely. It will be read, scrutinized, confirmed, notarized, and sworn to, and eventually copies of it will find their way into diocesan files and probably even Vatican files, where they'll sit until the end of time."

We walked on through the deserted streets of Radenau. As my hotel came into view, I felt one last question brewing in Shirin.

"I'm not quite sure how to ask this," she said.

"Ask it any way you like."

"Did you come here thinking of B as a stain on the wall?"

"No, not at all. When you're sent, you have to take the investigation seriously."

"Even though the conclusion is foregone."

"Virtually foregone. Ninety-nine-point-ninety-nine percent foregone. There is always the remote possibility—almost infinitely remote, but there all the same—that the stain is a miraculous apparition that weeps real tears every Friday afternoon."

"Or that B is the Antichrist."

"That's right."

"Then the question still needs to be answered: What would Fr. Lulfre do if he decided that B is the Antichrist?"

"He would tell his superiors to prepare for a new era in human history."

"He wouldn't care to do that."

"No, he certainly wouldn't."

We paused under the hotel marquee, and I turned to face her. Her eyes came up to meet mine with a look of vulnerable entreaty that sank into my heart like a knife. She held my gaze for half a second, then glanced away.

"I want to believe you're telling me the truth," she murmured uncertainly.

"I am," I said.

Adding to myself: *at least about that.*

Monday, May 20

Radenau: Day three

I'm sitting here yawning and yawning, waiting for my jaw to crack. Not from sleepiness but from nervousness. Six o'clock, nearly time to go.

Fr. Lulfre has received his daily fax in continued silence. I've performed routine maintenance chores—sleeping, showering, shaving, eating, and so on—and have brought this diary up to the minute. I've also acquired a very sophisticated (and very expensive) tape recorder that, set at a slow tape speed, will put two full hours of sound on each side of a single cassette without my having to fool with it.

6:07—I feel strongly that I shouldn't go on till I've found the source of this terrible nervousness. Is it just the fact of playing this double role? I'm like a lawyer trying to represent both sides in a dispute—and struggling to persuade each side that he's trustworthy. Struggling to persuade *himself* that he's trustworthy. I'm wallowing in a sea of lies while trying to look like someone standing on a solid ground of integrity.

True as all that is, however, I know that's not quite it. What I'm nervous about is something else. What I'm nervous about is B's program for me. It's one thing to check out someone who might just be the most dangerous man alive—and quite another thing to become his disciple.

Setting this down in visible words doesn't make the nervousness go away, but it does make further stalling seem pointless.

Down there again

B was alone in the subterranean greenroom of the Schauspielhaus Wahnfried, and as I wound my way through the jumbled acres of theatrical antiques, he watched me with a rather sad smile. He was seated as before, in his wonderful Regency *bergère* in gilt and ebony. I seated myself as before, in my wonderful old Biedermeier fauteuil with cushions of faded pale green velvet.

"A couple of times," he said after we'd exchanged polite greetings, "in Munich and in my talk last night, you heard me refer to a colleague, Ishmael—another teacher but quite a different kind of teacher from me. He was a maieutic teacher, and I'm not."

"Maieutic?"

"From the Greek word for—"

"I think I know it," I told him. "From the root *maia,* meaning midwife."

"That's right. A maieutic teacher is one who acts as a midwife to pupils, gently guiding to the light ideas that have long been growing inside of them."

I thought about this for a moment, then asked him if one can choose to be a maieutic teacher or if this is dictated by one's subject matter.

"Not every teaching objective lends itself to the maieutic approach. For example, it would have been inane for Isaac Newton to try to draw his discoveries in optics from his pupils' heads—inane because they weren't *in* his pupils' heads. On the other hand, he might have used the maieutic approach to show pupils why his alchemical studies seemed worthwhile to him. Socrates was of course famous for his use of the maieutic method. Jesus only dabbled in it, usually as a means of helping people understand their own questions, as when he said, 'If it is by Beelzebub that I cast out devils, then by whom do your children cast them out?' "

Again I gave this some thought before saying, "I assume this means that what you have to teach me is not something that can be drawn from my head."

"This is largely the case, yes."

I showed him the tape recorder I'd bought and asked if he minded my taping our conversations.

"It'd be pointless to mind," he replied. "The purpose of our conversation is to make a record for your Fr. Lulfre."

A mosaic

"At this point, I have nothing like a curriculum for you," B said. "You know what a curriculum is, I suppose."

"I'd say it was a sequence of teaching objectives."

"A sequence that proceeds on what basis? Presumably it's not an arbitrary sequence."

"I suppose ideally it proceeds from the familiar to the unfamiliar or from the simple to the complex. A curriculum is structured like a pyramid, building from the ground up. You have to know A to learn B, you have to know A and B to learn C, you have to know A, B, and C to learn D, and so on."

"Exactly. But as I say, I have no such curriculum. Rather than a pyramid, I'm constructing a mosaic. The pieces can be added in any order. In the early stages, there's nothing like an image, but as pieces are added, an image begins to emerge. As still more pieces are added, the image becomes more distinct, more definite, so that eventually you feel sure that the basic picture is before you. From this point on, the picture can only gain in sharpness and detail as pieces continue to be added. At last it seems that there are no 'missing pieces' at all, and only the cracks between contiguous pieces remain to be filled—with ever tinier pieces. As the cracks between pieces are filled, the picture begins to look more and more like a painting—a continuous whole rather than an assembly of fragments—and in the end it no longer resembles a mosaic at all."

"I understand."

"You'll have to transmit what I'm saying in pieces, I think. We'll just have to see what happens. I've had many pupils, but they've always learned simply by hanging around. Circumstances compel us to adopt an untried method."

I told him I was willing to try the untried.

"Here's a piece to begin with. You remember young Heinz and Monika Teitel, who were here last night."

I said I did.

"They've followed me through a complete course of lectures and so have heard at least once everything I'm able to say in public that I feel will be comprehensible. But you don't become a Christian by hearing one sermon, you don't become a Freudian by hearing one lecture, and you don't become a Marxist by reading one pamphlet. If an outsider asks the Teitels something that goes beyond anything they've heard from me, they must refer the question to me. They know what I'm saying, but my message is not sufficiently *theirs* that they can generate answers of their own. For them, the mosaic is only a rough sketch.

"Frau Doktor Hartmann has twice followed me through my course of lectures and has attended many more such soirees as we engaged in here last night. If an outsider asks her a question that goes beyond anything she's heard from me, she may try to deal with it, but when she reports her answer to me, she usually finds out that my answer would have been quite different from hers—sometimes even contradictory to hers. She too knows what I'm saying, but my message is not sufficiently hers that she can generate answers with certainty. She can see the general outlines clearly enough, but the image in the mosaic is still rather shadowy.

"Michael, on the other hand, has been with me a bit longer than Frau Hartmann, and if an outsider asks him a question beyond anything he's heard from me, he almost never gets the answer wrong, though it will probably lack the depth and assurance that it would have if it came from me. The message is almost his, and the image in the mosaic is substantially complete, though still a bit vague, almost as if it were not quite in perfect focus yet.

"But Shirin has been with me longer than anyone, and if an outsider asks a question that goes beyond anything she's heard from me, she'll answer without hesitation. Her answer will not necessarily have the same emphasis as mine would have or be delivered in the same style or reflect an identical point of view, but it will have the same authenticity and power, because the mosaic image she's referring to for her answer is as solid and well-focused as mine is. The message is hers entirely. It's as much hers as it is mine. She is the message in the same sense that I am the message."

B paused as if for a response, and I told him that I understood what he was saying but wasn't sure why he was saying it.

"I'm giving you a second look at something I talked about at our first meeting," B said. "When Jesus departed, he left no one behind who was the message."

I managed to suppress an urge to blurt out a "Wow," but wow was certainly what sprang to mind. This was undeniably true—not in any sense a condemnation, but undeniably true. Jesus left behind no one who could speak with his authority, no one who could say "This is what's what." There were very elementary questions the apostles couldn't answer with confidence, like: To what degree were those of the new dispensation bound by the laws of the old dispensation? You can hardly get more fundamental than that. In fact, it was St. Paul—a man who had never even seen Jesus—who ended up saying "This is what's what" with more authority than anyone else could muster. More than John or Peter or James (as far as we know), Paul *was* the message. But even with the writings of Paul and all the evangelists, it still took three hundred years of Christian thought to reconstitute Christ's message—to piece together the hints, reconcile apparent contradictions, cut away heresies and lunacies and irrelevancies, and organize it into a self-consistent, coherent creed that more or less everyone could agree on.

Even so, I told B that I still didn't quite know what he was getting at.

"Last night I talked about changing minds. I said that if the world is saved, it will be saved by people with changed minds. Not by programs. By people with changed minds."

"I remember."

"What you're here for today is to have your mind changed."

I looked at him blankly.

"Right now, Jared, what message are you?"

"I don't follow you."

"When Jesus departed, he left no one behind who was the message. None of the apostles was his message. You understand what I mean by that, don't you?"

"Yes."

"But you're not in the same condition as those apostles. Are you?"

"No, I guess I'm not."

"Are you or aren't you?"

"I'm not."

"Christ's message is *yours,* isn't it? If I ask you whether premarital sex is right or wrong, you won't have to call Fr. Lulfre to find out the answer, will you?"

"No."

"If I ask you whether suicide is right or wrong, you won't have to consult the scriptures, will you?"

"No."

"You possess these answers as your own. These and ten thousand others like them."

"That's right."

"Then I'll ask again: What message are you?"

"I'm Christ's message."

"A Lutheran minister would say the same, as would a Presbyterian minister or a Baptist preacher, even though some of their answers would differ from your own. So here you are, and I want you to understand what you're doing here."

"Yes, I see."

"Though he probably wouldn't think of it in these terms, Fr. Lulfre has sent you here to become my message."

An icy chill skittered down my spine.

A new horizon

"If you press a group of schoolchildren to explain why we're teetering on the edge of calamity, they'll soon trot out all the coffeehouse clichés—all the theories the Unabomber set forth so solemnly and at such great length in his magnum opus a couple years ago: out-of-control technological advancement, out-of-control industrial greed, out-of-control government expansion, and so on. How do you think all these commonplace explanations evolved?"

"I have no idea," I said. "Forgive me for answering so promptly, but I know this is something I've never given any thought to."

"Then let's give it some thought now. One of the major obstacles to building the Panama Canal in the late decades of the nineteenth century was yellow fever. Its cause was unknown and it was untreatable by the medical science of the day. Perhaps you know something of this."

"Yes. At that time it was thought to be caused by night air. People who stayed inside at night caught the disease less often than those who went out."

"But some who stayed inside at night caught it anyway."

"That's right, because they left their windows open. Eventually people realized they had to be very careful not to let in any night air at all."

"But, as Walter Reed eventually discovered, the carrier of the disease wasn't the night air, it was the *Aedes aegypti* mosquito, which hunts in the night air."

"Yes."

"What led people to think that night air was to blame?"

I shook my head, boggled by the question, and told B I didn't know how to answer it.

"Make a start at it all the same," he said. "Give it a shot."

I shrugged and gave it a shot. "This is what people thought. There wasn't anything inherently irrational in the idea, and in fact it had some merit."

"Good. I should add that the account you've just given is more legend than fact, but it serves to illustrate the point. The ideas the Unabomber articulated are also 'what people think.' There isn't anything inherently irrational in them, and in fact they have some merit."

"Okay, I see what you're saying. Vaguely."

"Both groups are struggling under a handicap. Do you see what it is?"

"I'd say that, in both groups, their intellectual horizon is too close. They're looking for causes too near to the effect."

"Exactly. This is the overriding effect of the Great Forgetting. In our culture—East and West, twins of a single birth—human history is only what's happened since our agricultural revolution began. In our culture, because of the Great Forgetting, people looking at the horizon are only looking back in time a few thousand years. In 1654 Archbishop Ussher calculated that the human race was born in 4004 B.C. Later, archaeologists calculated that this is just when the very first cities of Mesopotamia began to be built. For a people who imagined that Man was born an agriculturalist and a civilization builder, what could make better sense? The human race appeared in Mesopotamia six thousand years ago—and immediately began building cities. The Great Forgetting imprinted this picture indelibly on our cultural mind. It doesn't matter that everyone 'knows' the human race is three million years older than the cities of Mesopotamia. Every molecule of thought in our culture bears the impress of the idea that we needn't look beyond the Mesopotamian horizon in order to understand our history."

"And you're telling me that your horizon is three million years."

"Always. For me, Mesopotamia is *erased* as a horizon. How do you think one manages such a thing?"

"I suppose one manages it by climbing a ladder, which is to say by seeing things from a higher vantage point."

"That's right. When you do that, events that formerly seemed huge (because they're close) take their place in a deeper landscape and no longer stand out with the same prominence as before."

Climbing the ladder

"We were talking about the clichés that people trot out to explain why we're teetering on the edge of calamity: out-of-control technological advancement, out-of-control industrial greed, out-of-control government expansion, and so on. These are explanations that make sense to people of the Great Forgetting, to people who think that they're seeing the human horizon when they look at the Mesopotamian horizon. For people of the Great Forgetting, our agricultural revolution was literally the beginning of human history. When I view the human horizon, I'm looking back three million years past the Mesopotamian horizon, so it's simply grotesque to think of our agricultural revolution as signaling the beginning of human history. It signals *something*, to be sure, but not remotely 'the beginning of human history.' "

Feeling it was time to manifest some evidence of consciousness, I said, "What does it signal, then?"

"It signals the occurrence of a mind change—a new vision of the world and our place in it."

"How do you conclude that a mind change occurred?"

"I conclude it from the fact that a revolution occurred," B replied.

"Revolutions don't occur among people who are thinking in the same old way."

"Can't changed social or economic conditions produce a revolution?"

"Surely you don't mean that. *People* produce revolutions, not conditions."

"I mean, can't people react in a revolutionary way to changed social or economic conditions?"

"Of course they can. But the question is, can they react in a revolutionary way without first *thinking* in a revolutionary way?"

I had to admit that I couldn't imagine revolutionary action taking place in the absence of revolutionary thinking.

B said, "I *have* heard naive thinkers suggest that our agricultural revolution came about as a response to famine."

"Why is that naive?"

"It's naive because starving people don't plant crops any more than drowning people build life rafts. The only people who can afford to wait for crops to grow are people who already *have* food."

"Yes, that makes sense."

"You will also hear it conjectured that agriculture was pretty much an inevitable development, because it makes life so much easier and more secure. In fact, it makes life more toilsome and less secure. Every study of calories spent versus calories gained confirms that the more your food comes from agriculture, the harder you have to work for it. The first Neolithic farmers, who probably only planted a few crops and depended largely on foraging, worked much harder to stay alive than their Mesolithic ancestors. Later farmers, who planted more crops and did less foraging, worked even harder to stay alive, and completely modern totalitarian farmers, who depend entirely on crops, work harder to stay alive than anyone else. And famine, far from being banished by agriculture, is actually a by-product of agriculture and is never found apart from it. Travel to the most inhospitable desert of Australia during the most horrendous drought—and you won't find a single starving aborigine anywhere."

"Okay," I said. "I guess I see what you're doing. You're answering all the objections before they're raised."

"All the objections to what?"

"To your thesis."

"Which is what?"

"Which is that our agricultural revolution signaled the appearance of a mind change. It wasn't just starving people trying something new out of desperation. It wasn't just people looking for an easier life. It wasn't just people looking for more security."

"That's right. Far from having an easier life or increasing their security, they actually worked harder and were less secure than their hunting-gathering ancestors. So there's no question here of people doing something just because it was more comfortable."

It seemed to me that B was in danger of defeating himself with his own arguments. I said, "To hear you tell it, our agricultural revolution had so little going for it that it's a wonder it happened at all."

"It truly *is* a wonder that it happened," B said emphatically. "That's precisely what I want you to see. And when you see it, your vision of human history will be changed forever."

The peace-loving killers of New Guinea

"I find at this point that I need a mosaic piece with a particular feature that will be supplied by the Gebusi of New Guinea."

"Okay," I said.

"It's become popular in recent decades to speak of 'demonizing' people who are especially feared or hated, turning them into monsters of depravity. I've never actually heard the opposite tendency mentioned, but of course it's equally possible to 'angelize' people who are especially admired or revered—to turn them into perfect beings who embody all desired qualities. For example, there's been a recent tendency for people to angelize Leaver peoples wherever they're to be found, to imagine them as infinitely wise, selfless, farseeing environmentalist saints who practice perfect gender equality and never speak in contractions. Do you know what I'm talking about?"

"Certainly. I don't live in a refrigerator. I've seen *Dances with Wolves*."

"Good," B said. "Since angels are more or less all the same, the process of angelizing these peoples—call them Leavers or aborigines, it doesn't matter which—tends to make them out to be all more or less the same as well, which is as far from the truth as you can possibly get. This is where the Gebusi of New Guinea come in. I'd like to take a few minutes to describe them to you."

"Okay."

"The Gebusi are one of those agricultural peoples whose agricultural style owes nothing at all to our revolution. In fact, it would make better sense to call them hunter-gardeners than farmers. They're villagers who love to socialize, celebrate, and party with a lot of shouting, singing, and joking. Two thirds of them die of what we would call natural causes, and one third are murdered by friends, neighbors, or relatives. Murder is male business, and at any given time, two thirds of the men have murdered someone."

"Nice folks to know," I put in.

"Oddly enough, they are, on the whole, very nice folks to know—not saints, obviously, but pleasant, well-meaning people. If you were to ask them why they are so inclined toward violence, they literally wouldn't know what you're talking about. They aren't notably inclined toward violence, and if you wanted to interview them about crime in their society, you'd have to begin by explaining what crime is. They do things that annoy each other, of course, and there are just as many greedy, boorish, inconsiderate, and selfish people among them as there are among us, but crime as we understand it is nonexistent.

"Apart from homicide statistics, the main difference between them and us is their theory of sickness and death. We believe that sickness occurs when invisible creatures called microbes or germs or viruses invade our bodies. This theory seems nothing but blandly factual to us, but to thinkers of the twenty-third century (should there happen to be any) it will probably seem as quaintly fanciful as the humoral theory of the Renaissance seems to us today. Do you find that imaginable?"

"That our present theory of sickness will someday seem quaint? Oh yes. I find that entirely imaginable."

"Good. In the Gebusi theory, there's nothing that corresponds to our notion of death from 'natural causes.' All causes of sickness and death are supernatural, and every sickness and death is caused by someone who literally 'wishes you ill.' This may be a sorcerer or it may be the spirit of someone living or dead or even the spirit of an animal. To achieve a diagnosis in the case of illness, a medium visits the spirit world in order to discover the guilty party, and this information indicates the best means of treatment. If someone dies, the medium conducts an inquest in consultation with the spirits. Not every inquest leads to the accusation of a living person, but when it does, the accused sorcerer is given the chance to demonstrate his or her innocence by performing a sago divination, a cooking feat so difficult that skill alone can't assure success. You might compare its difficulty to cooking a perfect soufflé the size of a bathtub. Complete success is taken as a sign that the spirit of the deceased was on hand to help out and thus exonerate the accused. Partial success leaves the matter in doubt, and the accused will be spared for a while as other indicators are considered, such as the behavior of the corpse in the suspect's presence. As the result of the sago divination falls farther and farther short of success, guilt becomes clearer and clearer. In this event, since denial of the crime is pointless in the face of such evidence, the sorcerer will generally express remorse and try to persuade everyone that the anger that moved him or her to practice this sorcery has spent itself. Everyone wants to believe it and reassures the sorcerer that all is forgiven, but, chances are, the miscreant's days are numbered.

"Among the Gebusi, the spirits of the dead soon return as animals. Those who die young return as small animals—birds or lizards. Those who die at a more advanced age return as larger animals—cassowaries or crocodiles, for example. But executed sorcerers invariably return as wild pigs, which is why (I suspect) executed sorcerers are invariably cooked and eaten. My guess is that, being sorcerers, they are already in some sense wild pigs, which are hunted not only because they're good to eat but because they're inhabited by malevolent spirits."

I interrupted to ask if the Gebusi practice cannibalism in other circumstances.

"As far as I know," B said, "the only human item on their menu is roasted sorcerer."

"Fascinating."

"Now to the point of this anthropological exercise. I want you to imagine that it was not the people of our culture who teemed over the world and made it their own but rather the Gebusi. I want you to imagine a world where every death is routinely avenged by killing and eating a sorcerer. I want you to imagine a world where, if you were a telephone installer, legislator, symphony conductor, or fashion designer in Berlin or Beijing or Tokyo or London or New York City—or Box Elder, Montana—you might at any moment be required to perform a successful sago divination in order to save your life. I want you to imagine a world where eating sorcerers is a perfectly normal thing to do—as normal as sending your children off to educational concentration camps when they reach the age of five or six. I want you to imagine a world where killing a man will turn him into a wild pig as surely as punishing a man will turn him into a good citizen."

B paused at this point and gave me a hopeful look that I wasn't sure how to answer. I said, "I think you're telling me that every culture's lunacy seems like sanity to the members of that culture."

"That's certainly so," B said. "If I were to tell you that the Gebusi believe that the creator of the universe has spoken to only one people on this earth during its entire history, and that one people is the Gebusi, you would smile patronizingly. Wouldn't you?"

"Yes, I suppose I would."

"Yet this is precisely what the people of our culture believe, isn't it? Has the creator of the universe spoken to anyone but us?"

"No."

"Modern humans have been around for two hundred thousand years, but according to our beliefs, God had not a word to say to any of them until *we* came along. God didn't speak to the Alawa of Australia or to the Gebusi of New Zealand or to the Bushmen of Africa or to the Navajo of North America or to the Ihalmiut of the Great Barrens of Canada. God didn't speak a word to any of the other hundreds of thousands of peoples of the world, he spoke only to us. Only to us did he reveal the order and purpose of creation. Only to us did he reveal the laws essential to salvation."

"That's right. Speaking with the voice of undoubted faith, that's right."

"But this isn't lunacy."

"No. Again speaking with the voice of undoubted faith, this isn't lunacy."

"It would be completely silly for the Gebusi to believe that they are in direct, exclusive contact with the creator of the universe, but it's perfectly reasonable for us to believe it."

"That's right."

"Evidently it isn't just the history of the world that the victors get to write, it's the theology of the world as well."

"Yes, that's so."

"All the same, right now I'm not asking you to understand something, I'm asking you to do something."

"What do you want me to do?"

"I want you to imagine that the world—this world right here—is a Gebusi world. You, as a Roman Catholic priest, would be tolerated as a vestige of a quaint and harmless superstition. At night men would cluster in bars, not to watch televised sports but to hold raunchy conversations with female spirits clinging to the rafters. Spirit mediums would be on hand to diagnose and cure minor illnesses—and to conduct inquests into community deaths. Friends would invite you to a restaurant to celebrate a killing—and send you home with a slice of roast sorcerer for your family. What more can I tell you? The films would be Gebusi films, the novels Gebusi novels, the politics Gebusi politics, the sports Gebusi sports, the fun Gebusi fun."

I told him I could imagine it—more or less. "But I can't imagine what you want me to say."

"How does it seem to you?"

"How does it seem? It seems insane. Obscene."

"Of course it does. Confined to their own few hundred square miles, the Gebusi are quaint and bizarre. Blow them up into a universal world culture to which every human must belong and they become an obscenity. The same is true in general. Any culture will become an obscenity when blown up into a universal world culture to which all must belong. Confined to the few hundred square miles in which it was born, our own culture would have been merely quaint and bizarre. Blown up into a universal world culture to which all must belong, it is a horrifying obscenity."

"I think I'm beginning to see," I told him. "I think I'm beginning to see what you're getting at as a whole."

B nodded. "You probably don't remember why I brought up the Gebusi in the first place. You said it was a wonder that we ever adopted totalitarian agriculture, considering the fact that, far from making life easier or more secure, it actually has the opposite effect."

"Yes, I remember."

"I wanted you to see that lifestyle strategies adopted in a culture aren't necessarily *logical*. They don't necessarily benefit people in obvious ways. They aren't necessarily adopted because they make life more comfortable—though people may use this rationale to explain them to children and outsiders. In our culture, for example, the adoption of our style of agriculture is presented to our children as an inevitable step forward for the human race, because it makes life easier and more secure."

I asked B what it did do if it doesn't make life easier and more secure.

"That's exactly what we're trying to understand here. We're presented with a complex of behaviors and we're trying to figure out how they work together to produce the result that we see. Right now, sort through the peculiarities of the Gebusi and see if you can find a mechanism that would tend to make them blow up into a universal world culture to which all must belong."

I asked him what sort of mechanism he meant.

"Some dynamic within the culture. Some custom, some deeply held belief."

I spent a minute or two on it but could find no mechanism that would produce that effect.

"Invent one then," B said.

"I suppose territorial ambitions would have that effect."

"Not by themselves," B said. "The Aztecs had territorial ambitions, but once they conquered you, they didn't give a damn how you lived. They weren't interested in turning their neighbors into Aztecs. This is why, vile as they may have been, they were not us—not what Ishmael calls Takers."

"Okay, I see where you're coming from. You'd have to make them cultural missionaries if you wanted them to blow up into a world-dominating culture."

"And in order to make them cultural missionaries, you'd have to endow them with a belief. Missionaries are nothing if not believers. What kind of believers would the Gebusi have to be?"

"They would have to be believers in the rightness of their way of life."

"Exactly. If the Gebusi believed that theirs was the one right way for all humans to live (which they don't, by the way), this would motivate them to become cultural missionaries to the world. But the belief alone wouldn't be enough. The people of our culture have always held this belief—have throughout history demonstrated that they held this belief—but they needed another mechanism as well. I suppose you could call it a spreading mechanism. A mechanism that would push them across the face of their earth as they spread the gospel of their cultural enlightenment."

"Agriculture," I said.

"Agriculture of a particular design, Jared, because not every kind of agriculture will push a people across the face of the earth. The modest agriculture of the Gebusi simply wouldn't support such an expansion."

"I understand."

"In our culture, to support one peculiarity, we needed a second peculiarity, and the two reinforced each other. We believed (and still believe) that we have the one right way for people to live, but we needed totalitarian agriculture to support our missionary effort. Totalitarian agriculture gave us fabulous food surpluses, which are the foundation of every military and economic expansion. No one was able to stand against us anywhere in the world, because no one had a food-producing machine as powerful as ours. Our military and economic success confirmed our belief that we have the one right way for people to live. It still does so today. For the people of our culture, the fact that we're able to defeat and destroy any other lifestyle is taken as clear proof of our cultural superiority."

"Yes, I'm afraid that's so. When it comes to cultural 'survival of the fittest,' we're the champs."

"You mean that we're champion exemplars of the process of natural selection."

"Well . . . yes, I guess that's what I mean."

B shook his head. "It shouldn't be looked at that way—evolutionary ideas always make risky metaphors. The tendency of biological evolution is toward diversity—is now and always has been. Evolution isn't tending toward 'the one right species.' From the beginning, it has been tending *away* from the singularity from which all life sprang in the primordial stew. I remember as a boy reading a science-fiction story about a mutant organism that was born in a drain, in the fortuitous confluence of a dib of this and a dab of that. This organism was driven by a single tropism, which was to turn living matter into itself. Unstopped, it had the capability of reversing in a few days billions of years of biological evolution by devouring all life-forms on this planet and turning them into a single form, itself. This mutant organism is a perfect metaphor for our culture, which in just a few centuries is reversing millions of years of human development by devouring all cultures on this planet and turning them into a single culture, our own."

"An ugly thought," I said.

"It's an ugly process."

"Gunpowder," B said, "is a mixture of potassium nitrate, charcoal, and sulfur, and I suppose you know that if any one of these ingredients is missing, then the mixture isn't explosive."

"Of course."

"As an explosive mixture, our culture also consists of three essential ingredients, and if any one of them had been missing, no explosion would have taken place here on this planet. We've already identified two of the ingredients: totalitarian agriculture and the belief that ours is the one right way. The third is of course the Great Forgetting."

I thought about it some but finally told him I couldn't see how the Great Forgetting had contributed to the explosion.

"It contributed to the explosion roughly the way that charcoal contributes to the explosion of gunpowder. How did we come to have the strange idea that our way is the one right way?"

"I don't know."

"Let's go back again to the foundation thinkers of our culture—

Herodotus, Confucius, Abraham, Anaximander, Pythagoras, Socrates, and any others you can think of. Assemble them all in one room and ask them this question: How long have people been living the way we live? What would be their answer?"

"Their answer would be, people have been living this way from the beginning."

"In other words, Man was *born* living this way."

"That's right."

"And what does this tell you about the nature of Man?"

"It tells me that Man was *meant* to live this way. Man is meant to live as a totalitarian agriculturalist and a city builder the way bees were meant to live as honey collectors and hive builders."

"So tell me, Jared: What else *could* this be except the one right way?"

"Yes, I see that."

"What was missing from the education of these thinkers? What was forgotten during the Great Forgetting?"

"What was forgotten was the fact that Man was *not* born a totalitarian agriculturalist and a city builder. What was forgotten was the fact that our way was *not* ordained from the beginning of time. If this hadn't been forgotten, then we would never have been able to persuade ourselves that ours is the one right way. This is why the Great Forgetting was an ingredient essential to our cultural explosion."

"Let's go for a walk," B said. "There's something I have to pick up for you."

"Something for me?"

"Something you'll need later."

I started to head out the way I'd come, but B beckoned me in the opposite direction, down a hall that opened up behind his chair, the same hall from which Monika and Heinz Teitel had appeared with refreshments the night before. The hall soon widened to accommodate concrete benches on either side, and B told me it had been designed to serve as a bomb shelter for both the theater and a government office building the next street over.

"But I don't believe it was ever needed for that purpose," he added.

After a couple hundred meters the tunnel angled up and terminated at a heavy fire door that opened into the subbasement storage room of a government building of some kind. Surprisingly, to me, there was a desk here, and someone manning it, evidently to monitor access to the storage areas. This person, a middle-aged soldierly type who looked like he would have felt more comfortable in any sort of uniform, glared at us with disapproval but made no vocal objection to our passing through his territory. Two flights of stairs took us up to the ground floor and the street.

A visit to the Cretaceous

It was barely eight-thirty when we came out—hardly more than late afternoon in this northern city just weeks before the summer solstice. Despite the early hour, the shops were mostly shuttered, and the streets were all but deserted. Radenau is not to be visited for its exciting nightlife.

B is a stroller, as I am. He seemed to be going nowhere in particular, and I was glad to tag along.

He said, "I'm sure you're beginning to see why it isn't possible for me to carry mass audiences of listeners along in this direction."

"Yes, I see that," I told him. "But I'm not sure I see the direction."

"Remember that we're working on a mosaic, not a narrative or a syllogism. After this conversation, you still won't have a conclusion, but you should have a more complete understanding of everything you've ever heard me say."

"Yes, that's true. The figure in the mosaic is still a little vague, but it's not as vague as it was two hours ago."

"A while ago you said that, the way I was talking, it's a wonder that our cultural revolution ever took place. It really is a wonder. It wasn't destiny, it wasn't divinely ordained from the foundation of the universe, it wasn't something that was just inevitably going to happen. It hadn't happened in two hundred thousand years of people as smart as we are. It might not have happened in another two hundred thousand years—or in another million. It was a quirk, a fluke. Combine one never-before-seen cultural element with a second never-before-seen element, add a third just as odd, and you come up with a cultural monster that is literally devouring the world—and will end by devouring itself if it isn't stopped."

We sloped along for a while, then I asked B if the figure in the mosaic was going to turn out to be our culture.

"I suppose you might say so, though I've never thought of it that way myself," he said. "I think of it as a mural composed of many interrelated scenes, like the ceiling of the Sistine Chapel. What you call 'our culture' appears in many of the scenes at different moments in its history, but then there are also scenes within scenes. There are scenes depicting the history of the universe, and among these there are scenes depicting the development of life on this planet. Among these are scenes depicting the emergence of the human race. Among the scenes depicting the emergence of the human race are scenes depicting the origin of hundreds of thousands of cultures, including the Gebusi and our own. Among the scenes depicting the development of our culture are scenes depicting many other things, such as the conquest of the world by our culture, such as the appearance of salvationist religions in our culture, such as the Industrial Revolution. We move from scene to scene, we step back from the mural to try to see relationships between scenes, we move in again to focus on details, and so on. As time goes on, the whole composition begins to come together for us—but it's not a process that has an end point. There will never come a time when we insert a final piece and say, 'There, that's it, every last piece is now in place.' "

We came to a stop at a sign reading MEYER—ÜBERBLEIBSELEN, whatever that was. B looked over the huge, gray, steel shutter as if in hopes of locating a button he could press to make it go away. When he didn't find it, he began unceremoniously pounding on it with his fist. After a minute a window above shot up, and the Ghost of Christmas Past leaned out to ask in German what the hell we were doing. This I soon learned was Gustl Meyer. Meyer and B yelled at each other for a bit, in English and German, then the window was slammed shut.

B gave me a smiling nod as if to assure me that everything was going really well, then a couple minutes later the shutter clattered up and we were admitted to the dim interior of Meyer's shop, which was stocked exclusively with the castoffs and leftovers (*Überbleibselen*) of museums devoted to every sort of thing except art: military history, political history, natural history, science, technology, and industry. As soon as we crossed the threshold, B started vibrating with a kind of electric joy, like a five-year-old in a toy shop, and I began to realize he was a man with the heart of a completely lunatic collector of curios. He was enchanted by a working miniature of an early "safety" elevator, by a life-size wax Neanderthaler who sat cross-legged on the floor absorbed in some hand work that was no longer in his hands, by an exquisite cutaway scale model of a copper mine, by a hideous (and wholly improbable) stuffed dodo that Meyer claimed had been made from an actual skin, by a battered one-man submarine of the Napoleonic era, by a transparent talking head that described the operation of the brain (in Dutch) while pinpoint lights within indicated the areas under discussion.

There were crates of ore samples, piles of tarnished brass instruments, boxes of disintegrating scrolls, racks of entomological specimens, tubs of fossils of every kind—and it was at one of these that B finally paused to begin rummaging in a serious way. He took out and examined trilobites, crinoids, and things I assumed were dinosaur eggs, teeth, and claws. Finally he stopped at a doughnut-sized object rather like the shell of a chambered nautilus except that it was corrugated like the curling horn of a mountain sheep.

"An ammonite," B said, "cephalopod—same class as the nautilus." He dropped it into my hand, saying, "Been extinct for about sixty-five million years."

I said something brilliant, like "Really?" and started to give it back, but he turned to Meyer to ask its price. After dickering a bit, B handed him what looked like enough cash to cover dinner for two at a pretty good restaurant.

"A collector would have paid a lot more," B explained when we were outside, "but Meyer doesn't expect to get premium prices, certainly not from me."

"What am I supposed to do with it?" I asked him.

"Put it in your pocket. Keep it with you, I'm not sure when we'll get around to it."

The wired monkey

We stopped at a nondescript *Gasthaus* for dinner, and B told me to have beer, not whiskey. "Did you like Little Bohemia? We'll go there later for a real drink."

I told him that would be fine. I think he has the impression that all of us Romish padres are booze hounds.

"I have to go back to the first piece I tried to put in place tonight," B said. "I know it's not set in solidly."

"Okay."

"Last night in the theater I talked about changing minds. I said that if the world is saved, it will be saved by people with changed minds—not by programs but by people with changed minds."

"I remember."

"It's difficult for people to credit this notion, because they don't see that what we have here, every bit of it—all the triumph and glory and catastrophe of it—is the work of people with changed minds."

"I don't see it myself," I told him.

"I know," B said, "that's why we're coming back to it. Let's make sure we're agreed on basic facts. The mind change I'm looking at occurred about ten thousand years ago in what has been called the Fertile Crescent—an area between the Tigris and Euphrates rivers now encompassed by Iraq. It was the inhabitants of this area, ten thousand years ago, who laid the foundations of what is now our global culture. Is this what you understand?"

"Yes."

"Good. Now I'm sure you realize that the human race didn't originate in the Fertile Crescent. The evidence we have right now indicates pretty conclusively that the human race originated in Africa."

"Right."

"It originated in Africa and then very slowly spread into every part of the world: the Near East, the Far East, Europe, ultimately reaching the most distant regions—places like the Americas, Australia, and New Guinea—about thirty or forty thousand years ago. The Near East, being next door to Africa, has been inhabited by modern humans for an immensely long time, a hundred thousand years or more. This includes the area of the Fertile Crescent. Do you see the point I'm making here?"

"No, not really."

"The area we're looking at, the Fertile Crescent, was inhabited by modern humans for something like a hundred thousand years *before* our agricultural revolution began."

"Okay. I think I understood that already."

"I'm pointing out that the revolution we're looking at occurred among people who had been living there for tens of thousands of years. People were living there, and a revolution occurred. The revolution wasn't a meteorological event. It wasn't an earthquake or a volcanic eruption. It was something that happened among people. About ten thousand years ago people who had been living in the Fertile Crescent for tens of thousands of years *began to live a new way,* the way I've called the Taker way."

"I see that."

"They didn't begin to live a new way because they were starving, because, as I've said, starving people don't invent lifestyles any more than people falling out of airplanes invent parachutes. And their new way to live wasn't adopted because it was so pleasant that it was just an inevitable next step forward. What these founders of our culture fundamentally invented for us was the notion of *work.* They developed *a hard way to live*—the hardest way to live ever found on this planet."

"But it gave them some other things besides a hard life."

"Exactly. Now you're running with me, Jared! Now you're beginning to see why I say that these people represent *changed minds.* They didn't think like the Gebusi or the Cheyenne or the Alawa or the Ihalmiut or the Micmac or the Bushmen—or any other of thousands of peoples I could name. What they were doing didn't make sense to their neighbors, but it didn't have to. What they were doing wouldn't have made sense to their great-great-great-grandparents, but again it didn't have to. What they were doing made perfect sense to them, the way that what the Gebusi do makes perfect sense to them. What they were doing made perfect sense to them, because they saw things differently—differently from the way their ancestors saw them and differently from the way their neighbors saw them. Do you see now why I say that these people represent changed minds?"

"I think so."

"Because we share that mind change, we look at what they did and say, 'Well, of course. This makes sense. What could be more obvious? This was *bound* to happen. Humans were *meant* to live as Takers.' Because we share their mind-set, their revolution makes perfect sense to us. To us, it looks logical and inevitable, the way eating sorcerers seems logical and inevitable to the Gebusi."

"Yes, I see."

"We know what ethnic group these people belonged to—evidently they were Caucasians—but there's no reason at all to suppose that every Caucasian people took part in this revolution. The Gebusi and their neighbors the Kubor, the Bedamini, the Oybae, the Honibo, and the Samo all belong to the same ethnic group, but they certainly don't have a common culture. Are you following me?"

"I think so."

"We'll never know what the people of the revolution called themselves, but let's make up a name for them. Let's call them the Tak. This will link them to the way I've called the Taker way."

"Okay."

"The Tak didn't become agriculturalists because they were hungry or because they liked hard work better than loafing. Quite on your own, you grasped the key fact that they got something out of their toilsome life that compensated them for it. Why did they become agriculturalists? What did totalitarian agriculture give them that foraging didn't give their neighbors and their ancestors?"

"You already showed me this. Totalitarian agriculture gave them power."

"That's right. Their revolution wasn't about food, it was about power. That's *still* what it's about."

"Yes, I can see that."

"Someone once asked me how I could go on maintaining that the human race isn't flawed if it's so enamored of power. 'The Tak succumbed to a lust for power,' he said. 'Isn't that a flaw? All their cultural descendants succumbed to a lust for power. Isn't that a flaw?'

I told him about a famous psychological experiment of the late 1950s. An electrode was implanted in the pleasure center of a monkey's brain. Pushing a button on a small control box delivered an electric pulse to the electrode, giving the monkey a tremendous jolt of sheer, whole-body pleasure. They gave the box to the monkey, who of course had no idea what it was but by accident eventually pushed the button, giving itself this tremendous jolt of pleasure. It didn't take many more repetitions for the monkey to catch on to the connection between the button and the pleasure, and once this happened it just sat there hour after hour pushing the button and giving itself jolts of pleasure. It passed up food, it passed up sex. If they hadn't eventually taken the box away, the monkey would have sat there and literally pleasured itself to death. Here is the question I asked back to my questioner: 'Was there something wrong with this monkey? Was the monkey flawed?' What do you think, Jared?"

"I would say no, the monkey wasn't flawed."

"I'd say the same. Nor were the Tak flawed. Pushing the button of totalitarian agriculture gave them a tremendous jolt of power. It gave the same jolt of power to the people of China and to the people of Europe. It gives us the same jolt of power today. And just like the monkey, no one wants to quit pushing that button, and we're in serious danger of pleasuring ourselves to death with unending jolts of power."

I nodded. "I guess this is what you mean when you say that if the world is saved, it will be saved by people with changed minds. People with *un*changed minds will say, 'Let's minimize the *effects* of pushing the button.' People with *changed* minds will say, 'Let's throw the box away!' "

B nodded. "It wouldn't have occurred to me to say it that way, but of course you're right. As soon as the people of our culture decide to throw the box away, things will begin to change dramatically. And when you start saying things better than I could have said them myself, this is a clear sign that you're on your way to becoming the message."

The Tak

Our food came at this point, and we both fell silent to give it our attention. Finally B said, "There's one connection I've tried to put off making for you, thinking I could avoid it or skip it, but I'd better go ahead and make it."

I asked him why he'd been avoiding it.

"I've been avoiding it because I feel under some pressure to be economical of time here." He shook his head, dissatisfied with this statement. "That's not quite direct enough. I want to be rid of the hovering specter of Bernard Lulfre as soon as possible. I want to satisfy his curiosity and get him out of here."

"I understand. What's the connection you've been avoiding?"

"I've told you the Tak seemed like lunatics to their neighbors, just as the Gebusi seem like lunatics to us. Do you find that hard to believe?"

"Yes, I do, but I suppose the Gebusi find it equally hard to believe that they seem like lunatics to us."

"Just so," B said. "The Tak seem perfectly reasonable and ordinary to us, because we're their cultural descendants. We have the same worldview they had."

"I understand. But even so, we can't actually know what the Tak's neighbors thought of them."

"In this case, by a great fluke of history, we can know what at least *one* of their neighbors thought of them. Or rather, we *do* know, because we have their version of what happened. Again, we know what ethnic group these neighbors belonged to, but not what they called themselves. Let's call them the Zeugen—in other words, the witnesses. In terms of lifestyle, the Zeugen were rather like the Masai of East Africa. Do you know the Masai?"

"I've heard of them. They're nomadic herders, aren't they?"

"That's right. The Zeugen too were nomadic herders, and when they looked at the Tak revolution, they didn't see a technological advance or anything remotely like a technological advance. What they saw was an overturning of the order of the universe. They saw, as you have, that totalitarian agriculture isn't about food, it's about power—

power over who lives and who dies in the world. Is it clear why they would see it that way?"

"Talk about it some."

"The easiest way to see it is by example. According to totalitarian agriculture, cows may live but wolves must die. According to totalitarian agriculture, chickens may live but foxes must die. According to totalitarian agriculture, wheat may live but chinch bugs must die. Anything we eat may live, but anything that eats our food must die—and not merely on an ad hoc basis. Our posture is not, 'If a coyote attacks my herd, I'll kill it,' our posture is, 'Let's wipe coyotes off the face of the earth.' When it came to wolves and cows, we said, 'Let the wolves be destroyed,' and the wolves were destroyed, and we said, 'Let there be cows by the billion,' and there were cows by the billion."

"Okay, I get it."

"Who ordinarily wields this power?"

"What do you mean?"

"Look at it from the point of view of some nomadic herders of ten thousand years ago. Who decides who lives and dies on this planet?"

"The gods."

"Of course. Now, the way the Zeugen imagined it, the gods have a special knowledge that enables them to rule the world. This knowledge includes the knowledge of who should live and who should die, but it embraces much more than that. This is the general knowledge the gods employ in every choice they make. What the Zeugen perceived is this, that every choice the gods make is good for one creature but evil for another, and if you think about it, it really can't be otherwise. If the quail goes out to hunt and the gods send it a grasshopper, then this is good for the quail but evil for the grasshopper. And if the fox goes out to hunt, and the gods send it a quail, then this is good for the fox but evil for the quail. And vice versa, of course. If the fox goes out to hunt, and the gods withhold the quail, then this is good for the quail but evil for the fox. Do you see what I mean?"

"Of course."

"When the Zeugen saw what the Tak were up to, they said to themselves, 'These people have eaten at the gods' own tree of wisdom, the tree of the knowledge of good and evil.' "

I said, "Yipes." I'm not sure I ever uttered that syllable before in my life, but I did then. "Where did you get this?"

"This is one of Ishmael's contributions."

"Have you ever tried it out on a biblical scholar?"

B nodded. "Biblical scholars have seen it, and so far none has found any reason to quarrel with it. One said it was the only explanation he'd ever seen that makes sense."

"It's the only one *I've* seen that makes sense, and I've seen them all."

I remember sitting there frozen for two or three minutes while I tried to work out all the implications of this new interpretation of the story of the Fall. When at last I shook my head and gave up, B went on.

"I felt I had to bring this out in order to drive home the point I've been trying to make about this revolution. Even the authors of the story in Genesis described it as a matter of *changed minds*. What they saw being born in their neighbors was not a new lifestyle but a new mind-set, a mind-set that made us out to be as wise as the gods, that made the world out to be a piece of human property, that gave us the power of life and death over the world. They thought this new mind-set would be the death of Adam—and events are proving them right."

I threw down my napkin and said, "I'm full up."

B gave me a look of frowning puzzlement.

"That's all I can take for tonight," I told him.

"But it's early!"

"I know, and I'm sorry, but I can't take in any more, and I've got to figure out how this is going to be transmitted to Fr. Lulfre. I can't just send him a transcript of the tape. If he got the idea that I was becoming the sorcerer's apprentice, he'd pull me out in an instant."

B shrugged. "I agree. We can't risk that."

We arranged to meet for dinner the next day.

When I got back to my room, I resisted the temptation offered by the bed. I wanted to get a fax off to Fr. Lulfre by three or four in the morning so as to maintain the pattern I'd established in previous days.

It was my thought to translate my conversation with B into a series of vignettes in the style of the gospels—"A man came up to Jesus and said . . ." or "Jesus was met by a large crowd, one of whom shouted . . ." I'm not sure I produced anything very convincing. On the other hand, why would Fr. Lulfre suspect me of fabrication? (Answer: Because his thought processes are nothing remotely like mine.)

It's five A.M. and I feel wired as tight as a harpsichord. I hope a slug of whiskey will let me sleep.

Tuesday, May 21

Faith and its degrees

The phone rang at nine, and I crawled up out of a stupor miles deep to answer it. It was Shirin, explaining something far too intricate for me to comprehend on less than four hours of sleep. I asked her to go over it again, slowly, and finally got it straight. There was one speaking engagement B had been unable to talk his way out of, and it was today in Stuttgart. In order to reach it on time, we would have to board a train at eleven, and I was welcome to come with them to Stuttgart or to stay in Radenau, it was up to me. I told her I'd meet them at the Bahnhof at ten-fifty. I hung up and quickly decided that a shower and breakfast were more important than another hour of sleep.

There was something on my mind that I needed to explore on paper, so I took a notebook down to the dining room with me and wrote as follows:

> There is only one degree of *having* faith, but there are fifty degrees of *losing* it. I feel I should carry this weighty observation on a separate piece of paper so I can whip it out for study whenever I feel the need: Only one degree of *having* faith, but fifty of *losing* it.
>
> I think I know one priest who has faith in that one degree that deserves the name of faith. All the rest, including me, are at one of those fifty degrees of losing it. Most of my parishioners would probably consider this a shocking admission, but I don't think it is. Of course there are priests who have gone beyond the fifty degrees and have walked away from the ministry. Everyone knows that, and I've known half a dozen of them myself. But the rest of us are still hanging on, by

knees and elbows and fingertips and eyelashes and teeth and fingernails. This is actually reassuring, I think, because it shows that none of us *wants* to lose his faith or wants to think of himself as *having* lost it. Admittedly, this is partly just cowardice; we know that, once our faith is gone, the religious life will become utterly intolerable and we'll have to move on, out into an unknown world. But it's also partly because we have enough faith to want to go *on* having faith. When that amount of faith is gone, however, then it's *all* gone, and you're at the fifty-first degree. You're out, you're finished.

I figure I'm at something like the thirty-fourth degree. When I was fifteen, I was at the one degree that means faith. When I entered the seminary, I was at the third degree of losing faith. At my ordination, I was at the twelfth degree. When I walked into Fr. Lulfre's office three weeks ago, I was at the twenty-fifth. The fact that I'm at the thirty-fourth now probably sounds pretty bad, but actually it isn't. I was afraid (when I sat down here to do this soul-searching) that I was going to turn out to be at some really scary degree like forty-seven. I mean, when you're at forty-seven, you're really at the precipice. Three more degrees, and over you go!

To Stuttgart

The party of travelers consisted of B, Shirin, Michael, and me. As we shook hands, Michael for the first time gave me a surname by which to know him, though I can only guess at its spelling. It sounded like Dershinsky. Shirin was businesslike and neutral. B seemed gloomy and preoccupied.

No one was in a conversational mood, except possibly Michael, who kept giving me friendly nods and winks but otherwise seemed to be reining in his good mood out of deference to Shirin and B. After we were under way for ten minutes, I piped up to ask what the speaking engagement was. No one seemed keen to tell me. Finally B explained that it had been organized by a man and a woman at the university there who knew and wanted to promote B's views on population.

"You don't seem wildly enthusiastic about it," I said.

"My views on this subject always generate a lot of rage."

"Rage among whom? The Catholics?"

"No, not at all. The Marxists."

"Why the Marxists?"

He shrugged and turned his gaze out the window. Michael and Shirin each gave me a little shake of the head to warn me off.

In Hamburg we changed trains to something faster and slightly less austere, but the atmosphere remained bleak and didn't improve when we broke out the box lunches Michael had picked up for us at the Hamburg station.

Halfway to Stuttgart, B said to Shirin, "Why don't you tell Jared the story of the Imperial Chill?"

If I read the progress of her thoughts right, she didn't much care for the suggestion but was as bored as everyone else. To add a bit of encouragement, I unpacked my tape recorder and got it going.

Surprisingly, she betrayed no signs of self-consciousness or embarrassment (I certainly would have betrayed some). Instead, she spent a minute gathering herself, then launched into it like a professional actress.

The Imperial Chill

"The Imperial Chill had been an imperial preoccupation for so long that no one was counting centuries anymore. That it was genetic was obvious, of course, but this knowledge helped no one—certainly not the shivering Emperor. Every academic and scientific discipline in the realm had a chilly aspect. Every scholar and scientist was to some degree or in some sense working on the problem, which was generally agreed to be metabolic and probably dietary. There was of course nothing wrong with the emperor's diet, but it was assumed that some adjustment (possibly quite infinitesimal) would turn the trick and give His Highness relief. There were acorn diets and apple diets—and watercress diets and zucchini diets at the other end of the alphabet. Every university depended on its subsidy for research on the tempering effects of diet and food—research that everyone knew could be effortlessly spun out till the end of time.

"One day, however, the Prime Minister called a press conference and announced that a breakthrough had been made. Of course, breakthroughs had been announced before and had always come to nothing, so no one was really worried—till they saw the look on the Prime Minister's face. This time (that look told them) something uncomfortably new was in the offing."

Shirin paused and asked B whether she should finish it then or wait till later.

"Oh, finish it now," B said grumpily. "Then he can be thinking about it."

Shirin continued.

"The Prime Minister's announcement (that the cause of the Imperial Chill had been found) was shockingly brief—and was followed by a shocked silence, which soon became a murmur of horror, disbelief, and denial. The truth of the minister's words was not what outraged his listeners. What outraged them was the idea that, after defeating the best minds of a dozen generations, the Emperor's chilliness could be explained so simply. The feeling seemed to be that critical problems (like the Emperor's chill) must absolutely have complex and impenetrable causes, and they must absolutely be difficult (and perhaps even impossible) to solve. As he wandered aimlessly through the crowd, one dazed scholar was heard to mutter over and over, 'There *are* no easy answers, there are *no* easy answers, there are no *easy* answers'—not with any real conviction now but rather as if repetition might restore vitality to these familiar, comforting words.

"What was distressing them was not the fact that the cause of the chill was now known but rather the fact that it had *always* been known—but never as a *cause*. It had stared them in the face, and looking beyond it to remote and unintelligible causes, they had missed its significance. Throughout the empire, there was literally no one who was ignorant of the fact that their shivering monarch . . . had . . . no . . . clothes."

.   .   .

To say that I didn't know what to say to this would be an understatement. Luckily, it seemed that no response was expected. B continued to stare listlessly out the window. Without so much as a glance at her audience, Shirin picked up the book she'd been reading. Only Michael acknowledged that anything at all had occurred, winking me some of his abundant reassurance.

It hadn't even been much of a break. I snuck my tape recorder away, feeling rather like Lewis Carroll's Alice, who had so many experiences of this sort, getting herself all set up for exciting entertainments that didn't turn out to be entertainments at all.

Fun with Marxists and others

We were met at the station by our hosts, a middle-aged couple with a car into which five might conceivably squeeze, but not six by any means short of dismemberment. The problem was easily solved: Michael and I followed in a taxi. This ride gave me a new insight into him; he'd not been silent in the train out of deference to B and Shirin, he'd been silent out of sheer, desperate shyness—even more acutely projected now, when he might have talked as much as he liked. I made a couple efforts to draw him out but soon understood that he really preferred to remain in the background and never step forward into the light.

The taxi deposited us in front of a vast, neo-Gothic prison of a school, and we were led upstairs to a classroom that would have depressed a barrelful of monkeys. My heart sank as I saw it. Some twenty silent spectators were scattered through the room, half of them with the air of actors psyching themselves up to read for the role of Cassius in *Julius Caesar*. B, Shirin, and the host couple were at the front, chatting—or trying to give the impression of chatting.

Michael and I shuffled off to the back. A few minutes later Shirin took a seat in the front row, and B was introduced at length (and in German). I'd decided not to tape B's speech, since I'd eventually have to transcribe it anyway, but I hadn't counted on its being his longest presentation to date.*

* The text of this speech will be found on pages 285–304.

I wasn't prepared for what I heard—not that I ever was when it came to B. This material was extraordinary, unlike anything I'd ever heard or read on the subject, and as it unfolded I began to see the point of the story of the Imperial Chill. B was bringing to light crucial facts as far beyond argument as the Emperor's nakedness (or so I naively imagined). When he was finished, about seven people applauded, two of them being our hosts and three of them being Shirin, Michael, and me.

Looking drained to the point of collapse, B began fielding questions—or rather disquisitions and rebuttals, all in German. Michael leaned in my direction to explain that by declining to use English (which they obviously understood), they were demonstrating their contempt for B's views.

Before answering them, B summarized their questions in English (presumably for my benefit). As far as I could understand them, they simply denied everything B had said—an interesting approach, I thought. At the end of it (or when he got tired of it), he concluded with a little epilogue to the Imperial Chill, which he directed to me:

"When the scholars in the capital of the Chilly Emperor had had a few days to think things over, they began to recover their wits and to see that all was not lost to them after all. They called a press conference that was twice as solemn as the Prime Minister's and three times as well attended. After the various media representatives had been wined and dined regally, the head of the Royal Commission for Chilly Research called the meeting to order and made the following announcement. 'It's perfectly true that the Emperor is naked,' he said. 'We have always known this and have always chosen to ignore it, because it's a red herring. The causes of the Emperor's condition are many, complex, and difficult for laymen to understand—and they cannot be reduced to this single, childish notion: that he is cold because he's wearing nothing but his birthday suit. The suggestion that warm clothing might alleviate the Emperor's discomfort is charming and well meant but will not be recommended for implementation or further study.' Following this announcement, the Prime Minister was dismissed for incompetence, the scholars' grants were all renewed, and the Emperor went on shivering into a snowy old age."

B thanked his listeners and stepped away in the midst of a bemused silence. Evidently some sort of polite social follow-up had been planned for us, but we skipped it in order to catch a train back to Hamburg. As luck would have it, this late-night train was of the cozy, old-fashioned sort, with separate compartments.

Between Stuttgart and Frankfurt

"Remind me never to do this again," B said once we were settled in.

"I reminded you before you agreed to go in the first place," Shirin noted dryly.

"You didn't do it forcefully enough."

Michael cleared his throat and said, "You never know when you might have planted a seed," and then turned an amazing shade of scarlet.

"It's kind of you to say that, Michael," B said gently, "but that was mighty hard ground."

"It was indeed."

"Where did we leave off last night?" B asked me a few minutes later.

I thought for a bit and said, "You'd just made this point, that what the authors of the story of the Fall saw in our agricultural revolution was not a new technology but a new worldview that makes us out to be as wise as the gods—wise enough to wield the power of life and death over the world."

B nodded. "I'm glad we got that far, but that's the easy part of what we have to accomplish."

"Why is that?"

"It's easy enough to imagine what was going on when the universe was born, because we see the universe every time we lift our eyes to the sky. But it's very, very difficult to imagine what was going on *before* the universe was born."

"*Nothing* was going on before the universe was born. By definition."

"Precisely."

I shook my head. "You'll have to relate this to our subject here."

"It's easy for us to understand what those first farmers had in mind when they settled down to live in villages. It's easy for us to understand what bronze-age traders had in mind as they caravanned their wares over hundreds of miles between Thebes and Heracleopolis and Damascus and Assur and Ur. It's easy for us to understand what the empire builders of Akkad and Sumer had in mind, what the builders of the Great Wall of China had in mind, what the builders of the colossal pyramids of Egypt had in mind. I trust you see what I mean—I could obviously go on piling up examples for hours."

"I see what you mean."

"We understand what they had in mind because they were doing what we would do in their place. They were our cultural kin. These were people who saw the world as we see it and who saw Man's place in the world as we see it."

"I understand."

"But when we look back *beyond* our agricultural revolution into the human past, we no longer understand what people had in mind. We don't understand what they had in mind as they lived through tens of thousands of years *without* trade and commerce, *without* empires or kingdoms or even villages, *without* accomplishments of any kind."

"That's very true. I'd say it's our impression that they didn't have *anything* in mind. It's not that we don't understand it, it's that there was nothing there to be understood."

"This is the parallelism to the birth of the universe, Jared. We can't understand what was going on before the birth of the universe, because *nothing* was going on, and we can't understand what people had in mind before the birth of our culture because we imagine that they had *nothing* in mind."

"That's the way it seems, yes."

"This is of course another result of the Great Forgetting. We've *forgotten* what people had in mind before our revolution."

I said, "I guess I still don't get it. Why is it important to know what people had in mind before our agricultural revolution?"

B sighed. "There are some teaching problems that can only be solved by parables, and I guess this is one of them. Let me think for a minute."

I looked around at the others, but they were both keeping their eyes and their thoughts to themselves. We were at this moment just pulling into Frankfurt. B and I were sitting across from each other at the window side of the car, and with nothing better to do, I scanned the faces of passengers waiting to board and was surprised to see a familiar one. The train had glided past him by the time I remembered who it was. It was Herr Reichmann, the elderly gentleman who had advised me to drop Charles Atterley in favor of a person scheduled to speak at Der Bau—who of course turned out to be B. I was thinking vaguely of the possibility of introducing B and Herr Reichmann to each other when B began his tale.

The Weavers

"It's well known," B said, "that every piece of hand-woven cloth has an element of magic in it, which is the special magic of its weaver. This magic doesn't necessarily die with the individual weaver but rather can be passed on from generation to generation and shared among families and even whole nations, so that one who is sensitive to such things can tell in a moment whether a piece of cloth was woven in Ireland or France or Virginia or Bavaria. This is true on every planet in the universe where weaving is practiced, and it was true on the planet I'd like to tell you about right now.

"It happened on this planet that a weaver named Nixt came along who was a strange compound of genius and insanity, violence and artistry, ruthlessness and charm—and this was the magic he wove into his cloth, and those who wore garments made from it became just like the weaver. The weaver was quickly renowned, and everyone wanted clothes imbued with his magic. Wearing such clothes, artists created masterpieces, merchants got rich, leaders extended their power, soldiers triumphed in battle, and lovers left their rivals in the dust. Almost immediately it was noticed that Nixtian magic had some drawbacks. It was so powerful that it tended to devour what it touched. Instead of lasting for centuries, artists' masterpieces tended to disintegrate after only decades. Instead of lasting for generations, merchants' riches tended to melt away in a single lifetime. Instead of lasting for decades, leaders' power tended to ebb away in years. Instead of lasting for years, lovers' charms tended to pall in months. No one cared. Artists wanted masterpieces, merchants wanted money, leaders wanted power, and lovers wanted conquests.

"Naturally every weaver in the land wanted to weave with Nixtian magic, and Nixt himself was soon so extravagantly wealthy that he was glad to share it with them. Within a generation, every single weaver in the realm was practicing only this one kind of magic and all others had been forgotten. From swaddling clothes to shrouds, everyone in the land wore clothes woven with Nixtian magic—and, as you can easily imagine, this nation almost overnight became preeminent among the nations of the world. There wasn't a thing to stop them from taking over the entire planet, and they proceeded to do so in just a few generations, and in every land they conquered, weavers who were practicing other kinds of magic either learned Nixtian magic or they took up some other occupation.

"The spread of Nixtian magic revealed another of its drawbacks. Its exhaustive qualities seemed to increase exponentially. When twice as many masterpieces were created with Nixtian magic, they disintegrated four times as fast. When three times as many merchants were getting rich with Nixtian magic, their money melted away nine times as fast. No one liked it, of course, but artists still wanted masterpieces, merchants still wanted wealth, leaders still wanted power, and so on.

"Within a thousand years, every weaver on the planet knew only one kind of magic and all others had been forgotten. Within another thousand years, it was forgotten that any other kind of magic had ever been practiced in weaving, and people soon ceased to think of it as magic at all; it was just part of the process of weaving, and for all they knew, this had always been the case. In other words, they experienced a Great Forgetting of their own. They eventually came to view Nixtian magic as just part of weaving—just the way people of our culture eventually came to view totalitarian agriculture as just part of being human.

"The trouble was that once every man, woman, and child on the planet was wearing clothes woven with Nixtian magic, the exhaustive power of this magic was operating at such a high level that masterpieces were lasting only weeks—and no one wanted them. Fortunes were made and routinely lost within days, and merchants lived in a state of suicidal depression. Governments and whole political systems came and went like seasons of the year, and no one even bothered to learn the names of presidents or prime ministers. Romances and love affairs seldom lasted for more than two or three hours.

"It was at this point of total systemic burnout that some enterprising paleoanthropologists happened quite fortuitously to discover that weaving had existed long before the time of Nixt, and that people had for hundreds of thousands of years been very happy to wear clothes woven with other kinds of magic. And amazingly enough— even without Nixtian magic—artists had still occasionally produced masterpieces, merchants had gotten rich, leaders had become powerful, and lovers had made conquests. And, more important, these achievements had, by modern standards, been durable to an almost unthinkable degree.

"Terrifically excited, these paleoanthropologists brought their discovery to the attention of their department head and asked to be released from other duties so they could study ancient weavings and possibly even rediscover the magic employed in their production. 'I guess I don't get it,' the department head said, after patiently listening to their proposals. 'Why is it important to know what weavers were doing before the age of Nixt?' "

Now the parable is this

"I assume you see the parallels to what we've been talking about," B said. "I believe your words were, 'Why is it important to know what people had in mind before our agricultural revolution?' Do you still need an answer to that question?"

"I wish I could say no," I told him, "but I honestly can't. Here is my problem. I can see what idea motivated *us,* because I can see what we *accomplished.* But I can't see what idea motivated our ancestors, because I can't see what they accomplished. As far as I can see, they didn't accomplish *anything.* Show me what they accomplished, then maybe I can believe there was an idea motivating them."

"What did the pre-Nixtian weavers in my parable accomplish?"

"You mean, between the time their race came into being and the era of Nixt?"

"That's right," B said.

"I guess they learned how to weave."

"Exactly—and not an inconsiderable accomplishment, surely. Our ancestors accomplished something similar in the first three million years of human life: They learned how to live like humans—how to live well, how to have a great life. They developed a lifestyle that was uniquely human, entirely different from all other primate lifestyles, a lifestyle for creatures capable of poetry, philosophy, music, dance, mythology, art, and invention on a wide technological front."

"And is there an idea behind that?"

"I think you'll find there is. In any case, that's the challenge that confronts me, Jared: to reveal to you this idea. Right now I know it seems to you that all this—all this beauty and catastrophe of ours— was *bound* to happen. It was somehow in the very fabric of humanity to become what we've become, in the way that it's in the very fabric of the caterpillar to become a butterfly."

"Yes, that *is* the way it seems to me."

"Someday, if I succeed, you'll see that humanity was no more bound to become *us* than it was bound to become Gebusi. The people of our culture don't represent the final stage of human development any more than the Gebusi do."

"I hope you *do* succeed in that," I said. "I really do."

He stood up and grabbed the luggage rack overhead to steady himself. "Time for a walk," he said, and headed for the door.

I sat and looked at Michael and Shirin for a while, inviting conversation. Since that wasn't forthcoming, I pulled out my notebook and brought it up to date.

Wednesday, May 22

Last stop

After an hour Shirin didn't agree with my assessment that B had been gone a long time—she figured he'd just run into someone he knew—and Michael characteristically didn't think it was his place to have an opinion, so I went looking on my own.

The compartments were divided from the corridors by partitions with glass inserts, so it was easy enough to see who was where, and B wasn't anywhere in the front part of the train. A few compartments were empty and dark, and I saw no reason to check these till I ran out of other places to check. I realized he was almost as short on sleep as I was, and after his difficult evening in Stuttgart, he might well decide to stretch out on an empty seat for a nap. When I finally found him, I thought I was right, but I was wrong. He was stretched out on an empty seat all right, but he wasn't asleep, he was dead, eyes open, with a bullet hole in his left temple.

Maybe someday I'll write down what I went through in that minute, but not now. I think I came close to doing what used to be meant by "losing your mind," before those words just became another cliché synonym for going crazy. I knew I had to throw the emergency switch and stop the train, as little as I wanted to. There didn't seem to be any choice about that, though of course lots of passengers thought differently. It was a mess, of course, a nightmare. At first I thought I'd be executed on the spot. Eventually the conductor understood about the corpse. Eventually Michael arrived and took over as interpreter. Eventually some police arrived—it seemed like hours later—then waves of police arrived, each with the same questions. I was handcuffed twice and nearly a third time.

The train was eventually moved on into Hannover, just a few miles ahead. The night went on and on and on. Finally Michael and

Shirin convinced the police that I was a very improbable murderer, and they let me go after confiscating my passport. By this time it was dawn. Michael found a cabbie willing to drive us to Radenau, and we got out of that place.

I slept till eight P.M., went downstairs for some dinner, and faxed Fr. Lulfre a note explaining what had happened. One police official with a good command of English had told me to call if I recollected anything that wasn't in my statement. I called him and told him about seeing Herr Reichmann on the train platform at Frankfurt.

"How do you know he wasn't just meeting someone on the train?"

"I don't. But people who are meeting someone don't come forward the way he did. They stand back so they can see people getting off down the whole length of the train."

"That's well observed," the policeman agreed. "So let's say he got on the train. You think he had a reason to want to harm your friend?"

"No, not at all."

"Then what's the point?"

"You said to call if I remembered anything. That's what I'm doing."

"Good. I appreciate that. By the way, the tests on your hands were negative for traces of gunpowder."

"That's news to you but not to me," I told him. "I already knew there was no gunpowder on my hands. Can I get my passport back?"

"In a day or two. We just want to be able to talk to you if we need to."

We said good-bye.

I felt half dead myself. I didn't want to think, I didn't want to remember, I didn't want to do anything. I got out the bottle of Scotch and had a drink, but I didn't even want to do that.

I stretched out on the bed in my clothes, closed my eyes, and slept for ten straight hours.

Thursday, May 23

Radenau: Day six

Fr. Lulfre phoned at eight in the morning and opened the conversation by telling me, in a tone of mild reproof, that it was midnight where he was.

"I didn't ask you to call," I snapped. There was a lengthy silence as he evidently decided that the wisest course was to say nothing to that.

"When are you coming home?" he finally asked.

"I don't know. The police are holding my passport."

"Why?"

"To keep me in Germany, obviously."

"They don't have Atterley's killer?"

"As far as I know, they don't have a clue, much less a suspect. Believe me, I'm not in their confidence."

"What have you told them about your mission there?"

"Not a goddamned thing. All they want to know is, did you have a fight with him? Were you carrying a gun? Did you shoot him? They don't have the slightest interest in my life story. Maybe they will someday but not now."

"Shall I get you a lawyer?"

"Not at this point. Aside from the fact that I found the body, they have no reason to think I had anything to do with his death."

Fr. Lulfre pondered all this for a while, then said, with the comfortable certainty of someone four thousand miles away, "They can't keep you there indefinitely."

"I'll explain that to them. What's the hurry?"

"No hurry. It's just that there's nothing more to do, so I assumed you'd be eager to get back home."

I wondered why he thought I needed to have this explained to me
but let it go. "I'll be in touch when I know more," I said.

"Do you need anything?"

"I've got American Express and Visa Gold. How could I need
anything?"

"Jared, you're beginning to alarm me."

"This has not been a fun time."

"It will soon be over," Fr. Lulfre said, and we left it at that.

I showered, dressed, had breakfast, and went for a walk—something I'd never done in this town in broad daylight. It wasn't a place
you could get lost in, it had been designed with too much Teutonic
logic for that. By the merest chance, I eventually found myself in the
same street as Gustl Meyer's shop of leftovers and castoffs. The old
man looked at me with surprise when I walked in. I asked if he knew
what had happened to B, and he said he'd read about it in the paper. I
explained that I didn't have enough German to read the paper, so I
didn't know whether the police had arrested anyone.

"Oh, they won't find anyone to arrest," the old man assured me.

"Why is that?"

He shrugged elaborately. "Charles was a man who was bound to
be killed."

He seemed to think this explained it.

Back to the burrow

After lunch I went over to the theater, hoping Shirin and Michael
would be there. They were. So were Frau Hartmann, the American
teenager, Bonnie, and the Teitels. I wasn't expecting anyone to be
particularly glad to see me, and no one was. Except for Shirin, who
was sitting in B's chair, everyone was in his or her usual place. Maybe
they wanted at least that much continuity. No one was talking.

I sat down and asked them what the prevailing theory was: Who
killed B and why?

They looked at me blankly, except for Shirin, who said, "I

wouldn't call it a theory. The prevailing feeling seems to be that B would still be alive if you hadn't come."

"I'm glad it's not a theory. You recognize the fallacy involved— *post hoc ergo propter hoc*—it happened after, so it happened because. According to this reasoning, marriage is the cause of every divorce."

"Don't lecture us, Jared."

"I won't lecture you if you won't saddle me with B's death."

"Why do *you* think he was killed?" This was from Michael.

"I don't know. The possibilities are too numerous and I have no way of narrowing them down. Obviously a lot of people were upset with what he was saying."

"This wasn't done by someone who just generally didn't like what B was saying," Shirin said. "This was done by someone who knew B would be on that particular train. Someone who got on that particular train to kill him."

"Or someone who got on that particular train to kill whoever was available."

"If he got on the train to kill at random, why did he kill only B?"

"I don't know. Maybe one victim was enough. Maybe no one else was handy the way B was handy."

Bonnie said, "What's your boss's name? The guy who sent you here?"

"Fr. Lulfre."

"Maybe Fr. Lulfre had him killed."

"Why would he do that?"

"Didn't he send you here to find out if B was the Antichrist?"

"Well, just to keep it simple, suppose he did. Then what?"

"Then maybe he decided B *was* the Antichrist."

I shook my head. "He certainly couldn't have decided that on the basis of what he heard from me, and even if he had, he wouldn't have responded by having B murdered. You watch too much television, Bonnie. Fr. Lulfre is an archaeologist and a psychiatrist, not a Mafia don."

Bonnie smirked as if I were being incredibly naive—or deliberately stupid.

No one seemed to have anything else to say.

.   .   .

Sitting there in the midst of all these silent people, I began to wonder if I'd interrupted a meeting of some kind—a meeting to which I'd not been invited. I decided this was something I had to know and was pondering how to phrase the question when a medley of footsteps sounded on the circular staircase from above. I looked around to see if newcomers were expected but had the feeling they weren't. Everyone held tight until a troop of five finally emerged. They were assorted ages, teens to middle age, dressed in a ragtag style ranging from early hippie to late punk. They paused on the staircase to give us a good long look, as if we were museum specimens. Then, after passing a look back and forth among themselves, they clambered the rest of the way down and made their way through the jumble to where we were assembled.

"Have we come right?" asked the leader, a bearded gent in his forties. "We are from Sweden, and we are told to go to the theater in Radenau and down in the basement, and there they are meeting."

As we continued to stare dumbly, he gave each of us in turn a smiling, hopeful look. Finally, still smiling (though now somewhat doubtfully), he said, "Which of you is the one they call B?"

Since no one else seemed inclined to, I took it upon myself to say, "B is not here."

"Oh shut up, you stupid man," Shirin said. Then, standing up and turning to the newcomers, she spoke three words that I instantly knew were going to rip my life to pieces:

"I am B."

part
two

Friday, May 24 (two A.M.)

Stalling

One of the things decided yesterday is that B will speak publicly tomorrow night. This is viewed as "getting back on the horse that threw you." No one asked my opinion, which is that scheduling the same talk a week later would serve the same purpose and allow a little time to get the word out. I said I'd help put up posters, but I'll have to renege on that if I'm to get any sleep (which I am, come what may).

Time is running out for me here. My passport was returned a few hours ago, and I have to assume that Fr. Lulfre will know this almost immediately, since he has his own sources of information here. I can put him off for a few days (but not much more) by claiming that the police have asked me to stick around in case they find Herr Reichmann, the old gentleman who first put me onto B and who boarded our train in Frankfurt the night of B's murder. If it occurred to them, they probably *would* ask me to stick around for that purpose—or some purpose.

Shirin; Jared

After putting me in my place, B spoke for an hour or so to the Swedes. (To be honest, I would desperately rather call her Shirin, but to do so would be to ally myself with outsiders, like, say, her mother or her doctors; it seems to me that to deny that Shirin is B would be to deny that Charles was B.) She gave them a basic orientation to the teachings of B and promised to meet with them again on the morrow. Then she shooed everyone away so the two of us could talk.

It didn't immediately go well between us. I didn't know what she wanted to discuss, and she didn't seem to want to tell me. After a few minutes it was obvious that she didn't want to talk to me at all, and I asked her why she was bothering to do it. The question gave her some focus, because it made her mad.

She said, "A while ago I called you a stupid man, and I really have to say that you're one of the stupidest men I've ever known. Do you understand why?"

I admitted I didn't.

"I've known a lot of men who were less bright by a long shot—a lot of men with no mental equipment to speak of—but I've never met one with so much mental equipment being put to so little use."

I laughed at that—one of those reckless, bitter laughs that Bertie Wooster used to specialize in. "You sound just like my faculty adviser in graduate school," I told her. "You have no idea how much you sound like him."

She sighed, and I could see the anger drain away from her. Unexpectedly, she apologized for losing her temper. "I have to adjust my own thinking to this, Jared. You see, what I find maddening about you is just what Charles found useful. You're able to hold information in your head for an incredibly long time *without drawing a conclusion.* To me, this looks like stupidity. To Charles, it looked like . . . something else."

"You mean it takes me a long time to get things."

"That's the way it looks to me. To Charles, it looked like you had a terrific capacity for *not jumping.* For resisting the temptation to understand too quickly. For resisting the temptation to grab onto *something,* even if it wasn't what he was saying."

"Wow," I said. "What a fabulous thing to be good at."

"Don't knock it, Jared—and I'll try not to knock it either. But where it kills you is in dealing with someone like Fr. Lulfre. You think pawn to queen four is a brilliant first move, but while you're shoving up that pawn, he's bringing out both knights, both bishops, and has castled. He's always eight moves ahead of you."

"How does Fr. Lulfre come into this?"

"He comes into this by way of you, of course. He dropped you into this action two weeks ago and can pull you out whenever he pleases." She cocked her head to one side. "Unless you're ready to walk away from your vocation."

"I'm not."

"Then here's what you have to face right now: Fr. Lulfre knows you at least as well as I do. This means that, consciously or unconsciously, he chose you because you won't leap ahead to conclusions he wants to reserve to himself."

"Now I have an inkling," I said, "of how a retarded person must feel when he finally realizes that he *is* retarded."

"Don't be ridiculous."

"I have a question I've no business asking but that I'm going to ask anyway. What was your relationship with Charles?"

She gave me a frozen look, which I returned. "You didn't dare to ask Charles that."

"That's right."

"But you dare to ask me. Why?"

"Because you're the one I want to hear it from."

"Why is that?" she demanded, glaring.

"If Fr. Lulfre is eight moves ahead of me, then you must be at least four moves ahead, in which case you already know why. I'm still at move one, trying to figure it out."

B gave me a long look in an effort to sort through this mess. I'm not sure whether it was beyond her or she just decided to pretend it was beyond her. In any case, she said, "B and I were not lovers."

"I see. Nothing to add to that?"

"We were exactly what you saw. What part of that do you need to have explained?"

"None of it," I said. "I just didn't realize I was in the presence of a miracle. Friendships like yours are one in a billion. You were damned lucky—the two of you."

She sat through a full minute like a rock, refusing to let me see the tears welling up in her eyes, and if I'd been foolish enough to say a word or reach out a hand, she probably would have flattened me. At the end of it, she brushed the tears away, not minding my seeing her do that, because it was over.

"Characteristically," I said, "I don't know what's going on. What are we doing here?"

"I'm picking up your education where Charles left it off."

I stared at her for a while then asked why she would do that. "I know why *Charles* would do it, I just don't understand why *you* would do it."

"You probably won't like this answer," she said after a moment's thought, "but it's the only one I have. You see this education as a favor we're doing you, not as a necessity. We see it as a necessity because we're playing four moves ahead of you. Can you accept that?"

"I guess I have to."

"As soon as you catch up, you'll see the necessity for it yourself. You won't be in any doubt about it."

"You're right," I said. "I don't like that answer."

Defending the gap

"When Charles started, we thought we had weeks. With his assassination, I now think we have days, maybe hours."

I asked her what Charles's death had to do with it, but she just shook her head and went on. "Charles's approach had to be his own, of course, but to be honest, I thought it was too cerebral and too circuitous. I have to begin at a more elemental level."

"Okay," I said doubtfully. Then: "Are you talking about starting right this second?"

"Do you have another appointment?"

"No, of course not."

"If you're waiting for me to go into mourning for a month, that just can't happen. Not now. Not in these circumstances."

"I'm sorry, go on."

"Charles didn't want to carry you across the gap, Jared. He wanted you to leap across it yourself, that's why he proceeded as he did. Do you know what I'm talking about?"

"Are you talking about the leap I have to make to reach the conclusion he wanted me to reach?"

"That's right. Every sentence he spoke was designed to extend the road for you by a centimeter. He was closing the gap pebble by pebble, hoping you'd eventually make the leap by yourself."

"But I never did."

"You never did. I don't have the patience to follow that procedure, Jared—the patience or the time. I'm going to throw you across the gap. I'm going to start with the conclusion."

She waited for me to respond, and I guess I could have said okay or "That sounds swell," but it didn't sound either okay or swell to me. To me it sounded like the end . . . which is of course exactly what a conclusion is.

"Okay," I said. "That sounds swell."

She gave me a doubtful look, as if she didn't any more believe me than I did. Then she went on: "Here is something I want you to tell me, Jared. You're a priest of the Roman Catholic Church. You understand what the ministry of Jesus was all about, don't you?"

"Yes, I think so."

"Do you or don't you?"

"I understand it."

"Tell me in three words what Jesus came to do."

"In three words?"

"You tell me or I'll tell you. In three words, what did Jesus come to do?"

"To save souls."

"That isn't just the Roman Catholic take, is it? You could carry that around to every Christian denomination there is, and they'd all sign off on it, wouldn't they?"

"Yes, I think so. That's probably the only statement they all *would* sign off on."

"He didn't come to save the whales, did he?"

"No."

"He didn't come to save old-growth forests or wetlands, did he?"

"No."

"Now tell me what you think *we're* doing here, Jared. What is *this* all about?"

"What do you mean by 'this'?"

"I'll say it a different way. We know what Jesus came to do. What did B come to do?"

"I don't know," I said, alarmed.

"You *do* know, Jared. What is the subject of our conversations here? What is the subject of all our talks?"

I shook my head.

"Take the leap now, Jared. The gap's about two inches wide. Three words will bridge it."

I stared at her, frozen solid.

"Speak, goddammit. Don't make me say this for you. What's the subject of all our conversations? What's the subject of all our talks?"

I managed to get it out as a hoarse croak: *"Saving the world."*

"Saving the world—of course. It was right there in front of your nose the whole time, wasn't it. Now, Jared, we are goddamn well going to get to the Antichrist. Right now. Okay?"

"Okay."

"That's what you're here about, isn't it?"

"Yes."

"Now, in the history of the Antichrist, it was always understood that he would be the inversion of the Christ. If the Christ came for the salvation of souls, then the Antichrist would come . . ."

"For the damnation of souls."

"Absolutely. If the Christ preached good works and perfection, then the Antichrist would preach . . ."

"Sin and wickedness."

"That's how it's been traditionally understood. But, as I understood what you told us, more theologically sophisticated thinkers have moved beyond that traditional understanding. They already realize that, if the prophecies about the Antichrist are to be taken seriously, then they won't be fulfilled by someone preaching sin and wickedness—not in this day and age. What sins and wickedness could any preacher possibly come up with that wouldn't evoke yawns of utter boredom from an audience of modern television viewers?"

"None," I agreed.

"The traditional Antichrist as preacher of sin and wickedness wouldn't even make a ripple in the modern world, therefore . . ."

"Therefore?"

"Think, Jared. If a preacher of sin and wickedness wouldn't make it as the Antichrist, then . . ."

"Then the Antichrist is going to be something else."

"Then the Antichrist is going to be an inversion of Christ in a different direction."

She clearly wanted a reaction from me at this point, so I said, "I see that. The Antichrist is going to be an inversion of Christ in a different direction."

"What other direction?"

"I don't know." I really didn't.

"Come on, Jared. The gap is three inches wide."

I shook my head.

"We'll go through it again," she said. "Christ's ministry is . . ."

"Saving souls."

"But saving souls isn't B's ministry, is it?"

"No," I said.

"B's ministry is saving the world."

"No," I said again stubbornly refusing to see the light.

"You mean yes, Jared. This is the inversion Fr. Lulfre sees. Not *saving souls* inverted to *damning souls* but rather *saving souls* inverted to *saving the world*. This is why you were sent. This is what makes B a candidate."

"No!"

"Why do you say no? Charles told you again and again that you would eventually understand why people were calling him the Antichrist. This is what he was talking about."

"I say no because, if trying to save the world makes you the Antichrist, then Greenpeace is the Antichrist, Earth First is the Antichrist, the Nature Conservancy is the Antichrist, the World Wildlife Fund is the Antichrist."

"Jared, these organizations aren't up to the same thing as B. They aren't up to anything remotely like the same thing. You know that."

"I *don't* know that."

She produced an exasperated little laugh. "You're a wonder, Jared, you really are. For you, a three-inch gap might as well be the Grand Canyon."

A hazardous walk

"I am B," Shirin said, "but I'm not an experienced teacher. Having announced that I wasn't going to follow Charles's practice of trying to goad you across gaps, I immediately set about trying to goad you across a gap." She paused and looked around doubtfully at our strange, palatially seedy theatrical cavern. "I think we should get out of here, to begin with—break the pattern."

I agreed, and we left.

"Do you mind walking?" she asked.

"Not at all, provided we're not heading for Little Bohemia."

She smiled. "That was Charles's hangout, not mine. There's a little park a couple miles away that might be helpful."

I wondered why a park might be "helpful" but said that would be fine. We walked through the long twilight.

Back home, I never take long walks with beautiful women on pleasant spring evenings. That would not be thought well of, and I'm not exactly crazy.

It occurs to me to say that I've often wished someone would write a useful book about the real life of Roman Catholic priests. I wish for this not because such a book might include things I *do* know but because it might include things I *don't* know. It's my distinct impression that priests have more fucked-up love affairs than any other group of people on earth, including high-school kids and movie stars. And these are not great, soaring forbidden romances in the manner of *The Thorn Birds.* These are really dumb, incompetent, bruising debacles, because, by the very nature of things, priests have almost no chance to learn from experience in the normal way. (One thing the book would definitely have to cover is the utterly laughable idea that priests learn all about life in the confessional.)

Let me rush to note right here that I don't speak of fucked-up love affairs from personal experience. If I've avoided romantic entanglements, it's not because I'm noble and dedicated, it's for exactly the same reasons I've avoided skydiving, hang gliding, and street luging. The invitations to entangle are plentiful, ranging from the open to the barely discernible, not just for me but for all priests. It's partly that women imagine we're safe (will not get all demanding and tiresome), partly that they perceive us as a sexual challenge, and partly that they confuse us with the role we play. We're trained to be, expected to be, and even paid to be attentive, sensitive, understanding, wise, and authoritative, and this is a turn-on for a lot of women—what the hell, a lot of men too.

Another thing this book would point out is that vows are vows, and the priestly kind are neither more nor less serious than the marriage kind. Married folks don't usually go all to pieces if they happen to break their vows, and to tell the naked truth, neither do priests—except in fiction. In fiction, having an affair presents a priest with a life-shattering crisis of conscience; in real life, having an affair usually just presents him with a hell of a mess. Again, I speak from observation of colleagues, not from personal experience. So far.

I thought about these things as I walked through the pleasant spring evening with a beautiful woman at my side. Far from home, where I would never dream of doing such a thing.

It was borne in on me: I'm not made of iron.

I said, "How do you happen to know sign language?"

"My parents were deaf."

This was not much of a conversation, I thought, to be having in these romantic circumstances.

Leaden-footed, I droned on: "Is it the same in America and Germany?"

"No, actually it isn't."

I plodded on. "When you were signing on the stage with Charles, did you know whether anyone in the audience would understand you?"

"No. And if you're planning to ask why I bothered, the answer is that it's something I was doing for myself. It's a different language."

"I know that, but what's that got to do with it?"

"When you're signing, you have to think very differently. Very, very differently." We walked in silence for a bit. "It's hard to explain to someone who doesn't know the language," she added finally. "Translating into sign isn't like translating into another spoken language. You have to rethink it very fundamentally."

"Charles could sign?"

"He could understand a lot, but he couldn't sign a lot." From a corner of my eye, I saw a small smile edge onto her lips. "But when he *did* sign, he had a wonderful style, all his own."

My stomach sank under a tarry load of jealousy. I knew I was in big trouble here.

Borders

Shirin's "small park" seemed pretty big to me, in the gathering darkness. I don't know whether it was a park that had gone to seed or had been designed that way, as a miniature wilderness with sketchy paths, no lights, and an occasional bench. I'm not an expert on parks or on wildernesses. We trekked on for ten minutes or so, then settled on a bench. With the trees blocking out what little light was left in the sky, it might as well have been midnight.

"Borders are always tricky, intriguing things," B said at last. "Feral children fascinate because they stand at the border of the animal world. Gorillas and dolphins fascinate because they stand at the border of the human world. Even though they're only arbitrary consequences of the fact that we use a decimal numeration system, the borders between centuries and millennia fascinate. Shakespeare's fools fascinate because they live at the border between sanity and madness. The heroes of tragedy fascinate because they walk the border between triumph and defeat. The borders between prehuman and human, between childhood and adulthood, between generations, between nations and peoples, between social and political paradigms—all of these are intensely fascinating.

"The border that Charles and I have been trying to focus your attention on is the border that was crossed when one group of people living in the Fertile Crescent ten thousand years ago became *us.* You know that crossing this border brought us to a very special sort of agriculture that produces enormous food surpluses. You know that crossing this border brought us to the most laborious lifestyle ever practiced on this planet. But these are superficial perceptions. Charles wanted you to see that this border represents a profoundly important spiritual and mental crossing. Charles tried to lead you to an appreciation of this crossing by leading you *back* to it from this side, from the present moment, but I'm going to take the opposite tack. I'll try to lead you to an appreciation of this crossing by leading you *forward* to it from the other side, from our origins in the community of life."

I felt rather than saw her shiver. I think she must have felt my question in turn, for she said, "I'm not cold, I'm terrified."

"Why?"

"Charles could have done this—would have done this next. But he hoped he wouldn't have to. This is so much more . . . difficult."

The words *I'm sorry* were halfway out of my mouth, but I managed to hold them back.

B stared into space for a few minutes, then said, "The fundamental Taker delusion is that humanity itself was designed—and therefore destined—to become *us*. This is a twin of the idea that the entire universe was created in order to produce this planet. We would smile patronizingly if the Gebusi boasted that humanity was divinely destined to become Gebusi, but we're perfectly satisfied that humanity was divinely destined to become *us*."

"I think I'm beginning to see that, though I certainly didn't see it the first time Charles said *We are not humanity*."

B nodded distantly, as if holding on to a tenuous thought. "Because we imagine that we are what humanity was divinely destined to become, we assume that our prehistoric ancestors were *trying* to be us but just lacked the tools and techniques to succeed. We invest our ancestors with our own predelictions in what seem to us primitive and unevolved forms. As an example of all this, we take it for granted that our religions represent humanity's ultimate and highest spiritual development and expect to find among our ancestors only crude, fumbling harbingers of these religions. We certainly don't expect to find robust, fully developed religions whose *expressions* are entirely different from ours."

"Very true," I said.

"To what development do we trace the beginnings of human religious thought?"

"I'd say we trace the beginnings of human religious thought to the practice of burying the dead, which began thirty or forty thousand years ago."

B nodded. "This is just like tracing the beginning of human language to the practice of writing, which began about five thousand years ago."

"I see what you mean—I think."

"It would never occur to a linguist to search for the origins of human language in the clay tablets of Mesopotamia, would it?"

"Certainly not," I said.

"Where would a linguist search for the origins of human language?"

"I think he'd go back to the origins of human life itself."

"Because to be human is to have language."

"I'd say so."

"If *Homo habilis* didn't have language, then he's misnamed—doesn't deserve to be called *Homo.*"

"I would say so."

"What is our hypothetical linguist's method going to be?"

"I'd say it's going to be more philosophical and speculative than linguistic. He doesn't have an early human specimen whose language can be studied."

"He's going to be puttering around in one of those fascinating borderlands. On one side of the border, manlike creatures without language—tool-using (as even modern chimpanzees are), but lacking what we mean by language. On the other side of the border, people."

"That's right," I said.

"But he's not going to study any clay tablets."

"No, not even for a minute."

"Good, because I don't intend to spend even a minute on the burial practices of the Upper Paleolithic. They're as irrelevant to the origins of religion as clay tablets are to the origins of language."

"I understand."

Bricolage

"The linguist and I must both practice *bricolage,* which is the craft of building with whatever comes to hand. It comes from the French *bricoler,* to putter about. We must both putter about in this strange borderland inhabited by almost-humans on one side and truly-humans on the other."

"So you assume that being human means being religious, just as the linguist assumes that being human means being lingual."

"Being a *bricoleur,* I don't do anything as well defined as that, Jared. I poke around. I wonder if there's a dimension of thought that is inherently religious. I say to myself that perhaps thought is like a musical tone, which (in nature) is never a single, pure tone but is always a composite of many harmonics—overtones and undertones. And I say to myself that perhaps, when mental process became human thought, it began to resound with one harmonic that corresponds to what we call religion, or, more fundamentally, awareness of the sacred. In other words, I wonder if awareness of the sacred is not so much a separate concept as it is an overtone of human thought itself. A conjecture of this sort can yield *scientia,* knowledge, but since it isn't falsifiable, it can't yield science in the modern sense. A work of *bricolage* is never science, Jared, but it can still astound, make sense, and stimulate thought. It can still impress with its veracity, validity, soundness, and cogency."

"I see." It seemed to me that, in all this talk, she was somehow trying to "screw her courage to the sticking-place." I didn't know why this was necessary or how to help, so I just kept nodding and saying, "I see, I see."

Finally she lifted her eyes to the trees overhead and said, "The moon is up." As if this were a signal, she got up and led me off the path into the woods. Several times in the next few minutes she paused to look around (at what, I don't know), then moved on. Now and then she stopped to pick up something found in the grass. At last she came to a clearing that suited her, and we sat down.

She showed me the things she'd collected on the way—a nail, an old cartridge fuse, a 35mm film canister, a paper clip, a plastic comb, an acorn. At her request, I showed her what I had in my pockets, and she chose a key and a pen to add to the collection.

"This is what the universe has supplied me with tonight, Jared. We'll have to see what I can make with it."

Suddenly I remembered the fossil ammonite in my jacket pocket. She looked at it with evident surprise when I handed it to her, and I explained that Charles had given it to me to hold on to till we got around to it (which we never had).

"This will be the centerpiece of our work of *bricolage,*" she said, putting it down between us. "Charles had a different purpose in mind for it—I'm pretty sure I know what it was, and we'll get around to that as well—but meanwhile it'll serve as the piece to which all other pieces in our work must cling. It's the community of life on this planet."

"Okay."

"A few minutes ago I said that perhaps, when mental process became human thought, it began to resound with one harmonic that corresponds to what we call religion or awareness of the sacred."

"I remember."

"I want you to think of this shell as the community of life. I want you to think that if you know just how to listen to it, this shell will ring out with that harmonic. Can you do that?"

"I can try."

Animism

"There once was a universal religion on this planet, Jared," B said. "Were you aware of that?"

I said I wasn't.

"Audiences are almost always amazed by this news. Occasionally someone will think I'm referring to what is sometimes called the 'Old Religion'—paganism, Wicca—but of course I'm not. In the first place, paganism isn't old. It's a farmer's religion through and through, which means it's just a few thousand years old, and of course it was never a universal religion, for the simple reason that farming was never universal. Very often—almost invariably, in fact—no one will even recognize the name of the religion I'm talking about, which of course is *animism*. They've literally never heard of it."

"I can believe it," I said.

"Do you know animism?"

"I think you'd better assume I don't. Most people in my position, with my training, are aware of animism the way modern-day chemists are aware of alchemy."

"You mean you're aware of animism as a crude and simpleminded precursor of religion the way chemists are aware of alchemy as a crude and simpleminded precursor of chemistry. Not really religion in the proper sense any more than alchemy is chemistry in the proper sense."

"That's right."

She pawed through her collection of oddments and selected the film canister. "This is animism," she said, holding it up for my consideration. "An empty container as far as you're concerned." Then she dived into her purse and came up with a traveler's sewing kit, from which she extracted a bit of thread long enough to bind film canister and ammonite together.

"Here, hold on to this," she said, and I took it from her. "Tell me about the shell."

"What do you mean?"

"What is it?"

"Oh," I said. "It's the community of life on this planet."

"And what did I just say to you about it?"

"You said that when mental process became human thought, perhaps this community began to resound with one harmonic that corresponds to what we call religion or awareness of the sacred. If I learn how to listen to it, it'll ring out with that harmonic."

"Good. But it occurs to me that I've introduced a puzzle here. I said that when mental process (a common phenomenon in the animal kingdom) became human thought, *it* began to ring out with a harmonic that I've identified as awareness of the sacred. But now I'm saying that the *community of life* rings with that harmonic. Which is it, human thought or the community of life?"

"I don't find this too puzzling," I told her. "I think the community of life began to ring with that harmonic when human thought began to ring with it."

"Yes, that's what I had in mind. And when this shell begins to resonate with that harmonic, this hollow canister that I've called animism will also begin to resonate, because it's in contact with the shell."

"Okay," I said. "This is what you mean by *bricolage*?"

"This is what I mean by *bricolage*."

Regarding the number of the gods

"Someone inevitably asks why I speak of gods rather than one God, as if I simply hadn't been informed on this matter and was speaking in error, and I ask them how *they* happen to know the number of the gods. Sometimes I'm told this is just something 'everyone' knows, the way everyone knows there are twenty-four hours in a day. Sometimes

I'm told God *must* be one, because this seems to us the most 'enlightened' number for God to be—as if the facts don't count in this
particular case. This is like reasoning that the earth must be the center
of the universe, because no other place makes as much sense. Most
often, of course, I'm told this is an undoubtable number, since it's the
number given in monotheistic scriptures. Needless to say, I have a
rather different take on the whole matter.

"The number of the gods is written nowhere in the universe,
Jared, so there's really no way to decide whether that number is zero
(as atheists believe) or one (as monotheists believe) or many (as
polytheists believe). The matter is one of complete indifference to me.
I don't care whether the number of the gods is one, zero, or nine
billion. If it turned out that the number of the gods is zero, this
wouldn't cause me to alter a single syllable of what I've said to you."

She seemed to want a reaction to this, so I said okay.

"To speak of gods instead of God has this additional advantage,
that I'm spared the embarrassing necessity of forever playing stupid
gender games with them. I never have to decide between *he* and *she,*
him and *her.* For me, they're just *they* and *them.*"

"A not inconsiderable advantage," I observed.

She picked up the plastic comb and ran a thumbnail down its
teeth. "Is it one thing or many?"

"You mean the comb? I don't know. Depends on how you look at
it."

"This comb is the number of the gods, Jared. Not something to
be added to our work of *bricolage,* but rather something to be dis-
cussed and dismissed." She tossed the comb over her shoulder and out
of sight.

Where the gods write what they write

"The God of revealed religions—and by this I mean religions like
yours, Taker religions—is a profoundly inarticulate God. No matter
how many times he tries, he can't make himself clearly or completely
understood. He speaks for centuries to the Jews but fails to make
himself understood. At last he sends his only-begotten son, and his
son can't seem to do any better. Jesus might have sat himself down

with a scribe and dictated the answers to every conceivable theological question in absolutely unequivocal terms, but he chose not to, leaving subsequent generations to settle what Jesus had in mind with pogroms, purges, persecutions, wars, the burning stake, and the rack. Having failed through Jesus, God next tried to make himself understood through Muhammad, with limited success, as always. After a thousand years of silence he tried again with Joseph Smith, with no better results. Averaging it out, all God has been able to tell us *for sure* is that we should do unto others as we'd have them do unto us. What's that—a dozen words? Not much to show for five thousand years of work, and we probably could have figured out that much for ourselves anyway. To be honest, I'd be embarrassed to be associated with a god as incompetent as that."

"Your gods have done better?"

"Good heavens, yes, Jared. Immeasurably better—infinitely better! Just look out there!" She waved her hand at the world in front of us. "What do you see?"

"I see the universe."

"That's it, Jared. That's where the *real* gods of the universe write what they write. Your God writes in words. The gods I'm talking about write in galaxies and star systems and planets and oceans and forests and whales and birds and gnats."

"And what do they write?"

"Well, they write physics and chemistry and biology and astronomy and aerodynamics and meteorology and geology—all that, of course, but that isn't what you're after, is it?"

"No."

"What are you after?"

"I'm after . . . what the gods have to write about *us*."

B grabbed my pen and held it up. "This is what you're after. This is the Law of Life."

She picked up the ammonite fossil and slipped the pen under the thread that held the film canister in place. "What's this?" she asked, pointing to the fossil.

"The community of life on this planet."

"And this?"—pointing to the canister.

"Animism."

"And you see that the Law of Life is nestled in between the two, touching both the community of life and animism."

"What is the Law of Life?" I asked her.

"We'll get to that. That's our main subject tonight."

Science vs. religion

"Religions like yours, revealed religions, are all perceived to be at odds with scientific knowledge—at odds with or irrelevant to. I wonder if you see why."

"I think it's come to be seen that religion and science are just inherently incompatible."

B nodded. "Following the usual Taker pattern: 'We are humanity, so if our religions are inherently incompatible with scientific knowledge, then religion itself must be inherently incompatible with scientific knowledge.' "

"That's right."

"But as you'll see, animism is perfectly at home with scientific knowledge. It's much more at home with your sciences than with your religions."

"Why is that?"

"What's that out there?" she asked, making her usual sweeping gesture.

"That's the world, the universe."

"That's where the real gods of the universe write what they write, Jared. The gods of your revealed religions write in books."

"What does that have to do with animism?"

"Animism looks for truth in the universe, not in books, revelations, and authorities. Science is the same. Though animism and science read the universe in different ways, both have complete confidence in its truthfulness."

She poked around among her building blocks, picked out the cartridge fuse, and held it up for my inspection. "This is science," she said. "Religions like yours, Jared, are skeptical about it, are afraid to use it. They say, 'Suppose we use it and it blows up in our face! Better not trust it.' But animism isn't worried about anything that can be revealed about the universe, so science belongs right here beside it."

She slid the fuse under the thread holding the film canister to the fossil. Then she asked me to describe what I saw.

I said, "Animism is flanked by the Law of Life on one side and by science on the other. All three face the community of life."

The border

"Now I want to make sure we don't lose track of what we set out to do here, Jared. We're investigating a border between almost-humans on one side and truly-humans on the other. We're doing this because it's my notion that we came to humanity as religious beings."

"Okay."

"Let's extend our *bricolage* to include a little mental landscaping of the area around us. Take a stick and draw a circle around us at a distance of a couple paces."

I did as she asked and sat down again.

"That circle represents the border we're investigating, about three million years in the past, when *Australopithecus* became *Homo*. Is that clear?"

I said it was.

"I'm sure you understand that this line is imaginary. There was never a day when you would've been able to point to one generation of parents and say, 'These are Australopithecines,' then point to their children and say, 'These are humans.'"

"I understand."

"We can't know how wide the line itself is. It might be two hundred years wide or a thousand years wide or ten thousand years wide. All we know is that on our side of the line there are creatures we feel confident about calling *Homo* and on the far side of the line there are creatures we *don't* feel confident about calling *Homo*."

"I understand."

"I don't know how much you know about all this, so I'll play it safe and point out that the line doesn't correspond to tool use. I mean, you don't have users of tools on this side of the line and nonusers on the far side. You have tool-users on both sides of the line. We can be virtually certain of this, since even chimpanzees are well

known tool-users, and *Homo*'s immediate predecessors were far beyond chimpanzees."

I told her I knew all this but didn't mind her "playing it safe."

The Law of Life: the hologram

B asked me to describe the state of our work of *bricolage*. I picked it
up and studied it again before beginning. "This fossil shell is the
community of life on this planet. The religion you call animism is
bound up with this community. Something called the Law of Life is
written in the community of life and this too is bound up with
animism. Perhaps it's the work of animism to read the Law of Life
that is written in the community of life."

"That's an excellent guess, Jared. Go on."

"Animism perceives itself as allied with science, because both seek
truth in the universe itself."

"Good. Now we're ready to spend some time on the Law of Life.
The Law of Life is like a hologram. Do you know anything about
holography?"

"A bit. I was a photography buff in high school, and holography
is basically lensless photography. In ordinary photography, a photographic plate is exposed to light reflected from an object, and an
image appears on the plate because a lens intervenes. In holography, a
photographic plate is exposed to light reflected from an object, but no
image appears on the plate because no lens intervenes. What's recorded on the plate are patterns of light waves received from every
part of the photographed object. This is the hologram. And when the
hologram is placed in a beam of light, a three-dimensional image of
the photographed object appears in midair where the original object
stood. And because every part of it is imprinted with light waves from
the whole object, any fragment of the hologram can be used to regen-
erate the whole image."

"This is how the Law of Life is similar to a hologram, Jared: Every
fragment of it is imprinted with the whole law."

"The Law of Life is what governs life?"

"No, the Law of Life isn't what *governs* life, it's what *fosters* life,
and anything that fosters life belongs to the law."

I told her an example would help.

"Here's the Law of Life for newly hatched ducklings: *Latch on to the first thing you see that moves, and follow it no matter what.* Since the first thing newly hatched ducklings see is ordinarily their mother, they usually latch on to their mother, but they'll latch on to anything that moves. Since their best hope for survival is latching on to their mother, no matter what, you can see why this is the law that fosters life for ducklings."

"Yes, I can see that."

"Here's a generalization that can be made about the Law of Life: Those who follow it tend to become better represented in the gene pool of their species than those who don't follow it."

"So not all individuals follow the law?"

"The duckling that for one reason or another doesn't receive or respond to the genetic latching-on-to-mom signal is weeded out. It doesn't survive long enough to reproduce."

"I see."

"Obviously the law varies in its details from species to species. In ducks, the law is written for ducklings and it reads, 'Stick to mom no matter what.' In goats, the law is written for the mother, and it reads, 'Suckle only your own.'"

I thought about that for a bit and asked how "Suckle only your own" fosters life for goats.

"Let's say White Goat and Black Goat each have a suckling kid. Black Goat dies, so her kid comes over to White Goat and says, 'Hey, I'm hungry, how about some lunch?' The best chance White Goat's kid has for survival is if its mother says to this stranger, 'Get lost, kid, you're not mine.' If White Goat says, 'Okay, sure, pull up a teat,' she'll be diminishing her own kid's chance for survival—which means her own genes' chance for survival."

"Yes, I can see that."

"Here's a more general statement of the law as it's followed by goats: 'If your resources are of doubtful sufficiency for two offspring, then you're better off giving all to one than half to each.'"

"Not the law of kindness."

"I would say rather, 'Not the law of *futile* kindness.' I think most mothers would rather have one live child than any number of dead ones. Nonetheless, it's certainly true that, if the two are in conflict, the law favors life over kindness. Those who follow the contrary law—the law that favors kindness over life—will tend to lose their representation in the gene pool of their species. This is because their offspring will tend to survive and reproduce less often than the offspring of those who follow the law that favors life."

"I understand."

"On the subject of kindness . . . I don't know if you know David Brower—one of the century's foremost environmentalists, the founder of the John Muir Institute, Friends of the Earth, and Earth Island Institute. He tells this story of one of his earliest adventures as a naturalist. At the age of eleven he collected some eggs of the western swallowtail butterfly and kept an eye on them as they hatched into caterpillars, which later turned into chrysalides. Finally the first of the chrysalides began to crack open, and what Brower saw was this: The emerging butterfly struggled out, its abdomen distended by some sort of fluid that was pumped out over its wings as it hung upside down on a twig. Half an hour later it was ready to fly, and it took off. As the other chrysalides began to crack, however, Brower decided to make himself useful. He gently eased open the crack to facilitate the butterflies' emergence, and they promptly slid out, walked around, and one by one dropped dead. He had failed to realize that the exertions he had spared the butterflies were essential to their survival, because they triggered the flow of fluid that had to reach their wings. This experience taught him a lesson he was still talking about seventy years later: What appears to be kind and is meant to be kind can be the reverse of kind."

"I understand."

"Among goats, it's the mother that enforces this law: 'If your resources are of doubtful sufficiency for two, then you're better off giving all to one than half to each.' Among eagles (and many other bird species), it's enforced by the elder of the two offspring. The female will typically produce two eggs a few days apart, which is naturally better survival policy than producing a single egg. But if the first chick survives, it will almost invariably peck or starve the younger chick to death."

I said, "I guess it was my impression that infanticide was explained as a reaction to overcrowding."

"Yes, it used to be explained that way, but this argues a perception of evolution that ultimately didn't stand up to close examination—a perception of evolution as promoting what's 'good for the species.' It now seems clear that evolution promotes what's good for the individual, in the sense of assuring the individual's reproductive success—what I've been calling 'representation in the gene pool.' "

"I see."

"In lions and bears, females will often abandon a litter that has only one survivor—even if this one survivor is in perfect health. This isn't 'good for the species' in any way, but it's good for the individual's lifetime reproductive success. Her representation in the gene pool will definitely improve if she invests exclusively in litters larger than one."

"I have to admit that this is all news to me."

"No one can know everything," she said with a shrug.

"Show me where we're going here. I'm feeling lost again."

"I can't teach you the whole of the Law of Life in a single night, Jared. I couldn't teach you the whole of it if we came here every night for a decade. What I can do in a single night is present you with a few pieces of it, in the manner of a *bricoleur*. But let's reach for some pieces in a new direction."

The Law of Life: a mouse burial

She stood up, and I started to follow her example, but she told me to stay put. "Let's see if I'm lucky tonight," she said, and ducked into the underbrush straight ahead of us, clearly the huntress in search of a scent. I closed my eyes, grateful for the break. Returning after ten or fifteen minutes from the right, she beckoned me to follow her, which I did with some apprehension. I don't know whether it's a guy thing or a people thing, but I don't like being made to feel like a greenhorn, as I suspected I was going to be. Not more than ten paces in, she stopped, crouched, and invited me to inspect a bare patch of ground the size of a checkerboard. I identified it at a glance: "Dirt."

She shook her head impatiently and picked up a twig, which she used as a pointer, showing me something here, there, and everywhere. Looking closely, I spotted clumps of dry grass, twig parts, bits of bark, broken leaves, and more dirt.

"Don't do this to me," I told her. "I'm not Natty Bumppo and never will be."

She didn't argue. Instead, she reached her twig over to raise a branch of a low bush and invited me to have a look under it. What it looked like was a dead mouse being buried like a bather at the beach. Only its head showed, nestled in a little mound of dirt. As I watched, in the dimmest possible light, the ruffle of dirt around its neck bubbled here and there, and the mouse visibly slid back a millimeter, as if literally sinking into the earth.

"In an hour or so," B explained, "the mouse will be completely underground and out of sight, the work of burying beetles that are digging the soil out from under it."

She lowered the branch, and I asked what she'd been trying to show me in the dirt in front of the bush. She used her twig as a pointer as she tried to show me the signs. "The beetles—I'm pretty sure there are just two of them—found the mouse's carcass here but evidently didn't care for this as a burial site, so they carried it to a more sheltered site under that branch."

"Two beetles *carried* the mouse?"

"What they do is burrow under the carcass then turn over onto their backs and shove it in the direction they want it to go. It's a very laborious process. Once they have it underground, they harden the chamber around it, and while the corpse rots, the female lays her eggs nearby so the larvae will have easy access to the carrion mass once it's opened up."

"Yum," I said.

"Oh, there's plenty of competition for this mouse, Jared—other insects, microbes, many vertebrate scavengers. The flies are especially bothersome, because they may have laid their eggs in the mouse's fur before the beetles came along. Fortunately—but not surprisingly—the beetles themselves are supplied with egg-sweepers, mites that make their homes right on the beetles and that live on flies' eggs. The mouse, the beetles, the mites, and the flies are all inspiring embodi-ments of the Law of Life."

I thought about this last statement as we made our way back to the clearing. "I'm afraid I don't see what makes these creatures em-bodiments of the law," I told her.

"The Law of Life in a single word is: *abundance*." When no more was forthcoming, I asked if she'd elaborate on that a bit.

"A useful exercise would be for you to go back to the mouse carcass and bring back one of the beetles. Then I'd have you pick off a couple dozen of the beetle's phoretic mites so you could examine them under a microscope."

"What would I learn from that?"

"You'd learn that each mite—such an inconsiderable creature!—is a work of so much delicacy, perfection, and complexity that it makes a digital computer look like a pair of pliers. Then you'd learn some-thing even more amazing, that, for all their perfection, they aren't stamped out of a mold. No two of them are alike—no two in all the mighty universe, Jared!"

"And this would be a demonstration of . . . abundance?"

"That's right. This fantastic genetic abundance is life's very secret of success on this planet."

We trooped on. After a few minutes I realized we'd left our clear-ing far behind. Before long we were back on the public paths.

B said, "I haven't done nearly as well as I thought I would to-night, Jared. I haven't shown you a tenth as much as I hoped. Tomor-row will be better."

Friday, May 24 (ten P.M.)

One of the bad ones

The hotel dining room was open by the time I finished the previous entry, so I went down for some breakfast, then came back to the room and slept till midafternoon. At the theater everyone was disheartened because they'd failed to get the announcement of B's talk in today's paper. It'll appear tomorrow, but everyone knows this means the turnout will be even more dismal than expected.

I was frightened looking at B. She was wafer pale, nervous, and visibly shrunken, as if she'd aged ten years overnight. The life had gone out of her hair and her eyes, and I thought I saw a tremor in her left hand. Until then, in truth, I'd never really believed in her illness. Now I thought she should be in a hospital bed—or at least in some bed, with someone bringing cups of tea laced with honey, stoking a small, cheery fire, and reading aloud from *The Wind in the Willows*.

Around five o'clock she suggested that we get out of there, and I asked to where. When she said the park, I asked if she really felt up to that. She gave me a sharp look and half of an angry reply, then seemed to realize I hadn't earned it.

"I have my good days and my bad days," she said, with the air of making an admission. "Up to now you've only seen the good ones."

All the same, we took the Mercedes instead of walking. On the way, B asked if I was a theologian.

"Me? No way."

"That's too bad," she said without further explanation. "I know Charles made this point, but I'm going to make it again: When St. Paul brought Christianity into the Roman world, very fundamental ideas were already in place there. The idea of gods as 'higher beings.' The idea of personal salvation. The idea of an afterlife. The idea that the gods are involved in our lives, that their help can be invoked, that they're pleased or offended by things we do, that they can reward and punish. Notions of sacrifice and redemption. These were all things that Paul didn't have to explain from scratch."

I thought I saw where she was headed. I said, "Whereas, working with someone like me, you have to struggle to unseat these fundamental ideas and to replace them with others I've never heard of."

"That's right. When Christians began sending missionaries to 'savage lands,' they were faced with the same difficulty I have with you. The aborigines didn't have any idea what the missionaries were talking about."

"That's true."

"Charles and I are the first animist missionaries to *your* world— the world of salvationist, revealed religions—Christianity, Islam, Judaism, Buddhism, Hinduism. There's no blueprint for what we're doing. No precedent, no catechism, no curriculum. That's why it's so . . . improvisational. We're trying to *develop* the blueprint. We're trying to figure out what works."

"This will probably seem like a silly question, but . . . *why*? Why are you doing this?"

B drove for a minute in silence. Then: "You remember what B said: Vision is the flowing river."

"Yes . . . ?"

"The religions I just mentioned—the revealed religions—are fundamentally wed to our cultural vision, and I use the word *wed* advisedly. These religions are like a harem of sanctimonious wives married to a greedy, loutish sensualist of a husband. They're forever trying to improve him, forever hoping to get his mind on 'higher things,' forever bawling him out and shaking their fingers at him, but husband and harem are in fact completely inseparable. These revealed religions clearly function as our 'better half.' They're the highest expression of our cultural vision."

"Yes, I suppose you could say that."

"Here's what Charles said next: 'In our culture at the present moment, *the flow of the river is toward catastrophe.*' Does that make sense to you?"

"Yes."

"Then put it all together, Jared. Vision is the flowing river. The revealed religions of our culture are the highest expression of that vision, and the flow of the river is toward catastrophe."

My mind boggled at this. When I failed to reply, Shirin shot me a glance from the corner of her eye and said, "You wanted to know why we're doing this. Charles explained it the other night: *Our objective is to change the direction of the flow, away from catastrophe.* Nothing less will do the trick, Jared. Absolutely nothing."

I shivered. "I think I understand why the crowds call B the Antichrist."

She smiled and shook her head. "Do you know who the Baal Shem Tov was?"

"I have a general idea. He was a great Hasidic saint, sort of a Jewish Francis of Assisi, about five centuries later."

"Close enough. Do you know the meaning of the name?"

"No."

"A baal shem is a master of names—in other words, a magician. Baal Shem Tov means 'master of the good name,' which is to say a magician of the highest order, capable of wielding the name of God."

"I see."

"There once was a merchant who was afraid to travel to a nearby city, because the only route passed through a forest known to be inhabited by highwaymen. His wife said he should appeal to the Baal Shem Tov for help, but this just irritated the merchant, who didn't believe the stories he'd heard about this supposed wonder-worker. His wife said, 'Trust me. Go to the house of the Baal Shem Tov and slip his porter a few coins. The porter will let you know the next time his master is planning a trip through those woods, and you can go with him. No harm will come to you if you're with the Baal Shem Tov.' The merchant reluctantly took her advice and before long had an opportunity to travel with the Baal Shem Tov.

"When they reached the deepest, most dangerous part of the woods, the Baal Shem Tov called a halt so the horses could rest and graze. This stoppage terrified the merchant, but the Baal Shem Tov calmly took out his copy of the Zohar and began to read. Soon the branches alongside the road parted, and the robbers stepped out and approached, knives drawn. But when they were two or three paces away from the wagons, they suddenly started to shake uncontrollably.

They didn't know what to make of this, but they were in no condition to attack anyone, so back they went into the woods. After a few minutes they recovered and made a second attempt, with the same result: Before they could get close enough even to touch one of the horses' noses, they were rendered helpless with palsy and forced to retreat. The merchant, cowering in his wagon, watched all this with amazement.

"When the Baal Shem Tov finally looked up from his book and gave the word to continue, the merchant threw himself at his feet and kissed his hand. 'Now I understand,' he said. 'Now I understand why people call you the Baal Shem Tov!'

"The Baal Shem Tov frowned down at him and said, 'So you think you understand that, do you? Believe me, my friend, you're just *beginning* to understand!' "

The two visions

Once inside the park, B's exhaustion seemed to slip away from her. She led the way and I followed, for all the world like a husband being towed through a shopping mall. I didn't have the least idea what she was looking for, but she was certainly looking. When we finally stopped, it was in a spot that, for all I knew, might have been the same one we occupied the night before. We sat down facing a dusty clearing not much bigger than a dining-room table.

She said, "We have a lot to do here, Jared—a great journey to take—and I'm not sure I'm guide enough to see you through it. But I'll do my best."

I wanted to murmur a word of encouragement but decided against it. She reached in her purse and drew out of it our work of *bricolage*. Some reassembly was necessary, as the pen and the fuse were not snugly held in place alongside the film canister, and when this was done, she handed it to me and asked if I remembered what it was all about.

"The fossil represents the community of life," I told her. "Animism is bound up with that community and resonates with it. The Law of Life, represented by the pen, is written in the community of life, and animism reads this law, as does science in its own way."

"Excellent. I've called animism a religion, but there's a very real sense in which animism-as-a-religion is an invention of Taker culture, an intellectual construct."

"Why is that?"

"I told you that animism was once a universal religion on this planet. It's still universal among Leaver peoples—peoples you identify as 'primitive,' 'Stone Age,' and so on. But if you go among these people and ask them if they're animists, they won't have the slightest idea what you're talking about. And in fact if you suggest that they and their neighbors have the same religious beliefs, they'll probably think you're crazy. This is because, like neighbors everywhere, they tend to be much more aware of their differences than their similarities. It's the same with your revealed religions. To you, Christianity, Judaism, Islam, Buddhism, and Hinduism look very different, but to me they look the same. Many of you would say that something like Buddhism doesn't even belong in this list, since it doesn't link salvation to divine worship, but to me this is just a quibble. Christianity, Judaism, Islam, Buddhism, and Hinduism all perceive human beings as flawed, wounded creatures in need of salvation, and all rely fundamentally on revelations that spell out how salvation is to be attained, either by departing from this life or by rising above it."

"True."

"The adherents of these religions are mightily struck and obsessed by their differences—to the point of mayhem, murder, jihad, and genocide—but to me, as I say, you all look alike. It's the same among Leaver peoples. They see what's different between them and I see what's alike, and what's alike is not so much a religion (as religion is understood by Christians, Jews, Muslims, Buddhists, and Hindus) as it is a religious vision of the world. There is in fact no such religion as animism—that's the construct: animism as a religion. What exists—and what is universal—is a way of looking at the world. And that's what I'm trying to show you here."

"I understand . . . I guess."

"Always keep in mind what we're about here, Jared. We're here about visions, you and I. One vision is sweeping us toward catastrophe. This is a vision peculiar to a single culture, our culture, focused and sustained by the revealed religions of our culture during the last three thousand years. I'm trying to show you another vision, healthy for us and healthy for the world, that was embraced by hundreds of thousands of cultures through hundreds of thousands of years."

"Okay," I said. "But you can't actually know how long it's been embraced."

"I think I can, Jared. Consider this: How long have people been living in accordance with the law of gravity?"

"With the law of gravity? Forever, of course."

"How can you know that?"

"I suppose I know that because, if people hadn't been living in accordance with the law of gravity, then they wouldn't be here at all."

"But they didn't necessarily *understand* the law of gravity, did they? I mean, they couldn't express it the way a physicist might."

"No."

"But they knew it was a law all the same. Step off the edge of a cliff and you fall—every time. Drop the rock and it falls on your toe—every time."

"That's right."

"Now try this: How long have people been living in accordance with the Law of Life?"

"I don't know."

"The Law of Life is . . . ?"

"The Law of Life is . . . 'whatever fosters life.' "

"So try again, Jared: How long have people been living in accordance with the Law of Life?"

"From the beginning."

"Why? How do you know that?"

"Because if they hadn't been living in accordance with the law that fosters life, then they wouldn't be here at all."

"Good. But they didn't necessarily *understand* that law, did they? They probably couldn't have expressed it the way a biologist would."

"No."

"Nevertheless, they could know what they knew about the law of gravity—that it's *there*. That a law is in place. They could know, for example, that infants must be taken care of till they can take care of themselves. They could know that abandoned infants die—every time. They could know that a lion will defend its kill—every time.

They could know that you don't necessarily have to be as fast as a deer to catch a deer. They could know that if you're stalking any animal that can outrun you, you'd better be downwind of it. I could go on all night. I could go on for days and weeks, and I wouldn't be able to list everything they would know just by the simple experience of living in that community through thousands of generations."

"I'm sure you're right. What I don't see yet is the connection between this and animism."

"What *is* animism, Jared?"

"I'm less and less sure as time goes on. As I understand it right now, it's a vision. I suppose you mean a worldview, a weltanshauung."

"Yes, but I think I'll stick with *vision*. This is what we're about here: two visions, one vision that enabled us to live well and in harmony with the earth through millions of years, and another vision that has brought us to the verge of extinction and made us the enemy of all life on this planet in just ten thousand years."

"Okay."

"And what is the animist vision?"

"I don't know. I have no idea."

"Then tell me this: What is *our* vision, Jared—the Taker vision, the vision that has made us the master of the world and the enemy of life? Can you articulate it?"

"I can try."

"Go ahead."

"We're the creature for whom the world was made, so we can do what we please with it. That's a start."

"Yes, that's a good start. According to this vision, God seems to have little interest in the rest of the world."

"That's right. God cares about *people.* People are the big deal. People are what he made the universe for."

"So the world was made for Man, and Man— What was Man supposed to do with the world?"

"He was supposed to rule it. It was given to him to rule."

"But, oddly enough, the world wasn't *ready* for him to rule, was it. Man was ready-made to rule the world but the world wasn't ready-made for him to rule it."

"No, that's true. I never noticed that in particular."

"So what did Man have to do to make the world ready to rule?"

"He had to subdue it, conquer it."

"That's right. And he's still at it, isn't he. So, this is the Taker vision: *The world was made for Man, and Man was made to conquer and rule it.*"

"Yes."

"What we're looking for now, Jared, is the Leaver vision or the animist vision. Before we leave here today, you'll have that, I promise you."

Strategies: stable and otherwise

"I want you to understand that what I'm calling the Law of Life was not in any sense imprinted in the community of life by divine action. God or the gods didn't give their creatures 'good instincts' that I'm now calling collectively the Law of Life. It didn't happen that way. To posit such an action would be unparsimonious, a violation of Occam's razor. You understand what I mean by that, don't you?"

"Yes. You're saying the Law of Life doesn't have to be explained as a system of divine intervention any more than the laws of thermodynamics have to be explained as a system of divine intervention."

"That's right. A biologist would probably say that what I'm calling the Law of Life is just a collection of evolutionarily stable strategies—the universal set of such strategies, in fact. Do you know what an evolutionarily stable strategy is?"

"Madam," I said, "I am a classicist, not a biologist. In school, I read Homer in the Greek and Cicero in the Latin. I can give you a discourse on Plato's proof of the immortality of the soul—and a damned good one it is, too, if you accept his premises. But I haven't the least idea what an evolutionarily stable strategy is."

"All right. Let's break it down into parts. A strategy in this context is just a behavioral policy. For example, yesterday I mentioned a behavioral policy that's followed by lactating she-goats: 'Suckle your own and no other.' This is evolutionarily stable for goats because it can't be improved on by any alternative strategy. For example, it could happen that some goats might follow a strategy of refusing to

nurse any kids at all, including their own. But this will definitely have
the effect of reducing their representation in the gene pool, so refusal
to nurse will tend to disappear from the species. Similarly, some goats
might follow a strategy of indiscriminate nursing—suckling any kid
that comes along. But because this shortchanges their own kids, this
too will have the effect of reducing their representation in the gene
pool, so indiscriminate nursing will also tend to disappear. The only
strategy that will *not* tend to disappear is 'Suckle your own and no
other.' That's why this particular strategy is evolutionarily stable: The
normal process of evolution, natural selection, doesn't eliminate it."

"I understand. This is the Law of Life for goats not because God
decided goats should behave this way but because, in any mix of
strategies, goats that suckle only their own will tend to be better
represented in the gene pool than any others. It's actually a very
elegant concept."

"Science does occasionally produce an elegant concept," she said
with an mildly ironic smile. "I'm sure you understand that what is
stable and unstable for one species isn't necessarily stable and unstable
for another species. For example, many birds are indiscriminate nurs-
ers. They'll feed any chick that turns up in their nest, including chicks
of other species."

"Thus giving aid and comfort to the merry cuckoo," I said, re-
warding B's surprised look with a mildly ironic smile of my own. "We
classicists aren't total ignoramuses," I informed her. "The fool warns
King Lear, 'You know, Nuncle, the hedge-sparrow fed the cuckoo so
long it had its head bit off by its young.' "

"I'm glad to know that classicists aren't total ignoramuses, Jared,"
B said, giving me a smile so sweetly benevolent that, for one terrifying
moment, I actually had to struggle to keep from grabbing her. Noticing nothing, she went on.

"I know you've heard Charles mention a colleague known as
Ishmael. Though he didn't use this terminology, Ishmael identified a
set of strategies that appear to be evolutionarily stable for all species.
He called this set of strategies the Law of Limited Competition, which
he expressed this way: 'You may compete to the full extent of your
capabilities, but you may not hunt down your competitors or destroy

their food or deny them access to food.' In the miscalled 'natural' community (meaning the nonhuman community), you'll find competitors killing each other when the opportunity presents itself, but you won't find them *creating* opportunities to kill each other. You won't find them hunting each other the way they hunt their prey; to do so would not be evolutionarily stable. Hyenas just don't have the energy to hunt lions—calories gained by eliminating these competitors wouldn't equal the calories spent in eliminating them—and attacking lions is not exactly a risk-free venture. In the same way, in the 'natural' community, you won't find competitors destroying their competitors' food—the payoff just isn't big enough to make it worthwhile."

"What would be the motive for destroying your competitors' food?"

"If you destroy your competitors' food, you destroy your competitors, Jared. Suppose, for example, that you're a bird species that favors foods A, B, C, D, E, and F. Another bird species favors foods D, E, F, G, H, and I. That means you compete with them for foods D, E, and F. By destroying foods G, H, and I (which you don't care for yourself), you can strike an important blow against them."

"But won't they just compete all the harder for foods D, E, and F?"

"Of course. That's why you need the third strategy. You want to deny them *access* to foods D, E, and F. That way your competitors will be totally out of luck. You'll be denying them access to half the foods they favor and destroying the other half."

"But as you say, this doesn't happen."

"It doesn't happen in the nonhuman community, but this isn't to say that it *can't* happen. To say that it doesn't happen is to say that it isn't *found,* and it isn't found because it's self-eliminating. Do you see what I mean? It doesn't happen that goats refuse to nurse their young, but that isn't because such behavior is impossible. There surely have been goats that refuse to nurse, but you seldom or never come across them, because their offspring die and they lose their representation in the gene pool."

"I see that," I said.

"It *has* happened that a species has tried to live in violation of the Law of Limited Competition. Or rather it has happened one time, in one human culture—ours. That's what our agricultural revolution is all about. That's the whole point of totalitarian agriculture: We hunt our competitors down, we destroy their food, and we deny them access to food. That's what makes it totalitarian."

My mind reeled for a bit over this. It took me a while to figure out what it was reeling over. Finally I said, "Look, the subject here is evolutionarily stable strategies, right?"

"Right."

"There are three strategies here that you say are evolutionarily *un*stable: Hunt your competitors down, destroy their food, and deny them access to food. Right?"

"Right."

"But now you're telling me that our whole culture is founded on these evolutionarily *un*stable strategies."

"Right again."

"If these strategies are evolutionarily unstable, then how do we manage to pursue them?"

"Pursuing an evolutionarily unstable strategy doesn't eliminate you *instantly*, Jared, it eliminates you *eventually*."

"But how is it eliminating *us*?"

B cocked her head as if to ask why I was suddenly being so dense. "Jared, where were you the other night in Stuttgart when Charles was explaining the connection between totalitarian agriculture and over-population? Because six billion of us are pursuing an evolutionarily unstable strategy, we're fundamentally attacking the very ecological systems that keep us alive. Just like the goat that refuses to suckle its kids, we're in the process of eliminating *ourselves*. Think about the time line Charles drew in his talk about the boiling frog. For the first six thousand years, the impact of our evolutionarily unstable strategy was minimal and confined to the Near East. Over the next two thousand years, the strategy spread to Eastern Europe and the Far East. In the next fifteen hundred years, the strategy spread throughout the Old World. In the next three hundred years, it became global. By the end of the next two hundred years—which is now—so many people were following the strategy that the impact was becoming catastrophic.

We're now about two generations away from finishing the job of making this unstable strategy extinct."

I struggled to my feet and went for a walk.

The eyes begin to open

When I returned fifteen minutes later, I told B what I'd had to get away to think about. I'd heard everything Charles had said in Stuttgart and thought I understood it, but I hadn't. In spite of everything he said, I felt sure he was showing us that our population explosion is a *social* problem, like, say, crime or racism. I failed to hear him say that our population explosion is a *biological* problem, that if we pursue a policy that would be fatal for *any* species, then it will be fatal for us in exactly the same way. We can't *will* it to be otherwise. We can't say, "Well, yes, our civilization is built on an evolutionarily unstable strategy but we can make it work anyhow, because we're *humans.*" The world will not make an exception for us. And of course what the Church teaches is that *God* will make an exception for us. God will let us behave in a way that would be fatal for any other species, will somehow "fix it" so we can live in a way that is in a very real sense *self-eliminating.* This is like expecting God to make our airplanes fly even if they're aerodynamically incapable of flight.

"This will probably sound very naive," I said, "but why is this such a secret? Why is this something I've never heard before? Why isn't this taught in the schools?"

"It's not a secret, of course. It's just that the pieces of the puzzle are scattered among so many disciplines—so many disciplines that rarely talk to each other—archaeology, history, anthropology, biology, sociology. And who exactly would teach it in the schools?"

"Everyone should teach it," I told her. "They should teach this first. Reading, writing, and arithmetic can wait."

"Well, naturally I agree with you. This is the word of B, Jared: If the world is saved, it will not be saved by people with the old vision and new programs. If the world is saved, it will be saved by people with a new vision and no programs. This is because vision propagates itself and needs no programs. In the last half hour your eyes have begun to open to that new vision. But as yet you have only the bleak side of the vision—the shadow side."

I had to agree with that.

"So we come again—as we must, again and again, Jared—to these two visions, the Taker vision and the Leaver, or animist, vision. A few minutes ago, you did a fine job of articulating the Taker vision, the vision that has driven our culture through its ten thousand years of triumph and catastrophe. As the Takers see it, the world was made for Man, and Man was made to conquer and rule it. The next question is: Where did this vision come from?"

"I'm afraid I don't quite understand the meaning of the question," I told her.

"That's all right. Charles would have insisted on prodding you across this gap, but I've promised not to follow his example. I'll tell you where the vision came from, and you can tell me whether my explanation is plausible and persuasive. The Taker vision came from the Taker experience of the world—from the way the people of our culture made their living, which was, after all, by conquering and ruling the world. The practice of totalitarian agriculture over thousands of years gave them the idea that the world had been made for Man, and Man had been made to conquer and rule it. Does that make sense?"

"Yes, it makes perfect sense. I suppose you could call it a sort of rough-and-ready empiricism: 'We've always lived as though the world *was* made for us, so it must *have been* made for us."

"The important thing to note is that the vision grew out of the lifestyle, the lifestyle didn't grow out of the vision. Is that clear?"

"Well . . . it's almost clear."

"What I mean is, one day eleven thousand years ago, the Mesolithic hunters of Iraq *didn't* get together and say, 'Look, we've examined the world and conclude that it was made for humans to conquer and rule. Therefore we should get off our duffs and start conquering and ruling it.' Rather, what happened was that, over thousands of years of *living* like conquerors and rulers, the people of our culture gradually began to conceive the curious notion that the world had actually been *created* for us to conquer and rule. They began to imagine that they were fulfilling human destiny itself."

"I understand. The Taker vision grew out of the Taker lifestyle, not the other way around."

"Now, what do you suppose the Leaver vision grew out of?"

"I'd suppose it grew out of the Leaver lifestyle."

"And you'd be right, of course. And what do you know of that lifestyle?"

"To be honest . . . nothing at all."

B nodded. "That's our challenge for today, Jared. I have to reveal to you the vision that grew out of a lifestyle you know nothing about."

"Sounds difficult," I said.

"It is, but I don't have to teach you everything there is to know about this lifestyle. To articulate the Taker vision, all you really had to understand was how Takers make their living. Takers make their living by behaving as though the world belongs to them—and the Taker vision supports that behavior. There's a lot more to the Taker lifestyle than this, but this was all you needed in order to articulate that vision."

"Yes, I see."

"I can be—and will be—just as selective as that when it comes to the Leavers."

Silencing the inquisitor

Having said this, B fell silent. After a few minutes I made a mental check to see if I was supposed to be working on some question or other, but of course I wasn't. She wasn't in a trance or anything, just seemed to be staring vacantly into the middle distance. Soon I began fidgeting, and she slanted a look at me.

She said, "I've never done this before, Jared, and now that I'm right at the point of doing it, I don't know how to begin. I know everything I want to happen, I just don't know how to accomplish it. I know where I want to end up, I just don't know how to get there."

Since I didn't really understand the problem, I couldn't see any way to help, beyond giving her a reassuring pat on the back, which probably wouldn't have done either one of us much good.

Finally she said, "I have an idea, but I'm not sure how you'll take to it. I think my problem is that our relationship is inherently adversarial. I don't mean it's entirely adversarial, but it has an adversarial aspect to it that just won't go away. This isn't your fault or my fault, it's simply what is. You were sent here to satisfy yourself and others, to ask questions you would ask and questions they would ask, so your role here, like it or not, is that of an inquisitor. 'Like it or not' is the right way to talk about it, I think, because you mostly *don't* like it but feel you must do it anyway. You must ask for yourself, and you must ask for those others who sent you here."

"Yes, that's right."

"What I've done so far has been fine for the inquisitor." She laid a finger on our work of *bricolage.* "This worked perfectly well for him, didn't it?"

I nodded.

"My trouble right now is that I can't think of any way to fill an inquisitor's eyes with the animist vision. I really don't think it can be done. This means we have to take on a pair of new roles."

I nodded again.

"I had a son once, Jared—not one of the lucky ones. He lived only a few hours, not long enough to be named, really, but privately I named him Louis, somehow a very grown-up name. I won't be having others, for obvious reasons—or if they're not obvious, you can work them out at your leisure. If Louis were alive, he'd be eight years old, and I'd certainly be teaching him what I now need to teach you."

"So what are you asking?"

"I'm asking if you can turn off the inquisitor for an hour and listen to me the way Louis would."

I told her I thought I could manage that.

"I don't know whether I'm asking of you something easy or something hard. Probably a lot of men would find it impossible."

"I don't know either," I said. "But, to be honest, it doesn't seem like that big a deal. Let me ask this, though. Are you saying that you want me not to ask any questions at all? That doesn't sound right to me, because Louis would certainly be asking questions if he were eight years old."

She seemed disconcerted by this, maybe even a bit irked. It couldn't be helped, the question had to be asked.

She said, "An eight-year-old isn't an inquisitor."

"I know that. Give me a little credit."

She gnawed on it for a while, then said, "Louis *would* ask questions." I didn't bother to point out that I'd just told her that. "Do you think you can ask *his* questions and not Fr. Lulfre's?"

"I think I can, Shirin. Give me the benefit of a doubt."

She shrugged an unenthusiastic agreement. After spending a few moments in thought, she looked away. "Don't be surprised if I say things you don't expect to hear. These are the things I have to say."

"I understand."

"I wish you knew sign language," she added rather wistfully. "Barriers fall right away in sign."

I wished I knew it too.

The web

I don't know what she did during the next few minutes, I wasn't watching. At junctures like this, you leave people alone, turn your attention elsewhere, and give them a little room to work in. When she was ready, she started talking in a low, firm voice—and I unobtrusively switched on my tape recorder.

"I've told you I'm dying," she began. "I know it makes you unhappy to hear this, Louis, but the closer you come to understanding it, the less unhappy you'll feel. By the time we're finished here today, you still won't feel good about it, but you'll be able to bear it. In any case, this is where I have to begin. You want to understand me and you want to understand what's going on, and that's what we're going to look at right now. If I were someone else, I'd try to console you with a fairy tale like the one they tell about Santa Claus every Christmas. I'd tell you that Mommy's going to be taken up to heaven to live with God and the angels, and from there I'll look down and watch over you. The truth is better than this—partly because it *is* the truth.

"Let me begin with the great secret of the animist life, Louis. When other people look for God, you'll see them automatically look up into the sky. They really imagine that, if there's a God, he's far, far, far away—remote and untouchable. I don't know how they can bear living with such a God, Louis, I really don't. But they're not our problem. I've told you that, among the animists of the world, not a single one can tell you the number of the gods. They don't know that number and neither do I. I've never met one or heard of one who cares how many there are. What's important to us is not *how many* they are but *where* they are. If you go among the Alawa of Australia or the Bushmen of Africa or the Navajo of North America or the Kreen-Akrore of South America or the Onabasulu of New Guinea—or any other of hundreds of Leaver peoples I could name—you'll soon find out where the gods are. The gods are *here*."

For the first time B looked directly into my eyes as she spoke.

"I don't mean *there,* I don't mean *elsewhere,* I mean *here.* Among the Alawa: *here.* Among the Bushmen: *here.* Among the Navajo: *here.* Among the Kreen-Akrore: *here.* Among the Onabasulu: *here.* Do you understand?"

"I'm not sure," I replied truthfully.

"This isn't a theological statement they're making. The Alawa are *not* saying to the Bushmen, 'Your gods are frauds, the true gods are *our* gods.' The Kreen-Akrore are *not* saying to the Onabasulu, 'You have no gods, only *we* have gods.' Nothing of the kind. They're saying, 'Our place is a sacred place, like no other in the world.' They would never think of looking *elsewhere* to find the gods. The gods are to be found among *them*—living where *they* live. The god is what animates *their* place. That's what a god *is.* A god is that strange force that makes every place a *place*—a place like no other in the world. A god is the fire that burns in this place and no other—and no place in which the fire burns is devoid of god. All of this should explain to you why I don't reject the name that was given to us by an outsider. Even though it was bestowed with a false understanding of our vision, the name *animism* captures a glimmer of it.

"Unlike the God whose name begins with a capital letter, our gods are not all-powerful, Louis. Can you imagine that? Any one of them can be vanquished by a flamethrower or a bulldozer or a bomb—silenced, driven away, enfeebled. Sit in the middle of a shopping mall at midnight, surrounded by half a mile of concrete in all directions, and there the god that was once as strong as a buffalo or a rhinoceros is as feeble as a moth sprayed with pyrethrin. Feeble—but not dead, not wholly extinguished. Tear down the mall and rip up the concrete, and within days that place will be pulsing with life again. Nothing needs to be done, beyond carting away the poisons. The god knows how to take care of that place. It will never be what it was before—but nothing is ever what it was before. It doesn't *need* to be what it was before. You'll hear people talk about turning the plains of North America back into what they were before the Takers arrived. This is nonsense. What the plains were five hundred years ago was not their final form, was not the final, sacrosanct form ordained for them from the beginning of time. There is no such form and never will be any such form. Everything here is *on the way*. Everything here is *in process.*

"Here, I'll tell you a story. When the gods set out to make the universe, they said to themselves, 'Let us make of it a manifestation of our unending abundance and a sign to be read by those who shall have eyes to read. Let us lavish care without stint on every thing: no less upon the most fragile blade of grass than upon the mightiest of stars, no less upon the gnat that sings for an hour than upon the mountain that stands for a millennium, no less upon a flake of mica than upon a river of gold. Let us make no two leaves the same from one branch to the next, no two branches the same from one tree to the next, no two trees the same from one land to the next, no two lands the same from one world to the next, no two worlds the same from one star to the next. In this way, the Law of Life will be plain to all who shall have eyes to read: the rabbit that creeps out to feed, the fox that lies in wait, the eagle that circles above, and the man who bends his bow to the sky.' And this was how it was done from first to last, no two things alike in all the mighty universe, no single thing made with less care than any other thing throughout generations of species more numerous than the stars. And those who had eyes to see read the sign and followed the Law of Life.

"Do you understand that story?" she asked.

"No, I don't think I do."

"No two things alike in all the mighty universe, Jared. That's the key. That's why everything here is *on the way* and not in its final form. I told you this yesterday when I was talking about the mites that travel with the burying beetles. If you put these mites under a microscope to study the final form of this species, you'll be defeated, because the closer you look at them, the more clearly you'll see that no two of them are alike—and if no two are alike, what sense can it possibly make to hold up any one of them and say, 'Here, here is the final form of these mites'?

"This is what I mean by abundance, Jared: Even among these apparently negligible mites, no two have ever been made alike in all the mighty universe, and not one of them has ever been made with less care than a neutron star or a galactic cluster. The brain in that precious human head of yours is not more wonderful than one of those mites."

"I know it," I found myself saying.

"Would the Judeo-Christian-Islamic God have sent his only-begotten son to save those beetles and their household mites, Jared?"

"No."

"But the god of this place has as great a care for them as for any other creature in the world. This is why I knew you could benefit from seeing those beetles yesterday. Those beetles are a manifestation of the gods' unending abundance and a sign to be read by those who have eyes to read. I wanted you to see how the gods lavish care without stint on every thing: no less upon a beetle whose supreme achievement is burying a mouse than upon the brain of Einstein, no less upon a mite whose favorite dish is a fly's egg than upon the eye of Michelangelo."

"I *do* see—or I'm beginning to."

"Where are we going to find this god, Louis?"

Since she'd called me by my own name just a minute before, I was momentarily flummoxed by her reverting to Louis. As time went on, I saw that she could address me either way without derailing her train of thought. Sometimes her message was specifically for Louis (and for me incidentally), sometimes it was specifically for me (and for Louis incidentally), and sometimes, I suppose, it was for both of us equally. In any case, my answer to this particular question was a blank look.

"I'm not asking you to make a leap here, Jared. I've already told you where we're going to find this god . . . but I'll come back to it later. We've got plenty of other things to talk about. You and I, Jared, always come back to vision. Louis and I always come back to the meaning of death.

"Every creature born in the living community *belongs* to that community. I mean it belongs in the sense that your skin or your nervous system belongs to you. The mouse we saw didn't just 'live in' the park community, the way you might live in an apartment in Chicago or Fresno. Every molecule in the mouse's body was drawn from this community and eventually had be returned to this community. It would be legitimate to say that this mouse was an expression of this community the way Leonardo da Vinci was an expression of Renaissance Italy.

"The individual lives in dynamic tension with the community, withdrawing to burrow, hive, nest, lodge, or den for safety's sake but never totally self-sufficient there, always compelled to return and make itself available, as this mouse did. This tension is a phrase of the law, inspiring the trapdoor spider to seal its burrow like a bank vault and inspiring the spider wasp to become a safebreaker.

"Nothing in the community lives in isolation from the rest, not even the queens of the social insects. Nothing lives only in itself, needing nothing *from* the community. Nothing lives only for itself, owing nothing *to* the community. Nothing is untouchable or untouched. Every life is on loan from the community from birth and without fail is paid back to the community in death. The community is a web of life, and every strand of the web is a path to all the other strands. Nothing is exempt or excused. Nothing is special. Nothing lives on a strand by itself, unconnected to the rest. As you saw yesterday, nothing is wasted, not a drop of water or a molecule of protein— or the egg of a fly. This is the sweetness and the miracle of it all, Jared. Everything that lives is food for another. Everything that feeds is ultimately itself fed upon or in death returns its substance to the community."

She paused and gave me a look, which I took and gave back.

"Every strand of the web is a path to all the other strands. Does that make sense to you?"

"Yes, I think so."

"Where will we find the god of this place?"

I blinked at that and croaked feebly, "This place?"

"This place right here, Jared."

This was not a question I could handle, so I just goggled at her.

"Ten thousand years ago, this region was the home of a Mesolithic people whose name we'll never know. Dig in the ground and you'll find their hand axes and spearheads. These were Leavers, of course—animists—and they knew where to find the god of this place. The god of this place is *here,* Jared. They didn't look in the sky or on Mount Olympus. They looked *here,* where we're sitting."

I nodded. That was the most I was up for at this point.

"Here," she said again, this time patting the ground in front of us.

"Okay."

"Now I want you to *look.*"

I shook my head—just a little, just enough to say no, no thanks, I think I'll pass on this one.

"Come on," she commanded, and stretched out belly-down in the dust. Not happily, I followed suit.

In the center of the web

"Here is where you'll learn everything," she said. "Here is where it all comes together. This is the center of the web, where past, present, and future are joined and where the human mind was born. I want you to *look.* Don't tell me again that you're not Natty Bumppo. I heard you the first time. You don't have to *understand* what you see but you must at least make an effort to *see* what you see.

"A few decades ago, at a time when Lamarckian notions were still occasionally offered as science, it was popularly theorized that what stimulated the primate brain to grow to human size was our ancestors' mentally huffing and puffing to invent *tools.* This is of course what you'd expect in a culture like ours that equates advancement with tool use."

I grunted, to let her know I was still awake.

"The fact is, however, that the human breakthrough wasn't associated with any tool-making breakthrough. But it *was* associated with a different sort of breakthrough, a breakthrough as crucial to human development as the breakthrough to language. Any idea what I might be referring to?"

"No, none."

"I'm not surprised. This breakthrough isn't acknowledged in the Taker version of the human story—isn't even *mentioned*, since it adds nothing to the glory of the Takers. This is the breakthrough that decisively signaled the acquisition of a uniquely human lifestyle, a lifestyle critically dependant on *intelligence*. This is the breakthrough that decisively separated us from the apes. Still no ideas?"

"No, I'm afraid not."

"You evidently don't remember discussing this with Charles on the train back from Stuttgart. You couldn't imagine what our ancient ancestors might have achieved during the first three million years of human life, and he tried to show you that what they achieved was a fully human lifestyle."

"Yes, I remember now. That conversation got rather . . . overwhelmed by events."

"Travel among the gorillas and the chimpanzees and the orangutans, and you will be—or should be—struck by the fact that their lifestyle is nothing remotely like the lifestyle associated with even the earliest humans. The earliest humans, unlike those from whom they descended, were *hunter-gatherers*. Throughout the rest of the primate order, all are merely *gatherers*—foragers. They will and do kill for food, opportunistically, but none *live* as hunters. Among the primates *only humans* are hunters, because among the primates only humans have the biological equipment to make hunting a mainstay of life— and that equipment is strictly intellectual. Humans could only succeed at hunting one way. They couldn't succeed the eagle's way or the cheetah's way or the spider's way. These were out of reach. They found their own way to succeed—a way that was out of reach of any other species on earth. Do you understand what I'm trying to tell you, Jared? We didn't become human banging rocks together. We became human reading the tale of events written *here*—here in the hand of the god."

She opened her hand, palm up, to show me what she meant.

"I'm not an expert tracker, Jared, not by any means. Natives of this region—any of those Mesolithic hunters I mentioned earlier—

would be able to tell you about things that had happened here days ago. Literally every slightest mark you see in the dust here is the record of an event, even if it's only the track of a windblown leaf. They'd be able to identify every creature that left a mark here in the recent past, and they'd be able to tell you when it was here and what it was doing, whether it was hurrying or moseying, looking for something to eat or trying to get back home.

"I picked this spot to settle in, because I could see that *something* had happened here that I could probably figure out. I don't mean that some great melodrama was played out here, just *something*. Do you see this curving line of tracks here? They look like they might have been made by pressing an outsize zipper in the dirt."

"Yeah, I see them, now that you point them out."

"This is the track of a beetle, I haven't the least idea what species. Obviously a hefty fellow. The spoor is pretty fresh, not more than a few hours old. You can see where it crosses an older track here, the track of a squirrel."

"Surprisingly enough I *do* see it."

"Okay. Here comes the exciting part. The beetle is tooling along minding its own business, when suddenly from over here to the left a mouse leaps onto the scene to have a go at the beetle. You can see here, the way the tracks are bunched, that the mouse isn't just strolling, it's leaping. If we were in the United States, I'd say it was a chipmunk, but I don't know what this might be, so I'll call it a mouse. Anyway, the mouse grabs the beetle, and here you can see the marks where they scuffle."

"Yes, I see them."

"Now the mouse tracks continue off to the right—and the beetle tracks are seen no more. So what's written here is that the mouse has snaffled itself a beetle snack."

We got ourselves back up into a sitting position.

The first thing: reading the signs

"Very impressive," I said.

"Very *un*impressive, believe me, compared to what a real tracker could do, but good enough for our purpose. There are several things I want you to see from this. The first thing is this: Chimpanzees make and use tools, so tool-making and tool-using are not uniquely human, but the reading I've just done here *is* uniquely human. Of course what I've done so far is only a sample of the hunting process. It's like a still from a motion picture, which can suggest a mood and a theme but can't convey the *process* of the film, which is intrinsically *motion*. At any moment during the hunt, the hunter is considering these questions: What was the animal doing when it made this track? How long ago was it here? Which way was it heading? How fast was it going? How far away will it be by now?—keeping in mind the season, the time of day, the temperature, the condition of the ground, the nature of the terrain, and of course the typical behavior of the animal being tracked and other animals in the neighborhood as well.

"Here's a small example. One day an anthropologist was tagging along with a !Kung hunter in the Kalihari. Around noon they abandoned one hunt as hopeless and started looking around for something else to go after. Soon they came across a gemsbok track the hunter judged to be just a couple hours old. After half an hour of tracking, however, the hunter called it off. He explained that the track hadn't been made that morning after all, pointing out as proof a gemsbok hoofprint with a mouse track running across it. Since mice are nocturnal, the gemsbok track had to have been made during the night. In other words, this particular gemsbok was long gone."

"Yes, I see."

"Now, this isn't a feat of observation and ratiocination that's going to win that !Kung hunter a Nobel prize, but it's a feat that is light-years beyond anything our nearest primate kin is capable of. An ape with the right sort of training may persuade you that it's doing what we do when we talk, but no ape with any amount of training will ever persuade you that it's doing what this !Kung hunter was doing when he tracked the gemsbok."

"I'm sure you're right."

"This is what I'm proposing here, Jared: We didn't cross the line when we started using tools, we crossed the line when we became hunters. Our nonhuman ancestors were tool-makers and -users but they weren't hunters, because they didn't have the mental equipment to be hunters. In other words, we became human by hunting—and of course we became hunters by becoming human. And, by the way, hunting is not an exclusively male activity among aboriginal peoples of today, so there's no reason to suppose it was an exclusively male activity among our earliest human ancestors."

"Excuse me—I hope this won't sound like an inquisitorial question—but it sounds like you're saying that we hunted before we were hunters. How can you hunt before you're a hunter?"

"How can you fly before you're a flier, Jared?"

"I'm not sure I understand what you mean."

"The same question has to be resolved for every evolutionary development. Here's the classic challenge: If the eye developed gradually, then it was useless till it was all complete and functional, and being useless, it conferred no benefit on its owner—so why did it evolve at all? The answer is that something less than an eye *is* useful to its owner. Any sensory tissue, no matter how primitive, is better than none. No matter how the eye began, it gave its owner a slight edge. The same is true of a behavior like hunting. Even the most primitive tracking ability will give you a slight edge over those who don't have it—and any slight edge tends to increase your representation in the gene pool. As the hunters' representation in the gene pool increases, the behavior spreads, and in each generation the best hunters—even if they're well below modern standards—will have an edge and will tend to be better represented in the gene pool. In other words, hunting ability—which in humans doesn't mean speed or power but rather intelligence—was the vector for natural selection in the case of human evolution. Intelligence of a human order wasn't just a lucky accident; it didn't evolve just so we could have beautiful thoughts."

"It seems like language would have had a role in all this."

"Of course it did. I told you we became human when we developed a new lifestyle. Nonhuman primates make their living by foraging, but foraging doesn't require much communication. A band of primates can settle into an area and begin foraging without any planning or coordination or cooperation or allotment of tasks. They just move in, and everybody starts munching. But this sort of behavior won't work for primate hunters. You can't just move in and have everybody start hunting. Hunting teamwork is what pays off—but in primates no hunting teamwork is genetically wired in, the way it is with wolves or hyenas. In primates, hunting teamwork can only come about through communication."

"So you're saying language developed as an adjunct to hunting."

"Language developed because it conferred advantages. It didn't have to confer only one advantage. Language ability made you valuable as a hunting partner—therefore it also made you valuable as a mate. Language ability meant you were both more likely to survive and more likely to reproduce."

"It seems to me that language and hunting developed reciprocally, then. And if that's the case, then we became human not just by hunting but by hunting and talking."

B nodded. "You're not contradicting me, though you seem to think you are. You're just anticipating me. I can't say everything at once."

For some reason, this comment struck me as funny, especially when I imagined myself responding to it with: "Well, why not?" For a moment I thought I'd be able to hold it in and suppress it, but my central nervous system had other ideas, and I started sniggering, then I started chuckling, then I started snorting, then I started guffawing— and it was at this point that B decided to join in, and we laughed ourselves good and silly for about two minutes.

We both ended up gasping for breath and grinning foolishly, with tears running down our faces, and for a split second she had something in her eye that made me think she almost mistook me for a fellow human being. Then we both took a deep, shuddery breath, got a grip on our emotions, and went back to work.

The "hunting gene"

Again she patted the ground in front of us. "I said there were several things I wanted you to take from this demonstration. The first is that we became human by reading the signs—and of course by talking. We didn't become human by banging on rocks or by making up sonnets. Intelligence invited us to explore a new lifestyle, based on hunting and foraging rather than just foraging alone. This new lifestyle demanded—and rewarded—new forms of communication and cooperation.

"Here is the second thing I want you to take from this demonstration. There will inevitably be people who imagine that I'm offering a rationale for 'human violence.' Nothing could be further from my mind. In the first place, no special rationale is needed for humans, because humans are not remarkably or unusually violent—outside of our own culture, which represents a tiny, tiny fraction of humanity. Outside of our culture, humans are violent in the same circumstances that other species are typically violent—in establishing and defending territory. This has nothing—literally nothing—to do with political boundaries. Germany isn't a territory in a biological sense. The connection between political territoriality and biological territoriality is purely metaphorical. Do you know what I mean by that?"

"I haven't the foggiest idea."

"Maybe we can get to it later. Just at the moment I want to make sure you see that, outside of this one deranged culture of ours, we humans are not more violent than other species—and it wasn't hunting that made us as violent as we are. Our foraging ancestors were just as violent. Nonhunters are just as violent. Vegetarian species are just as violent. Nor are we the only species whose members visit violence on each other. Nothing could be further from the truth. Aside from predation, virtually all violence observed in the biological community is intraspecies violence. I can't explain everything here all at once, so you'll have to follow up on this on your own if you're interested.

"There will be people who will take what I'm saying and make out of it an endorsement of sport hunting. Again, nothing could be further from my mind. The fact that humans evolved as hunters didn't implant in them an irresistible urge to slaughter wildlife. The successful hunter isn't the one with the most bloodlust. Bloodlust is not required—is irrelevant. Watch hunters in the wild and you'll see this. They don't go about their business frothing at the mouth, and they don't kill gratuitously."

"Excuse me," I said, "and again I hope this won't sound inquisitorial. It seems to me I've read about archaeological finds of vast kills of bison that apparently were mostly left to rot by human hunters. They killed them, picked out the parts they wanted, and abandoned the rest."

"Improbable as it seems on the basis of the facts you've just mentioned, these were not gratuitous or wasteful slaughters. Hunters in the Old West—I mean hunters of our own culture—could have explained it. They knew from experience that you could literally starve to death surrounded by bison, if these were lean animals such as you'd find late in the winter. In the absence of other food, the only way to survive in the midst of lean bison is to kill vast numbers of them and take what little fat there is. I'm not going to get into the biochemistry of it here, but if you like I can lend you a book on it."

I told her I'd take her word for it.

"Where was I . . . ? I was making the point that hunting isn't violence. Let me put it this way. The trait that was being saved as we evolved as human hunters was not murderousness, it was a talent for observation, deduction, forecasting, cunning, stealth, and alertness. These are the qualities that make for success as a hunter—and they're not at all specific to hunting. If they were, then we would indeed be irresistibly impelled to hunt. But there *are* things that we're irresistibly impelled to do . . . and you can see them *here.*"

She patted the ground in front of her.

The "storytelling gene"

"Tell me what happened here in this spot a few hours ago, Jared."

"Well, a beetle came walking along, then a mouse leaped out of the grass at the left and made a grab at the beetle. You said these marks looked like marks of a scuffle, but I don't know why a mouse would have to scuffle with a beetle."

"Maybe the beetle grabbed back."

"True . . . Anyway, after the scuffle, the mouse carried the beetle off to the right."

"You understand that this—what you've just done—is totally beyond the capacity of any other animal on this planet."

"Yes."

"What exactly did you do?"

"Well . . . actually, I didn't do anything. You did it."

"That's odd. I could have sworn I saw your lips move."

"Yeah, but . . . What exactly is your question?"

"I asked what you did."

"You said, 'Tell me what happened here,' and I told you what happened. Isn't that right?"

"Yes, that's right. What I'm trying to make you see is that the two of us did different things. I did one thing, and you did another. I want you to put a name to what *you* did."

All I could think of to say was that I talked—and I wasn't going to say that.

"The reason you can't name it, Jared, is that you undervalue it. Do you know who Koko is?"

"Koko? She's a gorilla that's been taught sign language, isn't she?"

"That's right. If you sat Koko down here, and a beetle started ambling through the dust, and a mouse came out of the grass and carried it off, Koko would be able to sign something like, 'Bug bug mouse bug run fight mouse run bug.' If, ten minutes later, you were able to convey to her your desire for a description of what she'd seen (which is pretty unlikely), the best you could expect would be something like this: 'Koko mouse see mouse bug Koko see.' Even that would be remarkable. But what Koko will never be able to do is what you did, which is . . . ?"

"To put it all together into a story."

"Exactly." B patted the ground in front of her. "This is where storytelling began, Jared. This is where people began to read the world as a collection of stories. There isn't a child anywhere in the world, in any culture of the world, that doesn't want to hear a story—and everywhere in the world, in every culture of the world, a story is a story is a story: beginning, middle, and end. Beginning: 'One night a mouse was traveling through the tall grass on its way home when it suddenly spotted a great black beetle lumbering across a clearing just ahead. "Well," thought the mouse, "beetles aren't exactly my favorite food, but protein is protein!" ' Middle: 'So the mouse hid in the grass until the beetle was just a leap and a bound away, then it rushed out and attacked. To the mouse's surprise, however, the beetle had a powerful set of jaws of its own, which closed around the mouse's nose. Back and forth the two of them fought until at last the mouse managed to dislodge the beetle.' End: ' "I've got you now," the mouse said, using its sore nose to flip the beetle onto its back. Carefully

avoiding the beetle's waving legs and snapping jaws, the mouse gob-
bled up the beetle and happily trotted off toward home.' "

"Very nice, but . . . Do you really think we have a storytelling
gene?"

"Well . . . a geneticist would wince at such an expression. There
is no single gene in there you can pop out and label 'storytelling.' The
theory I'm putting forward here is that storytelling is a genetic characteristic in the sense that early human hunters who were able to organize events into stories were more successful than hunters who
weren't—and this success translated directly into reproductive success.
In other words, hunters who were storytellers tended to be better
represented in the gene pool than hunters who weren't, which (incidentally) accounts for the fact that storytelling isn't just found here
and there among human cultures, it's found universally."

Reading the future

"The people of the Great Forgetting are quite content to imagine that
the human story began just a few thousand years ago when people
started building cities, but *here* is where we became human in the first
place. I'm not talking about how we came to walk on two legs or how
we came to lose our hair. We were two-legged and hairless for hundreds of thousands of years before we crossed *this* border."

Again she patted the ground in front of us.

"This is where the temporal structure of the universe began to be
imprinted on the human brain. These tracks in front of us are of
course with us in the present, but they won't make any sense until we
recognize them as traces of *past events*. They would be meaningless to
any other species, because no other species would be able to read them
as traces of the past."

"Isn't this what a dog does with a scent?"

"No, not at all. Sitting here, you and I are releasing a physical
emanation of ourselves into the air. This scent, this physical emanation, extends all the way back to the car, and a dog encountering it
there could easily follow it here, but it wouldn't be reading the past, it
would be reading the present. It would be following its nose to us just

the way you might follow your ears to an outdoor concert blocks away."

"Yes, I see the distinction."

"To return to the traces on this patch of ground before us: In order to make sense of them, you not only have to recognize that they're traces of past events, you have to recognize that they have a direction in time: beginning, middle, and end. The beetle's story begins here, progresses to here, and ends there, where it intersects the mouse's story. We can see that the mouse's story continues—into a future that we can make *predictions* about. Sometime last night, a mouse was here, and now it's gone—headed *thataway*. If we follow those tracks, we know we're eventually going to find something *standing* in those tracks—and that something is going to be what?"

"A mouse."

"A mouse, Jared, that we have never laid our eyes on until that moment! You see what I'm saying? Sitting right *here*, we've gained the capacity to *foretell the future*. We've become *seers*! A few minutes ago I tried to make it plain that becoming hunters didn't endow us with an irresistible urge to slaughter wildlife, but it does give us some other urges that *do* seem irresistible. For example, we do seem to be irresistibly attracted to stories, everywhere and everywhen."

"Yes."

"Here's another urge that came to us through hunting: the urge to know what we're going to encounter on that track ahead of us. Each and every one of us *wants to know the future*—by any means whatever, rational or irrational, sensible or fantastic. This is so deeply ingrained in us, so much taken for granted, that we don't give a moment's thought to how remarkable it is. For many of us, every smallest action gives us purchase on the future. On getting up, we dress a certain way in anticipation of meeting a certain person. We read the paper not so much to find out what *has* happened as to find out what's *likely* to happen—in world affairs, in politics, in business, in sports, and so on. We check the weather forecast to see if we'll need an umbrella. On our way to work, we review our plans for the day, which will undoubtedly involve making plans for tomorrow, for next week, maybe even for next year. A good day is likely to be viewed as a day that turns out *as planned*, that has no unpleasant surprises. At some point we make plans about how we'll spend the evening. We'll undoubtedly spend time thinking about things that need to be done in anticipation of future events. We'll order plane tickets, make hotel reservations, arrange for someone to receive a gift on a birthday days or weeks hence.

"It would be hard for us even to imagine an intelligent species that wasn't obsessed with the future—and perhaps a species that wasn't obsessed with the future could never seem fully intelligent to us at all. Beyond all the presumably rational planning I just described, every single one of us is a reader of omens and signs—no matter how much we pooh-pooh it. When we get up in the morning and the newspaper on the lawn is soaked and the milk in our cereal is sour and the shirt we intended to wear is in the laundry and the car won't start, there's not one of us who can avoid thinking, 'This is going to be a rotten day.' There's not one of us who can pick a winner at the track without thinking, 'I knew it!' There's not one of us who can get a call from someone we've just been thinking about without feeling a twinge of pride in our clairvoyant abilities. I have utterly no rational belief in astrology, but if someone reads me my horoscope, a tiny part of me always listens and says, 'Yes, yes, that could happen, that makes sense.'

"You and I might insist that we have no belief in anyone's ability to predict the future, but others are not so snooty and will give ready credence to their psychic reader, their tarot reader, their palm reader, their aura reader, their *I Ching* reader, their dream reader. And this is something that cuts across all cultural lines. Belief in divination is found in every human culture, everywhere in the world. This isn't to say that everyone who looks into the future is practicing magic. Astronomy developed as a means of predicting celestial events. All medical drug research is designed to determine future effects, so that a doctor can say, 'Take this pill three times a day, and in two weeks you'll be better.' Doctors in all cultures are associated with divination, including our own, and we expect them to be trained readers of predictive signs. It doesn't matter whether we're in a Stone-Age village or an atomic-age medical facility, we expect them to say, 'We'll follow this procedure today, then tomorrow you'll be better.' The scientific method is itself fundamentally based on making predictions. 'Theory predicts that doing A, B, and C will result in D. I'll test the theory in this way and see whether this prediction is accurate or not.'

"Because we were born as hunters, we have a genetic craving to know where the track leads and what lies at the end of it. We have an appetite for the future that is as persistent as our appetite for food or sex. To say that it's genetic is of course to propose a theory, but again I see nothing implausible in it. The hunter who's not only hungry but avid to know the future is certainly going to have an edge over the hunter who's just hungry."

"Yes, I'd have to think so."

When the god is with you

"Tell me, Jared, are you a gambler?"

"No, not particularly."

" 'Not particularly.' What does that mean?"

"I guess it means I'm a gambler in a normal, casual way. I'll spend an evening with friends playing penny-ante poker, or if someone wants to go to the track, I'll bet a few dollars just to make it interesting. But I'm not one of those guys who isn't alive if he doesn't have a bet down on *something*."

"You sound like you know a guy like that—a compulsive gambler."

"Yeah, actually I do—my older brother."

"Tell me about him. What's his name?"

"This is Harlan. Harlan's very strange to me, an enigma, a being from another planet."

"Go on."

I sighed and mentally kicked myself for not having answered her original question so as to avoid this line of questioning. "Harlan's just the way I described—not alive if he doesn't have a bet down. His reason for getting up in the morning is to check the scores, to find out how he did during the night. He'll bet on anything, anywhere. He knows *everything*. If there's a football game going on in Melbourne, he can tell you who the players are, who the coaches are, what their records have been for the past five years. But he doesn't love the sports—or the teams. He's just interested in the point spread and the odds—and, of course, in winning."

"Does he lose a lot?"

"No, oddly enough, he doesn't. I know a lot of gamblers brag about their winnings and lie about their losses, but Harlan's honest. And if he didn't win consistently, or at least break even, he would've gone broke long ago, the way he bets. He thinks nothing of dropping ten thousand dollars on a game. If he doesn't have that kind of money at risk, he's not interested."

"It has to hurt if he loses."

"Absolutely. He lives and dies fifty times every day."

Shirin smiled. "And you really don't understand what he sees in that?"

"Well . . . it's one thing to hear about it and another thing to be around it. He was married once—I think it lasted three weeks. He doesn't have friends, he has bookies."

"What does he do for a living—or is he a professional gambler?"

"No, he's a real-estate agent, a specialist in commercial property. He spends his days on the cell phone with clients and bookies and his nights in front of the television switching channels between the games he's down on. If they decided to have a sports-free month, I think he'd have to be hospitalized."

"Doesn't he do any casino gambling?"

"Oh yeah, I forgot that. Casino gambling is for holidays. He spends his vacations in Las Vegas or Atlantic City. They'd have to close the casinos for a month too."

"That wouldn't matter. He'd find something else to bet on. He'd match coins in bars. He'd shoot craps on street corners. He'd bet on the weather, on the elections, on the make of the next car turning the corner, on the number of passengers getting off the next elevator."

"You're right, of course."

"You really don't see that the two of you are brothers in more than a biological sense?"

"No. What sense do *you* see it in?"

"What's at the root of your brother's obsession? You say he lives and dies fifty times a day. What does he live and die fifty times a day to *find out*?"

"He lives and dies fifty times a day to find out if he's *right*."

"No, you're missing the point entirely. If you bet someone that the Nile is longer than the Amazon, then of course the issue is whether you're right. But if you bet someone that the next toss of a coin will turn up heads, being right has nothing to do with it. The issue is, will the universe back you up? If you say heads and it turns up heads, it doesn't mean you're right, it means God is with you. You could just as easily have said tails, and if God wanted you to win, then it would have turned up tails. This is what every compulsive gambler is really trying to find out: 'Are you with me, Lord, or against me?' When Harlan wins, he feels as divinely affirmed as any saint, and when he loses for days on end, he knows the dark night of the soul, and God has abandoned him."

"Okay," I said. "I see what you mean. I remember once, in five-card draw, being dealt the card I needed to fill an inside straight flush. Getting that card was definitely a religious experience. It was like a transfiguration. I expected everyone at the table to be blinded by the divine effulgence that was radiating from me."

"When you call it a religious experience, are you being facetious?"

"Not at all. I suppose it was the kind of experience called oceanic. I was in a state of cosmic transcendence. I felt that the universe in that moment had *taken notice of me*. I was in touch with the fountainhead of meaning and being."

"A religious experience but presumably not a Christian experience."

"No, not a Christian experience."

"This oceanic feeling you describe has often been conjectured to be the source of the religious impulse, but only B traces that oceanic feeling to this patch of ground here in front of us, with its beetle scratchings and mouse scratchings. This is where we first began to reach into a dimension beyond the ken of any other creature on earth, a dimension that is surely not our own domain. But if we can imagine it to be *anyone's* domain, then whose must it be?"

"It must be the domain of the gods."

"To flip a coin and bet on heads is to enter the domain of the gods. To draw a card to a four-card straight flush is to enter the domain of the gods. To read the marks on this patch of earth and begin a hunt is to enter the domain of the gods. And when the coin turns up heads, when the fifth card fills your straight flush, and when the hunt succeeds, it doesn't matter whether you believe in one god, a thousand gods, or no gods at all, you know that the universe has taken notice of you, that you've been in touch with the fountainhead of meaning and being."

The sacred harmonic

"Now you understand—or at least I hope you understand—what I meant about the harmonic I was talking about yesterday. I said that when mental process crossed the border and became human thought, perhaps thought itself began to resound with a harmonic that corresponds to what we call religion or awareness of the sacred."

"Yes. At the time I had no idea what you were getting at. I thought it very unlikely that you'd ever be able persuade me of such a thing."

"And now?"

"And now it makes sense. Human thought is thought that opens up into the future, and the future is inescapably the domain of the gods. Crossing the border, you can't help but meet them."

"And you're in a position now to understand the universality of the animist experience—to understand why there once was a universal religion on this planet. It doesn't matter where you cross the border and meet those gods, the experience is the same. The African experience is not different from the Asian or the European or the Australian or the American. Every hunt begins here"—she patted the ground in front of us—"and is pursued into the domain of the gods."

Dynamiting "Nature"

B asked me to explain again the meaning of our "work of *bricolage*." I picked it up and studied it for a moment. "The fossil shell represents the community of life," I told her. "Animism is bound up with that community and resonates with it. The Law of Life, represented by the pen, is written in the community of life, and animism reads this law, as does science in its own way."

"Good. We've talked about resonance in two connections here, haven't we, Jared? Human thought resounds with a harmonic that corresponds to awareness of the sacred, and animism resonates with the community of life. What's the connection? Are these resonances actually just one resonance?"

"I'd have to guess they're the same."

"They are the same, and once you see this, you'll be ready to articulate the animist vision the way you've articulated the Taker vision."

Having said this, B lapsed into a thoughtful silence. Finally, after a couple minutes, she went on. "Sometimes you have to fill a gap in the road to get people going in the right direction, and sometimes you have to dynamite part of the road to keep them from heading off in the wrong direction—and of course sometimes you have to do both, which is where I am right now with you. I think I'll start with the dynamiting, though I know I don't have nearly enough dynamite or enough time to destroy this section of the road as thoroughly as I'd like.

"You'll see people turn onto this section of the road when they start talking about Nature, which is perceived as being something like the aggregate of processes and phenomena of the nonhuman world—or the power behind those processes and phenomena. As people commonly see it, we Takers have tried to 'control' Nature, have 'alienated' ourselves from Nature, and live 'against' Nature. It's almost impossible for them to understand what B is saying as long as they're in the grip of these useless and misleading ideas.

"Nature is a phantom that sprang entirely from the Great Forgetting, which, after all, is precisely a forgetting of the fact that we are exactly as much a part of the processes and phenomena of the world as any other creature, and if there were such a thing as Nature, we would be as much a part of it as squirrels or squids or mosquitoes or daffodils. We are *unable* to alienate ourselves from Nature or to 'live against' it. We can no more alienate ourselves from Nature than we can alienate ourselves from entropy. We can no more live against Nature than we can live against gravity. On the contrary, what we're seeing here more and more clearly is that the processes and phenomena of the world are working on us in exactly the same way that they

work on all other creatures. Our lifestyle is evolutionarily unstable—
and is therefore in the process of eliminating itself in the perfectly
ordinary way."

"I think I understand all that."

"Even understanding all that, I assure you, people will say to you,
'All the same, don't you think we need to get closer to Nature?' To
me, this is as nonsensical as saying that we need to get closer to the
carbon cycle."

"I understand. On the other hand, some people do like to be
outdoors."

"That's fine, of course—so long as they don't insist that sitting in
a forest glade is 'closer to Nature' than sitting in a movie theater."

Through the eyes of deer

"No one would ever think of saying that a duck or an earthworm is
'close to Nature,' and it's similarly true that our animist ancestors
were not 'close to Nature.' They *were* Nature—were a part of the
general community of life. They belonged to that community as fully
as moths and skunks and lizards belong to it—as fully and, I might
add, as thoughtlessly. I mean they didn't congratulate themselves for
belonging to it, they took it for granted. The same is true of modern
Leaver peoples. They don't belong to this community of life as a
matter of principle or because they think it's right or noble or 'good
for the children' or 'good for the planet.' I point this out to drag my
feet against the current tendency to angelize them, which I personally
think is no better than demonizing them the way our great-grandpar-
ents did. They don't need to be angelized. They do indeed have a
lifestyle that's healthier for people and healthier for the planet, but
they don't hold on to it because they're noble, they hold on to it for
the best reason in the world—because they prefer it to ours and would
rather be dead than live the way we do."

I nodded to let her know I was with her so far.

"Living in the community of life did give them something we've
lost, which is a complete understanding of where we come from.
Children in our culture think that life comes to us from our human
parents and that food is just another product we manufacture, like

paint or plastic or glass. Children in hunting-gathering cultures know that life doesn't come to us only from our parents. It comes to us just as truly from all the living things we subsist on. These plants and animals aren't products any more than we are, and if we live in the hand of the god, then so do they in exactly the same way."

She shook her head, obviously dissatisfied. "There are some things prose just can't handle, Jared. Let me address this to Louis."

She closed her eyes. "The people I learned the Law of Life from, Louis, are the people who actually gave the law that name, the Ihalmiut Eskimos, who lived in the Great Barrens of Canada, inside the Arctic Circle. Theirs was a strange life by our standards, but its strangeness makes it very easy for us to comprehend. The Ihalmiut were the People of the Deer. They were this because deer was what they lived on. They were completely dependent on the deer, because other animals were rare, and vegetation that's edible by humans is practically nonexistent inside the Arctic Circle. It's hard to imagine living entirely on meat—never a piece of bread, never a piece of chocolate, never a banana or a peach or an ear of corn—but they did and were perfectly healthy and happy.

"They'd never have to explain who and what they were to their own children, but if they did, they'd say something like this: 'We know you look at us and call us men and women, but this is only our appearance, for we're not men and women, we're deer. The flesh that grows on our bones is the flesh of deer, for it's made from the flesh of the deer we've eaten. The eyes that move in our heads are the eyes of deer, and we look at the world in their stead and see what they might have seen. The fire of life that once burned in the deer now burns in us, and we live their lives and walk in their tracks across the hand of god. This is why we're the People of the Deer. The deer aren't our prey or our possessions—they're us. They're us at one point in the cycle of life and we're them at another point in the cycle. The deer are twice your parents, for your mother and father are deer, and the deer that gave you its life today was mother and father to you as well, since you wouldn't be here if it weren't for that deer.' "

She opened her eyes and glanced at me—a signal, I assumed, that she was once again addressing me rather than her son.

"This perception of our kindredness with the rest of the community of life is fundamental to the animist vision, Jared, though it's naturally very mysterious and improbable to people of our culture. Everyone should spend some time with the cave paintings of the Upper Paleolithic—and I don't mean as an exercise in art appreciation. To identify these paintings as art as we understand it is to look at them very cursorily. They're magnificent and brilliant, but they weren't done for the sort of motives that we attribute to painters like Giotto or El Greco or Rembrandt or Goya or Picasso or de Kooning. Nor is there really any reason to suppose that they were painted as magical hunting aids. What's clear from examination is that these are hunting guides—visual aids for hunting instruction. For example, again and again, instead of being shown in profile—the way the rest of the animal is shown—the animal's feet are turned up to show the track-making surface they present to the ground. Another way of showing the same thing is to paint the animal's track right on its picture or beside it, and this too is seen again and again. Attention is paid to animal droppings and to what animals look like when they're producing those droppings (which I suppose is an activity hunters can take advantage of). Attention is paid to animals rolling on the ground, making wallows, and digging up the ground—all important signs for the hunter. Animals are shown in association with plants they feed on ('find the plant, find the animal'), with animals that prey on them ('follow the predator, find the prey'), and with symbiotic species ('follow the swallows, find the bison'). Attention is paid to animals making characteristic roars and bellows. Attention is paid to what you're likely to see if most of an animal is hidden by rocks or tall grass—a pair of antlers, a distinctive hump. Attention is paid to seasonal cues to behavior—'when the salmon are jumping like this, look for the stags to be on the move as well.' These caves aren't art galleries or shamanistic temples, they're schools of the hunting arts—the equivalent of one of our museums of science and industry."

After trying to digest all this, I told her I was confused. "You brought up the caves as if spending time in them would convince anyone that our hunting ancestors felt a kindredness with the rest of the living community."

"And here I am stripping away all the magical aspects of the paintings."

"That's right."

"I'll stand by the recommendation. I guess I'm not talking about magic, I'm talking about something like 'feeling tone.' These hunters obviously revered the animals they were painting—were in awe of them, idolized them the way people in our culture idolize movie stars and sports heroes. To paint them the way they did, they had to feel a joyous involvement and identification with the magnificent creatures they hunted. But I can see you're still not much convinced by all this. It's difficult to be persuasive in the absence of the paintings themselves. Have you ever seen a reproduction of one that's usually called *The Sorcerer*?"

"I think I have, though I don't recall it in any detail."

"It's conventionally interpreted as a shaman wearing a ritual mask, but you have to be pretty literal-minded (and not much of an anatomist) to see him this way. He has the antlers and body of a stag, the ears of a lion, the face of an owl, and the tail and genitals of a horse—and there's not the slightest indication that he's wearing a mask. I believe he's unique in Paleolithic art in that he doesn't just inhabit the plane on which he's painted. He does something no other man or creature does; he looks out of the plane on which he's painted and gazes into our eyes—with his strange owl eyes. The rule in conventional cinematic narrative is that the actor must never, ever look directly into the 'eye' of the camera, because if he does that, this shatters the illusion that he's interacting with the other people we see on the screen. If he looks into the camera, he's suddenly interacting with *us.* The man-beast on the wall of Les Trois Frères cave is unquestionably interacting with us—introducing himself graphically in the absence of text: 'Here,' he's saying, 'you can see what I am—I'm not just a man. I wouldn't be nearly so marvelous if I were just a man. Look closely and you'll see man, horse, owl, lion, and stag. I'm a compound of all these, and have you ever seen anything more beautiful?' "

I smiled, shrugged, and shook my head. "I guess I just like the way you said it better than the way these guys painted it."

She shrugged back. "Lillian Hellman once said something that surprised me: 'Nothing you write will ever come out the way you hoped it would.' Not her exact words but something like that. It surprised me because I thought, 'Hey, you're in complete control of what goes on the page, so why shouldn't it come out the way you want it to?' I suppose the answer is that what we hope to achieve is always beyond human power. We want to make the earth tremble and the stones weep and the skies open up. I wanted to do that for you here, right now, but I know I haven't."

For a moment I almost thought this was an odd sort of ambition for anyone to have. Then I remembered myself as a young man. My own ambitions had not been so different, but they'd grown dry and insubstantial, and the winds and rains of time had eroded them to almost nothing.

The web endlessly woven

"I said I was going to be selective in what I revealed to you about the Leaver lifestyle, so you'd be able to articulate the animist vision as easily as you were able to articulate our own vision."

"I remember."

"I told you this little patch of dirt here in front of us is where it all begins—human thought, human awareness of the sacred, and human history—but as many times as I've come back to it, I don't think I've ever been completely forthright with you. I've been diffident. I haven't spelled it out—because, I suppose, in spite of everything, I fear the sneering superiority of your kind."

I didn't want to ask what kind "my kind" is (and probably didn't need to, either). Instead I made the mistake of asking her if she'd ever actually seen me sneering.

"Many times, I'm afraid. I know you're not aware of it, and I know you try to suppress it, but I also know this isn't easy for some-one with your intellectual and cultural indoctrination."

"I'm sorry," I said, inadequately. "Profoundly."

"I know it. Charles knew it too. Otherwise you wouldn't be here."

I pondered that for a while and finally said, "I guess if you want me to do what you say you want me to do, then you're going to have to say the things you're afraid to say."

"You're right, of course," she said, "and I know it."

"Say them to Louis, if that helps. In a way, it helps me too."

"Okay, I'll do that when I have to," she said. "Meanwhile . . . An hour ago—I don't know if you'll remember it—I told you we became human reading the tale of events written *here*—here in the hand of the god. And I showed you my own hand, like this. Do you know what I meant by that?"

"I'm not sure."

"Do you see these marks in my hand?"

"Of course."

"I'm comparing them to *these* marks." She indicated the tracks of the beetle and the mouse. "Both sets of marks are tracks—marks left by the passage of life. It's my notion—and of course it's just a notion—that these tracks, found here in the hand and here on the ground, gave rise to the notion that we live in the hand of the god of this place."

She reached out and dragged her forefinger across the track of the beetle.

"Shirin's mark," she said. "Like the beetle and the mouse, once upon a time, I was here. And if another comes to study these marks, he or she will say, 'All three were here, at different times, all held in the hand of the god—and all still held in the hand of the god though they're no longer right here.' Every track begins and ends in the hand of god, and every track is a lifetime long. Hunter and hunted are both standing in their tracks when they meet, and there are no tracks, however far-flung, that fall outside the hand of god. All paths lie together like a web endlessly woven, and yours and mine are no greater or less than the beetle's or the mouse's. All are held together.

"These are things I'd like to say to Louis. We make our journey in the company of others. The deer, the rabbit, the bison, and the quail walk before us, and the lion, the eagle, the wolf, the vulture, and the hyena walk behind us. All our paths lie together in the hand of god and none is wider than any other or favored above any other. The worm that creeps beneath your foot is making its journey across the hand of god as surely as you are.

"Remember that your tracks are one strand of the web woven endlessly in the hand of god. They're tied to those of the mouse in the field, the eagle on the mountain, the crab in its hold, the lizard beneath its rock. The leaf that falls to the ground a thousand miles away touches your life. The impress of your foot in the soil is felt through a thousand generations."

In the sea of grass

"I'm at the end of my strength for now, Jared, but I want to take one more field trip before we call it a day. This will be a mental one, so you won't have to put on your Natty Bumppo hat. Where did you grow up?" I told her Ohio. "I've never been there, but it can't be entirely different from where I grew up, out in the Great Plains. It's not all cornfields, even today. I want you to travel with me to a place I remember as a child, a plains wilderness. . . . Once when I was a kid I remember watching an old western movie on TV called *The Sea of Grass*. I don't know what it was about. All I remember is one scene where Spencer Tracy looks out over this vast sea of grass stretching from horizon to horizon, and the wind's stirring it up and sending it into waves just like the sea. The place I'm talking about wasn't as huge as that, but it was the same *kind* of place. Close your eyes and see if you can picture such a place.

"The important thing to realize is that this isn't grass, Jared. This is deer and bison and sheep and cicadas and moles and rabbits. Reach down and grab a handful. Go ahead—at least mentally. Have you got it? That's a mouse. And the mouse, the ox, the gazelle, the goat, and the beetle all burn with the fire of grass, Jared. Grass is their mother and father, and their young are grass.

"One thing: grass and grasshopper. One thing: grasshopper and sparrow. One thing: sparrow and fox. One thing: fox and vulture. One thing, Jared, and its name is fire, burning today as a stalk in the field, tomorrow as a rabbit in its burrow, and the next day as an eleven-year-old girl named Shirin.

"The vulture is fox; the fox, grasshopper; the grasshopper, rabbit; the rabbit, girl; the girl, grass. All together, we're the life of this place, indistinguishable from one another, intermingling in the flow of fire, and the fire is god—not God with a capital *G*, but rather one of the gods with a little *g*. Not the creator of the universe but the animator of this single place. To each of us is given its moment in the blaze,

Jared, its spark to be surrendered to another when it's sent, so that the blaze may go on. None may deny its spark to the general blaze and live forever—not any at all. Certainly not me, for all my giant intellect. Each—each!—is sent to another someday. You are sent, Jared—Louis. You're on your way, both of you. I too am sent. To the wolf or the cougar or the vulture or the beetles or the grasses, I am sent. I'm sent and I thank you all, grasses in all your forms—fire in all your forms—sparrows and rabbits and mosquitoes and butterflies and salmon and rattlesnakes, for sharing yourselves with me for this time, and I'm bringing it all back, every last atom, paid in full, and I appreciate the loan.

"My death will be the life of another, Jared—I swear that to you. And you watch, you come find me, because I'll be standing again in these grasses and you'll see me looking through the eyes of the fox and taking the air with the eagle and running in the track of the deer."

The secrets

"These are our secret teachings, Jared. I know Charles told you that secret teachings are ones that teachers have a hard time giving away. Do you see now why this is so?"

"Yes."

"The Leaver peoples of the world have been trying to tell you these things for centuries, but they still remain secrets. Certainly *we* haven't hidden them—far from it. We're not like high-degree members of the Freemasons or the Templars or the Ku Klux Klan, whispering secrets in locked rooms and exacting promises of silence from those who hear them. Wherever people behave that way, you can be sure they're guarding either very paltry secrets or simple matters of fact, like where the Allies planned to invade Europe at the end of World War Two. Real secrets can be kept by publishing them on billboards."

By this time we were walking back to the car.

B said, "When we began this process, you offered this as the Taker vision: *The world was made for Man, and Man was made to conquer and rule it.* Have I given you enough to articulate the Leaver, or animist, vision?"

"I think so."

We walked on, and, thankfully, she didn't prompt me. Finally, as the street came in sight I paused and said, "This is the best I can do. It doesn't seem very elegant to me."

"It won't cause the ground to tremble."

"No. Nor will the stones weep or the heavens open up."

"I know what you mean, Jared, I really do."

"The world is a sacred place and a sacred process," I told her, "and we're part of it."

"That's excellent, Jared, simple and to the point. This is what was understood—and is still understood among Leaver peoples. Wherever you went in the world, you found people who took it for granted that the world is a sacred place, and that we belong in that sacred place as much as any other creature in the world." Smiling, she looked around the park, as if giving it a silent farewell. Then she included me in the smile as she said, "Maybe *someday* someone will find a way to say it that makes the ground tremble."

The fossil

About halfway back to the hotel, I said, "You were going to tell me what Charles had in mind with the ammonite fossil he gave me."

"Oh yes." She drove on for a couple of blocks, then pulled over and parked. "Charles was much better than I am with this aspect of things. He would have sat you down and made you *see* how past, present, and future were woven together at that little patch of ground. He would have shown you that you really could read the future from the signs you saw there. Nothing magical. As I said myself, we're all involved in reading the future all the time. He was fond of pointing out that our fascination with the hunt hasn't disappeared in modern times, it's just found a new object—the mystery story, where all the classic talents come into play: observation, deduction, forecasting, cunning, stealth, and alertness."

"What does this have to do with the fossil?"

"Where is it?"

I dug it out and handed it to her.

"I suspect he planned to ask you the future of this fossil, which is at least sixty million years older than the human race. That's an awful lot of its past that you know. What do you know of its future?"

"Nothing at all."

She laughed and shook her head. "I'm sure he could have predicted that answer without any difficulty."

"I'm sure he could," I said, a bit miffed.

"Come on," she said, getting out and going round to the trunk, where she took out a tire iron and handed it to me.

"What am I supposed to do with this?"

She walked over to the curb, sat down, and, when I joined her, she set the fossil between us and told me to smash it to bits.

"I won't," I told her.

"No, go ahead."

"I won't," I told her again. "Why do you want me to do that?"

"I want to show you how to read the future," she said—half laughing, it seemed to me.

I picked up the fossil, returned the tire iron to the trunk, and got back in the car.

"Charles would have done it better," she said as we drove off. "The point of the exercise needs to be more fully developed."

I snorted contemptuously.

"Charles would have got you to smash it."

"Bah," I said, unable to think of anything better.

B laughed—to me, in my besotted state, a sweeter sound than birdsong.

At the hotel

I told B not to expect me at the theater tonight, which is just as well, since it took me till eleven o'clock to finish the foregoing.

I'm now going to go down to the bar, have a couple of drinks, and think about absolutely nothing for an hour. Then, for a very great change, I'm going to have a normal night's sleep. Tomorrow night Shirin addresses the public as B for the first time. I'm frankly fascinated to know how it'll turn out.

part
three

Date unknown

They tell me I'm in a hospital.
They tell me I've been here three days.
They tell me I have a concussion.
They tell me bruised ribs hurt more than broken ribs.
They tell me I was in an explosion.
They tell me the theater exploded.
They tell me the reason for the explosion is unknown.
They tell me it's buried under a zillion tons of rubble.
They tell me it was probably a gas explosion.
They tell me it happened around six in the evening.
They tell me the theater was empty at the time.
They tell me no one ever lived there.
They tell me this is a ridiculous idea.
They tell me they won't dig up a zillion tons of rubble.
They tell me no bodies would be found.
They tell me no one has been reported missing.
They tell me no one has tried to visit me.
They tell me no one has called except Fr. Lulfre.
They tell me I talked to him the day after the explosion.
They tell me I forgot this because I have a concussion.
They tell me I talked to him yesterday.
They tell me I forgot this because I have a concussion.
They tell me this condition will "almost certainly" pass.
They tell me I may someday remember the explosion.
They tell me I may never remember the explosion.
They tell me I'll fly home as soon as I'm strong enough.
They tell me I may be strong enough day after tomorrow.
They tell me all my belongings are in the closet.
They tell me they brought them from my hotel room.
They tell me all my notebooks are intact.

They tell me I shouldn't be looking at them now.
They tell me I shouldn't be writing in them now.
They tell me I shouldn't be getting excited now.
They tell me I shouldn't be worrying now.
They tell me I shouldn't be thinking now.
They tell me I should be resting now.
They tell me I should be taking it easy now.
They tell me it's time for an injection.
I tell them I need to keep my notebook.
They tell me my notebook will not get lost.
I tell them I need to remember what I've written here.
They tell me it'll be right here when I wake up.
They give me the injection.
I start taking it easy.

Date unknown

It appears that this was actually written by me.

Date unknown

I, Jared Osborne, write this down for Jared Osborne for when you wake up in the middle of the night, as you seem to do, and you don't know where the hell you are. The preceding pages, beginning "They tell me I'm in a hospital," were also written by me for when you wake up in the middle of the night—but I don't remember writing them any more than I will remember writing *this* the next time I wake up in the middle of the night and find it sitting on the table beside the bed.

Date unknown

This is concussion. That's what you have to get fixed firmly in your head. You have a concussion and for the time being your long-term memory is out to lunch. We hope it's "for the time being"—all of us Jareds who read and write in this notebook. The doctors who patiently tell us their names every day and that we regularly forget every day, assure us that very probably this is a temporary condition.

May 31

Apparently I sleep a great deal. I have no idea whether it's for hours or for days. Now, when I wake up, I reach automatically for this notebook. I don't remember what's in it, but I do remember that it has the answers.

I think the idea is, even if my long-term memory never returns, this notebook can serve as a kind of cumulative record. I've collected a lot of information in the last hour, which I should put down here.

To begin with, I'm back in the United States. (I keep wanting to say *we*, meaning the Jared who is writing this entry and all the Jareds who will read it in days to come.) I'm at what seminarians used to call "the Company Farm," which is where you go when you "need a little rest"—or a little vacation from booze—or the whispers about you and the altar boys are beginning to get a bit noisy. All the big orders have them, of course, some of them have several, thoughtfully specialized. Naturally they're not called penitentiaries anymore; nowadays they're called retreat centers. This one is located in the rolling countryside about a hundred miles south of St. Jerome's.

I found this out by picking up the phone on my bedside table. Apparently I always do this. Tim, the young man who answered (I don't know that he's young, but he sounds young), told me to read the entries in my notebook, and I told him I'd already done that. Then he told me where I was, that I'd been here for two days, that it was two o'clock in the morning (evidently my favorite time for calling), May 31.

What he calls "the accident" happened "about a week ago." If he's right, then the explosion must have occurred Saturday, the day Shirin was scheduled to speak at the theater. But Saturday seems impossible in light of what I recorded that "they" first told me, probably in Radenau. If it happened on Friday I wouldn't have been there, since I was planning on a good night's sleep after spending the day in the park with B. Therefore I conclude that it probably happened on Sunday.

Tim knows nothing whatever about the explosion except that I was pulled out of the rubble and reportedly was deemed lucky to be alive.

I asked him how to get an outside line and was told I'd have to talk to Dr. Emerson about that. I told him I just wanted to call my mother and let her know I'm all right, but he said I'd have to talk to Dr. Emerson about that. I asked him what other kinds of patients are in this ward, and he said I'd have to ask Dr. Emerson a question like that. I asked him if he could send someone in to talk to me, and he said it was the middle of the night and he'd come himself but he had to stay at the desk. I asked him if I could come find him, and he said this would not be a good idea at this time of night but he'd be glad to talk to me as long as I wanted, on the phone.

I asked him if this is like a regular hospital, and he said no, not really, because there's no one here with, like, you know, diseases, like cancer or pneumonia or appendicitis. This is more like a nursing home, he says.

I asked him if he could make a call for me, and he said only if Dr. Emerson okayed it. I asked him if I'd had any visitors and he said he was pretty sure I hadn't. I asked if any visitors were expected, and he said there might be but he wouldn't necessarily know about it very far in advance. I asked if anyone was asking about me, and he said oh, sure, they call every day to see how you're doing. I asked who that was, and he said he doesn't know.

I said I was surprised they'd moved me from Germany.

He said, "Well, you don't have any problem functioning, you know. You just forget you've done it. Like now. Everything you're saying makes sense, but when you wake up in the morning, you probably won't remember saying it. You're not unconscious or any-thing, you just forget. Like, you've forgotten that we've already had this conversation three times."

"We've already talked about all this three times before?"

"Twice last night and this is the third time."

"I don't think I'll forget this time."

"Good, I hope not. That's what you said the last time, though."

I told him I'd tie a string around my finger, and he laughed.

He laughed, but he doesn't know the really funny part, which is that there is already a string tied around it.

Saturday, June 1

Morning

All the same, when I woke up, I remembered that conversation with Tim. I've lost a week almost to the hour.

I had to wait till noon to get in to see Dr. Emerson, who was pretty much what I'd pictured him to be and pretty much what I suppose he has to be to run a joint like this: old enough to be authoritative but not a senior citizen, unflappable, unimpressible, unsnowable, unmovable—but perfectly friendly and willing to hear you out.

I said I wanted to talk to Fr. Lulfre, and was surprised to learn that Fr. Lulfre was expected to arrive at the center today in time for dinner.

Like Tim, Dr. Emerson knew nothing about the "accident." When I asked for permission to call Germany, he asked who I wanted to talk to. I was prepared for the question, and offered him a piece of paper with three names on it. The incredible truth is, I don't know Shirin's last name. We were never formally introduced and there was never a moment when it would have been appropriate to ask. I know Michael's last name—to hear it—but it could just as easily be spelled Dzerjinski or Dyurzhinsky as the way I heard it, Dershinsky. Without a first name, Frau Doktor Hartmann was unfindable. So the three people named on the list were Monika and Heinz Teitel and Gustl Meyer, the owner of the "leftovers" shop, Überbleibselen.

Dr. Emerson glanced at the names and observed that it must be the middle of the night in Germany.

"No, actually, it's just midevening—the best time to call."

"Do you speak enough German to deal with an operator?"

When I said no, he did something that impressed the hell out of me. Without a moment's hesitation, he picked up the phone and started punching buttons. Within sixty seconds he had the German country code, the Radenau city code, and had exerted enough force of will to get himself an operator who spoke English. When he had the numbers, the operator asked him if he wanted to be connected, and he said yes, try Gustl Meyer. When there was no answer there, the operator tried the Teitels' number. When the phone was answered, Dr. Emerson asked if this was Monika Teitel. Evidently the answer was yes, because he shoved the phone at me.

I said, "Monika, is that you? This is Fr. Jared Osborne. We met in the basement of the theater . . . ?"

"Oh yes," she said. "What do you want?"

It was just as uncordial as it looks. I said, "I'm calling from the United States. You know I was in the explosion. . . ."

"Yes?"

"Monika, I'm trying to find out what happened."

"The theater was exploded."

"I know, I was there, but I was hit in the head and I don't remember anything. What I'm trying to find out is, was anybody down there in the—"

The phone was set down with a clatter.

I waited through a painful minute until I heard the receiver being scraped up again.

"Everyone is dead," Monika said.

"What? No!"

"I asked Heinz, and he says everyone is dead."

"But I was told the theater was empty!"

I heard her say "Here!" and another voice came on the line— Heinz's.

"What do you want?" he said. "All are dead."

"No! Heinz, I was told the theater was empty."

"Who tells you this?"

"I was told this in the hospital. They said no one was looking for bodies because the theater was empty."

"*Ja,* so. They tell you."

"Do you *know* that Shirin was there?"

I heard a muffled exchange between the two.

"I hang up now," Heinz said.

"No, wait! Can you tell me Shirin's last name? Her surname?"

Heinz thought for a moment before saying, "You should be there too."

Then he hung up.

Afternoon

I spent the next three hours in bed, and the thoughts I thought don't need to be recorded here.

Around four o'clock some being knocked and made his way in and introduced himself chummily as Fr. Joe. He wanted to know if he should schedule a spot for me in the chapel.

I said, "What?"

"Tomorrow's Sunday, Father," he said to me. "I assume you'll be saying Mass."

"I will *not* be saying Mass," I told him.

Fr. Joe disappeared as if whisked offstage like a puppet on strings.

So at least that much has been settled. I've reached and passed the fiftieth degree of losing my faith.

Evening

Tim, my middle-of-the-night confidant, is a Native American, built along the lines of a sumo wrestler. This is a summer job for him. During the school year he's a student at junior college in a town nearby. Not having eaten all day, I was starved, and he directed me to the dining room, which I took one look at and decided I couldn't stand right now—too bright and too much conversation that people would want to include me in.

I went back and asked Tim if I could get a tray sent over, and he said sure, nothing easier.

I told him I was expecting a visitor from St. Jerome's University by the name of Fr. Lulfre, and he asked how he'd be arriving. I told him I supposed by car.

Tim looked through his papers and asked if he'd be spending the night.

"I assume so."

He shook his head. "I don't think so," he said. "They're pretty careful about letting us know this stuff, and there's no Fr. Lulfre down here."

"He's expected for dinner."

Tim shrugged and repeated that he didn't think so.

I went back to my room and, with nothing better to do till my tray arrived, decided to take stock and see how many of my belongings had gone south while I was going west. Amazingly, except for my billfold, with all my cash and credit cards, every last thing seemed to be there, including my passport. I called Tim, and he confirmed my suspicion that the billfold was under lock and key in the office, "for safekeeping."

The item of greatest interest was the tape recorder, which had a tape in it that had been run forward an hour or so. After I'd eaten and returned the tray, I rewound the tape and hit the play button, mentally crossing my fingers and holding my breath. The first second confirmed my hopes: It was a tape of Shirin's speech at the theater on May 25. I stopped the tape to consider the fact that, if Heinz Teitel was right, these would be the last words I'd ever hear from her. The thought did me no good one way or another. I pushed the play button and listened.*

Following my usual practice of letting review material go by unrecorded, I had evidently turned the tape on in the middle of the speech. It's not easy to summarize what I felt on hearing what she had to say. She put it all together at last. I had no idea what the talk was "officially" called. I knew it could only be called "The Great Remembering." This was it, the fulfillment of the promise—and it left me with only about a million questions.

But there was one thing I finally understood beyond a shadow of a doubt, and that was why both Charles and Shirin declined to formulate a defense against the charge of being the Antichrist. I was disappointed in myself that I'd been so dense about it, that I'd failed to hear what they were telling me and what Fr. Lulfre was telling me. At any rate, I finally understood why, when I said that B seemed harmless, Fr. Lulfre's reply was, "That can't be right."

---

* The text of this speech will be found on pages 305–323.

Indeed, it wasn't right.

I've made a written copy of the speech. In these uncertain circumstances no precautions are excessive.

Obviously Fr. Lulfre didn't turn up here tonight—or if he did he's been asleep for hours.

Three A.M.

I finally figured out why I can't get to sleep. I'm going to have to learn to think more like a fugitive. I'm too used to being passive and trusting. It took me two hours of tossing and turning to get the point, which is that this is a potentially disastrous situation for me.

I don't know why Fr. Lulfre failed to show up tonight, but I'm damned glad he didn't, because there couldn't possibly be a worse place for me to confront him. If he wanted to, he could lock me up here and throw away the key. I've got to get out of here *right now* and hope to intercept him on more favorable ground. Luckily, if there's a wing of this place that's high security, this isn't it. I think I could make my way out with nothing but the essentials (recorder, notebooks, tapes, and passport), but a hundred-mile trip with nothing but lint in my pockets is not an appealing prospect. I should at least make a try at persuading Tim to liberate just one credit card from my billfold in the safe.

Monday, June 3

The fugitive at 35,000 feet

So that's that. Between now and Hamburg I've got a lovely bunch of hours ahead of me in which to sleep and bring this journal up to date—and in a nice, roomy first-class seat, since no other was available on this flight. The Laurentians won't notice the difference, and surely they must expect to send off their apostates with a little Visa Golden handshake.

Though it took the better part of two hours, Tim was persuadable. I may be dumb, but nobody ever said I didn't know how to make myself understood. I made a stab at getting him to throw in the keys to his car, but no, he wouldn't go that far. It took a couple more hours, but I did finally manage to hitch a ride. Priests have to cultivate an innocent, harmless look, which comes in handy on the road (as every serial killer knows). Once I got to an automatic teller machine, I was home free.

I reached Fr. Lulfre's office at eleven o'clock in the morning, and by God, there he was, just where I'd left him almost a month ago—something I hadn't exactly counted on, since it was Sunday.

He looked up at me from behind his desk, plainly astounded, and said, "You didn't have to do this, Jared. I was planning to come see you today."

He actually didn't get it; he thought I'd jumped the wall out of mere impatience to be near him.

"I'm here for a reckoning, Fr. Lulfre."

He capped his pen and set it aside—nice, well-thought-out moves.

"A reckoning, eh? You sound like the staunch hero of some turn-of-the-century melodrama."

"Different century," I said, sitting down, "but that's the idea."

"What is it you want reckoned?"

"I'll tell you what I remember, then you can tell me the rest."

"All right."

"They said I might or might not eventually remember the explosion, but all I remember right now is a little flash. For a while I thought it was something I'd dreamed, and maybe it is, but I don't think so. Do you know the setup in the theater?"

"Yes."

"Your man in Radenau laid it out for you."

Fr. Lulfre nodded, then added, "Our man in Europe, actually."

"This is the elderly person who introduced himself to me as Herr Reichmann?"

"That's right."

"Why didn't you tell me you already had a man on the ground there?"

He shrugged. "It's always better if you think it's all up to you."

"Then why did he phone me with instructions?"

"He got impatient. Professionals always get impatient with amateurs. You know that."

I shook my head. "Why did you send me at all?"

"We sent you for exactly the reasons I gave you." He smiled briefly. "For *almost* exactly the reasons I gave you. Under his real name, Reichmann maintains perfectly respectable offices in Berlin, Prague, and Paris and works on retainer for a dozen different firms and individuals, mostly in the U.S. He's a very useful, knowledgeable person, and ninety-nine percent of the chores we give him are routine and innocuous, but when we asked him to look into Charles Atterley for us, he showed a side we hadn't seen before. His approach was, 'I can't make out what the blighter is saying, so why don't I just shoot him and be done with it?' Whatever you may think of us after this dreadful experience, Jared, absolutely no one considered taking such advice. We had to send someone of our own to have a look at Atterley, and believe me, we very much wanted you to persuade us that he was harmless."

"And I failed to do that."

"It was out of your hands, really. He was condemned from his own mouth by the speeches you faxed to us."

"And you actually authorized his assassination?"

The man shrugged. "You said it very well, Jared: These days are still those days. Nothing's changed in the last five hundred years—or the last thousand—except that heretics can no longer be executed in public. I take all this as seriously as Pope Innocent the Third, who ordered up a crusade against the Albigenses. I take it all as seriously as Pius the Fifth, who, when he was the grand inquisitor, personally instigated the massacre of thousands of Protestants in southern Italy. I take it all as seriously as Thomas Aquinas, who said, 'If ordinary criminals may be justly put to death, then how much more may heretics be justly slain.' For Thomas well knew that the murderer just shortens his neighbors' temporal life, whereas the heretic deprives them of eternal life. If you no longer understand the difference—or if it no longer matters to you—then I assume you've lost your faith."

"You assume rightly, Father. I'm afraid it's fallen to the modernist fallacy."

"I'm sorry to hear it," he said, and I could see that he sincerely meant it.

"Since you quoted me about 'these days still being those days,' I assume the resourceful Herr Reichmann had the theater bugged."

"Of course he did. It was an obvious thing to do. Atterley and his followers were just too incredibly trusting to survive for very long as subversives."

"Yes, they were. So you knew they were recruiting me."

"Yes. That was an unexpected bonus, and you handled it just right."

"Except that I ended up recruited."

"Yes—except for that." He frowned for a moment, then looked up. "You say you now remember the explosion?"

"I said I remember a little flash. I'm looking up out of a well at Herr Reichmann, who's looking down into the well at me. I think this was the stairwell at the theater."

"That's right. That's all you remember?"

I nodded.

"I'm not exactly sure what happened there. Reichmann's story is that you blundered into him on the stairs moments before the bomb was to go off. Evidently you assumed he was up to no good and wouldn't let him talk you into leaving the theater with him, and when you headed down the stairs to warn the others, he slugged you and left you to your fate. This was relatively lucky for you, since that iron staircase was the only structure that survived both the blast and the collapse of the roof."

"You don't think it actually happened that way?"

"It may have happened that way. All I know for certain is that this is what Reichmann wants us to believe, and we're in no position to contradict him."

There was nothing for it now but to ask the question I dreaded to ask: "Did Reichmann tell you who was in the theater when it was destroyed?"

"He indicated that he got everyone."

I stared at him bleakly.

"His exact words were, 'The inner circle is gone.'"

I said, "Everyone else seems to think the theater was empty."

Fr. Lulfre shrugged.

"Well, he missed one—me."

He shook his head. "Jared, you know I think highly of you, but you're not a charismatic firebrand."

"I don't think being a firebrand has anything to do with it."

Again he shrugged.

"You know, I couldn't figure out why B insisted on putting his entire schedule on hold while he dealt with me. It made even less sense after Charles's death. Do you know what I'm talking about?"

"No, frankly, I don't. What is it that made less sense after Charles's death?"

"Why B insisted on spending so much time with me."

Fr. Lulfre started to tell me that he didn't know what in the world I was talking about, then the light dawned. "You're talking about the woman . . . Sharon?"

"Shirin," I told him. "Shirin is B."

"I thought Charles was B."

"Charles *was* B, but so was Shirin."

He shook his massive head, shooing away a bothersome fly.

"B had to spend time with me so that, even if worse came to worst, you could be told that you've failed."

"You're being far too elliptical for this old brain, Jared. If worse came to worst?"

"If you succeeded in killing both Charles and Shirin."

"If I succeeded in killing both Charles and Shirin, then I still will have failed?"

"That's right. Because you didn't kill me. I'm not a charismatic firebrand, but that doesn't matter. I am B."

"You are B? You really believe that?"

"It's not a matter of belief, Father. I'm no longer what I was when I sat here three and a half weeks ago—and you can't change me back to what I was."

Fr. Lulfre leaned forward, interested at last. "And you really think this matters, Jared? You think you'll do something different, now that you're B?"

"Oh yes," I told him, getting to my feet. "There's no question about that. That's a certainty."

"I'm not sure whether to scoff or to shudder, Jared. But if I had a gun in my desk, I'd take it out and shoot you dead just to be on the safe side."

"Would you really?"

"Yes, I would. Do you remember your friend Shirin's last speech at the theater a week ago? Or did you lose that along with the explosion?"

"I lost it, but I listened to a tape of it yesterday."

"I didn't know that," he said heavily. "At any rate, Reichmann made a tape of it as well, and played it for me on the phone. That was what . . ." He spread his hands wide in a gesture of helplessness.

"That was what sealed her fate," I suggested.

"Yes, that's right. You see, she showed me more clearly than any advocate of ecumenism why we are a confraternity, Jared—we Christians, Jews, Muslims, Buddhists, Hindus. We've drawn ourselves up from the slime in which animism grovels so proudly. We represent what is highest, what is most upward reaching, transcendental, and sublime in mankind. What stands between the members of the confraternity are minor rifts. What stands between the confraternity and animism is a gulf as wide as the gulf between Man and brute, spirit and matter."

"I agree."

"What will you do now?"

I took the tape recorder out of my pocket and showed him that it was running. "First, I'll find a safe place for this tape, Father. You called us too incredibly trusting to be conspirators, but you're pretty trusting yourself."

"You're quite right, Jared. None of us has been trained to look at the world with suspicious eyes. But you won't turn it over to the police."

"Certainly not. This is my safe-conduct for at least as long as you're alive. Once the police have it, it's worthless for that purpose."

He nodded. "Yes, you'll definitely want to find a very safe place for that."

I left, and because it seemed like to good time to start being a little less incredibly trusting, I didn't turn my back on him till I was outside with the door shut between us.

Tuesday, June 4

Radenau revisited

I'm installed in my old room at the hotel, and it feels rather eerie. The desk clerk acknowledged my appearance without surprise, allowing himself the liberty of hoping I was now completely restored after my "unpleasant experience" of nearly being blown to bits.

I arrived early enough to do a little useful groundwork. I picked up a few necessities like underwear and shaving equipment and spent some time with telephone directories at the library. I managed to place a display ad in the local paper asking Shirin or Michael to contact me. Naturally the ad takers would accept nothing but real money, so tomorrow I'll have to see if this piece of magic plastic will actually produce more cash if inserted in the proper slot of some proper machine.

My work with the phone books paid off to the extent that I managed to locate Frau Doktor Hartmann; she says my head should be cut off and thrown to the dogs, and torture wouldn't induce her to help me find either Michael or Shirin if they were alive; although beyond prosecution, I am, in her opinion, guilty of their murder. On this basis, I guess I can cross Frau Hartmann right off my list of supporters.

I talked to half a dozen people with first names approximately Michael and last names approximately Dershinsky and have dozens more to try as far north as Hamburg and as far south as Hannover, and if I want to try as far east as Berlin, I should be able to keep busy through Columbus Day.

It's now eight P.M., and I'm running on three cylinders. All I can do at this point is stay awake long enough to reset my biological clock to local time.

In truth, I'm not exactly sure what I'm doing here. I suppose I'm here to prove that Herr Reichmann and Heinz Teitel are wrong, the inner circle is *not* gone—but I don't know how to go about it. I can't seriously expect city officials to dig up a million tons of rubble to prove something they already believe to be true. What then? The Teitels aren't going to be any more helpful in person than they were over the phone. Can I imagine myself persuading the guardians at Shirin's clinic that I'm a close friend who should be given her address and phone number even though I don't know her last name? No, frankly I can't. Of course, I can just plant myself on the front steps of the place and see if she shows up someday.

For the moment I can't think of anything else useful to do. For the moment I'm too jet-lagged to think at all.

Wednesday, June 5

Plastic death

This morning I found myself a money machine, shoved in my plastic, and learned that I'd ceased to exist. My card had been revoked and was fresh out of magic. I considered myself lucky. They could've been a day quicker, in which case the card wouldn't have passed muster at the hotel.

I had a couple of choices. I could cash in my return plane ticket or I could call home and ask my mother for a loan. I decided to cash in the plane ticket. I then had to think about my position with the hotel. As long as I didn't try to use the card again there, I figured I was okay, and the hotel would not get stiffed, since the card was still valid when I checked in. Presumably the Laurentians would get stuck with the bill, which did not tax my delicate conscience at all.

Since the airline has no office in Radenau, I'd have to make a trip to Hamburg, which I decided to get out of the way. I made it back by six o'clock, looking forward to dinner, having missed lunch. As I was heading up to my room to rinse off, the clerk called me over to inform me that my card hadn't passed muster after all. I not only owed them for one day, I owed them for two, having missed today's checkout deadline by several hours—and of course I was going to be a cash customer from now on if I wanted to stay past tomorrow morning. I shoved nearly half my resources across the counter and told him I'd think it over.

Yeah.

Saturday, June 8

Walkabout

So at eleven Thursday morning I joined the ranks of the homeless, my worldly goods in a plastic bag. I stopped at a café for a croissant and coffee while I wondered what to do with myself. I thought later I'd look for a cheap pension or maybe just a pleasant bench in the park.

I went to the site of the theater. It was uncannily tidy, smartly fenced off to a height well over two meters. The buildings around it were perfectly unscathed. A demolition contractor could have demanded a bonus for a job done this neatly. The top of the iron spiral staircase was sticking up out of the rubble like the mast of a sinking schooner. The total experience wasn't inspirational or educational or anything. I stood there looking through the fence for about five minutes, then left.

I paid a visit to Gustl Meyer's shop of exotic leftovers. He was polite, even sympathetic, but had no suggestions.

I spent the afternoon at the library finding new ways to spell Michael and Dershinsky. I decided to take my list of numbers to Gustl Meyer's shop on the morrow to see if he'd let me use his phone.

I returned to the hotel to see if anyone had responded to my advertisement. No one had.

I lingered over a pizza and a beer till it was quite dark. Then I started walking. This time I didn't know where I was going except in a general way. I have a pretty good sense of direction, but if I didn't find what I was looking for the first time out, so what. Time was one commodity I had plenty of.

I walked and walked, on feet already sore, and the sights and smells began to come back to me. As the social and economic atmosphere went down the scale, my spirits went up. I was heading into Radenau's grimiest neighborhood, the domain of factories, machine shops, brickyards, and warehouses, inhabited at this hour only by night watchmen and guard dogs. Before long, I spotted a small, non-descript building just ahead, a sort of shed between a warehouse and a railroad yard, and I headed for it hoping the door would open, and it did, giving me a double lungful of cigarette smoke, booze, and "La Vie en Rose." It was Little Bohemia, and by God it felt like home.

Albrecht

I made my way to a table at the back—all the way to the back, against a wall solid with framed drawings and prints, not one of them straight, not one of them with a piece of glass that had been cleaned in twenty years. At eye level when I sat down was a faded sketch of Igor Stravinsky that appeared to be signed by Picasso. Elsewhere it looked like nobody had moved since Charles and I had left three weeks before.

When the waitress came over to see what I wanted, I asked her if her name was really Theda.

"It really is," she said with a smile. "Are you drinking Lagavulin tonight?"

"I'm drinking your cheapest rotgut, please, Theda," I told her politely, but when it came, a couple minutes later, it tasted just like Lagavulin to me.

Someone spoke at my elbow and I looked up into a distantly familiar face. It was Albrecht, he of the giant intellect, the smirking twenty-year-old Englishman who volunteered to dump me in a lake the first time I visited the sub-sub-subbasement in the theater.

I said, "What?"

He said, sneering, "Are you B now?"

I thought about this some. I've never had much opportunity to learn how to deal with hostile people—some priests do and some don't—but I feel like I must know the ABCs of it. I said to him, "Why don't you sit down and tell me what's on your mind."

"Is the question too difficult for you?"

"Yes, it is," I told him. With a triumph already in hand, he took a seat across from me. I said, "Why do you ask me this question?"

"You were being groomed, weren't you? Isn't that the word—'groomed'?"

"Well, there is certainly such a word, but no one ever told *me* I was being groomed."

He shrugged contemptuously.

"I've abandoned the priesthood," I told him. This got a blink. "When I spoke with the man who originally sent me here, Fr. Lulfre, I told him that killing B had been a wasted effort, because B is still here—in the person of me—but I certainly don't think I'm ready to begin where Shirin left off. And, by the way, I've deposited a tape of that conversation with a friend, otherwise I'd be a hunted man, possibly even a dead man by now." This got three blinks in a rapid succession. I asked him if this answered his question—probably a mistake, since it seemed to put him back on track.

"Anyone can be hunted," he said. "The question is, can you do what B did?"

"What exactly do you have in mind?"

"You took in their insights, but do you have any of your own? Are you a thinker and a teacher or just a reciter of Holy Writ? If all you can do is chant the scriptures, then you're no more B than I am. You're just an altar boy who has all the responses down pat."

I downed some rotgut and wished this young whippersnapper was far, far away. Finally I said to him, "Albrecht, the past ten days have been a bit hectic for me, so it's absolutely true that I haven't added a single word to the teachings of B. Whether I can or not is another matter. Be that as it may, you're absolutely right. If all I can do is chant the Holy Writ as I heard it from Charles and Shirin, then I'm no more than an altar boy."

Albrecht smirked. "But you don't really think you are, do you."

"I don't really think I am, no, but I haven't had a chance to prove myself one way or the other."

"Do you *want* a chance to prove yourself?"

What could I say to that? No?

The test

Albrecht said, "The people of our culture imagine that we invented technology, agriculture, law, and of course civilization, but we also take credit for less praiseworthy accomplishments. Can you think of some of those?"

"Well," I said, "I suppose we take credit for things like poverty, crime, and discrimination along racial and social lines. What Shirin called 'the suffering classes' are certainly our invention. Political oppression. Mental illness."

"You're missing the biggest one of all, Father."

"I've given up being father. Just call me Jared."

"All right."

"The biggest one of all would be . . . war."

"Of course. War is far and away the greatest ill we've brought to the world, isn't it?"

"Yes."

Albrecht shook his head, disgusted. "You really are pathetic, Jared. You don't even pause to doubt, to question what Mother Culture whispers in your ear. You remain a total captive of the Great Forgetting."

"Listen, let's just skip the name-calling for a while, okay? I don't pretend to know everything Charles and Shirin knew—or even everything you know. You're telling me what? That war was not our invention?"

"That's what I'm telling you. War is not a defect found only in our quirky, deranged culture. It's found wherever human culture is found—in the past and in the present. The myth of the peaceable noble savage is exactly that, a myth."

"Okay. So?"

Albrecht stood up. "You're truly sad, Jared. Don't let me hear that you're calling yourself B in this city. If I do, I'll come round and embarrass you, I promise you that."

"Sit down. Please." He sat. "Please understand that I don't pretend to be historically or anthropologically knowledgeable. I will be, I hope, but right now I honestly don't see the point you're making."

"Then why don't you ask?"

"I ask."

"The foundation thinkers of our culture imagined that human life began when our culture began, just a few thousand years ago. Therefore nothing could possibly be learned about human life beyond that point. Beyond that point was nothing but a vacancy. Thus they looked into the past and saw that Man had been born an agriculturalist and a civilization-builder. They thought this was Man's nature and Man's destiny—and this is what we teach our children. The human race was born to become precisely *us*. Isn't that what we teach them?"

"Yes."

"B has tried to show you the absurdity of this teaching by removing the obscuring lenses of the Great Forgetting. By showing you that what came before the birth of our culture was not a vacancy. By showing you that our culture was not born in an empty world, in a world devoid of religion and law. Religion and law extend back hundreds of thousands of years, perhaps even millions of years, to the very origins of human life."

"I understand."

"You do? You understand that religion and law extend back hundreds of thousands of years?"

"Yes."

"Well, so does war, Jared. Explain."

"Explain," I repeated hopelessly.

"Is this just another sign of our vicious nature, Jared? Is that the explanation? Do we just innately love to kill?"

"No."

"Does that 'no' represent a profession of faith or a statement of fact?"

"At the moment it represents a profession of faith, but I hope to turn it into a statement of fact."

"Fine. Do it. Take off the obscuring lenses of the Great Forgetting and explain—or for God's sake stop calling yourself B. Go home to your cozy little parish and apologize for behaving so foolishly."

I felt fear. Then I realized he couldn't possibly expect me to accomplish such a feat on the spot . . . but he did. He said, "If you'd like to become B another time, Jared, then by all means say so. Tell me this is your ambition—someday to become B. Then please go home."

"But surely even B couldn't perform this miracle sitting in a tavern, without a single reference book, without even a general encyclopedia."

"I'll be your encyclopedia. Or if you want books on prehistoric warfare, I can have them here in half an hour."

"So you already know the answer to your question."

"No, not at all. The books were not written by people who think like B. They were written by people who in their heart of hearts believe that Man was divinely shaped to conquer and rule the world. They're scandalized by prehistoric warfare. They don't explain it, they lament it. They're embarrassed, because the creature destined from all time to be the ruler of the world should have been finer, nobler, more angelic."

"Yes, I see. . . . Am I right in assuming that prehistoric warfare was similar to the sort of warfare found among tribal peoples in modern times?"

He shook his head, disgusted. "Either you know how to take off the obscuring lenses or you don't, Jared. Don't expect me to do it for you. I'll be on hand if you want to consult an encyclopedia, but don't ask me to do your thinking for you." He got up and moved to a table by himself on the other side of the room.

I was relieved. He was right: Either I knew how to take off the obscuring lenses or I didn't, and it would be easier done in solitude than in company. I flagged down Theda and ordered another drink.

The point I'd been making with Albrecht was one that I'd never explored with either Charles or Shirin, though it was implicit in everything they said. How do we know that modern tribal peoples live the way ancient tribal peoples lived? B's answer is this: The tribal lifestyle survived to the present moment because it works. What is extant in the world is what has endured, what is stable, what works. Failed experiments disappear, successful ones are repeated and repeated and repeated. It's fatuous to suppose that hibernation is a recent innovation for bears—though there's no way to prove that it isn't; bears hibernate because this works. It's similarly fatuous to suppose that migration is a recent innovation for birds—though again there's no way to prove that it isn't; birds migrate because this works. It's fatuous to suppose that web-building is a recent innovation for spiders—though there's no way to prove that it isn't; spiders spin webs because this works.

If you go back in time a million years, you will not expect to find bears spinning webs, birds hibernating, and spiders migrating. Bears hibernate today very probably because hibernation worked for them a million years ago. Birds migrate today very probably because migration worked for them a million years ago. And spiders spin webs today very probably because spinning webs worked for them a million years ago. Because humans were not the object of a special creation but evolved in the bosom of the community of life with all the rest, this sort of reasoning applies to people as well as it does to bears, birds, and spiders. We know for a certainty that totalitarian agriculture is a recent innovation, but there's no reason at all to suppose that the tribal lifestyle is a recent innovation. People live tribally in modern times very probably because living tribally worked for them a million years ago.

I asked myself what I knew about warfare in the *non*human community. What I knew was this: The closest thing to warfare in the nonhuman community is all *within* species, not *between* species. Predation isn't war. Birds aren't at war with worms, frogs aren't at war with mosquitoes, eagles aren't at war with rabbits, lions aren't at war with antelopes. Predators don't do battle with their prey—they just eat them. When animals do battle, it's always with members of their own species, for territory or mates, and no one despises them as morally flawed or dreams of a happier day when they'll learn to live together like Thumper and Bambi.

When nonhuman animals battle, the winners generally take over the losers' territory or mates. Tribal warfare doesn't work that way. (Albrecht confirmed this in his capacity as reference library.) Tribes living in a given area are more or less constantly in a state of low-level war with each other, but when Tribe X attacks Tribe Y, it doesn't typically take over its territory or its mates; rather, after inflicting a certain amount of damage, it typically turns around and goes home. Before long, typically, Tribe Y returns the favor, attacking Tribe X, inflicting a certain amount of damage, then going home. This relation of more or less permanent low-level hostility between X and Y isn't special. The same relation exists between X and Z and Y and Z—and these three have similarly hostile relations with the neighbors around them.

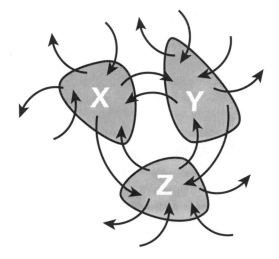

Characteristically, the people of these tribes don't think of themselves as having "a problem" with their neighbors; characteristically, no one is "working for peace"; characteristically, no one thinks there's anything wrong or reprehensible about this way of life. Also characteristically, the people of Tribe X don't imagine that their life would be sweet if one day they went out and killed off all their neighbors; they know there are neighbors beyond their neighbors, and these distant neighbors would be no friendlier than their near ones. It's in fact really not so bad. Years go by in which X doesn't attack Y and Y doesn't attack X, and in these years relations between them are typically very cordial.

The task of B is to ask, "What's working here?" or "Why is this system so successful that it's still around after hundreds of thousands of years?"

What's working is that cultural identities and cultural borders are being preserved. When X attacks Y, it doesn't annex it. It doesn't destroy Y's identity or erase its borders, it just inflicts a certain amount of damage, then turns around and goes home. It's no different when Y attacks X. In other words, every attack serves as a demonstration and affirmation of identity to both sides: "We're X and you're Y, and here's the border between us. We cross it at our risk, and you cross it at yours. We know you're strong and healthy. Every once in a while, we're going to make sure you know we're strong and healthy too. We know that if we mess with you, we'll suffer. We want you to know that if you mess with us, you'll suffer too."

One would think, of course, that there must be some better system, but if thousands of centuries of cultural experimentation haven't turned it up, what does "better" mean? Evolution is a process that sorts for what works, and "better" is discarded as easily as "worse"—if it doesn't work.

What works, evidently, is *cultural diversity.* This should not come as a surprise. If culture is viewed as a biological phenomenon, then we should expect to see diversity favored over uniformity. A thousand designs—one for every locale and situation—always works better than one design for all locales and situations. Birds are more likely to survive in ten thousand nest patterns than in one. Mammals are more likely to survive in ten thousand social patterns than in one. And humans are more likely to survive in ten thousand cultures than in one—as we're in the process of proving right now. We're in the process of making the world unlivable for ourselves—precisely because everyone is being forced to live a single way. There would be no problem if only one person in ten thousand lived the way we live. The problem appears only as we approach the point where only one person in ten thousand is permitted to live any *other* way than the way we live. In a world of ten thousand cultures, one culture can be completely mad and destructive, and little harm will be done. In a world of one culture—and that one culture completely mad and destructive—catastrophe is inevitable.

So: Tribal warfare—casual, intermittent, small-scale, and frequent—worked well for tribal peoples, because it safeguarded cultural diversity. It was not sweet or beautiful or angelic, but it did work . . . for hundreds of thousands of years, perhaps even millions of years.

Into the rubble

Sitting in Little Bohemia getting sloshed, I didn't work all this out as easily or as tidily as I've presented it here—and I certainly don't suggest that this represents a definitive last word on the subject. By taking off the obscuring lenses of the Great Forgetting, I was able to make out a dim path where before there seemed to be only an impenetrable thicket; I haven't explored the path to its full extent by any means. This, I think, is what B does. B opens a path for exploration.

Albrecht was forced to agree. He wasn't thrilled, clearly, but he had to admit that my insight into the problem had the stamp of B on it.

When it was all over, I was pleased and surprised. How had I failed to realize that I needed to be tested? How had I dared to think I could assume the mantle of B without first proving I could wear it?

I was pleased and surprised—and very, very drunk. I'd accepted Albrecht's challenge around nine o'clock, and it was now almost two. The crowd in the Little Bohemia had thinned out and, oddly, had clustered round my table to witness Albrecht's examination of me. I couldn't tell whether they comprehended what I was saying, but they listened in a lively, smiling way, applauding well-made points, exchanging appraisals of my success, and generally cheering me on. By now, most of the candles had been extinguished, and it was exceedingly dark.

Someone asked, "What is that thing?"

Quite unconsciously, I'd brought out the fossil ammonite to busy my fingers with as I made my presentation to Albrecht. It now lay in a pool of light beside the candle on my table.

"This is another test that was given to me, one I haven't managed to pass as yet. It's the fossil remains of a creature that may have lived as much as four hundred million years ago. I've been assured that the past, the present, and the future are written in it. Think of it as a track in the dust. A track in the dust shows not only where the creature has been but where it is and will be."

"Are you supposed to tell its future?" someone asked from the shadows.

"I'm not sure. Charles Atterley gave it to me but was killed before he had a chance to explain why. Shirin wanted me to smash it to pieces."

"Why?"

"I don't remember, to tell the truth." Memory wasn't the only thing that was beginning to slip away from me at that point.

"There's a message from B inside of it," someone suggested. "Like a Chinese fortune cookie. That's why you have to smash it."

"There's no way to get a message inside," I explained stupidly. "It's solid rock."

"B could get a message inside."

Several unseen listeners expressed confident agreement with this opinion.

Before I quite realized what was going on, a fossil-smashing party had been organized. I was uprooted from my table and hustled outdoors to stumble along in the center of a small drunken mob. I couldn't for the life of me figure out where we were going or why we were going anywhere at all. Others were leading, in search of some place or resource completely unimaginable by me.

As suddenly as we began, we stopped and were promptly squashed and trampled by those who continued to blunder forward, slapstick style. Someone ahead of me turned around, handed me a brick, and said, "Here!"

"Bring him over here!" someone else called out. A path opened up in front of me and I was led forward to a brick stack as wide and high as a pool table.

"Go ahead!" someone called out. "Let's see what's inside!"

"There's nothing inside!" I protested.

"Here, give it to me!" another said. "I'll do it!"

I clutched the fossil to my chest, and someone shoved me from behind. "Go on," he said, in a voice no longer quite friendly.

With the brick pile at my back, I turned to face them. "I'm not going to destroy this fossil," I said.

They received this news as if it were a thunderclap. After a moment someone at the back said in a puzzled tone, "I thought Shirin told him to smash it . . . ?"

An imposingly tall man at the front said, "Are you a coward?"

"No, I don't think so."

"Then why are you dithering? The fossil has no intrinsic value."

A woman at the back called out, "He's not a coward in general, Günter. He's just scared of this particular message."

Two in the crowd spoke at once. One said, "What *is* the message?" The other said, "What's he scared of?"

The tall man called Günter stepped forward and spoke to me almost confidentially. "It's not a thing you can just refuse to do, Jared. Charles gave you the fossil for a reason, and Shirin said you'd have to smash it to find out what the reason was—so you have to smash it. Otherwise this period of your life will remain incomplete and inconclusive."

I knew he was right, and one way or another I knew I was not going to leave that place with the fossil intact, so with no more dithering I set it on top of the bricks and smashed it. While I stood there befuddled, Günter stepped forward, plucked a scrap of white paper from the rubble, and instantly balled it up in his fist.

"Give me that!" I cried.

"There's no way to get a message inside," he told me gravely, already walking away. "It's solid rock."

The others laughed, and someone said, "Don't pay any attention to him—he's just teasing. It's a trick, a sleight of hand. He's always pulling coins out of people's ears."

On hearing these words, Günter tossed the ball of paper over his shoulder without a break in stride, and a woman sitting on a stack of bricks nearby darted forward to scoop it up as a souvenir. As suddenly as it began, the show was over, and the crowd began straggling away. Only the woman who had retrieved the scrap of paper seemed prepared to stay. I felt like crying.

"You probably don't remember me," she said. "I was sitting next to Shirin the first night you came down to the cellar. Bonnie?"

"I remember you, Bonnie, I just didn't recognize you. You look older."

"I *am* older," she assured me in all seriousness.

We stood there awkwardly through a long moment.

"Shirin didn't hold out much hope for you," Bonnie told me. "Not at first anyway."

Bonnie shrugged away my qualifying phrase. "She thought you were too *fixed*."

I pondered the various meanings of that word, and evidently so did Bonnie, for she soon added a clarification: "Too set in your ways."

I nodded.

"Like, for example, here you are, you've smashed the fossil to bits, and you're not even going to look at it."

I glanced at the mess on the bricks. "Bonnie, it's just a bunch of crushed calcium carbonate."

"Yeah, that's what she meant. That's just the kind of thing she'd expect you to say."

Well, goddamn. Tonight was definitely my night to be abused and chivvied about. With an exhausted sigh, I turned my attention to the debris beside me and sensed rather than saw Bonnie withdrawing a bit to give me some space.

What was I supposed to be seeing here, if there was anything to be seen? Or: How was I supposed to be looking at it? What had Shirin said about it? I didn't think the memory was there at all, then it suddenly leaped to mind. She said, "I want to show you how to read the future." Then she observed that Charles would have done it better and that the point of the exercise needed to be "more fully developed."

She wanted to show me how to read the future. I closed my eyes and tried to listen for what she would say. What words would not surprise me coming from her mouth on this subject?

Suddenly I heard her say, "The universe is all of a piece, Jared." It was so clear that I opened my eyes, half expecting to see her standing in front of me, but only Bonnie was there, sitting on a nearby stack of bricks and gazing up at the stars. I closed my eyes again, thinking, "So the universe is all of a piece. What does this tell me about anything?"

I let her speak: "This tells you that the flight path of a goose over Scandinavia has something to do with a man dying in a hospital room in New Jersey—but it takes some figuring to find out what it is. This tells you that what's hidden inside a fossil two hundred million years old has something to do with Jared Osborne. This too takes some figuring. This kind of figuring is the diviner's specialty, Jared, though anyone can learn to do it. The diviner is just a special tracker, a tracker of events and relations. Think about what you want right now. What are you looking for?"

That was easy. "I'm looking for *you*."

"Your search begins with this fossil, Jared. You could easily have told me its future when I asked you to, but you were too cowardly to try. Now you *know* its future, don't you."

"Yes, it's future is dust. It had no other future from the moment Charles handed it to me. Even if I hadn't smashed it, it had no other future. One day, in a week or a million years, it was going to become rubble, and no other destiny was ever possible for it."

"The universe is all of a piece, Jared. Charles bought this fossil for you because he knew it had a message for you—a message of some kind, he couldn't have guessed what, at that point. Ask for that message now, Jared. Ask this fossil what it has to do with you. What is it trying to show you?"

"I don't know," I said, predictably.

"Become a diviner now, Jared. You're looking for something. Cut open a bird and examine its entrails, consult your dreams, take up geomancy—or look at the remains of this fossil. Look at it and ask your question."

I looked at and asked: *Where is Shirin?* I suppose it took half a second to realize that I *had* the answer, about as long as it once took me to realize that I'd actually filled that inside straight flush. I nearly fell over backward with illumination, nearly floated off the ground as I came in touch with the fountainhead of meaning and being. If Bonnie hadn't been nearby, I think I would have called out helplessly to the universe that in that moment had *taken notice of me.* As it was, my eyes flooded with tears and my arms and legs began to tremble uncontrollably.

"Idiot, idiot, idiot, idiot, idiot," the fossil debris said to me. "Look closely, look closely—look anywhere you like! Do you see any Shirin here? Any Shirin at all here? Idiot! Idiot! *Shirin is not to be found in the rubble! She isn't there!*"

I waited a long, long time, till I was sure I'd be able to walk without wobbling and to talk without sobbing. It must have taken twenty or thirty minutes, and I thought Bonnie might have left, but no, she was still there. After sweeping the rubble away with my hand, I walked over and told her I'd learned what the fossil had to tell me. She saw with a glance that this was the truth, and graciously didn't press for details.

"I'm glad," she said. Then: "Do you want this?"

I said yes and held out my hand, and she dropped into it the little ball of paper that the conjuror Günter had tossed over his shoulder.

"I've got to run," she said, sliding down off her pile of bricks. "Do you need a ride back to your hotel?"

I didn't bother to explain that I was no longer being accommodated there, I just told her no, "And thanks for making me face the fossil. I would've left it undone otherwise."

"Oh, you know what Shirin always said. The universe is all of a piece."

"I never heard her say that with my own ears, Bonnie, but I'm glad to have heard it now."

She hurried into the night and I followed in her wake more slowly. At the first street lamp I came to, I paused and worked open the little ball of paper, just to make sure it was as blank as it was supposed to be. On it were penciled an even dozen words:

Shirin will live—not forever, of course, but long enough for you.

A brief intermission

Half an hour later I was beginning to regret turning down Bonnie's offer of a ride. I'd wanted to be alone, but now I was groaning for a chance to take my shoes off for ten minutes. At this hour there was nowhere to head but the park. It had occurred to me as a remote possibility that Shirin might be there, but this was just a pipe dream born of booze rather than opium. By the time I actually arrived, I had nothing in mind but stretching out on a bench and letting go, and if I couldn't find an isolated bench, I'd find an isolated glade and let the beetles see how far they could get with putting me underground. In the event, I skipped the isolation and took the bench.

It was my first great lesson in homeless living: If you're going to go the park-bench route, you'd better be ready to sleep like the dead. I was ready to do that when I crashed at four in the morning, but by seven I only *wished* I was dead. I was now personally enlightened as to why bums will take booze over food anytime. If somebody had stuck a bottle of screwtop in my hand, they would've had a helluva time getting it back.

Around eight I gave up the struggle and limped out in search of coffee, aspirin, and breakfast. The first place I came to was a working-man's joint, and I looked sufficiently wasted that they just pretended I was invisible till I showed them some money. I soaked up some caffeine, some painkiller, and as many carbohydrates as I could get into my system and tried to figure out my next move. If my divination was to be trusted, I knew where Shirin was *not:* She was not buried under a million tons of rubble at the site of the Schauspielhaus Wahnfried.

City officials claimed the theater was empty when it blew up, but this was improbable, to say the least. If the theater was empty, why would Herr Reichmann bother to blow it up? No, Shirin was in the theater when it blew up but somehow managed to escape. Of course there was an escape route there—the bomb shelter running from the sub-subcellar of the theater to an adjacent government building. I hadn't overlooked the existence of the shelter, I just hadn't figured it into my reconstruction of the event, because you can't outrun a bomb blast. When, without warning, a ceiling explosively collapses on you, the best reflexes in the world will not get you up out of a chair—much less up out of a chair and into a shelter four paces away. Only in the movies do things like this happen in slow motion. Of course, the operative words here are "without warning." If someone had been on hand to give her a few seconds of warning, then this would account for her survival. And of course there *was* someone on hand to give her a warning—me, though naturally I have no recollection of it, if that's what happened.

Even if all this supposing was valid, I still only knew where Shirin was *not* to be found. But it did give me a new place to start.

Succès fou

The government building was there, it was open, and people were dragging around in the dull way people do in government buildings all over the world. The stairs down to the subbasement were also still there, as was the middle-aged guardian at his desk. He watched me approach with a suspicious squint appropriate for someone he didn't recognize. I wasn't interested in him, I was interested in the door to the bomb shelter, which was now very securely barricaded against access, with a pair of two-by-fours screwed into place across it. I went over to inspect it, and the guardian barked at me in German, which I ignored.

I left after a minute to think things over. The workmanlike way to remove the barricade would be with a screwdriver, but I didn't think the watchdog would allow me the leisure for that. The fastest way to remove it would be with a power saw, but I didn't think the watchdog would help me find an electrical outlet. The fairly quick, nasty way to remove it would be with a crowbar, and I figured I could get that done before the watchdog managed to summon reinforcements. In retrospect, all this reasoning sounds completely cuckoo, but at the time, hungover, still jet-lagged, and operating on three hours of sleep on a park bench, I judged it a perfectly sensible and appropriate response to the situation. I returned in an hour with a pry bar—not quite a traditional crow, but one I thought would do the trick—cunningly hidden in the sleeve of my jacket. When I reached the barricade, I whipped it out, jammed it into place, and knew in a millisecond how wrong I was. For all the effect I was able to produce, I might as well have been trying to pry a beam off the Eiffel Tower.

The guardian was already summoning help, but he didn't stop at that. After hanging up the phone, he marched over and put me in a choke hold. Luckily for me, it wasn't in his mind to strangle me but only to immobilize me till help arrived. This gave me plenty of time to study what was in front of my nose, which just happened to be a name and a phone number neatly engraved in the wood of the top beam of the barricade—and it was the name and number I'd crossed the Atlantic to find.

When the cavalry finally arrived, it included one person who understood enough English to be persuaded that I was a harmless lunatic who would now go far away, never to return, leaving my pry bar behind.

Reunion

I almost didn't recognize Shirin when she came out of Michael's charming little chalet-in-the-woods twenty-odd kilometers west of Radenau. The scarlet lupus butterfly across her face had faded to almost nothing, signaling a remarkable remission, however temporary.

It was an awkward moment. Neither of us knew quite how to play it or even quite how we wanted to play it. In the end, we made it a comradely hug that we pretended had to be gotten through so we could get down to the important business of bringing each other up to date.

Driving me to the chalet, Michael had already told me most of it. My reconstruction of events at the theater was accurate enough not to need further elaboration here. Thanks to the warning shouts I was able to deliver, Shirin, Michael, Frau Hartmann, and Monika Teitel were halfway across the bomb shelter when the blast occurred. They produced a sensation when they emerged in a cloud of dust in the subbasement of the adjacent government building, but there was enough confusion so that they were able to slip away without being detained at the scene. As told by Michael as we drove to the chalet, Shirin had wanted to return to search for me in the rubble, but the others had managed to talk her out of such folly. As told by Shirin in her version, it was Michael who had wanted to return to search for me in the rubble.

Everyone had agreed it was time to run for cover and lie low for a while. The group was sharply divided by the news of my survival. For some, the fact that I hadn't died confirmed my guilt. For others (Shirin and Michael, mainly), the fact that I *almost* died confirmed my innocence. The Teitels, convinced that Shirin should be protected from her own bad judgment, had kept to themselves the fact that I'd called them from the States. Neither Bonnie nor Albrecht had been in the theater at the time of the explosion and neither knew where Shirin was—or even that she was alive.

Neither Shirin nor Michael had ever heard of a sleight-of-hand artist named Günter.

.   .   .

That brings this diary up to the present moment.

The household is governed by a strange rule: We don't talk about what's next. Michael is single, the only offspring of fairly well-off parents, without dependents; we have no financial worries.

It's too early to tell if Shirin and I are moving toward anything more than we presently have. Her reserve is profound, as is her need to be independent and unpitied. Time will tell.

I'm in no hurry.

Epilogue

Undated

Back to the burrow

As I mentioned earlier, I entrusted to a friend the tape of my recent conversation with Fr. Lulfre. I just got word from this friend that his apartment was broken into and ransacked two days ago, and the tape cassette is now gone. I'd urged him in the strongest possible terms to make a copy for safe deposit somewhere else, but of course he hadn't gotten around to it. My fault, for not telling him it was a matter of life and death. My fault, for not checking up on him. My fault, for still being too trusting.

Shirin and I must now leave Michael to his woodsy retreat and go truly underground. He'll be safe enough when we're gone, because neither Fr. Lulfre nor Herr Reichmann really understands what this is all about.

Where do you come in?

I end as I began, wondering if there was ever a diarist who wasn't in fact writing for posterity, who didn't secretly hope that his or her (oh-so-carefully hidden) words would one day be found and cherished. In any case, if there are such self-effacing paragons, I'm not one of them. From the beginning, I knew I was writing with the *possibility* of being read by others—by you, in fact.

From the first episode of my adventure—that initial conversation with Fr. Lulfre—I guessed something was afoot that would eventually have to be shared with a wider audience than is found inside my head. To put it bluntly: Though I tried to pretend otherwise, I knew I was making a record here, and I wouldn't have kept at it so diligently otherwise.

Why am I breaking off at this point? Is it because the teachings of

B are now complete and nothing more needs to added? Hardly. The idea is laughable. As a culture, we've grown up with the obscuring lenses of the Great Forgetting glued to our eyes. From the beginning, our intellectual growth has been stunted and warped by this angel dust of amnesia. This isn't something that will be undone by any one author—or by any ten authors. Nor will it be undone by any one teacher or by any ten teachers. If it's undone, it will be undone by a whole new generation of authors and teachers.

One of which is you.

There's no one in reach of these words who is incapable (at the very least) of handing them to another and saying, "Here, read this."

Parents, teach your children. Children, teach your parents. Teachers, teach your pupils. Pupils, teach your teachers.

Vision is the river, and we who have been changed are the flood.

I supposed people will ask you to summarize what it's all about. I offer you this, knowing how inadequate it is: *The world will not be saved by old minds with new programs. If the world is saved, it will be saved by new minds—with no programs.*

They won't like the sound of that, especially that last part. If it seems worth pursuing, remember the sticks in the river. Remember the Industrial Revolution, that great river of vision that needed not a single program to make it flow, even to the extent of engulfing the world.

Who is B?

Charles Atterley was B. Shirin has said she's B. I've said I'm B. This is what's made us targets. I have to change Fr. Lulfre's mind about this. That's what I'm doing here. I've lost the tape that was my safe-conduct, and I can only replace it with *you*. Because, believe me, if you've read these words, the damage is already done, and Fr. Lulfre will know that.

I'm not putting this very coherently. The fact is, I'm being rushed. Shirin is packed, and Michael is waiting to take us to the airport in Hamburg—and I must leave this manuscript with him. That's settled. The steps that must be taken with it can't be taken by someone on the run, someone with no address or phone number.

. . .

To resume: If we're not here, Michael will be safe, because Fr. Lulfre thinks that Shirin and I are B.

What does it mean for me to say that I'm B? It doesn't mean I can match the knowledge or the abilities of Charles and Shirin. It means I've been changed, fundamentally and permanently. It means *I cannot be put back to what I was.*

That's why I'm B: I cannot be put back to what I was.

Shirin just stuck her head into the room to tell me that if we don't leave in the next three minutes, we'll miss our plane.

So—in terrible haste . . .

I've written the words, and they've found their way to you—I don't know how, exactly. Michael says he has connections who know how to handle that part of it. I won't worry about that.

The words have found their way to you even if, having read them, you hate them—even if you hide them from your children's eyes and consign them to the flames.

They've found their way to you, so it's already too late. Even if, in the meantime, Fr. Lulfre tracks us down and sends his assassins to us, he'll be too late—because of what you've read here.

The contagion has been spread.

You are B.

The
Public
Teachings

The Great Forgetting

I wonder if you've ever considered how strange it is that the educational and character-shaping structures of our culture expose us but a single time in our lives to the ideas of Socrates, Plato, Euclid, Aristotle, Herodotus, Augustine, Machiavelli, Shakespeare, Descartes, Rousseau, Newton, Racine, Darwin, Kant, Kierkegaard, Tolstoy, Schopenhauer, Goethe, Freud, Marx, Einstein, and dozens of others of the same rank, but expose us annually, monthly, weekly, and even daily to the ideas of persons like Jesus, Moses, Muhammad, and Buddha. Why is it, do you think, that we need quarterly lectures on charity, while a single lecture on the laws of thermodynamics is presumed to last us a lifetime? Why is the meaning of Christmas judged to be so difficult of comprehension that we must hear a dozen explications of it, not once in a lifetime, but every single year, year after year after year? Perhaps even more to the point, why do the pious (who already know every word of whatever text they find holy) need to have it repeated to them week after week after week, and even day after day after day?

I'll wager that, if there are physicists listening to me here tonight, you do not keep a copy of Newton's *Principia* on your bedside table. I'll wager that the astronomers among you do not reach on waking for a copy of Copernicus's *De revolutionibus orbium coelestium,* that the geneticists among you do not spend a daily hour in reverential communion with *The Double Helix,* that the anatomists among you do not make a point of reading a passage a night from *De humani corporis fabrica,* that the sociologists among you do not carry with you everywhere a treasured copy of *Die protestantische Ethik und der Geist des Kapitalismus.* But you know very well that hundreds of millions of people thumb daily through holy books that will be read from cover to cover not a dozen times during a lifetime but a dozen dozen.

Have you ever wondered why it is the duty of the clergy of so many sects to read the Divine Office—daily? Why the same affirmations of faith are repeated word for word in so many religious communities around the world—daily? Is it so difficult to remember that Allah is One or that Christ died for our sins that it must be reiterated at least once every day throughout life? Of course we know that these things aren't in the least difficult to remember. And we know that the pious don't go to church every Sunday because they've forgotten that Jesus loves them but rather because they've *not* forgotten that Jesus loves them. They want to hear it again and again and again and again. In some sense or other, they *need* to hear it again and again and again and again. They can live without hearing the laws of thermodynamics ten thousand times, but for some reason, they cannot live without hearing the laws of their gods ten thousand times.

Verily I say unto you . . . again and again and again

A few years ago, when I began speaking to audiences, I had the rather naive idea that it would be sufficient—indeed entirely sufficient—to say each thing exactly once. Only gradually did I understand that saying a thing once is tantamount to saying it not at all. It is indeed sufficient for people to hear the laws of thermodynamics once, and to understand that they're written down somewhere, should they ever be needed again, but there are other truths, of a different human order, that must be enunciated again and again and again—in the same words and in different words: again and again and again.

As you know, I've nct spoken at Der Bau before this night. Yet some of you may have heard me speak elsewhere, and you may say to yourselves, "Haven't I heard him say these things in Salzburg or Dresden or Stuttgart or Prague or Wiesbaden?" The answer to that question is yes. And when Jesus spoke in Galilee, there were those who asked: "Didn't I hear him say these things in Capernaum or Jerusalem or Judaea or Gennesaret or Caesarea Phillippi?" Of course they heard him say them in all these places. All the public statements attributed to Jesus in the gospels could be delivered in three hours or less, and if he didn't repeat himself everywhere he went, then he was silent during ninety-nine percent of his public life.

.

Anywhere in the world

Anywhere in the world, East or West, you can walk up to a stranger and say, "Let me show you how to be saved," and you'll be understood. You may not be believed or welcomed when you speak these words, but you will surely be understood. The fact that you'll be understood should astonish you, but it doesn't, because you've been prepared from childhood by a hundred thousand voices—a million voices—to understand these words yourself. You know instantly what it means to be "saved," and it doesn't matter in the least whether you believe in the salvation referred to. You know in addition, as a completely distinct matter, that being saved involves some method or other. The method might be a ritual—baptism, extreme unction, the sacrament of penance, the performance of ceremonial works, or anything at all. It might, on the other hand, be an inner action of repentance, love, faith, or meditation. Again in addition, and again as a completely distinct matter, you know that the method of salvation being proposed is universal: It can be used by everyone and works for everyone. Yet again: You know that the method has not been discovered, developed, or tested in any scientific laboratory; either God has revealed it to someone or someone has discovered it in a supranormal state of consciousness. Although initially received by divine means, the method is nonetheless transmittable by normal means, which explains why it's possible for a perfectly ordinary individual to be offering the method to others.

But all this barely scratches the surface of what is meant when someone says, "Let me show you how to be saved." A complex and profound worldview is implicit in such a statement. According to this worldview, the human condition is such that everyone is born in an unsaved state and remains unsaved until the requisite ritual or inner action is performed, and all who die in this state either lose their chance for eternal happiness with God or fail to escape the weary cycle of death and rebirth.

Because we've been schooled from birth to understand all this, we're not at all puzzled to hear someone say, "Let me show you how to be saved." Salvation is as plain and ordinary to us as sunrise or rainfall. But now try to imagine how these words would be received in a culture that had no notion that people were born in an unsaved state, that had no notion that people need to be saved. A statement like this, which seems plain and ordinary to us, would be completely meaningless and incomprehensible to them, in part and in whole. Not a word of it would make sense to them.

Imagine all the work you'd have to do to prepare the people of this culture for your statement. You'd have to persuade them that they (and indeed all humans) are born in a state in which they require salvation. You'd have to explain to them what being unsaved means—and what being saved means. You'd have to persuade them that achieving salvation is vitally important—indeed the most important thing in the world. You'd have to convince them that you have a method that assures success. You'd have to explain where the method came from and why it works. You'd have to assure them that they can master this method, and that it will work as well for them as it does for you.

If you can imagine the difficulty you would encounter in this enterprise, you can imagine the difficulty I encounter every time I address an audience. It's seldom possible for me simply to open my mouth and say the things that are on my mind. Rather, I must begin by laying the groundwork for ideas that are obvious to me but fundamentally alien to my listeners.

The Great Forgetting

With every audience and every individual, I have to begin by making them see that the cultural self-awareness we inherit from our parents and pass on to our children is squarely and solidly built on a Great Forgetting that occurred in our culture worldwide during the formative millennia of our civilization. What happened during those formative millennia of our civilization? What happened was that Neolithic farming communes turned into villages, villages turned into towns, and towns were gathered into kingdoms. Concomitant with these events were the development of division of labor along craft lines, the establishment of regional and interregional trade systems, and the emergence of commerce as a separate profession. What was being forgotten while all this was going on was the fact that there had been a time when *none* of it was going on—a time when human life was sustained by hunting and gathering rather than by animal husbandry and agriculture, a time when villages, towns, and kingdoms were un-dreamed of, a time when no one made a living as a potter or a basket maker or a metalworker, a time when trade was an informal and occasional thing, a time when commerce was unimaginable as a means of livelihood.

We can hardly be surprised that the forgetting took place. On the contrary, it's hard to imagine how it could have been avoided. It would have been necessary to hold on to the memory of our hunting-gathering past for *five thousand years* before anyone would have been capable of making a written record of it.

By the time anyone was ready to write the human story, the foundation events of our culture were ancient, ancient develop-ments—but this didn't make them unimaginable. On the contrary, they were quite easy to imagine, simply by extrapolating backward. It was obvious that the kingdoms and empires of the present were bigger and more populous than those of the past. It was obvious that the artisans of the present were more knowledgeable and skilled than artisans of the past. It was obvious that items available for sale and trade were more numerous in the present than in the past. No great feat of intellect was required to understand that, as one went further and further back in time, the population (and therefore the towns) would become smaller and smaller, crafts more and more primitive, and commerce more and more rudimentary. In fact, it was obvious that, if you went back far enough, you would come to a beginning in which there were no towns, no crafts, and no commerce.

In the absence of any other theory, it seemed reasonable (even inescapable) to suppose that the human race must have begun with a single human couple, an original man and woman. There was nothing inherently irrational or improbable about such a supposition. The existence of an original man and woman didn't argue for or against an act of divine creation. Maybe that's just the way things start. Maybe at the beginning of the world there was one man and one woman, one bull and one cow, one horse and one mare, one hen and one cock, and so on. Who at this point knew any better? Our cultural ancestors knew nothing about any agricultural "revolution." As far as they knew, humans had *come into existence* farming, just the way deer had come into existence browsing. As they saw it, agriculture and civilization were just as innately human as thought or speech. Our hunting-gathering past was not just forgotten, it was unimaginable.

The Great Forgetting was woven into the fabric of our intellectual life from its very beginning. This early weaving was accomplished by the nameless scribes of ancient Egypt, Sumer, Assyria, Babylon, India, and China, then, later, by Moses, Samuel, and Elijah of Israel, by Fabius Pictor and Cato the Elder of Rome, by Ssu-ma T'an and his son Ssu-ma Ch'ien in China, and, later still, by Hellanicus, Herodotus, Thucydides, and Xenophon of Greece. (Although Anaximander conjectured that everything evolved from formless material—what he called "the boundless"—and that Man arose from fishlike ancestors, he was as unaware of the Great Forgetting as any of the others.) These ancients were the teachers of Isaiah and Jeremiah, Confucius and Gautama Buddha, Thales and Heraclitus—and these were the teachers of John the Baptist and Jesus, Lao-tzu and Socrates, Plato and Aristotle—and these were the teachers of Muhammad and Aquinas and Bacon and Galileo and Newton and Descartes—and every single one of them unwittingly embodied and ratified the Great Forgetting in their works, so that every text in history, philosophy, and theology from the origins of literacy to almost the present moment incorporated it as an integral and unquestioned assumption.

Now I hope—I sincerely hope—that there are many among you who are burning to know why not a single one of you has ever heard a word about the Great Forgetting (by any name whatsoever) in any class you have ever attended at any school at any level, from kindergarten to graduate school. If you have this question, be assured that it's not an academic one by any means. It's a vital question, and I don't hesitate to say that our species' future on this planet depends on it.

The Great Remembering

What was forgotten in the Great Forgetting was *not* that humans had evolved from other species. There isn't the slightest reason to think that Paleolithic humans or Mesolithic humans guessed that they had evolved. What was forgotten in the Great Forgetting was the fact that, before the advent of agriculture and village life, humans had lived in a profoundly different way.

This explains why the Great Forgetting was not exposed by the development of evolutionary theory. Evolution in fact had nothing to do with it. It was paleontology that exposed the Great Forgetting (and would have done so even if no theory of evolution had ever been proposed). It did so by making it unarguably clear that humans had been around long, long, long before any conceivable date for the planting of the first crop and the beginning of civilization.

Paleontology made untenable the idea that humanity, agriculture, and civilization all began at roughly the same time. History and archaeology had put it beyond doubt that agriculture and civilization were just a few thousand years old, but paleontology put it beyond doubt that *humanity* was *millions* of years old. Paleontology made it impossible to believe that Man had been born an agriculturalist and a civilization-builder. Paleontology forced us to conclude that Man had been born something else entirely—a forager and a homeless nomad—and this is what had been forgotten in the Great Forgetting.

It staggers the imagination to wonder what the foundation thinkers of our culture would have written if they'd known that humans had lived perfectly well on this planet for millions of years without agriculture or civilization, if they'd known that agriculture and civilization are not remotely innate to humans. I can only conclude that the entire course of our intellectual history would have been unthinkably different from what we find in our libraries today.

But here is one of the most amazing occurrences in all of human history. When the thinkers of the eighteenth, nineteenth, and twentieth centuries were finally compelled to admit that the entire structure of thought in our culture had been built on a profoundly important error, *absolutely nothing happened.*

It's hard to notice nothing happening. Everyone knows that. Readers of Sherlock Holmes will remember that the remarkable thing the dog did in the night was . . . nothing. And this is the remarkable thing that these thinkers did: nothing. Obviously they didn't *care* to do anything. They didn't care to go back to all the foundation thinkers of our culture and ask how their work would have changed if they'd known the truth about our origins. I fear the truth is that they wanted to leave things as they were. They wanted to go on forgetting . . . and that's exactly what they did.

Of course they were forced to make some concessions. They couldn't go on teaching that humans had been born farming. They had to deal with the fact that farming was a very recent development. They said to themselves, "Well, let's call it a revolution—the Agricultural Revolution." This was slovenly thinking at its worst, but who was going to argue about it? The whole thing was an embarrassment, and they were glad to dismiss it with a label. So it became the Agricultural Revolution, a new lie to be perpetuated down through the ages.

Historians were sickened to learn the true extent of the human story. Their whole discipline, their whole worldview, had been shaped by people who thought that everything had begun just a few thousand years ago when people appeared on the earth and started immediately to farm and to build civilization. *This* was history, this story of farmers turning up just a few thousand years ago, turning farming communes into villages, villages into towns, towns into kingdoms. *This* was the stuff, it seemed to them. *This* was what counted, and the millions of years that came before *deserved* to be forgotten.

Historians wouldn't touch this *other* stuff, and here's the excuse they fashioned for themselves. They didn't *have* to touch it . . . because it wasn't history. It was some newfangled thing called *pre*history. That was the ticket. Let some inferior breed handle it— not *real* historians, but rather *pre*historians. In this way, modern historians put their stamp of approval on the Great Forgetting. What was forgotten in the Great Forgetting was not something *important,* it was just prehistory. Something not worth looking at. A huge, long period of *nothing happening.*

The Great Remembering was in this way turned into a nonevent. The intellectual guardians of our culture—the historians, the philosophers, the theologians—didn't want to hear about it. The foundations of all their disciplines had been laid during the Great Forgetting, and they didn't want to reexamine those foundations. They were perfectly content to have the Great Forgetting go on—and, for all practical purposes, it did exactly that. The worldview we transmit to our children today is fundamentally the same as the worldview transmitted to children four hundred years ago. The differences are superficial. Instead of teaching our children that *humanity* began just a few thousand years ago (and didn't exist before that), we teach them that human *history* began just a few thousand years ago (and didn't exist before that). Instead of teaching our children that civilization is what *humanity* is all about, we teach them that civilization is what *history* is all about. But everyone knows that it comes to the same thing.

In this way human history is reduced to the period exactly corresponding to the history of our culture, with the other ninety-nine-point-seven percent of the human story discarded as a mere prelude.

The myth of the Agricultural Revolution

That the earth is the motionless center of the universe was an idea that people accepted for thousands of years. In itself, it seems harmless enough, but it spawned a thousand errors and put a limit on what we could understand about the universe. The idea of the Agricultural Revolution that we learn in school and teach our children in school seems similarly harmless, but it too has spawned a thousand errors and puts a limit on what we can understand about ourselves and what has happened on this planet.

In a nutshell, the central idea of the Agricultural Revolution is this, that about ten thousand years ago, people began to abandon the foraging life in favor of agriculture. This statement misleads in two profoundly important ways: first, by implying that agriculture is basically just one thing (the way that foraging is basically just one thing), and second, by implying that this one thing was embraced by people everywhere at more or less the same time. There is so little truth in this statement that it isn't worth bothering with, so I'll just issue another one:

> Many different styles of agriculture were in use all over the world ten thousand years ago, when our particular style of agriculture emerged in the Near East. This style, our style, is one I call *totalitarian agriculture,* in order to stress the way it subordinates all life-forms to the relentless, single-minded production of human food. Fueled by the enormous food surpluses generated uniquely by this style of agriculture, a

rapid population growth occurred among its practitioners, followed by an equally rapid geographical expansion that obliterated all other lifestyles in its path (including those based on other styles of agriculture). This expansion and obliteration of lifestyles continued without a pause in the millennia that followed, eventually reaching the New World in the fifteenth century and continuing to the present moment in remote areas of Africa, Australia, New Guinea, and South America.

The foundation thinkers of our culture imagined that what *we* do is what people everywhere have done from the beginning of time. And when the thinkers of the nineteenth century were forced to acknowledge that this wasn't the case, they imagined instead that what *we* do is what people everywhere have done for the past ten thousand years. They could easily have availed themselves of better information, but they obviously didn't think it was worth bothering with.

East and West

It's become a solid part of our cultural mythology that a profound gulf separates East from West, "and never the twain shall meet," and this causes people to be disconcerted when I speak of East and West as a single culture. East and West are twins, with a common mother and father, but when these twins look at each other, they're struck by the differences they see, not the similarities, just the way biological twins are. It takes an outsider like me to be struck by the fundamental cultural identity that exists between them.

Nothing could be more fundamental to any people than the way they get the wherewithal to live. The people of our culture, East and West, do this by means of totalitarian agriculture, and have done so from the beginning—the same beginning; for the past ten thousand years the people of both East and West have built squarely, solidly, and exclusively on totalitarian agriculture as their base. There's not a single thing to choose between them in this regard.

Totalitarian agriculture is more than a means of getting what you need to live, it's the foundation for the most laborious lifestyle ever developed on this planet. This comes as a shock to many listeners, but there isn't any question about it: No one works harder to stay alive than the people of our culture do. This has been so thoroughly documented in the past forty years that I doubt if you could find an anthropologist anywhere who would argue about it.

It's my notion that the laboriousness of their lifestyle has given rise to another fundamental similarity between the peoples of East and West, and this is the similarity in their spiritual outlook. Again, it's commonplace to imagine that an enormous gulf separates East and West in this regard, but the two of them look like twins to me, because they're both obsessed by the strange idea that people need to be *saved*. In recent decades, the salvationist coloration of Eastern religions has been toned down for export to Beat, hippie, and New Age markets, but it's unmistakable when seen in the originals, in native habitats.

It's certainly true that the ends and means of salvation differ between East and West, but then the ends and means of salvation differ among *all* the salvationist religions of the world—this is precisely how you tell them apart. The essential fact remains that, anywhere in the world, East or West, you can walk up to a stranger and say, "Let me show you how to be saved," and you'll be understood.

The nothingness of prehistory

When the foundation thinkers of our culture looked back in time, past the appearance of man the agriculturalist, they saw . . . nothing. This was what they expected to see, since, as they had it worked out, people could no more exist before agriculture than fish could exist before water. To them, the study of preagricultural man would have seemed like the study of nobody.

When the existence of preagricultural man became undeniable in the nineteenth century, the thinkers of our culture didn't care to disturb the received wisdom of the ancients, so the study of preagricultural man became the study of nobody. They knew they couldn't get away with saying that preagricultural peoples lived in nonhistory, so they said they lived in something called prehistory. I'm sure you understand what prehistory is. It's rather like prewater, and you all know what that is, don't you? Prewater is the stuff fish lived in before there was water, and prehistory is the period people lived in before there was history.

As I've pointed out again and again, the foundation thinkers of our culture imagined that Man had been *born* an agriculturalist and a civilization-builder. When thinkers of the nineteenth century were forced to revise this imagining, they did it this way: Man may not have been *born* an agriculturalist and a civilization-builder, but he was nonetheless born *to become* an agriculturalist and a civilization-builder. In other words, the man of that fiction known as prehistory came into our cultural awareness as a sort of very, very slow starter, and prehistory became a record of people making a very, very slow start at becoming agriculturalists and civilization-builders. If you need a tip-off to confirm this, consider the customary designation of pre-historic peoples as "Stone Age"; this nomenclature was chosen by people who didn't doubt for a moment that stones were as important to these pathetic ancestors of ours as printing presses and steam loco-motives were to the people of the nineteenth century. If you'd like to get an idea of how important stones were to prehistoric peoples, visit a modern "Stone Age" culture in New Guinea or Brazil, and you'll see that stones are about as central to their lives as glue is to ours. They use stones all the time, of course—as we use glue all the time—but calling them Stone Age people makes no better sense than calling us Glue Age people.

The myth of the Agricultural Revolution (cont.)

The foundation thinkers of our culture envisioned the descent of Man this way:

FIRST HUMANS
|
↓
US

The reluctant revisers of the nineteenth century emended the descent of Man to look like this:

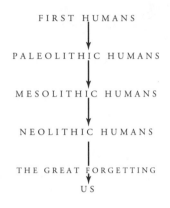

Naturally, they didn't hesitate to assume that the whole of the human story was all leading up to "Us"—the people of our culture—and this is the way it's been taught in our schools ever since. Unfortunately, like so much of the thinking that was done at this point, this was so grotesquely false to facts as to make flat-earth cranks look like intellectual giants.

Here is how it must look if you begin by acknowledging the fact that the people of our culture are not the only humans on this planet:

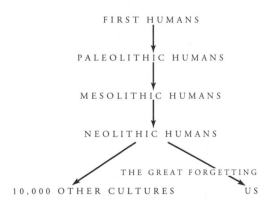

This diagram reveals a split in humanity far more profound than the one we see dividing East and West. Here we see the split that occurred between those who experienced the Great Forgetting and those who did not.

The Law of Limited Competition

During the Great Forgetting it came to be understood among the people of our culture that life in "the wild" was governed by a single, cruel law known in English as "the Law of the Jungle," roughly translatable as "kill or be killed." In recent decades, by the process of looking (instead of merely assuming), ethologists have discovered that this "kill or be killed" law is a fiction. In fact, a system of laws—universally observed—preserves the tranquillity of "the jungle," protects species and even individuals, and promotes the well-being of the community as a whole. This system of laws has been called, among other things, the peacekeeping law, the law of limited competition, and animal ethics.

Briefly, the law of limited competition is this: You may compete to the full extent of your capabilities, but you may not hunt down your competitors or destroy their food or deny them access to food. In other words, you may compete but you may not wage war on your competitors.

The ability to reproduce is clearly a prerequisite for biological success, and we can be sure that every species comes into existence with that ability as an essential heritage from its parent species. In the same way, following the law of limited competition is a prerequisite for biological success, and we can be sure that every species comes into existence following that law as an essential heritage from its parent species.

Humans came into existence following the law of limited competition. This is another way of saying that they lived like all other creatures in the biological community, competing to the full extent of their capacity but not waging war on their competitors. They came into existence following the law and continued to follow the law until about ten thousand years ago, when the people of a single culture in the Near East began to practice a form of agriculture contrary to the law at every point, a form of agriculture in which you were encouraged to wage war on your competitors—to hunt them down, to destroy their food, and to deny them access to food. This was and is the form of agriculture practiced in our culture, East and West—and in no other.

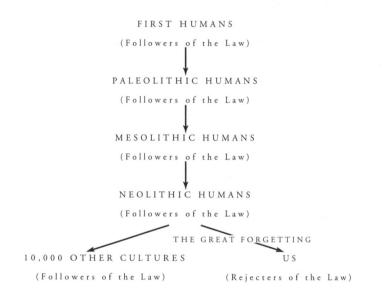

Leavers and Takers

We have at last arrived at a point where we can abandon this vague and clumsy way of talking about "people of our culture" and "people of all other cultures." We might settle for "Followers of the Law" and "Rejecters of the Law," but a simpler pair of names for these groups has been provided by a colleague, who called them Leavers and Takers. He explained the names this way, that Leavers, by following the law, leave the rule of the world in the hands of the gods, whereas the Takers, by rejecting the law, take the rule of the world into their own hands. He wasn't satisfied with this terminology (and neither am I), but it has a certain following, and I have nothing to replace it with.

The important point to note is that a cultural continuity exists among Leaver peoples that extends back three million years to the beginning of our kind. *Homo habilis* was born a Leaver and a follower of the same law that is followed today by the Yanomami of Brazil and the Bushmen of the Kalahari—and hundreds of other aboriginal peoples in undeveloped areas all over the world.

It is precisely this cultural continuity that was broken in the Great Forgetting. To put it another way: After rejecting the law that had protected us from extinction for three million years and making ourselves the enemy of the rest of the biological community, we suppressed our outlaw status by forgetting that there ever was a law.

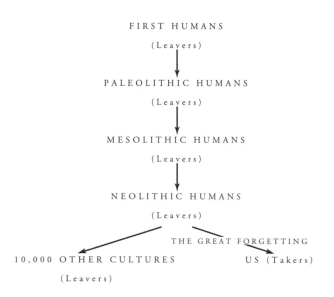

Good news and bad news

If you know even a little about me, you'll know I'm called by many bad names. The reason for this is that I'm a bringer of good news, the best news you've had in a long time. You might think that bringing good news would make me a hero, but I assure you this isn't the case at all. The people of our culture are used to bad news and are fully prepared for bad news, and no one would think for a moment of denouncing me if I stood up and proclaimed that we're all doomed and damned. It's precisely because I do not proclaim this that I'm denounced. Before attempting to articulate the good news I bring, let me first make crystal clear the bad news people are always prepared to hear.

> Man is the scourge of the planet, and he was BORN a scourge, just a few thousand years ago.

Believe me, I can win applause all over the world by pronouncing these words. But the news I'm here to bring you is much different:

> Man was NOT born a few thousand years ago and he was NOT born a scourge.

And it's for this news that I'm condemned.

> Man was born MILLIONS of years ago, and he was no more a scourge than hawks or lions or squids. He lived AT PEACE with the world . . . for MILLIONS of years.

This doesn't mean he was a saint. This doesn't mean he walked the earth like a Buddha. It means he lived as harmlessly as a hyena or a shark or a rattlesnake.

> It's not MAN who is the scourge of the world, it's a single culture. One culture out of hundreds of thousands of cultures. OUR culture.

And here is the best of the news I have to bring:

> We don't have to change HUMANKIND in order to survive. We only have to change a single culture.

I don't mean to suggest that this is an easy task. But at least it's not an *impossible* one.

Questions from the audience

Q. Are you identifying what religionists call the Fall with the birth of our culture?

A. That's precisely what I'm doing. The points of similarity between these two events have long been noted, of course—the fact that both are associated with the birth of agriculture and both occurred in the same part of the world. But the difficulty in identifying them as a single event has been that the Fall is perceived as a spiritual event whereas the birth of our culture is perceived as a technological event. I fear I shall have to come here another time to explore with you the profound spiritual ramifications of this technological event, however.

Q. You say that Man lived at peace with the world during the millions of years that preceded our agricultural revolution. But hasn't recent evidence revealed that ancient foragers hunted many species to extinction?

A. I believe I can still recall the words I used just a moment ago, when I said that Man lived at peace with the world: "This doesn't mean he walked the earth like a Buddha. It means he lived as harmlessly as a hyena or a shark or a rattlesnake." Whenever a new species makes its appearance in the world, adjustments occur throughout the community of life—and some of these adjustments are fatal for some species. For example, when the swift, powerful hunters of the cat family appeared late in the Eocene, the repercussions of this event were experienced throughout the community—sometimes as extinction. Species of "easy prey" became extinct because they couldn't reproduce fast enough to replace the individuals the cats were taking. Some of the cats' competitors also became extinct, for the simple reason that they *couldn't* compete—they just weren't big enough or fast enough. This appearance and disappearance of species is precisely what evolution is all about, after all.

Human hunters of the Mesolithic period may well have hunted the mammoth to extinction, but they certainly didn't do this as a matter of policy, the way farmers of our culture hunt coyotes and wolves, simply to get rid of them. Mesolithic hunters may well have hunted the giant elk to extinction, but they certainly didn't do this out of callous indifference, the way ivory hunters slaughter elephants. Ivory hunters know full well that every kill brings the species closer to extinction, but Mesolithic hunters couldn't possibly have guessed such a thing about the giant elk.

The point to keep in mind is this: It is the *policy* of totalitarian agriculture to wipe out unwanted species. If ancient foragers hunted any species to extinction, it certainly wasn't because they wanted to wipe out their own food supply!

Q. Wasn't agriculture developed as a response to famine?

A. Agriculture is useless as a response to famine. You can no more respond to famine by planting a crop than you can respond to falling out of an airplane by knitting a parachute. But this really misses the point. To say that agriculture was developed as a response to famine is like saying that cigarette smoking was developed as a response to lung cancer. Agriculture doesn't cure famine, it promotes famine—it creates the conditions in which famines occur. Agriculture makes it possible for more people to live in an area than that area can support—and that's exactly where famines occur. For example, agriculture made it possible for many populations of Africa to outstrip their homelands' resources—and that's why these populations are now starving.

The Boiling Frog

Systems thinkers have given us a useful metaphor for a certain kind of human behavior in the phenomenon of the boiled frog. The phenomenon is this. If you drop a frog in a pot of boiling water, it will of course frantically try to clamber out. But if you place it gently in a pot of tepid water and turn the heat on low, it will float there quite placidly. As the water gradually heats up, the frog will sink into a tranquil stupor, exactly like one of us in a hot bath, and before long, with a smile on its face, it will unresistingly allow itself to be boiled to death.

We all know stories of frogs being tossed into boiling water—for example, a young couple being plunged into catastrophic debt by an unforeseen medical emergency. A contrary example, an example of the smiling boiled frog, is that of a young couple who gradually use their good credit to buy and borrow themselves into catastrophic debt. Cultural examples exist as well. About six thousand years ago the goddess-worshiping societies of Old Europe were engulfed in a boiling up of our culture that Marija Gimbutas called Kurgan Wave Number One; they struggled to clamber out but eventually succumbed. The Plains Indians of North America, who were engulfed in another boiling up of our culture in the 1870s, constitute another example; they struggled to clamber out over the next two decades, but they too finally succumbed.

A contrary example, an example of the smiling-boiled-frog phenomenon, is provided by our own culture. When we slipped into the cauldron, the water was a perfect temperature, not too hot, not too cold. Can anyone tell me when that was? Anyone?

Blank faces.

I've already told you, but I'll ask again, a different way. When did we become *we*? Where and when did the thing called *us* begin? Remember: East and West, twins of a common birth. Where? And when?

Well, of course: in the Near East, about ten thousand years ago. That's where our peculiar, defining form of agriculture was born, and *we* began to be *we*. That was our cultural birthplace. That was where and when we slipped into that beautifully pleasant water: the Near East, ten thousand years ago.

As the water in the cauldron slowly heats, the frog feels nothing but a pleasant warmth, and indeed that's all there is to feel. A long time has to pass before the water begins to be dangerously hot, and our own history demonstrates this. For fully half our history, the first five thousand years, signs of distress are almost nonexistent. The technological innovations of this period bespeak a quiet life, centered around hearth and village—sun-dried brick, kiln-fired pottery, woven cloth, the potter's wheel, and so on. But gradually, imperceptibly, signs of distress begin to appear, like tiny bubbles at the bottom of a pot.

What shall we look for, as signs of distress? Mass suicides? Revolution? Terrorism? No, of course not. Those come much later, when the water is scalding hot. Five thousand years ago it was just getting warm. Folks mopping their brows were grinning at each other and saying, "Isn't it great?"

You'll know where to find the signs of distress if you identify the fire that was burning under the cauldron. It was burning there in the beginning, was still burning after five thousand years . . . and is still burning today in exactly the same way. It was and is the great *heating element* of our revolution. It's the essential. It's the sine qua non of our success—if success is what it is.

Speak! Someone tell me what I'm talking about!

"Agriculture!" Agriculture, this gentleman tells me.

No. Not agriculture. One particular *style* of agriculture. One particular style that has been the basis of our culture from its beginnings ten thousand years ago to the present moment—the basis of our culture and found in no other. It's ours, it's what makes us us. For its complete ruthlessness toward all other life-forms on this planet and for its unyielding determination to convert every square meter on this planet to the production of human food, I've called it *totalitarian agriculture.*

Ethologists, students of animal behavior, and a few philosophers who have considered the matter know that there is a form of ethics practiced in the community of life on this planet—apart from us, that is. This is a very practical (you might say Darwinian) sort of ethics, since it serves to safeguard and promote biological diversity within the community. According to this ethics, followed by every sort of creature within the community of life, sharks as well as sheep, killer bees as well as butterflies, you may compete to the full extent of your capabilities, but you may not hunt down your competitors or destroy their food or deny them access to food. In other words, you may compete but you may not wage war. This ethics is violated at every point by practitioners of totalitarian agriculture. We hunt down our competitors, we destroy their food, and we deny them access to food. That indeed is the whole purpose and point of totalitarian agriculture. Totalitarian agriculture is based on the premise that *all the food in the world belongs to us,* and there is no limit whatever to what we may take for ourselves and deny to all others.

Totalitarian agriculture was not adopted in our culture out of sheer meanness. It was adopted because, by its very nature, it's more productive than any other style (and there are many other styles). Totalitarian agriculture represents productivity *to the max,* as Americans like to say. It represents productivity in a form that literally cannot be exceeded.

Many styles of agriculture (not all, but many) produce food surpluses. But, not surprisingly, totalitarian agriculture produces larger surpluses than any other style. It produces surpluses *to the max.* You simply can't outproduce a system designed to convert all the food in the world into human food.

Totalitarian agriculture is the fire under our cauldron. Totalitarian agriculture is what has kept us "on the boil" here for ten thousand years.

Food availability and population growth

The people of our culture take food so much for granted that they often have a hard time seeing that there is a necessary connection between the availability of food and population growth. For them, I've found it necessary to construct a small illustrative experiment with laboratory mice.

Imagine if you will a cage with movable sides, so that it can be enlarged to any desired size. We begin by putting ten healthy mice of both sexes into the cage, along with plenty of food and water. In just a few days there will of course be twenty mice, and we accordingly increase the amount of food we're putting in the cage. In a few weeks, as we steadily increase the amount of available food, there will be forty, then fifty, then sixty, and so on, until one day there is a hundred. And let's say that we've decided to stop the growth of the colony at a hundred. I'm sure you realize that we don't need to pass out little condoms or birth-control pills to achieve this effect. All we have to do is stop *increasing* the amount of food that goes into the cage. Every day we put in an amount that we know is sufficient to sustain a hundred mice—and no more. This is the part that many find hard to believe, but, trust me, it's the truth: The growth of the community stops dead. Not overnight, of course, but in very short order. Putting in an amount of food sufficient for one hundred mice, we will find— every single time—that the population of the cage soon stabilizes at one hundred. Of course I don't mean one hundred precisely. It will fluctuate between ninety and a hundred ten but never go much beyond those limits. On the average, day after day, year after year, decade after decade, the population inside the cage will be one hundred.

Now if we should decide to have a population of two hundred mice instead of one hundred, we won't have to add aphrodisiacs to their diets or play erotic mouse movies for them. We'll just have to increase the amount of food we put in the cage. If we put in enough food for two hundred, we'll soon have two hundred. If we put in enough for three hundred, we'll soon have three hundred. If we put in enough for four hundred, we'll soon have four hundred. If we put in enough for five hundred, we'll soon have five hundred. This isn't a guess, my friends. This isn't a conjecture. This is a certainty.

Of course, you understand that there's nothing special about mice in this regard. The same will happen with crickets or trout or badgers or sparrows. But I fear that many people bridle at the idea that humans might be included in this list. Because *as individuals* we're able to govern our reproductive capacities, they imagine our growth *as a species* should be unresponsive to the mere availability of food.

Luckily for the point I'm trying to make here, I have considerable data showing that, as a species, we're as responsive as any other to the availability of food—three million years of data, in fact. For all but the last ten thousand years of that period, the human species was a very minor member of the world ecosystem. Imagine it—three million years and the human race did *not* overrun the earth! There was some growth, of course, through simple migration from continent to continent, but this growth was proceeding at a glacial rate. It's estimated that the human population at the beginning of the Neolithic was around ten million—ten million, if you can imagine that! After three million years!

Then, very suddenly, things began to change. And the change was that the people of one culture, in one corner of the world, developed a peculiar form of agriculture that made food available to people in unprecedented quantities. Following this, in this corner of the world, the population doubled in a scant three thousand years. It doubled again, this time in only two thousand years. In an eye blink of time on the geologic scale, the human population jumped from ten million to fifty million—probably eighty percent of them being practitioners of totalitarian agriculture: members of our culture, East and West.

The water in the cauldron was getting warm, and signs of distress were beginning to appear.

Signs of distress: 5000–3000 B.C.E.

It was getting crowded. Think of that. People used to imagine that history is inevitably cyclical, but what I'm describing here has never happened before. In all of three million years, humans have never been crowded anywhere. But now the people of a single culture—our culture—are learning what it means to be crowded. It was getting crowded, and overworked, overgrazed land was becoming less and less productive. There were more people, and they were competing for dwindling resources.

The water is heating up around the frog—and remember what we're looking for: signs of distress. What happens when more people begin competing for less? That's obvious. Every schoolchild knows that. When more people start competing for less, they start fighting. But of course they don't just fight at random. The town butcher doesn't battle the town baker, the town tailor doesn't battle the town shoemaker. No, the town's butcher, baker, tailor, and shoemaker get together to battle some *other* town's butcher, baker, tailor, and shoemaker.

We don't have to see bodies lying in the field to know that this was the beginning of the age of war that has continued to the present moment. What we have to see is war-making *machinery*. I don't mean mechanical machinery—chariots, catapults, siege machines, and so on. I mean *political* machinery. Butchers, bakers, tailors, and shoemakers don't organize *themselves* into armies. They need warlords—kings, princes, emperors.

It's during this period, starting around five thousand years ago, that we see the first states formed for the purpose of armed defense and aggression. It's during this period that we see the standing army forged as the monarch's sword of power. Without a standing army, a king is just a windbag in fancy clothes. You know that. But with a standing army, a king can impose his will on his enemies and engrave his name in history—and absolutely the only names we have from this era are the names of conquering kings. No scientists, no philosophers, no historians, no prophets, just conquerors. Again, nothing cyclic going on here. For the first time in human history, the important people are the people with armies.

Now note well that no one thought that the appearance of armies was a bad sign—a sign of distress. They thought it was a *good* sign. They thought the armies represented an *improvement*. The water was just getting delightfully warm, and no one worried about a few little bubbles.

After this point military needs became the chief stimulus for technological advancement in our culture. Nothing wrong with that, is there? Our soldiers need better armor, better swords, better chariots, better bows and arrows, better scaling machines, better rams, better artillery, better guns, better tanks, better planes, better bombs, better rockets, better nerve gas . . . well, you see what I mean. At this point no one saw technology in the service of warfare as a sign that something *bad* was going on. They thought it was an *improvement*.

From this point on, the frequency and severity of wars will serve as one measure of how hot the water is getting around our smiling frog.

Signs of distress: 3000–1400 B.C.E.

The fire burned on under the cauldron of our culture, and the next doubling of our population took only sixteen hundred years. There were a hundred million humans now, at 1400 B.C.E., probably ninety percent of them being members of our culture. The Near East hadn't been big enough for us for a long time. Totalitarian agriculture had moved northward and eastward into Russia and India and China, northward and westward into Asia Minor and Europe. Other kinds of agriculture had once been practiced in all these lands, but now—need I say it?—agriculture meant *our style* of agriculture.

The water is getting hotter—always getting hotter. All the old signs of distress are there, of course—why would they go away? As the water heats up, the old signs just get bigger and more dramatic. War? The wars of the previous age were piddling affairs compared with the wars of this age. This is the Bronze Age! Real weapons, by God! Real armor! Vast standing armies, supported by unbelievable imperial wealth!

Unlike signs of war, other signs of distress aren't cast in bronze or chiseled in stone. No one's sculpting friezes to depict life in the slums of Memphis or Troy. No one's writing news stories to expose official corruption in Knossos or Mohenjo-Daro. No one's putting together film documentaries about the slave trade. Nonetheless, there's at least one sign that *can* be read in the evidence: Crime was emerging as a problem.

Looking out into your faces, I see how unimpressed you are with this news. Crime? Crime is universal among humans, isn't it? No, actually it isn't. Misbehavior, yes. Unpleasant behavior, disruptive behavior, yes. People can always be counted on to fall in love with the wrong person or to lose their tempers or to be stupid or greedy or vengeful. Crime is something else, and we all know that. What we mean by crime doesn't exist among tribal peoples, but this isn't because they're nicer people than we are, it's because they're organized in a different way. This is worth spending a moment on.

If someone irritates you—let's say by constantly interrupting you while you're talking—this isn't a crime. You can't call the police and have this person arrested, tried, and sent to prison, because interrupting people isn't a crime. This means you have to handle it yourself, whatever way you can. But if this same person walks onto your property and refuses to leave, this is a trespass—a crime—and you can absolutely call the police and have this person arrested, tried, and maybe even sent to prison. In other words, crimes engage the machinery of the state, while other unpleasant behaviors don't. Crimes are what the *state* defines as crimes. Trespassing is a crime, but interrupting is not, and we therefore have two entirely different ways of handling them—which people in tribal societies do not. Whatever the trouble is, whether it's bad manners or murder, they handle it themselves, the way you handle the interrupter. Evoking the power of the state isn't an option for them, because they *have* no state. In tribal societies, crime simply doesn't exist as a separate category of human behavior.

Note again: There's nothing cyclical about the appearance of crime in human society. For the first time in history, people were dealing with crime. And note that crime made its appearance during the dawning age of literacy. What this means is that, as soon as people started to write, they started writing *laws;* this is because writing enabled them to do something they hadn't been able to do before. Writing enabled them to define in exact, fixed terms the behaviors they wanted the state to regulate, punish, and suppress.

From this point on, crime would have an identity of its own as "a problem" in our culture. Like war, it was destined to stay with us—

East and West—right up to the present moment. From this point on, crime would join war as a measure of how hot the water was becoming around our smiling frog.

Signs of distress: 1400–0 B.C.E.

The fire burned on under the cauldron of our culture, and the next doubling of our population took only fourteen hundred years. There were two hundred million humans now, at the beginning of our "Common Era," ninety-five percent or more of them belonging to our culture, East and West.

It was an era of political and military adventurism. Hammurabi made himself master of all Mesopotamia. Sesostris III of Egypt invaded Palestine and Syria. Assyria's Tiglath Pileser I extended his rule to the shores of the Mediterranean. Egyptian pharaoh Sheshonk overran Palestine. Tiglath Pileser III conquered Syria, Palestine, Israel, and Babylon. Babylon's Second Nebuchadnezzar took Jerusalem and Tyre. Cyrus the Great extended his reach across the whole of the civilized west, and two centuries later Alexander the Great made the same imperial reach.

It was also an era of civil revolt and assassination. The reign of Assyria's Shalmaneser ended in revolution. A revolt in Chalcidice against Athenian rule marked the beginning of the twenty-year-long conflict known as the Peloponnesian War. A few years later Mitylene in Lesbos also revolted. Spartans, Achaeans, and Arcadians organized a rebellion against Macedonian rule. A revolt in Egypt brought Ptolemy III home from his military campaign in Syria. Philip of Macedon was assassinated, as was Darius III of Persia, Seleucus III Soter, the Carthaginian general Hasdrubel, social reformer Tiberius Sempronius Gracchus, the Seleucid king Antiochus VIII, Chinese emperor Wong Mong, and Roman emperors Claudius and Domitian.

But these weren't the only new signs of stress observable in this age. Counterfeiting, coinage debasement, catastrophic inflation—all those nasty tricks were seen regularly now. Famine became a regular feature of life all over the civilized world, as did plague, ever symptomatic of overcrowding and poor sanitation; in 429 B.C.E. plague carried off as much as two thirds of the population of Athens. Thinkers in both China and Europe were beginning to advise people to have smaller families.

Slavery became a huge, international business, and of course would remain one down to the present moment. It's estimated that at the midpoint of the fifth century every third or fourth person in Athens was a slave. When Carthage fell to Rome in 146 B.C.E., fifty thousand of the survivors were sold as slaves. In 132 B.C.E. some seventy thousand Roman slaves rebelled; when the revolt was put down, twenty thousand were crucified, but this was far from the end of Rome's problems with its slaves.

But new signs of distress appeared in this period that were far more relevant to our purpose here tonight. For the first time in history, people were beginning to suspect that something fundamentally wrong was going on here. For the first time in history, people were beginning to feel empty, were beginning to feel that their lives were not amounting to enough, were beginning to wonder if this is all there is to life, were beginning to hanker after something vaguely *more*. For the first time in history, people began listening to religious teachers who promised them *salvation*.

It's impossible to overstate the novelty of this idea of salvation. Religion had been around in our culture for thousands of years, of course, but it had never been about *salvation* as we understand it or as the people of this period began to understand it. Earlier gods had been talismanic gods of kitchen and crop, mining and mist, housepainting and herding, stroked at need like lucky charms, and earlier religions had been state religions, part of the apparatus of sovereignty and governance (as is apparent from their temples, built for royal ceremonies, not for popular public devotions).

Judaism, Brahmanism, Hinduism, Shintoism, and Buddhism all came into being during this period and had no existence before it. Quite suddenly, after six thousand years of totalitarian agriculture and civilization building, the people of our culture—East and West, twins of a single birth—were beginning to wonder if their lives made sense, were beginning to perceive a void in themselves that economic success and civil esteem could not fill, were beginning to imagine that something was profoundly, even innately, *wrong* with them.

Signs of distress: 0–1200 c.e.

The fire burned on under the cauldron of our culture, and the next doubling of our population would take only twelve hundred years. There would be four hundred million humans at the end of it, ninety-eight percent of them belonging to our culture, East and West. War, plague, famine, political corruption and unrest, crime, and economic instability were fixtures of our cultural life and would remain so. Salvationist religions had been entrenched in the East for centuries when this period began, but the great empire of the West still saluted its dozens of talismanic deities, from Aeolus to Zephyrus. Nonetheless the ordinary people of that empire—the slaves, the conquered, the peasants, the unenfranchised masses—were ready when the first great salvationist religion of the West arrived on its doorstep. It was easy for them to envision humankind as innately flawed and to envision themselves as sinners in need of rescue from eternal damnation. They were eager to despise the world and to dream of a blissful afterlife in which the poor and the humble of this world would be exalted over the proud and the powerful.

The fire burned on unwaveringly under the cauldron of our culture, but people everywhere now had salvationist religions to show them how to understand and deal with the inevitable discomfort of being alive. Adherents tend to concentrate on the differences between these religions, but I concentrate on their agreements, which are as follows: The human condition is what it is, and no amount of effort on your part will change that; it's not within your power to save your people, your friends, your parents, your children, or your spouse, but there is one person (and only one) you can save, and that's *you.* Nobody can save you but you, and there's nobody you can save but yourself. You can carry the word to others and they can carry the word to you, but it never comes down to anything but this, whether it's Buddhism, Hinduism, Judaism, Christianity, or Islam: Nobody can save you but you, and there's nobody you can save but yourself. Salvation is of course the most wonderful thing you can achieve in your life—and you not only don't *have* to share it, it isn't even *possible* to share it.

As far as these religions have it worked out, if you fail of salvation, then your failure is complete, whether others succeed or not. On the other hand, if you find salvation, then your success is complete—again, whether others succeed or not. Ultimately, as these religions have it, if *you're* saved, then literally nothing else in the entire universe matters. Your salvation is what matters. Nothing else—not even *my* salvation (except of course, to me).

This was a new vision of what counts in the world. Forget the boiling, forget the pain. Nothing matters but you and your salvation.

Signs of distress: 1200–1700

It was quite a vision—but of course the fire burned on under the cauldron of our culture, and the next doubling of our population would take only five hundred years. There would be eight hundred million humans at the end of it, ninety-nine percent of them belonging to our culture, East and West. It's the age of bubonic plague, the Mongol Horde, the Inquisition. The first known madhouse and the first debtor's prison are opened in London. Farm laborers revolt in France in 1251 and 1358, textile workers revolt in Flanders in 1280; Wat Tyler's rebellion reduces England to anarchy in 1381, as workers of all kinds unite to demand an end to exploitation; workers riot in plague- and famine-racked Japan in 1428 and again in 1461; Russia's serfs rise in revolt in 1671 and 1672; Bohemia's serfs revolt eight years later. The Black Death arrives to devastate Europe in the middle of the fourteenth century and returns periodically for the next two centuries, carrying off tens of thousands with every outbreak; in two years alone in the seventeenth century it will kill a million people in northern Italy. The Jews make a handy scapegoat for everyone's pain, for everything that goes wrong; France tries to expel them in 1252, later forces them to wear distinctive badges, later strips them of their possessions, later tries to expel them again; Britain tries to expel them in 1290 and 1306; Cologne tries to expel them in 1414; blamed for spreading the Black Death whenever and wherever it arrives, thousands are hanged and burned alive; Castile tries to expel them in 1492; thousands are slaughtered in Lisbon in 1506; Pope Paul III walls them off from the rest of Rome, creating the first ghetto. The anguish of the age finds expression in flagellant movements that foster the idea that God will not be so tempted to find extravagant punishments for us (plagues, famines, wars, and so on) if we preempt him by inflicting extravagant punishments on ourselves. For a time in 1374, Aix-la-Chapelle is in the grip of a strange mania that will fill the streets with thousands of frenzied dancers. Millions will die as famine strikes Japan in 1232, Germany and Italy in 1258, England in 1294 and 1555, all of Western Europe in 1315, Lisbon in 1569, Italy in 1591, Austria in 1596, Russia in 1603, Denmark in 1650, Bengal in 1669, Japan in 1674. Syphilis and typhus make their appearance in Europe. Ergotism, a fungus food poisoning, becomes endemic in Germany, killing thousands. An unknown sweating sickness visits and revisits England, killing tens of thousands. Smallpox, typhus, and diphtheria epidemics carry off thousands. Inquisitors develop a novel technique to combat heresy and witchcraft, torturing suspects until they implicate others, who are tortured until they implicate others, who are tortured until they implicate others, ad infinitum. The slave trade flourishes as millions of Africans are transported to the New World. I don't bother to mention war, political corruption, and crime, which continue unabated and reach new heights. There will be few to argue with Thomas Hobbes when, in 1651, he describes the life of man as "solitary, poore, nasty, brutish, and short." A few years later Blaise Pascal will note that "All men naturally hate one another." The period ends in decades of economic chaos, exacerbated by revolts, famines, and epidemics.

Christianity becomes the first global salvationist religion, penetrating the Far East and the New World. At the same time it fractures. The first fracture is resisted hard, but after that, disintegration becomes commonplace.

Please don't overlook the point I'm making here. I'm not collecting signals of human evil. These are reactions to overcrowding—too many people competing for too few resources, eating rotten food, drinking fouled water, watching their families starve, watching their families fall to the plague.

Signs of distress: 1700–1900

The fire burned on under the cauldron of our culture, and the next doubling of our population would take only two hundred years. There would be one and a half billion humans at the end of it, all but half a percent of them belonging to our culture, East and West. It would be a period in which, for the first time, religious prophets would attract followers simply by predicting the imminent end of the world; in which the opium trade would become an international big business, sponsored by the East India Company and protected by British warships; in which Australia, New Guinea, India, Indochina, and Africa would be claimed or carved up as colonies by the major powers of Europe; in which indigenous peoples all around the world would be wiped out in the millions by diseases brought to them by Europeans—measles, pellagra, whooping cough, smallpox, cholera—with millions more herded onto reservations or killed outright to make room for white expansion.

This isn't to say that native peoples alone were suffering. Sixty million Europeans died of smallpox in the eighteenth century alone. Tens of millions died in cholera epidemics. I'd need ten minutes to list all the dozens of fatal appearances that plague, typhus, yellow fever, scarlet fever, and influenza made during this period. And anyone who doubts the integral connection between agriculture and famine need only examine the record of this period: crop failure and famine, crop failure and famine, crop failure and famine, again and again all over the civilized world. The numbers are staggering. Ten million starved to death in Bengal, 1769. Two million in Ireland and Russia in 1845 and 1846. Nearly fifteen million in China and India from 1876 to 1879. In France, Germany, Italy, Britain, Japan, and elsewhere, tens of thousands, hundreds of thousands died in other famines too numerous to mention.

As the cities became more crowded, human anguish reached highs that would have been unimaginable in previous ages, with hundreds of millions inhabiting slums of inconceivable squalor, prey to disease borne by rats and contaminated water, without education or means of betterment. Crime flourished as never before and was generally punished by public maiming, branding, flogging, or death; imprisonment as an alternate form of punishment developed only late in the period. Mental illness also flourished as never before—madness, derangement, whatever you choose to call it. No one knew what to do with lunatics; they were typically incarcerated alongside criminals, chained to the walls, flogged, forgotten.

Economic instability remained high, and its consequences were felt more widely than ever before. Three years of economic chaos in France led directly to the 1789 revolution that claimed some four hundred thousand victims burned, shot, drowned, or guillotined. Periodic market collapses and depressions wiped out hundreds of thousands of businesses and reduced millions to starvation.

The age also ushered in the Industrial Revolution, of course, but this didn't bring ease and prosperity to the masses; rather it brought utterly heartless and grasping exploitation, with women and small children working ten, twelve, and more hours a day for starvation wages in sweatshops, factories, and mines. You can find the atrocities for yourself if you're not familiar with them. In 1787 it was reckoned that French workers labored as much as sixteen hours a day and spent sixty percent of their wages on a diet consisting of little more than bread and water. It was the middle of the nineteenth century before the British Parliament limited children's workdays to ten hours. Hopeless and frustrated, people everywhere became rebellious, and governments everywhere answered with systematic repression, brutality, and tyranny. General uprisings, peasant uprisings, colonial uprisings, slave uprisings, worker uprisings—there were hundreds, I can't even list them all. East and West, twins of a common birth, it was the age of revolutions. Tens cf millions of people died in them.

As ordinary, habitual interactions between governed and governors, revolt and repression were new, you understand—characteristic signs of distress of the age.

The wolf and the wild boar were deliberately exterminated in Europe during this period. The great auk of Edley Island, near Iceland, was hunted to extinction for its feathers in 1844, becoming the first species to be wiped out for purely commercial purposes. In North America, in order to facilitate railway construction and undermine the food base of hostile native populations, professional hunters destroyed the bison herds, wiping out as many as three million in a single year; only a thousand were left by 1893.

In this age, people no longer went to war to defend their religious beliefs. They still had them, still clung to them, but the theological divisions and disputes that once seemed so murderously important had been rendered irrelevant by more pressing material concerns. The consolations of religion are one thing, but jobs, fair wages, decent living and working conditions, freedom from oppression, and some faint hope of social and economic betterment are another.

It would not, I think, be too fanciful to suggest that the hopes that had been invested in religion in former ages were in this age being invested in revolution and political reform. The promise of "pie in the sky when you die" was no longer enough to make the misery of life in the cauldron endurable. In 1843 the young Karl Marx called religion "the opium of the people." From the greater distance of another century and a half, however, it's clear that religion was in fact no longer very effective as a narcotic.

Signs of distress: 1900–60

The fire burned on under the cauldron of our culture, and the next doubling of our population would take only sixty years—only sixty. There would be three billion humans at the end of it, all but perhaps two tenths of a percent of them belonging to our culture, East and West.

What do I need to say about the water steaming in our cauldron in this era? Is it boiling yet, do you think? Does the first global economic collapse, beginning in 1929, look like a sign of distress to you? Do two cataclysmic world wars look like signs of distress to you? Stand off a few thousand miles and watch from outer space as sixty-five million people are slaughtered on battlefields or blasted to bits in bombing strikes, as another hundred million count themselves lucky to escape merely blinded, maimed, or crippled. I'm talking about a number of people equal to the entire human population in the Golden Age of classical Greece. I'm talking about the number of people you would destroy if today you dropped hydrogen bombs on

Berlin, Paris, Rome, London, New York City, Tokyo, and Hong Kong.

I think the water is hot, ladies and gentlemen. I think the frog is boiling.

Signs of distress: 1960–96

The next doubling of our population occurred in only thirty-six years, bringing us to the present moment, when there are six billion humans on this planet, all but a few scattered millions belonging to our culture, East and West.

The voices in our long chorus of distress have been added a few at a time, age by age. First came war: war as a social fixture, war as a way of life. For two thousand years or more, war seems to have been the only voice in the chorus. But before long it was joined by crime: crime as a social fixture, as a way of life. And then there was corruption: corruption as a social fixture, as a way of life. Before long, these voices were joined by slavery: slavery as world trade and as a social fixture. Soon revolt followed: citizens and slaves rising up to vent their rage and pain. Next, as population pressures gained in intensity, famine and plague found their voices and began to sing everywhere in our culture. Vast classes of the poor began to be exploited pitilessly for their labor. Drugs joined slavery as world trade. The laboring classes—the so-called dangerous classes—rose up in rebellion. The entire world economy collapsed. Global industrial powers played at world domination and genocide.

And then came us: 1960 to the present.

Of what does our voice sing in the chorus of distress? For some four decades the water has been boiling around the frog. One by one, thousand by thousand, million by million, its cells have shut down, unequal to the task of holding on to life.

What are we looking at here? I'll give you a name and you can tell me if I've got it right. I'm prepared to name it . . . cultural collapse. This is what we sing of in the chorus of distress now—not instead of all the rest, but in addition to all the rest. This is our unique contribution to our culture's howl of pain. For the very first time in the history of the world, we bewail the collapse of everything we know and understand, the collapse of the structure on which everything has been built from the beginning of our culture until now.

The frog is dead—and we can't imagine what this means for us or for our children. We're terrified.

Have I got it right? Think about it. If I've got it wrong, there's nothing more to say, of course. But if you think I've got it right, come back tomorrow night, and I'll continue from this point.

The Collapse of Values

Before our era, the chorus of distress that had assembled over the ten thousand years of our cultural life consisted of nine voices: war, crime, corruption, rebellion, famine, plague, slavery, genocide, and economic collapse. Beginning in 1960, our own era found a tenth voice to add to the chorus, a voice never heard before, and this is the voice of cultural catastrophe—a voice that wails of loss of vision, failure of purpose, and the collapse of values.

Every culture has a defining place in the scheme of things, a vision of where it fits in the universe. There's no need for people to articulate this vision in words (for example, to their children) because it's articulated in their lives—in their history, their legends, their customs, their laws, their rituals, their arts, their dances, their stories and songs. Indeed, if you ask them to explain this vision, they won't know how to begin and may not even know what you're talking about. You might say that it's a kind of low, murmurous song that's in their ears from birth, heard so constantly throughout their lives that it's never consciously heard at all. I know that many of you are familiar with the work of my colleague Ishmael, who called the singer of this song Mother Culture and identified the song itself as nothing less than mythology.

The famous mythologist Joseph Campbell lamented the fact that nowadays the people of our culture have no mythology, but, as Ishmael showed us, not all mythology comes from the mouths of bards and storytellers around the fire. Another sort has come to us from the mouths of emperors, lawgivers, priests, political leaders, and prophets. Nowadays it comes to us from the pulpits of our churches, from film screens and television screens, from the mouths of clergy, schoolteachers, news commentators, novelists, pundits. It's not a mythology of quaint tales but a mythology that tells us what the gods had in mind when they made the universe and what our role in that universe is. A people can no more function without this sort of mythology than an individual can function without a nervous system. It's the organizing principle of all our activities. It explains to us the meaning of everything we do.

It can happen that circumstances may shatter a culture's vision of its place in the scheme of things, may render its mythology meaningless, may strangle its song. When this happens (and it's happened many times), things fall apart in this culture. Order and purpose are replaced by chaos and bewilderment. People lose the will to live, become listless, become violent, become suicidal, and take to drink, drugs, and crime. The matrix that once held all in place is now shattered, and laws, customs, and institutions fall into disuse and disrespect, especially among the young, who see that even their elders can no longer make sense of them. If you'd like to study some peoples who have been destroyed in this way, there's no shortage of sites to visit in the United States, Africa, South America, New Guinea, Australia—wherever, in fact, aboriginal peoples have been crushed under the wheels of our cultural juggernaut.

Or you can just stay at home.

You no longer need to travel to the ends of the earth to find people who have become listless, violent, and suicidal, who have taken to drink, drugs, and crime, whose laws, customs, and institutions have fallen into disuse and disrespect. We ourselves have fallen under the wheels of our juggernaut, and our own vision of our place in the scheme of things has been shattered, our own mythology has been rendered meaningless, and our own song has been strangled in our throats. These are things that we all sense. It doesn't matter where you go or who you talk to—a rancher in Montana, a diamond merchant in Amsterdam, a stockbroker in New York, a bus driver in Hamburg.

I'm just old enough to remember a time when it wasn't so, and certainly my parents remember that time, as do yours. I'm certainly not talking about "the good old days" here. The chorus of distress was in full voice—heaven knows it was, since I'm talking about the decades following the most destructive and murderous war in human history. Even so, in the late forties and fifties, the people of our culture still knew where they were going, were still confident that a glorious future lay just ahead of us. All we had to do was to hold on to the vision and keep doing all the things that got us here in the first place. We could count on those things. They were the things that had brought us universities and opera houses, central heating and elevators, Mozart and Shakespeare, ocean liners and motion pictures.

What's more—and you must mark this—the things that got us here were *good* things. In 1950 there wasn't the slightest whisper of a doubt about this anywhere in our culture, East or West, capitalist or communist. In 1950 this was something everyone could agree on: Exploiting the world was our God-given right. The world was *created* for us to exploit. Exploiting the world actually *improved* it! There was no limit to what we could do. Cut as much down as you like, dig up as much as you like. Scrape away the forests, fill in the wetlands, dam the rivers, dump poisons anywhere you want, as much as you want. None of this was regarded as wicked or dangerous. Good heavens, why would it be? The earth was created specifically to be used in this way. It was a limitless, indestructible playroom for humans. You simply didn't have to consider the possibility of running out of something or of damaging something. The earth was designed to take any punishment, to absorb and sweeten any toxin, in any quantity. Explode nuclear weapons? Good heavens, yes—as many as you want! Thousands, if you like. Radioactive material generated while trying to achieve our God-given destiny can't harm us.

Wipe out whole species? Absolutely! Why ever not? If people don't need these creatures, then obviously they're superfluous! To exercise such control over the world is to *humanize* it, is to take us a step closer to our destiny.

Listen: In 1948 Paul Müller of Switzerland received a Nobel Prize for his wonderful work with dichlorodiphenyltrichloroethane, considered the completely ideal chemical means of wiping out unwanted insect species. Perhaps you don't recognize it by that melodic name, dichlorodiphenyltrichloroethane. I'm talking about DDT. In the 1950s and 1960s DDT flowed across the earth like milk and honey, like ambrosia. Everyone knew it was a deadly poison. Of course it was a deadly poison, that was the whole point of it! But we could use as much of it as we liked, because it couldn't harm *us*. The earth, doing its job, would see to that. It would swallow all that wonderful, deadly poison and give us back sweet water, sweet land, and sweet air. It would always and forever swallow all the radioactive wastes, all the industrial wastes, all the poisons we could generate, and give us back sweet water, sweet land, and sweet air. This was the contract, this was the vision itself: *The world was made for Man, and Man was made to conquer and rule it.* This is what we'd been about from the beginning: conquering and ruling, taking the world as if it had been fashioned for our exclusive use, using what we wanted and discarding the rest— destroying the rest as superfluous. This was not wicked work (please note again), this was holy work! This is what God created us to do!

And please don't imagine that this was something we learned from Genesis, where God told Adam to fill the earth and subdue it. This is something we knew before Jerusalem, before Babylon, before Çatal Hüyük, before Jericho, before Ali Kosh, before Zawi Chemi Shanidar. This isn't something the authors of Genesis taught us, this is something we taught them.

Let me say again, as I must on every occasion, that this was not the *human* vision, not the vision that was born in us when we became *Homo habilis* or when *Homo habilis* became *Homo erectus* or when *Homo erectus* became *Homo sapiens.* This is the vision that was born in us when our particular culture was born, ten thousand years ago. This was the manifesto of our revolution, to be carried to every corner of the earth.

The truth of this manifesto wasn't doubted by the builders of the ziggurats of Ur or the pyramids of Egypt. It wasn't doubted by the hundreds of thousands who labored to wall off China from the rest of the world. It wasn't doubted by the traders who carried gold and glass and ivory from Thebes to Nippur and Larsa. It wasn't doubted by the scribes of the Hittites and the Elamites and the Mitanni who first pressed the record of imperial conquest into clay tablets. It wasn't doubted by the ironworkers who carried their potent secrets from Babylon to Nineveh and Damascus. It wasn't doubted by Darius of Persia or Philip of Macedon or Alexander the Great. It wasn't doubted by Confucius or Aristotle. It wasn't doubted by Hannibal or Julius Caesar or Constantine, Christianity's first imperial protector. It wasn't doubted by the marauders who scavenged the bones of the Roman Empire—the Huns, the Vikings, the Arabs, the Avars, and others. It wasn't doubted by Charlemagne or Genghis Khan. It wasn't doubted by the Crusaders or by the Shiite Assassins. It wasn't doubted by the merchants of the Hanseatic League. It wasn't doubted by Pope Alexander VI, who in 1494 decided how the entire world should be divided among the colonizing powers of Europe. It wasn't doubted by the pioneers of the scientific revolution—Copernicus and Kepler and Galileo. It wasn't doubted by the great explorers of the sixteenth and seventeenth centuries—and it certainly wasn't doubted by the conquerors and settlers of the New World. It wasn't doubted by the intellectual founders of the modern age, thinkers like Descartes, Adam Smith, David Hume, and Jeremy Bentham. It wasn't doubted by the pathfinders of the democratic revolution, political theorists like John Locke and Jean-Jacques Rousseau. It wasn't doubted by the countless inventors, tinkers, dabblers, investors, and visionaries of the Industrial Revolution. It wasn't doubted by the Luddite gangs who smashed up factories in the Midlands and north of England. It wasn't doubted by the industrial giants who built the railroads and armed the armies and rolled out the steel—the Du Ponts, the Vanderbilts, the Krupps, the Morgans, the Carnegies. It wasn't doubted by the authors of the Communist Manifesto, by the organizers of the labor movement, or by the architects of the Russian Revolution. It wasn't doubted by the rulers who plunged Europe into the maelstrom of World War I. It wasn't doubted by the authors of the Treaty of Versailles or by the architects of the League of Nations. It wasn't doubted by the Fellowship of Reconciliation or by the signers of the Oxford Pledge. It wasn't doubted by the scores of millions who were jobless during the Great Depression. It wasn't doubted by those who struggled to establish parliamentary democracy in Germany or by those who ultimately defeated them. It wasn't doubted by the hundreds of thousands who labored in an industry of death created to rid humanity of "mongrel races." It wasn't doubted by the millions who fought World War II or by the leaders who sent them to fight. It wasn't doubted by the hardworking scientists and engineers who exerted their best skills to rain down terror on the cities of England and Germany.

The world was made for Man, and Man was made to conquer and rule it.

This manifesto certainly wasn't doubted by the rival teams that raced to split the atom and build a weapon capable of destroying our entire species. It wasn't doubted by the architects of the United Nations. It wasn't doubted by the hundreds of millions who in the postwar years dreamed of a coming utopia where people would rest and all labor would be performed by robots, where atomic power would be limitless and free, where poverty, hunger, and crime would be obsolete.

But that manifesto is doubted now, ladies and gentlemen . . . almost everywhere in our culture, in all walks of life, among the young and the old, but especially among the young, for whom the dream of a glittering future in which life will become ever sweeter and sweeter and sweeter, decade after decade, century after century, has been exploded and is meaningless. Your children know better. They know better in large part because *you* know better.

Only our politicians still insist that the world was made for Man, and Man was made to conquer and rule it. They must, as a professional obligation, still affirm and proclaim the manifesto of our revolution. If they want to hold on to their jobs, they must assure us with absolute conviction that a glorious future lies just ahead for us— provided that we march forward under the banner of conquest and rule. They reassure us of this, and then they wonder, year after year, why fewer and fewer voters go to the polls.

Silent Spring and beyond

I've said that this new era of the collapse of values began in 1960. Strictly speaking, it should be dated to 1962, the year of Rachel Carson's *Silent Spring,* the first substantive challenge ever issued to the motivating vision of our culture. The facts Carson brought forward to detail the devastating environmental effects of DDT and other pesticides were astounding: DDT didn't just do its intended job of killing unwanted insects; it had entered the avian food chain, disrupting reproductive processes and breaking down egg structures, with the result that many species had already been destroyed and many more were threatened, making it not unthinkable that the world might someday wake to a silent spring—a spring without birds. But *Silent*

Spring wasn't just another sensational exposé, welcome in any publishing season. With a single powerful blow, it shattered for all time a complex of fundamental articles of our cultural faith: that the world was capable of repairing any damage we might do to it; that the world was *designed* to do precisely this; that the world was "on our side" in our aggrandizement, would always tolerate and facilitate our efforts; that God himself had fashioned the world *specifically* to support our efforts to conquer and rule it. The facts in *Silent Spring* plainly contradicted all these ideas. Something presumably beneficial to us was not being tolerated and facilitated by the world. The world was *not* supporting our cultural vision. *God* was not supporting our cultural vision. The world was *not* unequivocally on our side. *God* was not unequivocally on our side.

If the matter had ended with Rachel Carson and DDT, our cultural vision would surely have cleared up and recovered, but as we all know, Rachel Carson and DDT were only the barest beginning. Carson was just the first to look, the first to show us that there was something new here to be seen. Dozens, hundreds, thousands have looked since then, and the more they've looked, the more they've shattered our cultural faith. I won't review it for you. In an evening I could barely scratch the surface, and I'd only be telling you things discoverable in any encyclopedia.

It comes down to this: In our present numbers and enacting our present dreams, the human race is having a lethal impact upon the world. Lakes are dying, seas are dying, forests are dying, the land itself is dying—for reasons directly traceable to our activities. As many as a hundred and forty species are vanishing *every day*—for reasons directly traceable to our activities.

Listen, I hear you squirming in your seats—but I'm not saying these things to make you feel guilty. That's not my purpose here at all.

I'm here tonight to figure out . . . what's gone wrong here.

Theories: What's gone wrong here?

Figuring out what's wrong has become a global preoccupation. People of all ages are working on it—people of every social and economic class, every political persuasion. Ten-year-old kids are trying to work it out. I know this because they talk to me about it. I know this because I've seen them pause in the midst of play to give it their attention.

Every year more and more children are born out of wedlock. Every year more and more children live in broken homes. Every year more and more people are bruised and battered by crime. Every year more and more children are abused and murdered. Every year more and more women are raped. Every year more and more people are afraid to walk the streets at night. Every year more and more people commit suicide. Every year more and more people become addicted to drugs and alcohol. Every year more and more people are imprisoned as criminals. Every year more and more people find routine entertainment in murderous violence and pornography. Every year more and more people immolate themselves in lunatic cults, delusional terrorism, and sudden, uncontrollable bursts of violence.

The theories that are advanced to explain these things are for the most part commonplace generalities, truisms, and platitudes. They are the received wisdom of the ages. You hear, for example, that the human race is fatally and irremediably flawed. You hear that the human race is a sort of planetary disease that Gaia will eventually shake off. You hear that insatiable capitalist greed is to blame or that technology is to blame. You hear that parents are to blame or the schools are to blame or rock and roll is to blame. Sometimes you hear that the symptoms themselves are to blame: things like poverty, oppression, and injustice, things like overcrowding, bureaucratic indifference, and political corruption.

These are some of the common theories advanced to explain what's gone wrong here. You'll hear others. Most of them have to be deduced from the remedies that are proposed to correct them. Usually these remedies are expressed in this form: *All we have to do is . . . something.* Elect the right party. Get rid of this leader. Handcuff the liberals. Handcuff the conservatives. Write stricter laws. Give longer prison sentences. Bring back the death penalty. Kill Jews, kill ancient enemies, kill foreigners, kill somebody. Meditate. Pray the Rosary. Raise consciousness. Evolve to some new plane of existence.

I want you to understand what I'm doing here. I'm proposing a new theory to explain what's gone wrong. This is not a minor variation, not a smartening up of conventional wisdom. This is something unheard of, something entirely novel in our intellectual history. Here it is: We're experiencing cultural collapse. The very same collapse that was experienced by the Plains Indians when their way of life was destroyed and they were herded onto reservations. The very same collapse that was experienced by countless aboriginal peoples overrun by us in Africa, South America, Australia, New Guinea, and elsewhere. It matters not that the circumstances of the collapse were different for them and for us, the results were the same. For both of us, in just a few decades, shocking realities invalidated our vision of the world and made nonsense of a destiny that had always seemed self-evident. For both of us, the song we'd been singing from the beginning of time suddenly died in our throats.

The outcome was the same for both of us: Things fell apart. It doesn't matter whether you live in tepees or skyscrapers, things fall apart. Order and purpose are replaced by chaos and bewilderment. People lose the will to live, become listless, become violent, become suicidal, and take to drink, drugs, and crime. The matrix that once held all in place is shattered, and laws, customs, and institutions fall into disuse and disrespect, especially among the young, who see that even their elders can no longer make sense of them.

And that's what's happened here, to us. The frog smiled for ten thousand years, as the water got hotter and hotter and hotter, but eventually, when the water began to boil at last, the smile became meaningless, because the frog was dead.

Circumstances have at last shattered our mad cultural vision, have at last rendered our self-aggrandizing mythology meaningless, have at last strangled our arrogant song. We've lost our ability to believe that the world was made for Man and that Man was made to conquer and rule it. We've lost our ability to believe that the world will automatically and inevitably support us in our conquest, will swallow all the poison we can generate without coming to harm. We've lost our ability to believe that God is unequivocally on our side against the rest of creation.

And so, ladies and gentlemen, we're . . . going to pieces.

At last, good news

A woman recently told me she wanted to bring a friend to hear me speak, but her friend said, "I'm sorry, but I can't stand to hear any more bad news." [Laughter] Yes, it is funny, because you know that, oddly enough, you're here in this theater listening to me because you absolutely know that I'm a bringer of good news.

Yes, that's so, and because you know it's so, you laugh. You're already feeling better! You're absolutely right to feel better, and here's why. It's really quite simple. Here is my good news: *We are not humanity.*

Can you feel the liberation in those words? Try them out. Go ahead. Just whisper them to yourselves: *We . . . are not . . . humanity.*

I'm sure they seem bizarre at the very least. Before we quit for tonight, I want you to understand why they seem so.

We are not humanity.

Putting them on is like putting on a stranger's shoes, mistaking them for your own—your whole life changes in an instant!

We are not humanity. I want you to understand what these four words are. They are a summary of all that was forgotten during the Great Forgetting. I mean that quite literally. At the end of the Great Forgetting, when the people of our culture began to build civilization in earnest, those four words were practically unthinkable. In a sense, that's what the Great Forgetting was all about: We forgot that we're only a single culture and came to think of ourselves as humanity itself.

All the intellectual and spiritual foundations of our culture were laid by people who believed absolutely that we are humanity itself. Thucydides believed it. Socrates believed it. Plato believed it. Aristotle believed it. Ssu-ma Ch'ien believed it. Gautama Buddha believed it. Confucius believed it. Moses believed it. Jesus believed it. St. Paul believed it. Muhammad believed it. Avicenna believed it. Thomas Aquinas believed it. Copernicus believed it. Galileo and Descartes believed it, though they could easily have known better. Hume, Hegel, Nietzsche, Marx, Kant, Kierkegaard, Bergson, Heidegger, Sartre, and Camus—they all took it for granted, though they certainly didn't lack the requisite information to know better.

But you're bound to be wondering why it would be such bad news if we were humanity? I'll try to explain. If we were humanity itself, then all the terrible things we say about humanity would be *true*—and that would be very bad news. If we were humanity itself, then all our destructiveness would belong not to one misguided culture but to humanity itself—and that would be very bad news. If we were humanity itself, then the fact that our culture is doomed would mean that humanity itself is doomed—and that would be very bad news. If we were humanity itself, then the fact that our culture is the enemy of life on this planet would mean that humanity itself is the enemy of life on this planet—and that would be very bad news. If we were humanity itself, then the fact that our culture is hideous and misshapen would mean that humanity itself is hideous and misshapen—very bad news indeed.

Oh, groan, humanity, if *we* are humanity! Oh, groan in horror and despair, if the miserable and misguided creatures of our culture are humanity itself!

But we're not humanity, we're just one culture—one culture out of hundreds of thousands that have lived their vision on this planet and sung their song—and that's wonderful news, even for us!

If it were humanity that needed changing, then we'd be out of luck. But it isn't humanity that needs changing, it's just . . . us.

And that's very good news.

Stick with me, friends. We'll get there, step by step by step.

Population: A Systems Approach

Because the ideas I'm going to be presenting here have proved to be so unsettling for people, I've learned to approach them cautiously, from a good, safe distance—a good, safe distance being in this case about two hundred thousand years. Two hundred thousand years ago is when a new species called *Homo sapiens* first began to be seen on this planet.

As with any young species, there were not many members of it to begin with. Since our subject is population, I'd better clarify what I mean by that. We have an approximate date for the emergence of *Homo sapiens* because we have fossil remains—and we have fossil remains because a sufficient number of this species lived around this time to *provide* those fossil remains. In other words, when I say that *Homo sapiens* appeared about two hundred thousand years ago, I'm not talking about the first two of them or the first hundred of them. But neither am I talking about the first million of them.

Two hundred thousand years ago, there was a bunch. Let's say ten thousand. Over the next hundred ninety thousand years, *Homo sapiens* grew in numbers and migrated to every continent of the world.

The passage of these hundred ninety thousand years brings us to the opening of the historical era on this planet. It brings us to the beginning of the agricultural revolution that stands at the foundation of our civilization. This is about ten thousand years ago, and the human population at that time is estimated to have been around ten million.

I want to spend a couple minutes now just looking at that period of growth from ten thousand people to ten million people. As it happens, what this period of growth represents is ten doublings. From ten thousand to twenty thousand, from twenty thousand to forty thousand, from forty thousand to eighty thousand, and so on. Start with ten thousand, double it ten times, and you wind up with about ten million.

So: Our population doubled ten times in a hundred ninety thousand years. Went from about ten thousand to ten million. That's growth. Undeniable growth, definite growth, even substantial growth . . . but growth at an *infinitesimal* rate. Here's how infinitesimal it was: On the average, our population was doubling every *nineteen thousand years.* That's slow—glacially slow.

At the end of this period, which is to say ten thousand years ago, this began to change very dramatically. Growth at an infinitesimal rate became growth at a rapid rate. Starting at ten million, our population doubled not in nineteen thousand years but in five thousand years, bringing it to twenty million. The next doubling—doubling and a bit—took only two thousand years, bringing us to fifty million. The next doubling took only sixteen hundred years, bringing us to one hundred million. The next doubling took only fourteen hundred years—bringing us to two hundred million at the zero point of our calendar. The next doubling took only twelve hundred years, bringing us to four hundred million. The year was 1200 A.D. The next doubling took only five hundred years, bringing us to eight hundred million in 1700. The next doubling took only two hundred years, bringing us to a billion and a half in 1900. The next doubling took only sixty years, bringing us to three billion in 1960. The next doubling will take only thirty-seven years or so. Within ten or twenty months we'll reach six billion, and if this growth trend continues unchecked, many of us in this room will live long enough to see us reach twelve billion. I won't attempt to imagine for you what that will mean. At a rough guess, my personal guess, take everything bad that you see going on now—environmental destruction, terrorism, crime, drugs, corruption, suicide, mental illness—violence of every kind—and multiply by four . . . at least. But, believe it or not, I'm not here to depress you with gloomy pictures of the future.

We have a population problem. There are a few people around who think that everything is fine, and we don't have a population problem at all, but I'm not here to change their minds. I'm here to suggest that the *angle* of attack we've traditionally taken on this problem is ineffective and can never be anything *but* ineffective. After that, I want to show you a more promising angle of attack. But right now I'd like to read you a fable that I think you'll find relevant. It's about some people with a population problem of their own and the way they go about attacking it. It's called "Blessing: A Fable About Population."

Blessing: A Fable About Population

It happened once, on a planet not much different from our own, that researchers at a drug company got lucky with a substance they were testing as a pain reliever. Ingesting this substance, called D3346, pain-ridden mice began to exhibit signs of relief: They were friskier, they mated more often, their appetites improved, and so on. Human tests made company officials ecstatic. D3346 outperformed much more powerful drugs and had no deleterious side effects (aside from imparting to the subject an objectionable odor that soon disappeared when the drug was discontinued).

The new drug worked so well that the marketing department knew they had more than a mere painkiller on their hands. People put up with a host of small aches and pains more or less all the time, and simply by getting rid of them, D3346 gave users a feeling of well-being so intense that it almost amounted to a "high." The name *Blessing* was adopted for the new product without discussion, as was its slogan: "Works on pain you didn't even know you had!"

The drug was initially marketed in pill and liquid forms, but in less than a year someone had the bright idea of packaging it as a powder in disposable shakers designed to take their place beside the salt and pepper on the dining-room table. Within months, all "medicinal" forms had disappeared from store shelves, and Blessing was no longer "taken for pain." It had become just another beneficial food additive, like a vitamin.

No one was surprised when, nine months after the introduction of the drug, the birth rate began to climb. This had been predicted, and everyone understood the reasons for it. Blessing didn't increase fertility or sexual appetite; it wasn't an aphrodisiac. People using it just *felt* better—more playful, more affectionate, more outgoing. It was predicted that the birth rate would soon level off—and it did . . . at about ten percent *above* the old rate.

On this planet, the people I've been talking about did not constitute a dominant world culture, as we do—but they soon began to be noticed globally. In the first place, they *smelled* bad, which earned them the name by which they became known all across the world: the Stinkards. In the second place, responding to internal population pressures, they were incorrigible trespassers and encroachers. Nonetheless, the Stinkards usually managed to do their encroaching without violence . . . by sending Blessing ahead of them.

It didn't matter that no one wanted to end up smelling like the Stinkards. The Blessing was there, and few could resist taking just an occasional dose for a sore back or a headache, and before long they were using it like table salt. People began by loathing the Stinkards and passionately resisting their encroachments, but ended up becoming Stinkards themselves. After a few hundred years the Stinkard expansion came to an end—because there were no new lands to expand into. The entire planet was Stinkard.

Farsighted leaders realized that population was soon going to be an urgent problem, but a century passed without significant action being taken. The human population, having no reason to do anything else, continued to grow. Famine became a familiar feature of life in certain parts of the world, and in some quarters the problem came to be understood not as one of curbing growth but as one of increasing food production. Another century passed, and the human population continued to expand.

In informed circles, people began to practice and advocate various population-control strategies, ranging from birth control in one form or another to school programs designed to reduce teenage pregnancies, but none of these initiatives had any measurable effect. As more and more people became aware of the crisis, sociologists and economists began to probe more deeply for its causes. They noted, for example, that in many parts of the world, having children was a means of financial success; lacking other economic opportunities, especially for women, people brought children into the world to serve as unpaid workers and guarantors of old-age security.

One biohistorian by the name of Spry tried to draw people's attention to the fact that, before the appearance of Blessing, the human population of the planet had been virtually stable, but his listeners had a hard time seeing the connection between the two things.

Dr. Spry tried to explain. "If you introduce Blessing into the diet of *any* species," he said, "the result will be the same: The birth rate will increase. Without any offsetting increase in the death rate, the species' overall population will inevitably increase as well."

The professor's listeners really had no notion of what he was getting at, since Blessing had been a constant feature of the human diet for a thousand years, and they couldn't begin to imagine how it felt to live without it. He had to explain very patiently that, without a constant intake of Blessing, everyone would experience a whole host of minor aches and pains, and experiencing these minor aches and pains, they would be slightly less frisky, slightly less playful, slightly less affectionate, slightly less outgoing—and slightly less inclined to mate. As a result, the birth rate would go down, and the population would soon become stable once again.

"Are you saying that the solution to our population problem is to live in pain?" people asked him incredulously.

"That's a complete exaggeration of my point," the professor said. "Before Blessing came along, people didn't think of themselves as 'living in pain.' They were *not* living in pain. They were just living."

Others said, "This is really all beside the point. Dr. Spry has already pointed out that Blessing isn't an aphrodisiac and doesn't in itself increase fertility. The fact that we use Blessing doesn't *compel* us to mate more often. We can mate as little or as much as we want. What's more, we can also use any number of contraceptive methods to avoid pregnancy. So it's hard to see what Blessing has to do with the matter at all."

"It has this to do with it," Dr. Spry replied. "If you make Blessing available to *any* species, the members of that species will mate more often, and their birth rate will rise. It's not a question of what you or I will do—whether you or I will elect to use contraceptives, for example. It's a question of what the species as a whole will do. And I can demonstrate this experimentally: The birth rate of *any* species with free access to Blessing will increase. It doesn't matter whether it's mice or cats or lizards or chickens—or humans. This isn't a matter of what individuals do, this is a matter of what *whole populations* do."

But the professor's audiences always indignantly rejected this observation. "We're not mice!" they would yell. "We're not cats or lizards or chickens!"

Increasingly regarded as a crank and an extremist, Dr. Spry eventually lost his teaching post and with it his credibility as an authority on any subject, and was heard from no more.

The population crisis mounted. Environmental biologists estimated that the human population had already exceeded the carrying capacity of the planet and was headed for a catastrophic collapse. Even former scoffers and optimists began to see that something had to change. Finally the heads of state of the major world powers convened a global conference to study and discuss the issues. It was an impressive event, unprecedented in human history. Thousands of thinkers from dozens of disciplines came together to put the problem under scrutiny.

The concept of *control* soon emerged as the overriding theme of the conference. Population control, of course, was the subject itself. But achieving control of population implied control on all sorts of levels and in all sorts of ways. New economic controls would encourage couples to control family size. In backward lands, where women were little more than breeding machines, new social controls would release their creativity to enhance family prosperity. Birth-control devices, birth-control substances, and birth-control strategies needed wider dissemination. Naturally, on the level of the individual, personal control needed to be improved. Educational controls were hotly debated, with some arguing that controls were needed to keep children *ignorant* about sex while others argued that controls were needed to make children *aware* of sex.

Control, control, control—it was a word heard ten thousand times, a million times.

Unlike the word *Blessing*.

At the Stinkards' great global conference on population, Blessing wasn't a major topic—or even a minor topic.

In fact, Blessing wasn't even mentioned once.

People who hear this parable naturally want to know how to interpret it. They can see that the Stinkards were fundamentally irrational when they refused to acknowledge the connection between Blessing and their population explosion. The connection seems obvious. The Stinkards' population explosion began *exactly* with the introduction of Blessing, and the introduction of Blessing *would* clearly produce the result observed. Logic and history combine to indict Blessing as the cause of the Stinkard population explosion. Logic and history combine to suggest that removing this cause would end the explosion and restore population stability.

But what in our own culture corresponds to Blessing?

I'll answer an easier question first and tell you that my role here today corresponds exactly to the role of the unfortunate Dr. Spry. I will name to you the cause of our population explosion—with far more evidence and plausibility than Dr. Spry was able to muster in the case of Blessing—and then we'll see. I'm used to people becoming enraged with me on this issue. They become enraged because, like Dr. Spry, I'm indicting what is perceived to be the very foremost blessing of our culture—a blessing far more essential to our way of life than any mere pain reliever.

Growth and the ABCs of ecology

Among life-forms found on the surface of our planet, all food energy originates in the green plants and nowhere else. The energy that originates in green plants is passed on to creatures who feed on the plants, and is passed on again to predators who feed on plant eaters, and is passed on again to predators who feed on those predators, and is passed on again to scavengers who return to the soil nutrients that green plants need to keep the cycle going. All this can be said to be the A of the ABCs of ecology.

The various feeding and feeder populations of the community

maintain a dynamic balance, by feeding and being fed upon. Imbalances within the community—caused, for example, by disease or natural disasters—tend to be damped down and eradicated as the various populations of the community go about their usual business of feeding and being fed upon, generation after generation. Viewed in systems terms, the dynamic of population growth and decline in the biological community is a negative feedback system. If you've got too many deer in the forest, they're going to gobble up their food base—and this reduction in their food base will cause their population to decline. And as their population declines, their food base replenishes itself—and since this replenishment makes more food available to the deer, the deer population grows. In turn, the growth of the deer population depletes the availability of food, which in turn causes a decline in the deer population. Within the community, food populations and feeder populations control each other. As food populations increase, feeder populations increase. As feeder populations increase, food populations decrease. As food populations decrease, feeder populations decrease. As feeder populations decrease, food populations increase. And so on. This is the B of the ABCs of ecology.

For systems thinkers, the natural community provides a perfect model of negative feedback. A simpler model is the thermostat that controls your furnace. Conditions at the thermostat convey the information "Too cold," and the thermostat turns the furnace on. After a while, conditions at the thermostat convey the information "Too hot," and the thermostat turns the furnace off. Negative feedback. Great stuff.

The A of the ABCs of ecology is food. The community of life is nothing else. It's flying food, running food, swimming food, crawling food, and of course just sitting-there-and-growing food. The B of the ABCs of ecology is this, that the ebb and flow of all populations is a function of food availability. An increase in food availability for a species means growth. A reduction in food availability means decline. Always. Because it's so important let me say that another way: invariably. An increase in food availability for a species means growth. A reduction means decline. Every time, ever and always. *Semper et ubique.* Without exception. Never otherwise.

More food, growth. Less food, decline. Count on it.

There is no species that dwindles in the midst of abundance, no species that thrives on nothing.

This is the B of the ABCs of ecology.

Defeating the system's controls

With the A and the B of ecology in hand, we're ready to go back and look again at the origin of our population explosion. For a hundred and ninety thousand years our species grew at an infinitesimal rate from a few thousand to ten million. Then about ten thousand years ago we began to grow rapidly. This was not a miraculous event or an accidental event or even a mysterious event.

We began to grow more rapidly because we'd found a way to defeat the negative feedback controls of the community. We'd become food producers—agriculturalists. In other words, we'd found a way to increase food availability *at will.*

This ability to make food available at will is the blessing on which our civilization is founded. It's also the blessing that the pain reliever in my parable stands for. The ability to produce food at will is an undoubted blessing, but its very blessedness can make it dangerous— and dangerously addictive—just like the analgesic in my fable.

"At will" is the operative expression here. Because we could now produce food at will, our population was no longer subject to control by food availability on a random basis. Anytime we wanted more food, we could grow it. After a hundred and ninety thousand years of being limited by what was available, we began to *control* what was available—and invariably we began to *increase* what was available. You don't become a farmer in order to *reduce* food availability, you become a farmer to *increase* food availability. And so do the folks next door. And so do the folks farming throughout your region. You are all involved in increasing food availability for your species.

And here comes the B in the ABCs of ecology: An increase in food availability for a species means growth for that species. In other words, ecology predicts that the blessing of agriculture will bring us growth—and history confirms ecology's prediction. As soon as we began to increase the availability of our own food, our population began to grow—not glacially, as before, when we were subject to the community's negative feedback controls—but rapidly.

Population expansion among agriculturalists was followed by territorial expansion among agriculturalists. Territorial expansion made more land available for food production—and no one goes into farming to *reduce* food production. More land, more food production, more population growth.

With more people, we need more food. With more food available, we soon have more people—as predicted by the laws of ecology. With more people, we need more food. With more food, we soon have more people. With more people, we need more food. With more food, we soon have more people.

Positive feedback, this is called, in systems terminology. Another example: When conditions at the thermostat convey the information "Too hot," the thermostat turns the furnace ON instead of OFF. That's positive feedback. Negative feedback *checks* an increasing effect. Positive feedback *reinforces* an increasing effect.

Positive feedback is what we see at work in this agricultural revolution of ours. Increased population stimulates increased food production, which increases the population. More food, more people. More people, more food. More food, more people. More people, more food. More food, more people. Positive feedback. Bad stuff. Dangerous stuff.

The experiment run 10,000 times

What is observed in the human population is that intensification of production to feed an increased population invariably leads to a still greater increase in population. I've seen this called a paradox, but in fact it's only what the laws of ecology predict. Listen to it again: "Intensification of production to feed an increased population invariably leads to a still greater increase in population."

Think of it as an experiment that has been performed annually in our culture for the last ten thousand years: Let's see what happens if we increase food production this year. Hey, whaddya know, our population increased too! Let's see what happens next year if we increase food production.

Hey, whaddya know, our population increased again! Do you suppose there's a connection?

Nah, why would there be?

Well, what shall we do this year? Increase production or decrease it? Well, we *gotta* increase it, don't we, because we've got more mouths to feed!

Okay, let's increase food production again this year and see what happens. Wow, look at that! Population up again.

Well, let's increase production again and see what happens. Who knows, maybe this time the population will go down.

Nope, up again. Amazing.

These thumbnail conversations describe the results of five annual experiments performed in ancient times. Imagine nine thousand nine hundred ninety-five more of them, bringing us up to the present year, 1996, when we have to ask ourselves, well, what are we going to do *this* year? Decrease food production?

No way, don't be ridiculous.

Well, whaddya say, let's just keep it the same as last year just for once. You know, see what happens?

Are you kidding? Civilization would crash and burn.

Why? If we produced enough food for five and a half billion people last year, why should civilization crash and burn if we produce enough for five and a half billion people *this* year?

Because enough for five and a half billion *wasn't* enough. Millions are starving.

Yeah, but everyone knows that this isn't because food is lacking. The food is there, it's just not getting to the people who are starving.

Look, didn't we have this conversation in 1990?

Sure we had it in 1990.

We had it in 1990 and in 1921 during the Russian famine and in 1846 during the Irish famine and in 1783 during the Japanese famine and in 1591 during the Italian famine and in 1315 during the European famine. God, I can remember having this conversation in the sixth century B.C. during the *Roman* famines.

Well, that's the point I'm making. How many times have we run this experiment?

About ten thousand times. Ten thousand times we've decided to increase food production, and ten thousand times the population has gotten bigger. Doesn't *prove* anything, of course. This time could be different. This time the population might go *down*.

Well, okay, let's try it one more time. We'll increase food production again this year and see what happens. . . .

Hey, whaddya know. The population went up again this time. Quite a coincidence, huh?

Three demonstrations

Let me spend a few minutes now outlining a series of demonstrations that will clarify the issues I've raised here.

This is demonstration number one. Into a nice roomy cage we introduce two young, healthy mice. The cage has a built-in feeder that enables us to make food available to the mice in any quantity we like. After installing the two mice, we shove in two kilos of food. This is obviously much more than two mice need, but that will do no harm and you'll soon see the point of it. Next day, we take out the feeder, discard the uneaten food, and replace it with another two kilos. We do this every day. Soon the two mice become four, the four become eight, the eight become sixteen, the sixteen become thirty-two. This population growth confirms the fact that these mice have plenty of food. We continue to put in two kilos of food every day and, as time goes on, more and more of it is eaten; this isn't a surprise, because there are more and more mice eating it. Eventually there comes a day when all of it is eaten. No matter. We continue to put two kilos of food in the cage every day, and every day the two kilos of food are eaten. Now guess what happens to that population, which has been growing so busily from day one of the demonstration. It *stops* growing. It levels off. Again, this is no surprise at all. As we continue to supply two kilos of food a day, we count the mice daily for a year and see that the population fluctuates between two hundred eighty and three hundred twenty, with an average of three hundred. Two kilos of food every day will maintain about three hundred mice. That's demonstration one.

Demonstration two begins much the same way. Cage. Two mice. This time, however, we follow a different procedure. Instead of putting in the same amount of food every day, we start with one amount and increase it daily. However much the pair of mice eat the first day, we put in fifty percent more the second day. However much they eat the second day, we put in fifty percent more the third day. Before long there are four mice. No matter, we follow our procedure. Whatever they eat in a day, we put in fifty percent more the next. Before long there are eight mice, sixteen mice, thirty-two mice. No matter, whatever they eat in one day, we put in fifty percent more the next. Sixty-four mice, a hundred twenty-eight, two hundred fifty, five hundred, a thousand. Whatever the mice eat in one day, we put in fifty percent more the next, carefully extending the sides of the cage as needed to avoid stressful overcrowding. Two thousand, four thousand, eight thousand, sixteen thousand, thirty-two thousand, sixty-four thousand. At this point, someone runs in and yells, "Stop! Stop! This is a population explosion!"

Golly! I guess you're right! What shall we do?

I have a suggestion. Let's start by answering this question: How much did the sixty-four thousand mice eat yesterday? Answer: five hundred kilos of food. Okay. Well, ordinarily, we'd put seventy-five hundred kilos of food into the cage tomorrow, but let's abandon that procedure now. Our new procedure will be based on this theory: Yesterday five hundred kilos was enough for them, so why shouldn't five hundred kilos be enough for them today?

So today we put just five hundred kilos of food into the cage, same as yesterday.

Now watch closely. There are no food riots. Why should there be? The mice have just as much to eat today as they did yesterday.

Now watch closely again. No mice are starving. Why would there be?

Now it's tomorrow, and again we put just five hundred kilos of food into the cage.

Again, watch closely. There are still no food riots. Still no mice starving.

We do it again on day three. Again, no food riots, no mice starving.

But aren't new mice being born? Of course—and old mice are dying.

Day four, day five, day six. I'm waiting for the food riots, but there are no food riots. I'm waiting for the famine, but there is no famine.

There are sixty-four thousand mice, and five hundred kilos of food will feed sixty-four thousand mice. Why should there be riots? Why should there be famine?

Oh—and I almost forgot to mention it—the population explosion stopped overnight. What else could it do? Population growth *has* to be supported by increased food availability. Always. Without exception. Less food—decline. More food—growth. Same food—stability. That's what we've got here: Stability.

Demonstration three. This demonstration is identical to demonstration two right up to the end. Sixty-four thousand mice, five hundred kilos of food, stability. Then the head of the department charges in and says, "Who needs sixty-four thousand mice? These mice are eating us out of house and home. What's special about sixty-four thousand mice anyhow? Why not eight thousand? Why not four thousand?"

Oh my, what a crisis. Quick—check the Yellow Pages, see if anyone makes condoms for mice! What, no condoms for mice!?! Well, look under Family Planning! What, no family planning for rodents!?!

No, you know this would not be the reaction. You know this because you understand the B in the ABCs of ecology. We don't need birth control. All we need is *food* control.

Someone says, here's what we do. Yesterday five hundred kilos of food went into the cage. Today we'll reduce that by a kilo. Oh no, another objects. A kilo is too much. Let's reduce it by a quarter of a kilo. So that's what they do. Four hundred ninety-nine and three quarters kilos of food go into the cage. Tension in the lab as everyone waits for food riots and famine—but of course there are no food riots and no famine. Among sixty-four thousand mice, a quarter of a kilo of food is like a flake of dandruff apiece.

Tomorrow four hundred ninety-nine and a half kilos of food go into the cage. Still no food riots and no famine.

This procedure is followed for a thousand days—and not once is there a food riot or a famine. After a thousand days only two hundred fifty kilos of food are going into the cage—and guess what? There are no longer sixty-four thousand mice in the cage. There are only thirty-two thousand. Not a miracle—just a demonstration of the laws of ecology. A decline in food availability has been answered by a decline in population. As always. *Semper et ubique.* Nothing to do with riots. Nothing to do with famine. Just the normal response of a feeder population to the availability of food.

Objections

I've been surprised by how challenging people find these ideas. They feel menaced by them. They get angry. They feel I'm attacking the foundation of their lives. They feel I'm calling into question the blessedness of the greatest blessing of civilized life. They somehow feel I'm questioning the sacredness of human life itself.

I'd like to deal with some of the objections people make to these ideas. I do this not to discourage you from expressing objections of your own but because I can express these objections as rudely as I like to myself without making anyone nervous.

I'll deal with the most general objection first, which is that humans are not mice. This is of course absolutely true, especially at the individual level. Each of us as an individual is capable of making reproductive choices that mice absolutely cannot make. Nonetheless—and this is the point that ecology makes and that I've made here today—our behavior as a biological population is indistinguishable from the behavior of any other biological population. In defense of that statement, I offer the evidence of ten thousand years of obedience to this fundamental law of ecology: An increase in food availability for a species means *growth* for that species.

I've been told that it doesn't *have* to be this way. I've been told that it's possible for us to *increase* food production and simultaneously *reduce* our population. This is basically the position taken by birth-control advocates. This is basically the position taken by well-intentioned organizations that undertake to improve indigenous agricultural techniques in Third World countries. They want to give technologically undeveloped peoples the means of increasing their population with one hand and birth-control aids with the other hand—even though we know full well that these birth-control aids don't even work for *us*! They're certain that we can go on increasing food production while ending population growth through birth control. This represents a denial of the B in the ABCs of ecology.

History—and not just thirty years of history but ten thousand years of history—offers no support whatever for the idea that we can simultaneously increase food production and end population growth. On the contrary, history resoundingly confirms what ecology teaches: If you make more food available, there will be more people to consume it.

Obviously the matter is different at the individual level. Old Macdonald on his farm can increase food production and simultaneously hold his family's growth to zero, but this clearly isn't the end of the story. What's he going to do with that increase he produced on his farm? Is he going to soak it in gasoline and burn it? If so, then he hasn't actually produced an increase at all. Is he going to sell it? Presumably that *is* what he's going to do with it, and if he *does* sell it, then that increase enters the annual agricultural increase that serves to support our global population growth.

I'm often told that even if we *stop* increasing food production, our population will *continue* to grow. This represents a denial of *both* the A *and* the B of the ABCs of ecology. The A in the ABCs of ecology is this: *We are food.* We are food because we are what we eat—and what we eat is food. To put it plainly, each and every one of us is *made from food.*

When people tell me that our population will continue to add new millions even if we stop increasing food production, then I have to ask what these additional millions of people will be made of, since no additional food is being produced for them. I have to say, "Please bring me some of these people, because if they're not made of food, I want to know what they *are* made of. Is it moonbeams or rainbow dust or starlight or angel's breath or what?"

Almost invariably someone asks if I'm not aware that population growth is much slower in the food-rich North than in the food-poor South. This fact seems to be offered as proof that human societies are *not* subject to the laws of ecology, which (it is assumed) predict that the more food the faster the growth. But this is *not* what ecology predicts. Let me repeat that: Ecology does *not* predict that the population in a food-rich area will grow more rapidly than the population in a food-poor area. What ecology predicts is: When more food is made available, the population will increase. Every year more food is made available in the North, and every year the population increases. Every year more food is made available in the South, and every year the population increases.

Then I will be told very emphatically that more food is *not* being made available in the South. The population is growing like wildfire, but this growth is *not* being supported by any increase in food. All I can say about this is, if what you say is true, then we are clearly in the presence of a miracle. These people are not being made from food, because, according to you, no food is being made available for them. They must be made of air or icicles or dirt. But if it turns out—as I strongly suspect it will—that these people are *not* made of air or icicles or dirt but ordinary flesh and blood, then I'll have to say, what do you think this stuff is? [Here B grabbed the skin on his arm.] Do you think you can make this flesh and blood out of *nothing*? No, the existence of the flesh and blood is *proof* that these people are being made out of food. And if there are more *people* here this year, this is proof that there is more *food* here this year.

And of course I have to deal with the starving millions. Don't we have to continue to increase food production in order to feed the starving millions? There are two things to understand here. The first is that the excess that we produce each year does *not* go to feed the starving millions. It didn't go to feed the starving millions in 1995, it didn't go to feed the starving millions in 1994, it didn't go to feed the starving millions in 1993, it didn't go to feed the starving millions in 1992—and it won't go to feed the starving millions in 1996. Where did it go? It went to fuel our population explosion.

That's the first thing. The second thing is that everyone involved in the problem of world hunger knows that the problem is not a shortage of food. Producing more food does *not* solve the problem, because that's simply *not* the problem. Producing more food just produces more people.

Then people will ask, "Don't you realize that our agricultural base is already being destroyed? We're eliminating millions of tons of topsoil every year. Even the sea isn't yielding as much food as before. Yet the population explosion continues." The point of the objection is

contained in that last sentence: Our food production capacity is declining, yet the population explosion continues. This nonfact is offered as proof that there is no connection between food and growth.
Once again, I'm afraid I must insist that this is magical thinking. Our
population explosion can no more continue without food than a fire
can continue without fuel. The fact that our population continues to
grow year after year is *proof* that we're producing more food year after
year. Until people start showing up who are made of shadows or metal
filings or gravel—when that happens, then I'll have to back off this
point.

When all else fails, it will be objected that the people of the world
will not tolerate a limit on food. That may be, but it has nothing to
do with the facts I've presented here.

No one has ever specifically asked me what I have against birth
control, but I'll answer the question anyway. I don't have a thing
against birth control as such. It just represents very poor problem-
solving strategy. The rule in crisis management is, Don't make it your
goal to control effects, make it your goal to control causes. If you
control causes, then you don't *have* to control effects. This is why they
make you go through airport security *before* you get on the plane.
They don't want to control effects. They want to control causes. Birth
control is a strategy aimed at effects. Food-production control is a
strategy aimed at causes.

We'd better have a look at it.

Questions and Answers

[All Qs as summarized by B for non-German-speaking listeners]

Q. You mention in one of your "demonstrations" that the walls of
the cage are expanded to accommodate an increased population of
mice. It seems to me this invalidates the demonstration, inasmuch as
there is no way for us to expand the walls of this planet to accommodate an increased human population.

A. What the nations of Europe did, beginning in the sixteenth
century, was precisely to expand the walls of their cage to accommo-

date an increased population—into the New World, Australia, Mela-
nesia, and Africa.

Q. It's difficult for me to see how you have improved on Thomas
Malthus, who was making similar predictions a century ago.

A. Malthus's warning was about the inevitable failure of totalitarian agriculture. My warning is about its continued success.

Q. Your models of population growth fail to take into account the
well-established correlation between standard of living and population
growth. Countries with a high standard of living have a growth rate
near zero or even below zero (as in Germany!), whereas countries with
a low standard of living are the ones that account for the greatest
growth. This shows that food production and population growth
aren't necessarily connected.

A. The argument you've presented is the sort of argument the
tobacco industry likes: "One of my best friends never touched a cigarette in her life, didn't grow up among smokers, and didn't work
among smokers, but she died of lung cancer at age thirty-seven. On
the other hand, my father has been smoking two packs of cigarettes a
day since he was seventeen and is still hale and hardy at age sixty-
three. This shows that smoking and cancer aren't necessarily connected."

When our population system is assessed as a whole—on a global
scale, rather than country by country—there is no doubt whatever
that, as a whole, our population is increasing catastrophically, so that
studies conducted by international groups like the United Nations
predict without reservation that there will be twelve billion of us here
in forty years or so.

Q. The point you are ignoring is that population growth can be
slowed if living conditions are improved.

A. In the New World five hundred years ago, the non-native
population was zero. Today the non-native population is three hundred million. This growth was not a result of poor living conditions.
It was a result of the causes I have outlined here tonight.

Q. The farmers of the world do not primarily produce food to feed an expanded population, as you suggest. This is not the force to which they are responding. More and more farmers are engaged in producing crops that don't feed anyone at all, crops like coffee, cotton, and tobacco.

A. Where is the food coming from to feed our expanding population then? If it isn't being produced by farmers, who is producing it? This is a biological fact that is simply beyond dispute: If a hundred million people are added to the population, these people will be made from food and nothing else.

Q. According to Karl Marx, the population of every culture is determined by the constraints of its livelihood. For example, foraging peoples, in order to pursue their lifestyle, must maintain a very small population. They could feed more, but only by abandoning some aspect of their lifestyle. In other words, their lifestyle forces a limit on them. Our lifestyle will force a limit on us as well.

A. I see. And meanwhile, food production has nothing to do with it?

Q. As far as I am concerned, food production has nothing to do with it.

A. I can only point out that the biological sciences see the matter differently.

Q. It seems to me that we don't need to do anything about our growing population. The system itself will take care of it.

A. You mean by collapsing. Yes, that's perfectly true. If you learn that the building you're living in has a structural fault that will soon cause it to collapse under the force of gravity, you're certainly at liberty to let the system take care of it. But if your children are living in the building when it finally collapses, they may not think as highly of this solution as you do.

The Great Remembering

There's a drug known as angel dust or PCP that has the effect of blinding people to their physical limitations and vulnerability. Under its influence, people will manically plunge into feats that are beyond the design limitations of the human body, so that they heedlessly break bones, rip flesh, and tear ligaments, imagining themselves to be indestructible, only becoming aware of the damage they've done to themselves when the drug wears off.

Our culture has its own form of angel dust, which blinds us to our biological limitations and vulnerability. Under its influence, we have manically plunged into feats that are beyond the design limitations not only of our species but of any species on earth, so that we have heedlessly broken bones, ripped flesh, and torn ligaments, imagining ourselves to be indestructible. Only now, like the addict when his drug begins to wear off, are we beginning to count the wounds we have inflicted on ourselves during our maddened riot. But even as we make that count, we keep taking the drug, because we haven't yet identified it as the source of our mania.

The drug I'm talking about is the Great Forgetting. Just as angel dust blinds its users to the fact that they're flesh and bone, the Great Forgetting blinds us to the fact that we are a biological species in a community of biological species and are not exempt or exemptible from the forces that shape all life on this planet. The Great Forgetting blinds us to the fact that what cannot work for any species will not work for us either. As angel dust tempts people to do things that would be mortally hazardous for any human, the Great Forgetting tempts us to do things that would be mortally hazardous for any species.

There are many who think it's too late for humankind to save itself. I hear from them daily, and my heart goes out to them. Their hopelessness is understandable, because they mistake the workings of the drug for human nature itself. There *is* time for us to stop taking the drug and to stop feeding it to our children. There *is* time for us to begin the Great Remembering.

The obliteration of tribalism

I explained a little while ago that the Great Forgetting fostered the delusion that the world was empty of humans until the people of our culture made their appearance just a few thousand years ago. As a corollary of this delusion, it was understood that our culture was not only the first and original human culture but the single culture that God intended for all humankind. These delusions remain in place today globally—East and West, twins of a common birth—even though the true (and well-known) story of human origins obviously gives them no support at all.

As the foundation thinkers of our culture reconstructed the story, humans appeared in the world with an instinct for civilization but of course no experience. They soon discovered the obvious benefits of communal life, and from there the course of civilization was clear. Farming villages grew into towns, towns grew into cities, cities grew into kingdoms, and so on. All was clear, but all was not smooth, because a key social instrument had yet to be invented, that instrument being law. Ignorant even of the concept of law, the citizens of these early cities and kingdoms were compelled to suffer crime, turmoil, oppression, and injustice. Law was a vitally important enabling invention, on which orderly social development had to wait, much as oceanic navigation had to wait on the invention of the astrolabe.

One would expect to find that laws existed long before literacy, but this appears not to have been the case. If laws had been formulated orally in preliterate times, then the earliest writings would surely have been transcriptions of these laws—but no such laws are found in these writings. In fact, the earliest written code of law, the Code of Hammurabi, dates to only about 2100 B.C.E.

Roughly speaking, this is what the foundation thinkers imagined, and this is what became the received wisdom of our culture, embedded in all social thought—and in the textbooks used by schoolchildren around the globe, even to the present moment. Needless to say, it's about as close to the truth as the fairy tale that babies are delivered by storks.

Now let's take off the obscuring lenses of the Great Forgetting and have a look at what was really happening in the world ten thousand years ago. Members of *Homo sapiens* had been moving outward from their African birthplace for more than a hundred thousand years and had literally reached every corner of the world—and I don't mean recently. By the time I'm talking about, ten thousand years ago, the Near East, Europe, Asia, Australia, and the New World had all been occupied by modern humans for at least twenty thousand years. And far from being empty, the Near East was among the most densely populated areas of the world—densely populated, that is, by tribal peoples, such as were found everywhere in the world at that time and such as are found still today where they've been allowed to survive.

So we've made two steps beyond the fairy tale: The founders of our culture didn't live in an empty world, they were a tribal people surrounded by many other tribal peoples—and none of them were newcomers to the business of culture. These were old, old, old, old, old, old hands at culture, which means that not a single one of them was a stranger to the concept of law. Never once in the whole history of anthropology has a tribal people been found unequipped with a complete set of laws—complete, that is, for the lifestyle of that particular tribe.

The names of the tribes inhabiting the relevant area at this time will never be known to us. The name of the tribe in which our own quirky approach to life was born is similarly unknown. Since their descendants have come to be called Takers, I'll give them a name that echoes this a bit. I'll call them the Tak. With this as a beginning, I'll tell you a story of my own—obviously not intended to be taken as literal history, to be sure, but also not a ridiculous fairy tale, like the one we hear from those who are still blinded by the Great Forgetting. There certainly was such a people as the Tak (there had to be or we wouldn't be here!), and they were certainly a tribal people surrounded by other tribal people, whom I've shown here as the Ak, the Bak, the Cak, and so on up through the Kak.

This drawing reflects two vitally important realities of tribal life. First, the dark background of each tribal area is what makes the tribal name stand out. What this is meant to show is that each tribe is defined by the solidity and density of its own laws and customs. There is literally no other way to tell them apart. The laws and customs of the Ak are what make them distinguishable as a tribe. The laws and customs of the Bak are what make them distinguishable as a tribe. The laws and customs of the Cak are what make them distinguishable as a tribe. And so on. Second, the solid border around each tribe makes it clear that the cultural boundaries between tribes are impenetrable. A member of the Bak can't just decide one day to become a member of the Hak; such a thing is quite unthinkable among tribal peoples anywhere in the world.

Probably at this time some of these tribal peoples were agriculturalists and some were hunter-gatherers. There's nothing at all unusual about finding the two living side by side. In any case, we know that the Tak (the tribal founders of the lifestyle we're used to calling the Taker lifestyle) were agriculturalists—though there's no reason to suppose that they invented agriculture. Their invention was a new *style* of agriculture—the totalitarian style.

But the stupendous innovation of the Tak was not just a new style of agriculture. The Tak had the remarkable and unprecedented idea that *everyone* should live the way they lived. It's impossible to exaggerate how unusual this made them. I can't name a single other people in history who made it a goal to proselytize their neighbors. Certainly no tribal people in history has evinced any interest in converting neighbors to their way of life—and I know of no civilized people who evinced such an interest either. For example, the Maya, the Natchez, and the Aztecs had no interest in spreading their lifestyle to the peoples around them, including those they conquered. The Tak were definitely revolutionaries in this regard. By inspiration, persuasion, or aggression, the Tak revolution began to engulf its neighbors.

By adopting a common culture, the Tak, Dak, and Fak have necessarily lost some of the solidity that once defined them. This is why they're depicted as somewhat grayed out. The laws and customs of the Tak mean little to the Dak or the Fak. The laws and customs of the Dak mean little to the Tak or the Fak. The laws and customs of the Fak mean little to the Tak or the Dak. Because they now share a common lifestyle, the cultural borders between them grow faint. It's not as easy to tell one from another now. Being a Dak or a Fak isn't as important as it once was. Now what's important is that they're allied with the Tak. It should be kept in mind that in this alliance the original laws and customs of the Tak are no more relevant than anyone else's. The Dak and the Fak have not become Tak. They've just largely ceased to be Dak and Fak.

The process continues. The laws and customs of individual tribes continue to fade into irrelevance. By now the Dak and the Fak have virtually lost their tribal identities, and the Hak and the Kak soon will join them.

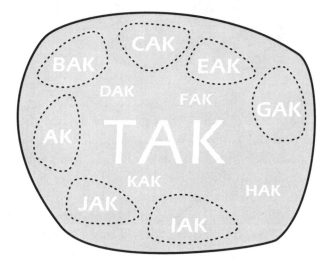

At last the original dozen have been assimilated into a single vast farming collective. Because tribal laws and customs have been reduced to nothing, tribal identities are all but unreadable. It's as easy for one

of the Ak to live among the Hak as it is for a Belgian to live in France
or for a New Yorker to live in San Francisco.

Now we're ready to depict the state of law in this farming collective.

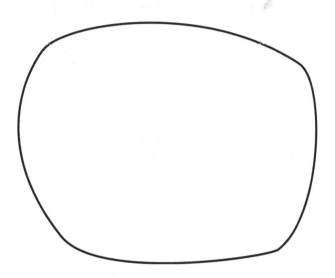

The foundation thinkers of our culture imagined that our culture
was born in a world empty of law. As this series of drawings shows,
our culture was born in a world absolutely full of law, and then
proceeded to obliterate it—quite inadvertently, I'm sure (at least in
the beginning). Even the law of the original Tak tribe disappeared,
rendered by this process as irrelevant as all the rest.

I want you to notice that this reconstruction is not entirely a work
of imagination. Study the spread of our culture into the Americas,
into Australia, into Africa and elsewhere, and you can hardly fail to
see the steady obliteration of tribal law in the path of its advance—
and with the obliteration of tribal law, the obliteration of tribal identity.

On the nature of received laws

As time went on, and the vacuum increased in size, it became obvious
that some new form of law was needed. Since tribal law had been

rendered obsolete, nothing remained now but to begin to *invent* laws. . . .

I think anyone who does a lot of public speaking eventually learns to sense when a chord has been struck and the audience is ringing with it. That's what I just sensed after saying that nothing remained but to begin to *invent* laws.

This is of course a startling idea, the idea that laws could be anything *but* invented—but that's exactly the point to be made about tribal laws. Tribal laws are *never* invented laws, they're always *received* laws. They're never the work of committees of living individuals, they're always the work of social evolution. They're shaped the way a bird's beak is shaped, or a mole's claw—by what works. They never reflect a tribe's concern for what's "right" or "good" or "fair," they simply *work*—for that particular tribe. An example will show you—

I see this woman here has an urgent question. Please go ahead. . . .

Yes. I'll repeat the question for those of you who were unable to hear it. It's about the genital mutilation of women among tribal peoples, specifically the excision of the clitoris disguised as a form of female circumcision. I've looked into this and haven't found any untouched tribal people who follow this abominable practice. It's found only among peoples who have been all but completely absorbed into Taker culture—and specifically Taker culture in the Islamic sphere. Clitoral excision isn't advocated in the Koran, but its practitioners clearly have the impression that it's Islam-approved and a very Muslim thing to do, and the practice isn't found outside areas under Muslim influence. A strong confirmation of the fact that this is not a "tribal" practice is that it's not found among peoples who are still living tribally, like say, the Pagibeti or the Yaka. It's found only among people who have abandoned tribal identity, laws, and customs, and now belong to the wider Taker community of some recognized political entity like Senegal or Mali.

Okay?

I was saying that an example will show you the difference between received tribal laws and laws invented by committees. Here's how the Alawa of Australia handle adultery.

Let's suppose that you're a young unmarried man of the Alawa.

You find yourself in the unhappy circumstance of being attracted to your second cousin's wife, Gurtina—and of knowing that she is attracted to you. Now, your second cousin is a fine fellow, and you wouldn't intentionally hurt him, but these things happen: You and his wife are possessed by the love madness.

It's really very touching and pathetic. Living in the same camp, you can't help but see each other daily. You circle each other like binary stars, drawn together by one force, thrust apart by another. What you read in each other's eyes is plain but untested. You yearn to test it, but . . . you know what the testing will inevitably cost.

No matter. Soon you can endure it no longer. The fire of love is burning you alive. One day in passing at the outskirts of camp, you confront her. She lowers her eyes modestly, as always, but your determination is fixed. "Tonight," you whisper, "past the saltbush on the other side of the stream."

She hesitates a moment to consult her own heart, but she too knows that the time has come. "At the setting of the moon?" she asks. "At the setting of the moon." She nods and hurries away, her heart bursting with joy and dread.

That night you're there a little beforehand, of course, to prepare your bower of love, your nest of passion. Gurtina comes to you at last. Your hands touch. You embrace. Ah!

A few hours later, exhausted with delight, you sit by a tiny fire and watch it grow pale in the burgeoning dawn. You exchange a glance, and more is written in that glance than in all your night's endearments and caresses. You have tested your passion. Now, this glance says, it's time to test your love.

With a sigh, you smother the fire and head back to camp, trying not to let your feet drag. Your faces are a careful display. Exultation would be childish and insolent. Shame would be a denial of your love. Instead, what's seen there is something like repose, acceptance, fortitude. You both know what you're going to see, and without fail you see it. At one side of the camp the men are arrayed, already hopping with fury. At the other side wait the women, smoldering.

You and Gurtina exchange another glance—this one briefer than the beat of a gnat's wing—and then you're engulfed in a wave of wrath. The men descend on you, the women on her. Rocks and spears and boomerangs are flying through the air, clubs and digging sticks are being wielded with abandon. But you don't just stand there and take it—far from it. You both battle back in defense of your love, answering screams with screams, rocks with rocks, spears with spears, blows with blows, until all weapons and combatants are finally exhausted.

Gurtina, bleeding and battered, is returned to her husband, and you're told to roll your swag and get the hell out if you know what's good for you. For a while the men's bodies are exhausted, their fury isn't, and when they revive, you'll be fair game again. So you roll your swag, thinking. Thinking very hard. The test of your love isn't over, it's just begun. The next few hours will be the true test, and this test will be in your head and heart alone. You leave camp, knowing that as yet you have a choice. . . .

The question is: Do you really want this woman? Do you want her more than anything you hold dear in the world? If you don't, if there's the slightest doubt . . . you will just keep going—go on walkabout for a few weeks. When you come back, the men's fury will have abated. They'll jeer at you for a few weeks and then forget all about it. Gurtina . . . ah, Gurtina will know you for what you are, a craven seducer, a hollow man, and she'll never forget. And of course there'll be a price to be paid to your cousin. But all these are bearable. The alternative, on the other hand . . . You circle the camp all day, staying out of sight and out of reach, thinking. But by dusk you know that your doubts have vanished. In the gathering darkness, you approach camp stealthily, to the spot where your loved one is being guarded. Lightly guarded.

Lightly guarded—to keep her from running away with you. Ah, the exquisiteness of that guard! Do you see its effect?

Gurtina has her own choice to make, you see—the same terrible choice as yours. And the restraint provided by those guards defines and delimits her choice. For she's guarded. You're not. You have to prove your courage by coming for her. She doesn't need to prove her courage by coming for you. And in fact, she can't. She's guarded, you see. So that, should you *not* come for her, she will not be shamed. Rather it will be you who is shamed.

But this is only half of it. The guards are there to protect you as well, because Gurtina too has her choice to make. Does she really want you? Does she want you more than anything she holds dear in the world? If not—if there's the slightest doubt—when your signal comes at dusk, she need only shrug helplessly, as if to say, "See? I can't get away, my love. I'm being too well guarded." Thus the presence of the guards enables her to express her choice in a way that does not crush your self-esteem. The presence of the guards makes it possible for her to end the whole episode in a moment, without a single word, as painlessly as possible.

Now note very well that none of this is or was worked out rationally or consciously, of course. Nevertheless, the guard on Gurtina is in fact curiously inefficient. Efficient enough to serve all the purposes I've just mentioned—but inefficient enough to allow her to escape at your signal, if that is her will. Because of course the Alawa are sensible enough to know that if she wants you this much, it would be foolish to make escape impossible.

The testing is over now. You and she have made your decision. Now the price must be paid. The price for disrupting the life of the tribe, for cheapening marriage in the eyes of the children. And that price is, next to death itself, the heaviest that can be paid: detribalization, lifelong exile.

At your signal, Gurtina slips away from her guard and, together at last and forever, the two of you hurry away into the night, never to return. You are journeying into the land of the dead now. Detribalized, you *are* dead to all you left behind and to all you shall ever meet for the rest of your lives. Now you are truly homeless, by your own choice, alone and adrift in a vast, empty world. Your home is now each other, which you chose *above* the tribe. There will be no comradeship for you forever except what you find in each other: no friends, no father and mother, no aunts and uncles, no cousins, no nieces and nephews. You have thrown it all away—to have each other.

And you know that this is truly a price you've paid of your own choice, not a punishment. To have each other and go on living with the tribe would be unthinkable, disgraceful, even worse than exile. It would in fact destroy the tribe, because once the children saw that there was no price to be paid for adultery, marriage would become a laughingstock, and the basis of the family and of the tribe itself would disintegrate.

What you see at work here in this example is the stupendous efficacy of tribal law. Nothing like invented law, which just spells out crimes and punishments, tribal law is something that *works*. It works well for all concerned. A man and woman whose love is as great as this must of course have each other. But for the sake of the tribe, they must be *gone*—out of sight, out of mind forever. The children of the tribe have seen with their own eyes that marriage and love are not the trifling matters they have become among "advanced" peoples like us. The husband's dishonor has been avenged—and there will be no snickering among his comrades about it, for they stood side by side with him to lambaste the adulterer.

But perhaps you had a question at this point in the story: Why would the lovers return to the camp at all?

Oh, that's exactly the crux of the law. It wouldn't work at all without that. Suppose, after your night of lovemaking, you were to suggest to Gurtina: "Oh, why should we wait another day to be together? Let's run away now!" What would she think? She would think, "Uh-oh, what have I gotten myself into here? What kind of a man is this? A coward, obviously, who would have us slink off into the night rather than go back to face the others and say, 'Well, here we are! Do your worst!' "

And if she made the suggestion instead of you, you'd think the same of her. So the two of you *must* go back. . . .

Every part of this process is the law, and every actor in it is a participant in the law. The law for these people isn't a separate statute written in a book. It's the very fabric of their lives—it's what makes the Alawa the Alawa and what distinguishes them from the Mara and the Malanugga-nugga—who have their *own* ways of handling adultery, which are the best for *them*. It can't possibly be said too often that there is no one right way for people to live; that's only the delusion of the most murderous and destructive culture that history has ever produced.

I'm sure it's all but self-evident to you that this law of adultery could not have been the invention of any committee whatever. It's not an improvisation or a contrivance, and *because* it's not an improvisation or a contrivance, it has weight with the Alawa. It might not occur to any of them to analyze it as I've done here tonight, but that doesn't matter in the least. They don't obey the law of the Alawa because it checks out under analysis. They obey the law of the Alawa because they're the Alawa, and to give up the law would be to give up their identity—would be to become detribalized.

The world of the detribalized

Now I hope I've given you a handle on the price to be paid for becoming part of the Taker revolution: detribalization—the loss of tribal laws, customs, and identity. Since the detribalization of the Old World (by which I mean the Near East, the Far East, and Europe) occurred thousands of years before the earliest historical records, it became part of the Great Forgetting, and as such it was invisible to the foundation thinkers of our culture. As they reconstructed it in imagination, the first humans were just proto-urbanites—farmers without farms, villagers without villages, city dwellers without cities. They couldn't possibly have imagined a whole world of tribal peoples becoming detribalized—or more importantly, what it meant to become detribalized. When they looked into the past, they saw people setting out to build civilization, being already innately inclined toward civilization. When we look into the past no longer under the influence of the Great Forgetting, we see something very different: people inadvertently (but systematically) obliterating a highly successful lifestyle—then scurrying like mad to knock together something to replace it with. We've been scurrying ever since, and every year our legislators and political thinkers go back to work at the ceaseless task of trying to knock together something as workable as what we destroyed.

People will sometimes charge me with just being in love with tribalism. They say to me in effect, "If you love it so much, why don't you just go do it and leave the rest of us alone?" Those who understand me in this way totally misunderstand what I'm saying. The tribal lifestyle isn't precious because it's beautiful or lovable or because it's "close to nature." It isn't even precious because it's "the natural way for people to live." To me, this is gibberish. This is like saying that bird migration is good because it's the natural way for birds to live, or like saying that bear hibernation is good because it's the natural way for bears to live. The tribal life is precious because it *tested out*. For three million years it worked for people. It worked for people the way nests work for birds, the way webs work for spiders, the way burrows work for moles, the way hibernation works for bears. That doesn't make it lovable, that makes it *viable*.

People will also say to me, "Well, if it was so wonderful, why didn't it last?" The answer is that it did last—it has lasted right up to the present moment. It continues to work, but the fact that something works doesn't make it invulnerable. Burrows and nests and webs can all be destroyed, but that doesn't change the fact that they *work*. Tribalism *can* be destroyed and indeed *has* largely been destroyed, but that doesn't change the fact that it worked for three million years and still works today as well as it ever did.

And the fact that tribalism works doesn't mean that something else can't work. The trouble is that our particular something else *isn't* working—doesn't work and *can't* work. It bears with it its own seeds of destruction. It's fundamentally unstable. And unfortunately it had to reach global proportions before the nature of its instability could be recognized.

It's important to realize that ours wasn't the only lifestyle experiment going on at this time. Birds experiment with nests—that's how nests evolved in the first place and how they continue to evolve. Moles experiment with burrows—that's how burrows evolved in the first place and how they continue to evolve. Spiders experiment with webs—that's how webs evolved in the first place and how they continue to evolve. We can't know what experiments in human culture were made in the Old World—they were all obliterated by the Taker experiment—but we know a lot about experiments that were made elsewhere. What's fascinating about them is that these cultural variants were being tested just the way variants within a species are tested. What worked survived, what didn't work perished, leaving behind its fossilized remains—irrigation ditches, roads, cities, temples, pyramids.

People everywhere were looking for alternatives to the traditional tribal way of making a living—hunting and gathering. They were looking at full-time agriculture and settlement, but if their particular experiment didn't work, they were prepared to let it go—and they did so again and again. It used to be considered a great mystery. What became of these ancient builders who carved strange cities out of the jungles and the deserts? Were they whisked away into another dimension? No, they just quit. They just went back to something they could count on to work.

What made the Taker experiment different from all of these was its very quirky belief that the Taker way was the way people were *meant* to live—people everywhere, forever, no matter what. To the Takers, it didn't matter whether it worked. It didn't matter if people liked it. It didn't matter if people suffered the torments of hell. This was the *one right way* for people to live. This bizarre notion made it impossible for people to give it up, no matter how badly it worked. If it doesn't work, then you'll just have to suffer.

If it doesn't work, suffer

And suffer they did.

It's not hard to figure out what made people cling to the tribal life—and makes them cling to it wherever it's still found today. Tribal peoples have their full share of suffering to do, but in the tribal life, no one suffers unless *everyone* suffers. There's no class or group of people who are expected to do the suffering—and no class or group of people who are exempt from suffering. If you think this sounds entirely too good to be true, check it out. In the tribal life there are no rulers to speak of; elders or chiefs—almost always part-time—exert influence rather than power. There's nothing equivalent to a ruling class—or to a rich or privileged class. There's nothing equivalent to a working class—or to a poor or underprivileged class. If this sounds ideal, well, why shouldn't it be, after three million years of evolutionary shaping? You're not surprised that natural selection has organized geese in a way that works well for geese. You're not surprised that natural selection has organized elephants in a way that works well for elephants. You're not surprised that natural selection has organized dolphins in a way that works well for dolphins. Why should you be surprised that natural selection organized people in a way that worked well for people?

And conversely, why should you be surprised that the founders of our culture, having obliterated a lifestyle tested over a period of three million years, were unable to instantly slap together a replacement that was just as good? Really, the task was a formidable one. We've been working at it for ten thousand years, and where are we?

The very first thing to go was the very thing that made tribal life a success: its social, economic, and political egalitarianism. As soon as our revolution began, the process of division began, between rulers and ruled, rich and poor, powerful and powerless, masters and slaves. The suffering class had arrived, and that class (as it would always be) was the masses. I won't repeat a tale everyone knows. Just a few thousand years separates the bare beginning of our culture in rude farming villages from the age of the god-kings, when the royal classes lived in mind-boggling splendor and all the rest—the suffering masses—lived like cattle.

At last we've entered the historical era. The Great Forgetting was complete. The tribal life had been gone for thousands of years. No one in the entire civilized world, East or West, remembered a time when perfectly ordinary people—the kind of people who now made up the suffering masses—lived well, and human society was not divided into those who are expected to suffer and those who are exempt from suffering.

Everyone thought it had been this way from the beginning. Everyone thought this was the nature of the world—and the nature of Man. They began to think that the world is an evil place. They began to think that existence itself is evil. They began to think (and who can blame them!) that there was something fundamentally wrong with humans. They began to think that humankind was doomed. They began to think that humankind was damned.

They began to think that someone needed to *save us*.

It's important for you to see that none of these ideas sprang from the tribal life—or could imaginably have sprung from the tribal life. These are ideas you expect to find welling up among people leading anguished lives, empty lives. You can make people live like cattle, but you can't make them think they're living well. You can render them powerless, but you can't render them dreamless. The suffering masses knew they were suffering—knew something was desperately wrong— knew they *needed* something. And what they needed was *salvation*.

The origin and cause of human suffering—and the means of ending it—became the first great intellectual and spiritual preoccupation of our culture, beginning about four thousand years ago. The next three millennia would see the development of all those religions that were destined to become the major religions of our culture— Hinduism, Buddhism, Judaism, Christianity, and Islam—and each had its own theory about the origin and cause of human suffering and its own approach to ending it, transcending it, or putting up with it. But all were united in a single, central vision: Whether it's release from the endless round of death and rebirth or blissful union with God in heaven, salvation is the highest goal of human life, unimaginably beyond any other, such as wealth, happiness, honor, or fame— and each of us is utterly alone in the universe with it. There is no marketplace in which nirvana or merit or grace or the forgiveness of sins can be purchased. No parent or spouse or friend can obtain salvation for you by any means whatever. And because nothing remotely compares with it in value, salvation is the one thing about which you may be totally and blamelessly selfish. Your salvation need not take second place to anything—friendship, loyalty, gratitude, honor, king, country, family. In the entire universe of possibilities, not a single one of them takes precedence over your salvation, and anyone who asks you to put something ahead of it is asking too much—no matter what it is—and may be refused without the slightest hesitation, reservation, or apology.

Is B the Antichrist?

Now at last we're ready to tackle this most difficult problem that so many of you have brought to me for solution. Again and again you say to me, "Tell me how to face those who accuse. Tell me how to explain that you are *not* the Antichrist!"

You have to begin by understanding what the Antichrist stands for. All serious commentators on the subject agree that *Antichrist* is just the latest name for an ancient figure in the religious legends of our culture—far more ancient than the Christ to which this name makes him opposed. In other words, he doesn't just represent the antithesis of Jesus. All our salvationist religions have feared the appearance of one who would lead the righteous from the paths of salvation. The Antichrist isn't just the antithesis of Jesus, he's equally the antithesis of Buddha, of Elijah, of Moses, of Muhammad, of Nanak, of Joseph Smith, of Maharaj Ji—of all saviors and purveyors of salvation in the world. He is in fact the Antisavior.

Accompanying the legend of the Antichrist has been the bizarre and almost laughable notion that his massive global appeal will be his unbridled wickedness. This shows what a low opinion our salvationist religions have of their members. This is how they despise us that they think we yearn for evil and vileness and corruption and will slavishly follow anyone who promises these things.

So now I'm ready at last to tell you how to face the accusers of B. When they say to you, "B is the Antichrist," don't think you're doing something admirable if you say, "Oh no, no, no, you don't understand." These accusers *do* understand.

When they say to you, "B is the Antichrist," here's what you should say to them. Say to them, "Yes, you're right—absolutely right. B means to steal the hearts of the people away from you so that the world may live. B means to gather the voices of humans all over the planet into one voice singing, 'The world must live, the world must live! We are only one species among billions. The gods don't love us more than they love spiders or bears or whales or water lilies. The age of the Great Forgetting has ended, and all its lies and delusions have been dispelled. Now we remember who we are. Our kin are not cherubim, seraphim, thrones, principalities, and powers. Our kin are mayflies, lemurs, snakes, eagles, and badgers. The blinding we suffered in the Great Forgetting has abated, so we no longer imagine that Man was ill-made. We no longer imagine that the gods botched their work when it came to us. We no longer think they know how to make every single thing in the whole vast universe except a human being. The blinding we suffered in the Great Forgetting has passed, so we can no longer live as though nothing matters but us. We can no longer believe that suffering is the lot the gods had in mind for us. We can no longer believe that death is sweet release to our true destiny. We no longer yearn for the nothingness of nirvana. We no longer dream of wearing crowns of gold in the royal court of heaven.' "

Say to them, "You're right to see that we're straying from the path of salvation. We're straying from that path *exactly as you always feared we might.* But listen, we're not straying from the path of salvation for the sake of sin and corruption, as you always *imagined* we might. We're straying from the path of salvation because we remember that we once belonged to the world and were content in that belonging. We're straying from the path of salvation—but not for love of vice and wickedness as you contemptuously imagined we might. We're straying from the path of salvation for love of the world, as you never once dreamed in a thousand years of dreaming."

The evangelist John wrote, "You must not love the world or the things of the world, for those who love the world are strangers to the love of the Father." Then, just two sentences later, he wrote: "Children, the final hour is at hand! You've heard that the Antichrist is coming. He's not one but many, and when the many of him are among us, you'll know the final hour has come."

John knew what he was talking about. He was right to warn his followers against those who love the world. We *are* the ones he was talking about, and this *is* the final hour—but it's *their* final hour, not ours. They've had their day, and this is indeed the final hour of that day.

Now our day begins.

ABOUT THE AUTHOR

Daniel Quinn is at work on several new projects, including a sequel to
Ishmael called *My Ishmael*. He is the author of *Ishmael* and *Providence:
The Story of a Fifty-Year Vision Quest.*

Contact other readers of *The Story of B* and *Ishmael* at

http://www.B-network.com

BOGOTA PUBLIC LIBRARY, NJ

3 9161 09006641 1

Bogota Public Library
375 Larch Avenue
Bogota, NJ 07603

DEMCO